The "Satyr" by Edd Cartier for Nelson Bond's *Occupation: Demigod*

The Far Side of Nowhere

Nelson Bond

Arkham House Publishers
2002

Copyright © 2002, Nelson S. Bond
Frontispiece: "The Satyr" copyright © by Edd Cartier. From *Unknown Worlds*, December 1941. Reprinted by permission of the artist.
"Command Performance," copyright © 1951 by Orb for *ORB*, vol. 2, no. 3.
"Parallel in Time," copyright © by Better Publications, Inc., for *Thrilling Wonder Stories*, June 1940 issue.
"Time Exposure," copyright © 1951 by McCall Corp., for the July 1951 issue of *Blue Book*.
"Private Line to Tomorrow," copyright © 1951 by McCall Corp., for January 1951 issue of *Blue Book*.
"The Castaway," copyright © 1940 by Love Romances Publishing Co., for *Planet Stories*, Fall 1940 issue.
"The Message From the Void," copyright © 1939 by Western Fiction Publishing Co., for *Dynamic Science Stories*, February 1939.
"The Battle of Blue Trout Basin," copyright © by Esquire, Inc., for May 1937 issue of *Esquire*.
"The Unusual Romance of Ferdinand Pratt," copyright © 1940 by Short Stories, Inc., for *Weird Tales*, September 1940.
"The Ballad of Blaster Bill," copyright © 1941 by Love Romances Publishing Co., for *Planet Stories*, Summer 1941 issue.

(Acknowledgments continued on next page.)

LIBRARY OF CONGRESS CATALOGING-IN-PUBLICATION DATA

Bond, Nelson Slade, 1908–
  The far side of nowhere / Nelson Bond.
    p.   cm.
  ISBN 0-87054-180-3 (alk. paper)
  1. Science fiction, American. I. Title.
PS3503.O4286F37 2001
813'.54—dc21   2001055971

All rights reserved. No part of this book may be reproduced in any form without the permission of Arkham House Publishers, Inc., Sauk City, Wisconsin 53583.

Manufactured in the United States of America
First Edition

(Acknowledgments continued from copyright page.)

"Case History," copyright © 1958 by King-Size Publications, for *Fantastic Universe*, April 1958.
"Herman and the Mermaid," copyright © 1943 by McCall Corp. for *Redbook*, July 1943.
"Double, Double, Toil and Trouble," copyright © 1942 by Street & Smith Publications, for *Astounding Science Fiction*, April 1942.
"Proof of the Pudding," copyright © 2002 by Nelson S. Bond.
"Pawns of Tomorrow," copyright © 1957 by King-Size Publications, for *Fantastic Universe*, May 1957.
"Magic City," copyright © 1941 by Street & Smith Publications, for *Astounding Science Fiction*, February 1941.
"The Masked Marvel," copyright © 1943 by McCall Corp., for *Blue Book*, December 1943.
"The Scientific Pioneer Returns," copyright © 1940 by Ziff-Davis Publishing Co., for *Amazing Stories*, November 1940.
"Miracles Made Easy," copyright © 1942 by Popular Publications, Inc., for *Argosy*, April 15, 1942.
"The Amazing Invention of Wilberforce Weems," copyright © by Ziff-Davis Publishing Co., for *Fantastic Adventures*, September 1939.
"Brother Michel," copyright © 1942 by Ziff-Davis Publishing Co., for *Fantastic Adventures*, May 1942.
"Pipeline to Paradise," copyright © 1955 by Nelson S. Bond, *Wheel of Fortune*.
"The World Within," copyright © 1942 by Fictioners, Inc., for *Super Science*, May 1942.
"The Geometrics of Johnny Day," copyright © 1941 by Street & Smith Publications, for *Astounding Science Fiction*, July 1941.
"Mr. Snow White," copyright © 1941 by McCall Corp., for *Blue Book*, March 1941.
"The Unpremeditated Wizard," copyright © 1951 by McCall Corp., for *Blue Book*, March 1951.
"The Secret of Lucky Logan," copyright © 1942 by Ziff-Davis Publishing Co., for *Amazing Stories*, April 1942.
"The Fertility of Dalrymple Todd," copyright © 1940 by Ziff-Davis Publishing Co., for *Fantastic Adventures*, August 1940.
"The Man Who Weighed Minus Twelve," copyright © 1940 by Ziff-Davis Publishing Co., for *Fantastic Adventures*, March 1940.
"Occupation: Demigod," copyright © 1941 by Street & Smith Publishing Co., for *Unknown Worlds*, December 1941.

To Lisa and Emily, Michael and Kelsey;
To Charles and Michelle, and to Wils and Rénee;
To Leigh, Slade and Marybeth I dedicate
this book. They're the kids of the kids of my kids:
They're not just <u>grand</u> children, they're all of them *<u>great!</u>*

Contents

"It's About Time"
Command Performance 3
Parallel in Time 11
Time Exposure 26
Private Line to Tomorrow 45
The Castaway 58
The Message from the Void 74

"Odds Without End"
The Battle of Blue Trout Basin 81
The Unusual Romance of Ferdinand Pratt 84
The Ballad of Blaster Bill 93
Case History 101
Herman and the Mermaid 105
Double, Double, Toil and Trouble 117
Proof of the Pudding 123
Pawns of Tomorrow 127

"Family Circle"

Magic City 157

The Masked Marvel 192

The Scientific Pioneer Returns 207

Miracles Made Easy 236

"In Uffish Thought"

The Amazing Invention of Wilberforce Weems 249

Brother Michel 266

Pipeline to Paradise 282

The World Within 297

The Geometrics of Johnny Day 314

"Wild Talents"

Mr. Snow White 331

The Unpremeditated Wizard 342

The Secret of Lucky Logan 359

The Fertility of Dalrymple Todd 381

The Man Who Weighed Minus Twelve 393

Occupation: Demigod 405

Epilogue 423

"It's About Time"

The nature of time is a problem that has troubled me for . . . may I say quite some time?

It is an oxymoron to ask, "Does time exist?" But does it? Is there really such a thing as the "passage of time" or is time a dimension of space? In the stories that follow you will find my numerous efforts to explore this mystery, some sensibly or others, perhaps in desperation, humorously.

And another thing . . .

You will also find that many of the stories in this book are dated. True, I had the option of rewriting them and updating all their timely references. But upon reflection I decided that unfair. It were better, I think, that you should read them in their original form, as they were read by a wartime generation.

When villains appear in these stories they are almost always our foes of World War II: a period when Herr Doktor Werner Von Braun was not a brilliant American rocket scientist but a Hitler hireling; when the Japanese were the infamous attackers of Pearl Harbor, not the respected manufacturers of America's most popular low-cost automobiles.

So as you read them I urge you exercise the virtues of faith, hope and charity. But do read them. For if you have not already done so, it's about time!

Command Performance

YOU CAN SAY WHAT YOU WANT TO, I DON'T LIKE IT. Some newspapers tell you one thing and others tell you another; one radio commentator says it's the real McCoy, and the government Johnnies pooh-pooh the whole business. I still don't like it. It's mysterious, and it's inexplicable, and maybe it's sinister —I don't know. But I keep thinking about Hartmann. And every time I think of *him* I think about *them*, and then I worry all the more. Maybe I'm off base, but that's the way it is. I'll tell you about it . . .

I've acknowledged that I may be off base. That's a possibility. But here's a fact. Hartmann *was* off base. *Way* off. He was out in left field without a glove. I guess that's why they wished him off on me. I was a new man at the hospital. The Chief said, "Take over, Preston, and do what you can for him—short of surgery. The family refuses to let us try shock treatment or surgery."

I asked, "What's his trouble?"

"Schizophrenia. And with the *damnedest* delusions in the alter ego. He thinks—but you'd better find out for yourself. If I told you, you'd have *me* locked up."

Cute clinical joke, see? But you get that way after you've

3

worked in a mental institution for a while. And the Chief has been king cobra in this snake pit for almost twenty years.

So I went to see Hartmann. I spent an hour in his room. I might just as well have spent that hour calling on a maiden aunt, or sipping tea with the curate. Hartmann was as gentle as either of these, as pleasant and well-behaved. And as rational. He was a quiet little man in his middle fifties, intelligent and—until this thing had struck him—reasonably successful. He spoke well on a diversity of subjects, and I rather enjoyed my visit. We didn't speak of his illness until just as I rose to leave. Then he asked me suddenly, "Doctor—why am I here?"

I gave him the stock reply. "You've had a nervous breakdown," I told him. "Nothing to worry about. It seems to be all over now. But we'd like you to stay with us for a little while longer. For routine observation."

That seemed to satisfy him, and I left, promising I would come to see him again the next day. And I did. But he didn't see me.

That's right. He literally didn't *see* me. When I entered the room I found him huddled in a ball on the floor, cowering in the corner behind his bed. His eyes were open, but they looked right through me, beyond me, as if I weren't there. There was terror in his eyes. Sheer panic terror.

I put on my best consulting-room manner. I asked, "What's the matter, Hartmann? What are you hiding from?"

That's when I discovered that he couldn't *hear* me. Actually. It wasn't that he chose to ignore my question, or pretended not to hear my voice. To all practical purposes, he was completely deaf. He couldn't hear my words, the scrape of my footsteps, the jingle of my keys, or the sharp crack of a ruler slapped on the wall beside him.

You find that hard to swallow? Well, chew on this one a while. He couldn't *feel* me, either! I contacted him physically in all degrees short of actual brutality. I tried everything from gentle pats and pinches to a fairly stiff slap in the face. They didn't register. It was like trying to rouse a reaction from a sofa cushion. He yielded as readily to the force of my actions—and showed as much response.

In short, only Hartmann's body was in that room with me. The senses envitalizing that body were—well, you tell *me* where they were. I think I know. And I don't like it.

One thing Hartmann could do. That was hallucinate. Those absentee senses of his—sight, hearing, feeling and the rest—were hammering away on all eight in whatever sphere his alter ego inhabited. All the time I was in the room with him he kept up a constant, fearful, running-fire of chatter—a jabberwocky that made no sense, yet caused the duck bumps to rise and march on my back.

"The Twisted Ones!" he whimpered. "The ships; the ships of flame. They won't take me. They won't! I'm not a beast!"

Frenzy, here, and scuttling attempts to dig himself still farther into the corner. Then:

"Go home. Let us alone. This world is ours. Go back to whatever hell you came from. Leave us in peace!"

That sort of thing. There was nothing I could do to order or persuade him out of his delirium. I simply couldn't make any impression on his sensory apparatus. I lingered for a while, observing his actions, taking notes on what he said, then I left.

The next day the Chief asked, "How are you coming along with Hartmann?"—which was the opening I wanted. I'd spent a lot of time checking the patient's case history, and knew his previous physicians had tried everything in the textbooks on him—to no avail. Everything but one. That was a brand new therapy, so new and so radically different from all the older methods that I wasn't sure I'd be allowed to try it. Anyway, I decided to ask.

"I've familiarized myself with the case," I replied, "and decided on a line of approach. If it's all right with you, I'd like to use dianetic therapy on him."

"Dianetic therapy? What's that?"

"A new technique for disclosing and releasing the aberrating power of subconscious memories."

My statement was not completely accurate. There's a lot more to dianetics than that. But I didn't want to upset the Chief by leading him to believe I intended to employ something other than the old standby methods. I was counting on the fact that he doesn't keep up with the latest wrinkles, that as Chief of Staff he's more an administrator than a practicing physician. I succeeded. He took it in stride.

"Very well. He's your patient. Let me know if you make any progress."

So I started working with Hartmann. I waited till he regained his prime personality, then had a cozy chat with him. I told him something of the basic principles of dianetics: that it was a new science of the mind which, practiced therapeutically, could improve his mental health and bodily vigor; that it was unlike any form of psycho-analytical therapy he had ever heard of before; that it did not employ drugs, hypnotism, or any such artificial aids; that it could not possibly harm him in any way, and probably would help him.

He said simply that to the best of his knowledge he was in no need of treatment of any kind—all unknowing, poor devil, that a few hours earlier he had been cringing in a corner, screaming his dread of unearthly enemies—but that he would be happy to cooperate with me. So I led him into dianetic reverie.

There's nothing occult about this "reverie." It's not, as the word may suggest, a form of sleep. The patient is wide awake and in complete command of himself. At any time he chooses, he may open his eyes, rise, and end the session.

I told Hartmann this. I told him further that were I to give him any orders or instructions during the course of therapy, such suggestions were to be invalid and without force when at the end of the session I uttered the word *Cancelled*. This was to guard against the possibility that he might be a natural hypnotic subject. I wasn't seeking hypnotic trance, but there was always the chance it might turn up.

He voiced his understanding, and we began searching for the cause of his derangement.

I'll spare you the tiresome details. Dianetics is an exact science, but its methods can be tedious. Opening a case takes time; time and patience. There are routine tests to be made for visual and sonic recall. I won't bore you with a recountal of these. I'll come right to the point of that first session.

A good dianetic technique is to indoctrinate the patient in the use of his time-track by asking him to re-experience increasingly remote episodes of pleasure in his life, then shifting to an early pain encounter. Some therapists call this the "dry run" because it merely serves as prelude to the longer, more intensive session that follows.

But in Hartmann's case, the run was far from dry. I had let him relate, successively, pleasurable experiences occurring within the past twenty-four hours, several months ago, and during his early childhood. Then, quite casually, I asked him to contact a painful episode in his infancy—and all hell broke loose! Where a moment before I had had a sedate, cooperative patient lying on the cot beside me, now I had a wild-eyed little mouse of a man shrinking into his corner, wholly impervious to me and his surroundings, bleating his horror at creatures out of nightmare.

"I'll hide from them; they'll never find me here! The Twisted Ones! Oh, God—their ships of flame!"

The Hartmann I had started working with was gone. On the turn of a single phrase I had uncovered his other personality.

There was nothing further I could do that day. So I went back to the records of Hartmann's case. I was looking for any known facts or incidents which might conceivably give rise to his illusory "Twisted Ones" or "ships of flame."

I found nothing. Hartmann seemed to have led an exceptionally placid and commonplace existence. He was not addicted to the reading of outré or fanciful tales, as I had half suspected, but was pretty much a Book-of-the-Month type person. He was a church member, but no religious zealot; I dismissed the fear of hell-fire as the root-source of his aberration.

Indeed, I could find *no* dread of fire or flame apparent in his background. He had lived a most uneventful life until some six months ago when he had been involved in a minor train accident. Not even a wreck. Just a simple derailment, in the course of which no one had suffered the slightest injury. But a day or so after this incident, he had gone into the first of his hallucinatory periods. These had increased in strength and frequency from that time on until finally his family had felt compelled to send him to us for treatment.

It looked as if there should be something there. I waited again, perforce, until Hartmann had regained his normal valence, then approached him for a second therapy session. I found him pleasant and cooperative as before, but dubious.

"I appreciate your efforts, Dr. Preston," he said, "but I see no purpose to them. Aside from these annoying spells of unconsciousness which you tell me is a natural result of my nervous condition, I have no sense of illness. Are you sure you're not wasting your time?"

"Hartmann," I asked him, "what are Twisted Ones?"

He stared at me in frank bewilderment.

"I'm sure I don't know. Corkscrews, perhaps? Or those long sugared doughnuts?"

"How about—ships of flame?"

He shrugged. "It sounds like the title of a movie. But I can't recall having seen any such picture. Why?"

I gave him no answer. I had none to give. I took him into therapy, instead.

This time I was careful not to repeat the error of our first session. I didn't try to take him back to infancy, but played around gingerly in the later areas of his timetrack. I moved him through non-somatic episodes of the past week and the past month, all with good results. Then, mentally bracing myself for a repeat performance of that pussy-wants-a-corner maneuver of his, I made a deliberate try for the railroad accident that had keyed-in his aberration.

"Let's return now," I suggested, "to that railway accident of six months ago. Pick it up as you're getting on the train, and run the incident."

Silence. Then, querulously:

"What accident?" asked Hartmann.

You don't argue with a patient in dianetic therapy. You don't argue with him, bulldoze or browbeat him. Gentle insistence is the keynote of the technique. I repeated my request.

"Let's return to that railway accident six months ago. Contact the incident and recount."

Hartmann sighed. "I'm sorry," he said apologetically. "I'm very sorry, doctor, But I have no idea what you are talking about. I wasn't in any railway accident six months ago."

You think that was bad, perhaps? You think so flat a denial dismayed me? Far from it. That was the most encouraging thing I'd heard Hartmann say. I knew now, and with certainty, that I was on the right track. Such a dead cold occlusion in his mind meant only one thing: that the railway accident *was* important, was probably the reactivator I suspected it to be.

All this I thought. All this I *knew*. But I told Hartmann nothing. I said, "Very well. Then let us go back to an earlier *similar* accident in your life. Let's return to another railway—"

I got that far. I got just *that* far and Hartmann was in the corner!

Do you see the picture developing? Do you begin to understand the nature of his madness? I did. But the battle was far from won. So far I knew only that somewhere in Hartmann's infancy there had been a railway accident, an episode containing pain and terror, perhaps unconsciousness and certainly words. Words that formed part of the engram which caused his aberration. The big job lay before me. The job of uncovering that incident, getting Hartmann to relive the experience and hear again those words.

I promised I wouldn't bore you with details. And frankly, my two closely-written books of notes on Hartmann's case don't make exciting reading. It took more than forty hours of therapy to ease him to the point, gradually, painstakingly, where at last I was able to contact that accident.

And then one day it happened. One day, when many locks had been removed, Hartmann rode down the time-track to find himself on that other train—that wooden-coached local that had cracked up before the turn of the century!—and the story came tumbling out.

I'll make it short, because it's not important now. Not to you, who never before heard of the accident, nor to Hartmann, to whom it has ceased to be an aberrating factor. But essentially the story was this:

The young Hartmann, a child of three, had been riding in a coach beside his mother. An old wooden coach with green plush seats. It was a hot and dusty day, he said. In the engram were perceptions of the rattle of train wheels . . . childish prattle . . . the musty smell of old velour . . . a mother's loving smile.

Then came the crash. The screech of brakes . . . the splintering of wood . . . screams, and a dizzy sense of headlong flight as the child plunged forward, striking his head on the seat before him.

What happened next must have been pure, unadulterated hell. Even in dianetic therapy, where no pain is more intense than one-thousandth of the original somatic, sweat poured in streams from Hartmann's forehead, his body writhed in terror, and his face was lined with agony. He lay there reliving the past, and beside him lay his mother, conscious and unhurt—but crushed to the floor, her legs pinned by the warped seat that pressed her down, trapped, unable to escape, thrusting at her son and crying orders. Screaming commands that burned their way into his memory along with the other sights and sounds and smells of that dreadful moment: the hiss of steam, the frenzy of fleeing passengers, a scrap of ticket on the floor beside him, the sting of wood-smoke in his nostrils as crackling flame leaped from the rear of the coach to lick at him with hungry, scorching breath. And over all, his mother's desperate screams . . .

Well, we cleared it. We dredged the memory out of his engram bank, and he ran it and ran it again until it lost its sting. He ran it in terror and tears, then in sober comprehension. Then finally in dull acquiescence, experiencing no pain, feeling only a sympathy for that brave, misguided parent who in seeking but to save him had unwittingly sowed in him the germ of an insanity years removed.

And when the engram had been totally erased, Hartmann was cured. Oh, not cured of all ills; I don't mean that. But released from this prime factor of his trouble. Able to return to the workaday world a sane man, a man as normal as the next one you may meet upon the street. So it all ended in peace and quietude.

Then why, you wonder, do I tell this tale? One man's case history, you say. Mildly interesting. But what possible reason for my passing it along in all its tedious detail to the world?

Well—simply this. I have not told you yet what it was that Hartmann's mother said. I have yet to tell you the exact words she used, the words that when reactivated turned him schizophrenic, caused him to obey her command literally, gave him an alter ego with strange powers.

"Go forward!" were the words his mother cried, she lying there confronted with sure death, seeking only to save the child she loved. "Go forward! You've got to get out of here in time!"

Go forward—in time. A literal command. And one to be obeyed unquestioningly by the reactive mind of a stunned child. Forward in time—to see the Twisted Ones. The ships of flame. The enemies of man, come from elsewhere to cause strong men to shrink and hide in corners, cowering in fear.

I don't know just what to make of it. But I don't like it. I read of ships of flame from time to time. Too often. Some newspapers tell you one thing and others tell you another. One radio commentator says it's the real McCoy, and the government Johnnies pooh-pooh the whole business. A lot of people scoff at flying saucers. But I don't. I keep thinking about Hartmann. And every time I think of *him* I think about *them*. And then I worry all the more.

Go forward in time, Hartmann. Go forward in time—and huddle in a ball, fearful of Twisted Ones who ride in ships of flame.

Only—how far forward did you go? A hundred years? Or ten? Or to tomorrow?

Parallel in Time

AT 11:40 P.M. ON THE FOURTEENTH OF JANUARY, 1941, there was a momentary interruption in the program of dance music being broadcast over the N.B.C. network. An announcer's voice burst through excitedly.

"Ladies and gentlemen, we interrupt this program to bring you a special news bulletin from the observatory at Mount Palomar, California. At ten-fifty-one tonight, activity was reported from the vicinity of the planet Mars. A series of seven flashes of light, spaced at equal intervals, were seen to come from that section of the planet known to astronomers as 'Fontana Land'.

"From the United States Naval Observatory in Washington comes the request that all observers, professional or amateur, who witnessed this event communicate their findings to Dr. Elmer Lockring at the Mount Palomar Observatory. Meanwhile, the public is assured that a speedy effort will be made to ascertain the cause of this unusual stellar phenomenon. This concludes our special bulletin."

In the living room of a private home in Frankford, two young people resumed their interrupted dance as the strident brasses of Goosie Greer's band once more outraged the loudspeaker. There was a frown on the girl's face as her feet followed the intricate maneuverings of her partner's lead.

"Mars, Joe?" she asked plaintively. "Did he say 'Mars'? What's he talking about?"

Joe shrugged. "Oh, a star, I guess. What difference does it make? Boy! Listen to Bugs Dooley take off on that gobble-pipe! Ride away, Bugs! We're with you!"

He heaved his partner an ecstatic two feet ceilingward. The girl shuddered deliciously.

In a tap-room in Cincinnati, bartender Bud McGuire sloshed an indignant rag at a puddle of stale beer.

"You hear that?" he snarled. "More of that stuff. I thought the commission ruled them kind of programs off the air. They ought to be ashamed of themselves, that's what."

One of his listeners nodded sagely. "Sure," he agreed. "Orson Welles, that's what it is. Another one of them 'men from Mars' fakes."

On a farm twelve miles beyond Fargo, an elderly woman dropped her knitting to her lap, reached out and shook her husband's shoulder, gingerly.

"Goodness, Aaron! What do you think of that! Did you ever—?" Then she stopped despairingly.

Aaron was sound asleep.

In the small attic room of a small private lodging house in Huntington, West Virginia, a young man reached over and flicked on the radio as the strains of Goosie Greer's band assailed his eardrums. He had no appetite for music; not after what he had just heard.

He walked across the floor to the only window of his little room, looked south and eastward to a bright, unwinking dot of red that hung low upon the horizon. His eyes glowed happily. He did not even know that at his side his fists were clenched with tense expectancy. His lips formed words.

"Seven flashes of light in Fontana Land," he repeated slowly. Then he grinned. "You made it! You darned little rebel, you made it! Okay. It's a date then. I'll be seeing you—darling!"

And suddenly eager, he turned again to a work-bench strewn with confused sections of blueprint, pencil sketches, and a small scale model of something that looked amazingly like a submarine without a conning tower.

Hank Morgan went to work.

* * *

Almost a year had passed since Hank Morgan had conceived the brilliant idea which he fervently hoped would bring him fame and fortune. It was almost a year ago that he had sat across the desk from Henry P. Armbruster, Sr., President of the Nationwide Broadcasting Company.

"It's simple, really, Mr. Armbruster," he had said. "So simple it's astounding that no one ever thought of it before. We've been attacking the problem the wrong way, that's the trouble. We've been trying with short waves, but not short enough. What we should do—"

The corporation president had frowned. "Just a moment, young man. Not so fast, please. What is it that's so—ah—simple? You've neglected to mention the problem you claim to have solved."

"Oh, didn't I?" Hank had said. "Well, it's that about interstellar communication. You know, sending messages to the people on other planets. Scientists have been trying to devise a means of doing it for years. They've thought of all sorts of methods—some fantastic, some fairly logical. They tried radio waves, but radio impulses won't work; the Heaviside bounces them back. Short waves aren't strong enough."

Henry Armbruster had nodded. "Why on earth should we want to send messages to the other planets?"

"*Why?*" Hank stared at him bewilderedly a moment. "Why—why because they're there, I suppose."

"The planets are, yes!" Armbruster said reasonably. "But people?" He shook his head.

"But you can't say that, sir," protested the younger man. "We don't know. I'll grant that the new telescope found no evidence of life on—well, say Mars, for instance. But that still doesn't prove that Mars doesn't support life. Excellent as it is, the telescope can't decide that for us. The solution lies either in space ships or communication. So far, our civilization hasn't progressed to the point of developing a space ship. But it will—when we discover the means of getting power."

Hank paused, then went on.

"But, communication—that's the thing. Here's my idea. Super-short waves; waves whose radiation length is stripped down to one-twenty-billionth of an inch. Or down to one-one-millionth Angstrom units.

"Cosmic rays! They are the only thing that, in our positive knowledge, do possess the power to bridge interstellar space. By using my cosmic frequency condenser—"

"Did you say *cosmic* rays?"

"Yes, why not?"

"Young man," Henry Armbruster had said gravely, "are you trying to tell me you've found a method of producing cosmic rays in your laboratory?"

Hank flushed. "No," he had confessed ruefully, "I can't produce them. But I have devised a trap for them. A sort of cosmic ray condenser, in which I can store them until needed. From the condenser they can be released at will, directed toward any given point in space. They are—well, sort of bounced back into space. But first we superimpose on them the ordinary long waves of normal speech."

Armbruster looked interested. He also looked puzzled.

"If you can do these things," he had said, "why are you here?"

"That's just it. I can't do them—yet. All I have is the theory. Before I can go ahead, I need assistance—"

Armbruster smiled faintly. "Oh, I see! Assistance! Now we're getting somewhere."

"Yes. You see, I haven't the means or the laboratory in which to complete my studies. But with your resources to back me—"

"I'm sorry, young man," Armbruster apologized.

"You mean—" Hank's hopes dwindled. "You mean you won't help me?"

"I'm sorry. I confess your idea of reflecting cosmics intrigues me—but only from a theoretical point of view. It has no practical application. The time and money we might waste on such an experiment would be—"

Armbruster was not an unkindly man. He was merely a business man.

"However, Morgan," he had gone on, "I do like your spirit and your enterprise. If you'd care for a job in our laboratories—"

Hank Morgan rose, shook his head gruffly. "No, thanks. I'm not interested in any job but this one. I'm going to finish it somehow. And if I do I'll—"

Armbruster rose, too. "If you do," he had offered, "come back and see me, Morgan."

During the ensuing months, Hank Morgan thought often of Henry Armbruster's offer. As time went on he found himself no nearer the solution of his self-imposed problem than he had been on that day on which he had boasted success was so near.

While his frequency modifier would achieve the results he had predicted for it, in actual practice it wouldn't work!

The principle was sound. On the plates of his modifier he

received and stored the surcharge of those mysterious, infinitesimal quanta which man has named "cosmic rays." It was unimportant that no man knew the exact nature of these rays, that opposing and equally brilliant scientists claimed in their respective camps that these rays emanated from the birth and death of matter.

Hank's theory was that these rays could be trapped on his galvano-condenser and subsequently released toward any given point in space to bear along with them through the ether superimposed long waves of speech.

It had been in December that Hank had had his conversation with Henry Armbruster. Now it was June. Outside his twilight-darkened room the world was warm and fragrant; the green West Virginia hills bright with promise. But inside the little third floor laboratory was only despair as for the thousandth time Hank snapped off his master switch and stared at his machine moodily.

"No good," he muttered to himself. "No good! I guess I ought to—" He stopped. He wanted to abandon this crazy idea of attempting communication with a planet which scientists did not even know was inhabited.

But still burning within him was that strange spark which carries inventors on and on, even in the face of assured defeat.

Hank turned again to his machine. His fingers touched a screw here, a wire there; made a slight adjustment on the intricate dialing of its panels.

His minor corrections made, Hank snapped the master switch. Once more the dim bulb lighted, the needles on the panel hopped like wild things to their charge positions. A phosphorescent glow rose from the sealed and cloudy place which was Hank's ingenious cosmic ray trap.

Hank Morgan spoke wearily, almost hopelessly. He spoke in English, knowing that even if his message should attain its objective, its recipients would not understand him.

"Calling CQ," he said. "Earth calling CQ. Earth calling CQ."

Then he threw the switch over into the receive position, and waited. Again as many times before, he realized the incredible optimism of this gesture. It would take three and a half minutes for his message to reach its destination.

Then, granting there was an intelligent being on Mars, who could understand that Earth was calling and who had the instrument with which to reply, it would be another three and a half minutes before an answer could return to him through the vast, unknown void.

He waited, Five minutes. Ten minutes. Fifteen. Failure again.

Blind, unreasoning rage seized Hank Morgan. He reached out for the master switch, wrenched at it as though to tear it from the instrument rather than to turn it off. He achieved just that.

There was a sudden blinding flash of light from the interior of the instrument, and a pulsating streamer of blue bridged the damaged gap between his positive post and the cosmic wave trap. The hum deepened to a roar.

Morgan leaped back, startled. "What's happened now?" he shouted bitterly. "I've half a notion to—"

Suddenly his body stood rooted to the spot, and his jaw sagged. For from the receiving unit of the damaged set drawled a soft, sweet voice! A voice that said:

"Coming on the O-Two wave. Who's calling, please? Where are you?"

For a moment Hank was completely frozen into immobility. A host of wild thoughts surged through his mind. Then common sense came to his rescue, and despair poured through him again like a cold, debilitating wave. He smiled, but there was no humor in his smile.

This was the end of his high hopes! He had built a machine that would talk across the void to Mars—and it had succeeded only in picking up an Earth "ham!" Not only that but the hammiest of Earth hams! A girl who did not even speak in the approved short wave communication terminology.

"Oh, hell!" he said, loudly and clearly, and again reached for the switch. But before his fingers had a chance to touch it, the voice spoke again, querulously.

"Coming on O-Two. Am picking up your signals. But you might try to speak like a gentleman!"

Hank's fingers dropped away from the switch nervelessly. There was something fantastically wrong here. He had not thrown the switch over to audio-reception. There was no reason a voice should be reaching him. Unless—

Again the strange discoloration of his cosmic ray unit caught his eye. Its silky, blue chamber was alive with tiny, darting, yellow flecks of light.

His heart gave a great lurch. Perhaps he was on the right trail after all! At least, for the first time he had brought in a listener.

"Calling CQ!" he cried hoarsely. "Calling CQ! This is W-two-CX-three-Y calling. Who are you? Come in, please!"

Instantly, that sweet, drawling voice came back to him. "Hello, there! What are all those letters and numbers about? I don't understand you at all! This is Mary Lou Beaufort calling from Hunter's Fort, Virginia. Who am I talking to?"

Hank grinned wryly. A woman ham. She didn't even understand the meaning of call signals or CQ. But that was odd. What was she doing with a short wave set of her own unless she had passed a federal test?

"Hello, Mary Lou Beaufort!" he said. "This is Hank Morgan calling from Huntington, West Virginia—"

A gasp from the audio interrupted him. The girl's voice said excitedly:

"From *where?*"

"Huntington, West Virginia."

"*West* Virginia! You mean *western* Virginia?"

"I mean West Virginia," Hank snapped impatiently.

There was a long pause.

"I—I don't know what you're talking about Hank Morgan," she said, confusedly. "The state of West Virginia? But there isn't any such thing!"

Hank snorted. Not only a lady ham but a moron as well.

"You'd better not tell Governor Hope that! Listen, Mary Lou Beaufort, I don't have time to monkey around tonight. This is Hank Morgan at Huntington, West Virginia, W-Two-CX-Three-Y signing off." And for the third time that evening his fingers sought the switch.

And for the third time that evening he was interrupted. Brought to a jolting pause by the girl's next words.

"Wait, Hank Morgan! There must be some mistake. Where is this—West Virginia?"

"In the United States, of course. Where did you think? Where do you live that you never heard of West Virginia?"

When the girl spoke again, her voice was so low with shock and something akin to horror that Hank had to strain his ears to hear her.

"Hank Morgan," she whispered. "I'm buzzing from Hunter's Fort, Virginia—in the Confederate States of America!"

It was Morgan's turn to be startled. Confederate States of America! This was stark raving madness!

He stared at this machine, a strange feeling of horror mingling strangely with elation. There was only one explanation. Somehow he had succceded in bridging a gap that he had never anticipated. The dimension of Time!

Words spilled from his mouth in an excited flood.

"Mary Lou Beaufort! For God's sake, don't sign off now! We've got something here, you and I! We've accomplished something that man never dreamed of! Do you know we're talking across Time? Confederate States of America—you must be speaking from a period around Eighteen-sixty-three, aren't you? And I'm speaking in June of Nineteen-thirty-nine!"

Then the wild theory was exploded abruptly.

"So am I, Hank Morgan," the girl's plaintive voice said. "This is June Third, Nineteen-Thirty-Nine."

Either he was crazy or she was. As a matter of fact, he wasn't altogether sure he wanted to find out.

The girl continued talking. "Now you have me guessing, Hank Morgan. What do you mean by saying it must be about Eighteen-sixty-three? And where is this West Virginia you keep talking about?"

Hank answered almost mechanically. "The Confederate States ceased to exist in Eighteen-sixty-five. Is this a joke of some sort?"

He was not prepared for the fury of the voice that stormed back at him. "Confederate States ceased to exist! Why, you—Yankee! We're just as great a nation as you are!"

"Wh-what!" Hank said.

"Just because you have six more stars in your flag than we do, you think you own the earth!"

"Six more stars?" said Hank bewilderdly.

"Oh, you don't need to be sarcastic! You've been kidding me all along, haven't you? You *are* from the United States?"

A dawning suspicion gripped Hank Morgan. His discouragement vanished in sharply reawakening eagerness.

"Mary Lou, you're right," he said. "There is something funny about this. I've been perfectly sincere in all I've said and I think you have been too. Let me tell you something."

He took a deep breath, then continued.

"I, Hank Morgan, am now speaking to you from the town of Huntington which is in the state of West Virginia, one of the forty-eight states of the United States of America. The date is June third, Nineteen-thirty-nine. The hour is—" Hank glanced at his wristwatch "—exactly twelve-o-three A.M. The United States is a great nation extending between the Atlantic and Pacific Oceans, with Canada as its northern boundary and Texas its southernmost state, bordering on Mexico. Is there anything in these statements that you find strange?"

The instrument spluttered with the girl's swift answer. "*Any-*

thing, Hank Morgan! Well, most *everything!* I agree with you perfectly about the date and the hour, but what you say of the United States is fantastic. There are only twenty-seven states. The country, as you say, runs from the Atlantic to the Pacific Oceans, bounded on the north by Canada. But its southern boundary is the twenty-one states of the Confederacy—Virginia, North and South Carolina, Georgia, Jackson, Tennessee, Mississippi, Alabama, Lee—"

"Jackson? Lee?" Hank interrupted.

"Of course. The far western states on the old Mexican border just before you reach South California."

Hank's hands sought his scalp, and he scratched vigorously for a moment.

"Arizona, New Mexico," he muttered to himself, "but with different names. Because those names were given under different circumstances. It can mean only one thing. Mary Lou—"

"What are you muttering about?" demanded the girl.

"Tell me something. When did the Civil War end?"

The girl snorted indignantly. "The War of the Secession ended in Eighteen-sixty-four, of course. A year after General Lee's glorious victory at Gettysburg."

"*Victory!*" Hank shouted the word.

"Certainly. Any school child knows that Pickett's charge broke Meade's lines. And a year later the United States granted the Confederacy the right to secede. Certainly you know—"

"I know everything now!" shouted Hank. "Everything. Mary Lou—"

"Yes?"

"Prepare yourself for a shock. Do you know where you are?"

"Of course I know where I am!" Mary Lou snapped. "I've already told you twice."

"I know you have. But I didn't understand it till just now. Mary Lou, you're in the same place that I am. Somehow my group frequency modifier has found a way to bridge a gap that man never even dreamed existed until this moment. The gap of probability. Somehow we've connected two different worlds. Two completely different civilizations, and one of which you are a member, and I the other.

"Listen carefully, Mary Lou, and see if you don't understand now when I tell you that in my history books it is written that Pickett's charge failed; that the Southern forces were defeated in Eighteen-sixty-five. And in the world I live in there is no such thing as the Confederate States of America. Now do you understand?"

The girl's voice was shaken and uncertain. "Hank Morgan, do you mean—?" she said.

"I do. We are the children of chance, you and I, who live on two different planes of probability, at the same moment on the same world. The pathways of our lives lie parallel in time."

How long Hank Morgan talked to Mary Lou Beaufort that night he never remembered. One thing they ascertained early in their conversation. That was that historical events prior to July 3, 1863, they shared as common knowledge and background. But upon that date had come the change, the great change. How or why it had come about neither could venture to say.

"There's just this," said Hank. "All our mathematics and philosophies teach us that the history of mankind is one of cause and effect. That from any given point in time, an infinitude of things can happen. One small action is sufficient to divert the world's history.

"Perhaps the time stream down which we humans drift is like a river with a multitude of tributaries. We can take any one of these, but we never can return back the branch down which we floated. The current is too strong.

"Some time back there in Eighteen-sixty-three, *your* ancestors won the decisive battle of Gettysburg. From that moment on the probability of the Confederate States of America became an actuality. From my viewpoint, Mary Lou, you and your friends in that strange world of yours are of the stuff that dreams are made of. I'm not even sure that you actually exist."

The girl's laughter floated to him over the audio. "I've been wondering the same thing about you, Hank Morgan. But I assure you, I do exist."

"Yes," Hank said, "and beside ourselves, Mary Lou, there may be a thousand, a million, other civilizations concurrent with our own, lying in diverse planes. One in which Christopher Columbus never made his voyage. Another in which there was no Caesar. A third in which no Maximilian ever sought the new world—"

"Maximilian?" interrupted the girl.

Hank continued, unmindful of her interruption.

He spoke of the growth and development of machine civilization. Of the Wright Brothers. The invention of the telephone. The World War. Of radio. Television. Motion pictures. Up to the very present he carried her.

Her story was no less strange to him than his must have been to her. She, too, spoke briefly of the "other" history. She told him all about the twenty-seven great United States sprawling across the northern part of North America. The equally great twenty-one Confederate States which dominated the lower half of the continent.

She told how victory at Gettysburg had brought to the Confederacy an ally—England. How the South had won through to ultimate victory. How after the war a self-dependent new nation had been forced to develop great mills and manufacturing plants, shipping ports and banking houses.

She told how the necessity of assuring economic independence for the Confederacy had caused southern inventors to find new uses for King Cotton. Before the turn of the century, rayon and cellulose products were in common usage in the C.S.A. Southern agrarians swiftly discovered the potentialities in peanuts, tung oil, and ground waste.

"We use phenoloids for almost everything today," the girl explained. "Don't you?"

Hank had to confess that his world did not, until he discovered that "phenoloids" were known to his world as "plastics."

Many more things Mary Lou told him. How, after the Civil War had been settled, the twin republics rose to a position of world dominance. In her time there had been no Spanish-American War, no World War. But there had been other conflicts. The dramatic upheaval in Germany, in 1886, when the Teutonic people had overthrown their Emperor and established a republic like that in the western hemisphere. Twelve years later, France followed suit.

All through the night they talked, these wondering young people from worlds that lay on different planes of probability. And that was but the beginning.

These nightly meetings soon came to something toward which Hank Morgan looked expectantly. Never once did either he or Mary Lou express a desire to introduce a third party into their discussions.

Across the transverse mystery of Time, two young people had met. They knew each other's voices only—yet from this meager contact they had derived something that less gifted mortals often live a life's span without achieving. Love.

And so, inevitably, there came a day when Hank Morgan knew that the medium of speech was not enough to satisfy his curiosity about Mary Lou Beaufort. It was at this time that he set about adding new, strange gadgets to his already involved machine.

He installed a visiplate on which he hoped to capture the image of Mary Lou. And with hopeful, trembling fingers one night he pressed the button that should activate its screen. . . .

He thought he saw her for an instant, but it was a dismal failure. And it was Mary Lou who guessed the reason why.

"It can't work, Hank," she said. "It can't ever work. We can hear each other speak; yes. Because the sound waves we emanate are not really a part of ourselves, but are simply the air currents stirred into motion by our vocal activities. But as for seeing each other that is impossible."

Mary Lou paused, went on.

"As you yourself pointed out, days ago, we co-exist on different planes. Possibly even intersecting planes. We are like children playing with a gyroscope. We have discovered a miraculous toy—but we don't know how it works. Possibly in your plane, light is polarized in one direction; in mine its polarization is at a different angle."

"But Mary Lou," Hank said bitterly, "we can't admit defeat. Not now. I *must* see you!"

The girl laughed. "The heart of a true scientist. Never satisfied. Isn't this success enough, Hank?"

"No!" stormed Hank. "Success? It's utter failure if I can only talk to you each night, never seeing you. Never—" He stopped abruptly, and his voice was unnaturally gentle when he resumed. "Heart of the scientist, Mary Lou? It's not the scientist in me that wants to see you. It's the man."

There was a long silence.

"Is it that way with you, too, Hank?" the girl asked, in a low, husky voice.

"It's that way—" Hank started to say. "You mean—do you mean you feel that way?"

"Yes, Hank. But I'm afraid we're the world's unhappiest people. Or perhaps I should say the unhappiest people in two worlds. Because we can never meet. There is no mutual station at which we can get off and—"

"Wait a minute!" Hank's voice lifted to a shout. "Two trains! A mutual station! By golly, Mary Lou, there's a chance—a faint chance—"

The girl's voice was excited, too. "What do you mean, Hank?"

Hank laughed in sheer exultation. "I see a way out, Mary Lou. We *can* meet—if we go outside our individual closed systems to find a mutual station!"

"What?"

"Time," explained Hank swiftly, "is nothing but a fourth dimension of space. But any man's recognition of it is purely artificial; dependent on his remaining within the particular 'closed system' wherein his Time obtains. If systems to a common meeting ground—say another planet. Mars, for instance—"

Then he groaned, enthusiasm fading.

"I must be mad, Mary Lou. Listen! As if spaceflight were a simple problem to be solved by any school child! Men have spent lifetimes working on the problem, never nearing a solution.

"Oh, if we had only met thirty . . . forty . . . fifty years in the future! Then they'd have it. Then we could meet. Scientists have the principles of space drive all figured out now. Oberth and Goddard have laid the foundation. But the fuel. Until men find a way of releasing atomic energy—"

It was at this moment, as Hank's despair was at its ebb that unexpected help came from the girl. "Atomic power, Hank? But have I never told you? *We* have atomic power!"

"What?"

Morgan was amazed.

"But of course. It had to come. With the rapid growth and development of the Confederacy, we soon used all our oil fuel reserves. A scientist named Toomey discovered a way to harness the atom in Nineteen-eleven—my time! If you have the other part, the design for a ship that will navigate in free space—"

"I have!" cried Hank. "But, Mary Lou, how is it that your science has not constructed a spaceship? Since the secret of atomic power is known?"

"Why, goodness, Hank," the girl said ingenuously, "we have had no time for such abstract dreaming! We are a young nation. We are practical."

"Then it's high time," exulted Hank, "you began to get gloriously impractical! Mary Lou—go get your plans! Be back with them tomorrow night. We must start working. There is so much to be done. . . ."

Thus it was that, three months later, Hank Morgan and Mary Lou Beaufort spoke for the last time over the temporal-abberant carrier wave they had discovered by accident.

Theirs should have been a joyful conference. They had succeeded in their aims. But it was not so. At the last moment, Hank suffered misgivings.

"Mary Lou," he pleaded, "we've been over this before, I know. But for the last time I ask you—won't you wait? Let me finish my ship and be the first to make the trial? It isn't fair that you should take all the risk, endure the possible hardships. Just because—"

The girl's laughter floated to him.

"What difference does it make, Hank, who makes the first flight? We know our ships will work. And yours is not quite finished yet. Mine is."

"My scale model is finished," Hank said. "I'm taking it to Armbruster tomorrow. He'll finance me; I know he will. He must! When he sees your design for the atomic motor."

"Of course." The girl's voice was tender. "Anyway, Hank, our reasoning may be wrong. Despite your convictions, there's a possibility that Mars is not a 'mutual station' for our two times. There may be two Marses, an infinitude of Marses, looking down upon us. One that winks upon your time, another that peers into mine. If so, even though I land successfully upon Mars and set off the signal, you never will see it."

"No Mary Lou! I know I'm right. The time synapse is peculiar only to the closed system which is Earth. It is as though you and I are passengers in twin elevators, traveling up and down in the same shaft. We can never meet so long as we remain in our own carriages. But when we get off at the same floor, the mutual station, Mars—"

"I'll come anyway!" he ended grimly. "Mary Lou, I'll find you somewhere, somehow, if I have to tear the Universe apart and put it together again with my bare hands."

"Now you're really being silly," the girl chided. "Silly and romantic. But I love it. It shouldn't take me long, Hank. Ten days at the most. You'll be watching for my signal?"

"Seven atomic flares," Hank said, "spaced at equal intervals, released from a point as near the center of Fontana Land as you can reach. I'll be watching Mary Lou."

"And I'll be waiting," said Mary Lou Beaufort. Her breath caught.

At 11:40 P.M. on the fourteenth of January, 1941, there was a momentary interruption in the program of dance music being broadcast over the nation-wide network of the N.B.C. An excited announcer brought to an incurious world a bewildering message.

In the living room of a private home in Frankford two young people resumed their interrupted jitterbugging as the message ended. In a Cincinnati taproom, an indignant bartender forgot himself so far as to set 'em up for the house. On a farm twelve miles beyond Fargo, an elderly woman wondered dully if all men looked like stupid brutes when they slept.

But in a small attic room in Huntington, West Virginia, the one young man in the world who knew the meaning of that message, smiled as he looked at a bright, unwinking dot of red that hung low over the horizon.

"Seven flashes of light in Fontana Land," repeated Hank Morgan slowly. "You made it! You darned little rebel, you made it! Okay. It's a date, then. I'll be seeing you—darling!"

And, suddenly impatient, suddenly eager, he turned once more to the workbench on which lay the plans for the spaceship which, two days ago, Henry Armbruster had agreed to build for him. There were a host of tiny details to be completed before he could keep his rendezvous through space, beyond the tremendous confines of stifling mundane time. . . .

Hank Morgan went to work.

Time Exposure

NO, MA'AM, I'M NOT BEING UNREASONABLE. THAT IS, I don't mean to be. I *am* a little impatient, yes. After all, I've been haunting outer offices for the past three weeks now, trying to find someone with the authority to—

Yes ma'am, I *know* it's not easy to get a passport nowadays. But I've got to have one. Got to! If you'll just give me five minutes with your boss—

Business? I've already stated my business to half the private secretaries in Washington, and it never does the least— Oh, all right—if that's the way it's got to be. But I'm wasting my time and yours. You won't believe me. Nobody does. You'd have to know Joe Dorry to—

Joe Dorry. My partner. Or erstwhile partner. If I can just get to see him, I can straighten things out in jig time. He's confused, that's all. You see, he didn't realize Jean and I—

From the beginning? Well, okay. But you've got to go back a full year. To the day when Joe Dorry first entered my life—and my hair.

My title was Chief Photographer, which meant that I was sole dictator, drudge and janitor of the oversized stall shower the *Times-News* fatuously calls a darkroom. I had just finished making a layout for the Sunday society section when the Managing Editor buzzed me to his lair.

"Gray," he growled, "meet Mr. Joseph Dorry."

I swapped squeezes with the lanky, wide-eyed youngster standing beside the desk, and queried the Old Man with a hoisted brow.

"Your new assistant," he added, "if you want him."

This was good news. I had been pleading vainly for a relief man for the past two years.

"Does Sears want Roebuck?" I chortled. "Does roast beef want Yorkshire pudding? Welcome to Headache Hall, Dorry. Got your equipment with you?"

Dorry nodded at a scuffed case.

"Then what are we waiting for?" I demanded. "Leave us go hence and make like a photographic staff. Yoicks, view halloo, not to mention tally-ho!"

Together we left the office.

Outside, Joe Dorry said hesitantly; "There's one thing I maybe ought to tell you Mr. Gray—"

"Ted."

"There's one thing I ought to tell you, Mr. Ted. I haven't had any previous experience in this field. I'm not a trained news photographer, like you."

"Few," I told him modestly, "are. But you'll learn. And there's no time like the present to begin your training." I glanced at my watch. "Eleven-thirty. Do you know the City Auditorium?"

"That big building over by the railroad station?"

"Right. That edifice is at the moment hideously alive with yips, yaps and yelps as a bevy of bleating beldames parade their perfumed pooches around the arena. Today is the final day of the annual Dog Show. How about gallivanting over there and getting a few snaps of, not from, the winner?"

"Gosh," gulped Dorry, "can I *really*? That would be wonderful, Mr. Ted. I love dogs."

I handed him my press pass.

"Just get the Best of Show. Never mind the rest. And be back no later than twelve-thirty. We put the sheet to bed at two-forty-five."

"Oh, I'll be back before that," he said excitedly. "I'll hurry, Mr. Ted. I'll hurry real fast."

"Maybe *you* will. But how about the judges? Here's an idea, Dorry. If the decision is delayed, get a picture of the Bidawee Kennels Cairn, Bonny Dundee o' Lochinvar. He's favored to win, so we'll have some protection."

"Don't worry. I'll bring back the winner's picture," Dorry pledged. "It sure is nice of you to give me this break, Mr. Ted. I certainly do appreciate it."

"Down, Dorry!" I said absently. I patted his head, resisted an impulse to scratch behind his ears, and unleashed him. He scampered happily away, his coattail wagging behind him, and I plunged myself into the serious problem of picking a winner in the fourth at Pimlico. It sure was wonderful, I thought, finally to have an assistant to take the unimportant details off my hands.

Twenty minutes later the door of my cubby flew open and Dorry entered, glowing like an overgrown sunbeam on legs. I stared at him in surprise.

"What's the matter?" I asked. "Run out of film?"

"No sir."

"Then what did you come back for? See here, kid," I reprimanded, "this is no way to handle your first assignment. I told you to get a picture of the dog-show winner."

"I did," said Dorry.

"Huh?"

"I got a swell shot of the winner. That is, I suppose it's swell. They usually are," he finished incomprehensibly.

"You mean," I frowned, "the show is over already?"

"No sir. Not quite. It's still going on. Gosh, it's a wonderful show. They have some beautiful dogs. There was one little dachshund I just *loved*, but the judges—"

"Wait a minute!" I interrupted. "Let me get this straight. The show's not over yet, but you've got a shot of the winner?"

"That's right."

"What," I demanded narrowly, "is the dog's name?"

Dorry's smile faded. His fingers laced and unlaced slowly. He quavered: "Well, I—I don't exactly know—yet."

"You don't *know!*"

"Not yet. But I will in a few minutes. As soon as I—" He paused, gulped, and wrestled film-pack from his bag. "If you'll excuse me, Mr. Ted, I'll develop these pix. Then I'll show you what I mean."

"Okay," I said stonily. "You do that. Help yourself to the hypo, sonny—internally, if you wish. I'll see you when this red mist fades from my eyes."

I stalked into the city-room, stood there brooding for a few minutes, then dialed the Auditorium. The secretary of the Kennel Club barked greeting.

"Pete?" I said. "This is Ted Gray. Judges picked the winner yet?"

"Not quite, Ted. They're still in the ring."

"I figured!" I said grimly. "Pete, do you want to buy some dog meat? About a hundred and forty pounds? On the hoof? Cheap?"

Dorry appeared beside me, flapping a moist print.

"Mr. Ted," he said breathlessly, "here he is. The winner. His name is—"

"Ted?" called Pete from the other end of the wire. "Ted, are you still there?"

"Yes," I said. "Shuddup, you!"

"What? Now, see here, Gray—"

"Not you, Pete—this hunk of mayhem-bait beside me. Go ahead. You were saying—"

"I've got a flash for you. The judges just brought in their decision."

"Bonny?"

"No. A surprise winner. The Best of Show goes to an Irish terrier named Castle of Blarney Brian. Got that?"

"Yes," I said. "Thanks. I'll be over in a minute to get a picture of him. See you, Pete."

I hung up, turned savagely on Dorry.

"Out of my way, buster," I growled. "Thanks to you, I've just barely got time to catch a shot of the winning hydrant-sprinkler before deadline. If you're smart, you'll leave before I get back. It's been nice having you for an assistant—but not too nice."

I started to brush by him, but he clutched my arm.

"But, Mr. Ted, I've *got* the picture. Here! This is Castle of Blarney Brian."

I took the damp oblong with which he was massaging my nose, stared at it dazedly. There was no doubt about it. It was an Irish terrier. I gaped at Dorry.

"Well, I'll be darned!" I mused. "Crooked, eh?"

"I beg your pardon?"

"The show was rigged. Somebody got to the judges. But how did you find out about it?"

Dorry looked horrified.

"Oh, no sir! Nothing like that. The judges were completely honest."

"Then how in blazes did you—" I paused, viewing him with new respect. "I get it. You're a dog expert? You figured Brian to cop the prize?"

Dorry wriggled uncomfortably.

"Not that either, Mr. Ted. As a matter of fact, I don't know the first thing about show dogs. If the selection had been left to me, I would have picked that little dachshund I told you about. She was the *sweetest* little creature—"

"Then how did you know? How?"

"Well, I tried to tell you once before, Mr. Ted. I mean—well, I haven't had much experience as a cameraman, but there are certain things— It's sort of—that is—"

We were getting nowhere. And deadline was close. I had no time to listen to his fumbling explanations.

"Okay," I sighed. "I don't know how you did it, but who am I to argue with results? Label this, sonny, and let's roll it upstairs."

Perhaps I should have guessed the truth right then and there. But I didn't. With a happy ending to the incident, I chalked up Dorry's accomplishment as a lucky guess and proceeded to forget all about it. The light of comprehension did not begin to penetrate the fog-bank of my brain until the next day. That was the day of the big accident.

We had just reported in that afternoon, when there came a screech from the police shortwave radio, announcing a General Fourteen in the midtown area. I didn't even wait for the bawl to rise from the newsroom. The minute I heard it, I was up off my brains and yelling to Dorry.

"That's the emergency call, Joe. Load up and let's get rolling."

He reached for his case and I for mine; I crammed a pocketful of cut film into my jacket, and in two clicks of a shutter we were on our way to the scene of the accident.

It was a mess, all right. There's this grade crossing in our town, right in the heart of the business district. For the past twenty years, thoughtful citizens had been urging that something be done about it—but nothing ever *had* been done, partly because the crossing was so obviously dangerous that no major accident had ever happened there, and mostly because the railroad packs a weighty political punch in our fair city.

Today, however, the law of averages had finally asserted itself. A fast freight had highballed down the main to tangle with the automotive traffic. The solid line of motor-driven vehicles had scattered desperately in all directions, trying to get out of the way. Most of the panicky drivers had succeeded, but one bus had failed. Loaded with passengers, it had matched tonnage with the locomotive—and lost. The result was grisly.

Dorry and I had literally to claw our way through the mob to reach a vantage point; and after I got there, I was sorry I'd made it. I may be a sissy, but I'm allergic to useless slaughter—and that's what this was. Police were trying to hold back the crowd; ambulance crews and rescue squads were working like demons, the air was tortured with mingled shouts, screams and sobs—but why go on? I summarized the situation in my first phrase. It was a mess.

Dorry and I separated. For the next thirty minutes I didn't even know where he was, or what he was doing. I went into action. I got some terrific shots, ghoulish, but newsworthy: A woman finding her husband under one of the blankets that lined the tracks; a man desperately struggling with his remaining sound arm to release from the twisted wreckage of the bus a girl whose need for assistance was long since past. . . . That sort of thing. When I returned to the car, I found Dorry waiting for me. His jowls were as green as my own. Without exchanging a word, we threw ourselves into the crate and raced back to the plant, where we immediately tossed our cargo into the soup. Then, in our first free minutes of a hectic hour, we took time out for a cigarette. We went into the cityroom to talk things over with the reporters.

Those who were not hunched over typewriters batting out eyewitness accounts of the tragedy were huddled together in a sober little knot trying to figure out what had happened. There was a considerable amount of disagreement about this.

"It was clearly the bus driver's fault," said Wally Thornton. "He must have rushed the gates after they started down, then got trapped in the traffic snarl."

"That's not the way I got it," denied Chad Osborne. "The witnesses I talked to say the bars didn't start down until the bus was already on the crossing. That makes it the gatetender's fault and the railroad's responsibility."

"Maybe," said someone else dubiously. "I found witnesses who claim just the opposite."

"In that case," fumed Phil Harrison, "we'll *never* know. This case will drag on in the courts for years, and no one will ever be tagged with the liability."

Dorry cleared his throat, spoke up hesitantly.

"Then it's important to establish whether the gates were down at the time of the accident?"

"Important! It's the key to the whole case!"

"In that case," said Dorry, "I'm glad."

"Glad of what? That you weren't in the bus?"

"That I took that shot," said Dorry cryptically. He turned to me. "Mr. Ted, isn't it about time for our stuff to come out of the developer?"

We went back to the darkroom. Dorry ran the films through

the hypo, blew up the negatives and set prints. When he had dipped the prints in a stop bath and washed them, he pulled out a dripping sheet.

"This should settle the question, shouldn't it, Mr. Ted?" he asked.

"Hmm?" I said. "What question?"

"The matter of the gate. You see, it *wasn't* down. It was just starting to descend when the bus—"

"What the hell are you talking about?" I demanded. "You and I didn't even *get* there till after the—after—you and I— Holy sweet bald-headed saints!"

My yammering ended in a stunned ejaculation as the picture's meaning registered on my gray cells. Dorry's shot was of the *locale* we had just left, but not the *scene*. There were differences—important differences. This was no hectic scene of carnage. This shot showed a breaking phalanx of automobiles scuttling out of the way of a looming freight locomotive. Halfway across the grade crossing was the crosstown bus. The picture was so clear that you could see the frozen look of horror on the driver's face as with one futilely gesticulating arm he strove to fend off the impending impact.

Most significant of all, the picture showed that at this moment —which must have been split seconds before the collision—the bars of the grade-crossing gates were only halfway down across the opening!

I croaked at Dorry: "Where—where did you get this shot?"

He wriggled.

"At the scene of the accident."

"I know. But *when*? We didn't get there till after it was over. This must have been taken when you and I were still here in the office."

"No," said Dorry slowly. "That's not when it was *taken*. That's when it happened. There's a difference, you know."

"I don't know," I told him flatly. "I don't know anything about that. But I *do* know three other things. The first is that I'm shooting this picture upstairs, but fast! It's the hottest news snap ever to hit this sheet. The second is that I'm filing the negative in the office safe for protection. It will be the plaintiff's number one piece of evidence that pegs the railroad with responsibility for this accident and—unless the town fathers of this village are even more stupid than I think they are—will finally compel the railroad to do something about that death-trap."

"And the third?" asked Dorry.

"Will wait," I said, "but not for long. As soon as this matter is tidied up, pal, you and I are going to have a nice little conversation. I want to know the truth, the whole truth, and nothing but the truth, about that crazy camera of yours!"

An hour later, I ushered Dorry into my digs, poured him a stiff bourbon, settled him on a seat opposite my own, and said: "Okay, pal—give!"

Dorry squirmed uncomfortably. He said: "Well, it's kind of hard to understand, Mr. Ted—"

"Many things are! Women, the administration's foreign policy, the Einstein theory—"

"It's sort of like that," said Dorry. "Einstein, I mean. Perhaps I'd better show you the camera first."

He drew it from its carrying case. I stared at it with some surprise. It wasn't the Graflex or Speed-Graphic news photographers commonly use. It wasn't one of those foreign makes, either. I didn't know *what* it was. It looked very much like one of those Brownie box cameras you used to use when you were a kid. Only larger. And something new had been added. It did not have just one lens aperture. There were eyeholes on each of the six sides of the cube! Also, it had a gimmick I'd never seen on any other camera. In addition to the conventional range-finder, speed, and trigger mechanisms, it had a circular dial scored off in time segments completely meaningless to me. I studied it thoughtfully, arched questioning eyebrows at Dorry.

"What kind of a camera is *this?*"

"It's my own invention," he answered. "It's a tesseractional camera."

"A which?"

"Tesseractional. Do you know what a tesseract is?"

"Pass," I told him.

"A tesseract," he interpreted, "is a hyper-cube."

"Still pass. How about a new deal?"

"A hyper-cube," he continued desperately, "is to a cube what a cube is to a square. Does that make sense?"

"In a meaningless sort of way. Let's make like I'm a Grade A dope, and take it from there. Can you explain it in words of one syllable?"

"Well, I'll try." He paused, brooding quietly for a moment. Then: "A line," he said. "How many dimensions does it have?"

"A straight line? Why, just one. Length."

"That's right. Now, a line is made up of—"

"Points."

"Yes. And if you were to extend the points in that line in right angles to the direction of the line, what would you get?"

"A square?" I hazarded.

"Correct. Now, if you extend all the points in the plane of that square once more at right angles to the two dimensions of the square, what do you get?"

"A cube," I said, more certainly this time.

"Of course. A cube—a three-dimensional object." Dorry nodded gravely. "Now comes the hard part. What I want you to do next will seem intuitively impossible. And so it is, from a practical point of view. But it is a mathematical possibility, none the less.

"Extend the points of that cube once more at right angles to the three dimensions of the cube, and *now* what do you get?"

"A headache," I told him promptly. "It can't be done. You'd be moving in the fabled fourth dimension."

"Exactly!" agreed Dorry. "And that's precisely what this camera of mine *is*. It's a fourth-dimensional figure known to scientists as a hyper-cube, or tesseract. A closed object bounded by eight cubes, having sixteen vertices, twenty-four faces, and thirty-two edges. They are all *there*. The reason you cannot see them is simply that you are looking at them through three-dimensional eyes. In other words, you can no more visualize what this camera *really* looks like than could a Flatlander—a man who lives in a world of two dimensions—visualize the finger we thrust through his sheet-of-paper world. He would see only a circle, a cross-section of that finger. Now do you understand?"

I rubbed my chin.

"Dimly," I said. "But we're off the main point. I'm willing to accept the theory briefly on faith. But what I want to know is— how does the camera work?"

"Well, I'll show you." He fingered the dial of his curious box, frowned at me mildly, then asked: "Were you home last night?"

"Yes."

"What were you doing?"

"Me? Oh, nothing much. Couple of the boys dropped in for a game of stud," I lied cheerily. "Why?"

"I just wanted to make sure." He finished setting his stops. "All right. Watch the camera."

"The traditional phrase," I said, "is, 'Watch the birdie!' However—"

A flash bulb flared, blinding me briefly. So to be utterly truthful, I'm not positive of what I saw. But for an instant I got the *impression* that Dorry's camera weirdly and mysteriously blossomed in his hands. Yes, *blossomed.* It appeared to grow, leaping, expanding, into an incredible and monstrous something which looked like a lopsided tower of adjacent cubes. Then the flash faded, my eyes stopped burning, and the box in his hands was its normal self. Dorry asked: "Do you have a darkroom?"

"In there," I nodded. "Don't slip on the soap."

He disappeared into my combination lav and laboratory. I sat moodily nursing my drink, wondering how anyone could possibly construct a fourth-dimensional object out of three-dimensional materials, and finally deciding he could not. I further decided, as I sipped my second drink, that there was something very wacky about Mr. Joseph Dorry, and that I intended to find out what it was. I poured myself a third drink and decided that if wheedling wouldn't work, I could always try the more direct approach of a swift punch in the nose.

Then there was an apologetic cough from the bathroom doorway, and Dorry entered, bearing in his hand a damp print.

"I'm sorry, Mr. Ted," he said.

I leered at him. "Didn't work, eh? I thought it might flop on a test run. Okay, sonny. Suppose we cut out the stalling, now, and you tell me how you *really* got the inside dope on those two events?"

"Oh, no sir. You don't understand. I mean I'm sorry about *this*. I wasn't trying to be nosey. But you told me you were playing poker—"

I took one horrified glance at the picture he held forth. Maybe I'm a gentleman after all, because my face got as red as his. I snatched the considerably-too-candid shot from him.

"See here, you!" I snarled. "What's the big idea? Is this a new twist on the badger game? What were you snooping around here for last night? And how long have you known Flossie?"

"Flossie?" he repeated. "Is that her name?"

"You mean you didn't know? You didn't shoot this last night?"

"No sir. That's the picture I took five minutes ago."

I stared at him numbly for a long moment. I looked at the picture again. Like Dorry, it was honest—and disturbing. Gallantly I tore the print into confetti and tossed the incriminating evidence into my wastebasket. Then I fumblingly poured nerve-tonic number four.

"Okay, chum," I conceded, "you've sold me. You've invented a fourth-dimensional camera that can perform miracles. But I still want to know—*how* does it work?"

He elaborated then. I could repeat most of what he told me, but what would be the use? You wouldn't understand much more of it than I did, and I didn't understand *any* of it. Boiled down to rock-bottom essentials, here's what it amounted to: Dorry had invented a camera which took pictures through the fourth dimension. The fourth dimension is the *time* dimension. Dorry proved this. He pointed out that we arrange our everyday engagements in four dimensionals. We agree to meet a friend at such-and-such a corner (length and breadth), on the ground level or a certain floor (depth), and at a certain hour (time). It sounded good when he said it, and I couldn't give him a rebuttal.

Well, then, Dorry's tesseractional camera took its pictures in time as well as the other three dimensions. The circular dial was its time-selector. By setting it, he could focus the lens on any event that had happened, was happening, or was going to happen before that lens at any instant, past, present or future.

"That's how I got the picture of the show winner," he explained, "and of the exact moment of the accident. Also of—"

He blushed and faltered to embarrassed silence.

That's when I got my bright idea. I said: "Dorry, one more question: Why in the name of all that's holy, did you ever decide to become a news photographer?"

"Oh, I don't know. Because I've always admired you newspaper men, I guess. It's such a romantic profession—"

"I know a doughnut manufacturer," I told him, "who will buy those holes in your head! In addition to being the world's most wistful dreamer, you're a dope! Didn't it ever occur to you that your incredible gizmo is worth approximately umpteen billion bucks, plus sales tax?"

"You mean I could make and sell these cameras? Oh, I'm planning to do that—later. When I've ironed out a few wrinkles. There are still some things—"

"Sell it, yes. But not yet. First feather your own nest with gold fleece. If you can take pictures of future events, why not clean up a tidy fortune by betting on the results of impending certainties: horse-races, baseball games, stock-market rises, and the like?"

Dorry shook his head sadly.

"I've thought of that, Mr. Ted. But it won't work. That's one of the things my camera still can't do."

"But you took a picture of Castle of Blarney Brian before he won the dog show!"

"Yes. But the picture wouldn't come out of the developer until the moment the decision was made. You see, the image is latent on the film, but it can't emerge until whatever it portrays actually happens."

"And the railroad accident—"

"Had already happened. I can shoot anything out of the past, but the future remains a blank until it becomes the present. That's one of the things I'm still working on. If I can find a way actually to peek into the future—"

"We'll be set for life," I gloated. "As it is, the camera's good enough to make us financially independent."

"We?" puzzled Dorry.

"We," I repeated firmly. "Joseph, my lad, you're a brilliant young man, but you need a manager. Someone who has been around and knows all the angles. Namely, myself. We'll form a partnership and parlay this hyper-cube of yours into the surplus-income brackets."

"You really mean it?" he cried delightedly. "You'll be my partner? Gosh, Mr. Ted, that's wonderful! You sure are good to me. What shall we call ourselves? Gray and Dorry?"

"And miss a title opportunity that comes once in a millennium?" I snorted. "Not on your life, chum! Did you ever hear of a character named Oscar Wilde? We're using the name he gave us years before we were born. Tomorrow we resign our jobs at the dear old *Times-News* and go into business together—snapping the pictures of Dorry & Gray!"

So that's how it all started. And it was just as I had predicted; it took no time at all for the results of our photography to make us famous. The pictures of Dorry & Gray— Oh, you have seen some of 'em? The tornado shots, eh? We got those the day *after* the big blow knocked the town apart, but our pictures were taken as at the moment of impact from the heart of the twister. And the Third National holdup—*that* was a funny one. Just a lucky break for us. It caused the bank robbers to be captured, but we didn't even know we had a picture of them until the story broke, and a previously blank negative swimming in Dorry's soup bowl suddenly formed an image.

Cabinet photography, too. That was a fat source of revenue. We had a fine old time snapping pictures of pudgy females and balding brothers who cheerfully paid through the nose to recapture semblances of themselves in the Good Old Days before crow's feet and gray hair.

Meanwhile, Dorry continued tinkering with his gizmo, constantly experimenting to find some way of actually viewing tomorrow before it got here. In this I encouraged him. And so we were rolling along beautifully, cashing checks from our private clients, from the news agencies and picture journals, from advertising agencies and practically everyone else with a bank account—when the roof caved in. Dorry fell in love.

I've got no one but myself to blame for that. I'm the one who introduced him to Jean Conroy. I brought her to our studio to pose for some swimsuit art. One of our agency accounts. After I'd shot a few stills, I got the bright idea of getting Dorry to snap one of the same gal with a slightly younger face. Not that Jean *needed* any Elizabeth Arden treatment, understand! At twenty-three, she was a pulse-palpitator in any man's league. But there's a freshness, an eagerness, a verve to the eighteen-year-old that she loses after she's been fighting off metropolitan wolves for a while—you know what I mean?

I called to Joe, who was working in the back of the shop, and he came in lugging his camera. He took one look at Jean, and it was Katy-bar-the-door. You could see by the laboring of his gills that he had been hooked, landed and dipped in bread-crumbs for frying the instant he laid eyes on her.

I made polite talk-talk for a moment, trying to give his eyes time to retract into their sockets.

"Jean, this is my partner, Joe Dorry. Joe—Jeanie Conroy, sister of an old flame of mine. For whom," I added truthfully, "the home fires never have stopped burning. Where is Jane now, Jeanie? Still in Hollywood?"

"Oh, no. She came back a few months ago. Haven't you seen her?"

"Are you kidding? After what happened the last time we had a date—"

"Oh, *that!*" sniffed Jean. "Jane's forgiven you for that long ago. Why don't you call her sometime, Ted?"

"Well, if I thought she wouldn't hang up on me—"

"She won't. She still thinks of you, I know. In fact, your picture's on her dressing-table. So you see—"

"P-pup!" Dorry broke in suddenly. "Pup-pup-pup—"

We both turned to stare at him, Jean with something like alarm. She asked me anxiously: "What is it, Ted? Does he think he's a motorboat?"

"Pup-picture!" managed Toe explosively. "Take your picture!"

I studied Dorry shrewdly. There was nothing wrong with him, I realized, that could not be cured by a dosage of moonlight and roses, music and a medley of sweet nothings. I said. "Look, Jean—I can't work up to this reconciliation too quickly. But if you could help me out a little—"

"How?"

"Well, perhaps you could make a date or two with Joe? Then after a week or so you could suggest a double date to Jane—a blind date with Joe's partner. You wouldn't have to mention my name. Once she had committed herself—"

Jean asked demurely: "Well, if Mr. Dorry would not mind being forced into my company that way—"

"P-pup!" strangled Dorry. "Pup-pup-pup—"

"His motor's revving again," I sighed.

"Pup-pleasure!" gasped Dorry. "Tonight?"

"Very well. Tonight," grinned Jean impishly. And for some incomprehensible reason, the amused glance she gave my gangling partner was not at all unkind.

Love is not only blind; it's deaf and dumb, as well. There was no earthly reason why a harmful armful like Jeanie should have warmed to a lunk like Joe Dorry. But that's just what happened. The wench who could have had her pick of the crop wasted no time in making it clear that she was one brief ceremony short of signing her charge accounts *Mrs. Joseph T. Dorry.*

Which was all right with me, mind you! I was glad the kids had gone for each other like that. I liked both of them, and Joe was my partner. But all I mean is, women are peculiar. So ridiculously— Oh, pardon me ma'am.

Dorry was so topsy-turvy with the stuff that makes the world go round that he forgot all about my plan to renew auld acquaintance with Jean's sister. He had suddenly discovered the truth of the adage that three's a crowd; I guess he figured four would be a mass demonstration. So we didn't ever get around to attempting that double date. In fact, so engrossed were Jean and Joe with each other that Dorry never even got to meet Jean's sister.

This was a big mistake—because if he had merely been introduced to her once—

But I'm getting off the main line. I'll rush it to a conclusion, now, because it's getting late, and I want to talk to that boss of yours before he gets out of here today.

I waited impatiently for three weeks for Dorry and Jean to arrange that double date. Nothing happened. Finally I decided to do something about it myself. After all, Jean had said my picture was still on her sister's bureau. Girls don't usually frame for reference their nominations to the Man-I-Wouldn't-Be-Caught-Dead-With presidency. So one afternoon I clutched my courage in two hot little hands and dialed the Conroy apartment. The voice that answered the telephone retained its never-forgotten power to send little hot caterpillars crawling up and down my spine. After I had stopped tingling I said, "Jane, this is Ted—Ted Gray."

I held the phone a safe distance from my ears so my drums wouldn't be shattered by the crash of descending bakelite. But my fears were unfounded. To my vast surprise and delight, Jane's reply was encouraging.

"Ted! Why, how nice to hear from you again!"

And well, after that it was smooth sailing. Our conversation ended with an invitation to come see her, a fast acceptance of the suggestion for that very night, and all of a sudden *my* private universe took on a hue to match the rosiness of that in which Dorry had been cavorting for the past few weeks. I was singing gayly when Joe came back from the supply shop with some new equipment. He stared at me in astonishment.

"Gosh, Mr. Ted, what's the matter with you? Sick?"

"Sick? My dear boy, I—"

"I heard you moaning halfway down the street, so I hurried as fast as I could. Here! Sit down and let me—"

"Dolt!" I snorted. "Unreasoning, unreasonable mortal, gitten yore filthy paws offen me afore I plug ya! Don't you have any of the finer sensibilities? Don't you recognize *l'amour, toujours l'amour* when you see it?"

He stared at me nervously.

"Is it catching?" he asked.

"Very likely. I probably got it from you. Dorry, my boy, behold a rejuvenated man. I am in love!"

"You *are?*"

"Please!" I winced. "Need you sound so completely incredulous, Joe? Yes, little man, I have succumbed to the lure of Daniel J. Cupid, Esq. I feel burning within me the flame of a sweet and wholesome passion—and I think the feeling is shared by the party of the second part."

"Golly!" gulped Joe. "That's wonderful. Now both of us, huh? Who is she, Mr. Ted?"

"She—" I began. Then caution asserted itself. I didn't want to make an utter fool of myself. Perhaps it had been wishful thinking on my part to believe that Jane's voice was so very warm, so more-

than-friendly. "Well, I—I'd rather not tell you that just now, Joe."
"Not even *me*?" He sounded hurt. "Your partner?"
"*Particularly* you. I have a good reason. Believe me, lad. I wouldn't want to hurt your feelings, but—well, later, perhaps?"
"Okay," he shrugged. "Whatever you say, Mr. Ted."
"And Joe," I went on seriously, "this makes a big difference in our lives. Yours, mine, Jean's—all of us—it has become doubly important, now, that we increase our efforts to make good. No struggling marriage for me. My wife must have the best of everything—which means you and I must step up our income. Tell me, how are you coming along with that future-focusing feature on your camera?"

"You know, I think I'm beginning to get somewhere with that, Mr. Ted. I'm not *certain*, but if my figuring is right, a new improvement I added just this afternoon might do the trick. Do you want to try it?"

"Sure. What do we do?"

"You just stand still. I'm going to take a picture of you *here;* but if my new idea is correct, the time-warping shutter I just installed will throw a shunt across the space dimensions and take a picture of you wherever you're going to be at the time I set the dial for.

"Just for example," he continued, "where will you be at—oh, let's say nine o'clock tonight?"

I grinned at him secretively. "No comment," I said.

"Well, okay. Then at ten tomorrow morning?"

"Breakfast, probably."

"All right. Let's try it and see what happens."

He uncrated his box, set the dial, snapped me. Then he scowled. "Aw, heck! Made a mistake. Let's try it again, Mr. Ted." This time, after resetting the dial, he was satisfied. "All right. Got it. Now you snap me."

"At any particular time?"

"No. A couple of weeks from now, maybe? Then we can find out where I'm going to be, and what I'll be doing. That should be fun, huh?"

"I hope so," I agreed dubiously. "I'm just beginning to realize that this improvement could prove a bit embarrassing from time to time. But okay. Here goes!"

I set the time dial for one month later, snapped the shutter. It was the first time I had ever used Dorry's gadget; I felt a curious tremor of emotion when I felt the camera twist and somehow *grow* under my grasp. But the sensation ended almost before I began to experience it, and Dorry reclaimed his instrument.

"Fine," he said. "Now I'll develop these, and we'll see what comes out. Want to watch?"

"No, thanks. I've got to dress. That heavy date, you know!" I grinned at him. "Good luck, kid. I hope you've got it this time."

He disappeared into the darkroom.

Ten minutes later he emerged. I grunted a query at him from my doubled position over my shoelaces. "Well, Joe?"

His voice was gray, colorless, dejected. So was his expression, when finally I lifted to behold it.

"No," he said slowly. "It didn't work, Mr. Ted."

"Too bad," I sympathized. "But don't worry. You'll get it sooner or later, pal. Keep trying. Hey—hadn't you better start getting dressed?"

"What for?" he asked dully.

"What *for!* Don't you have a date with Jean tonight?"

He winced, and for an instant the look of pained resignation in his eyes was replaced by one of anger. Then the petulance died. He merely said reproachfully: "That was sort of a mean thing to say, Mr. Ted."

"Mean? What are you talking about? I merely—hey! Hey, Joe, come back here! What—"

I was talking to a still-quivering door. Dorry had left in a gangling, stiff-legged huff. I stared after him a moment or two, then resumed dressing. Lovers' quarrel—that was the way I figured it. Well, it would pass. Such things do in time. As witness my own renascence, my own date with Jane tonight.

I started singing again. Anybody who says my singing sounds like moaning is crazy. I was terrific.

So was Jane. We didn't go out that evening. There were too many things we had to talk over, too much lost time we had to make up for. We said all the things we should have said months ago; then there was a little weeping on her part and a little promising on mine, and some salty kisses which were strangely sweet— and what with one thing and another I didn't even realize how late it was getting to be, until Jean came in and caught us making like two toasted marshmallows on the divan.

I didn't even try to wipe the lipstick off. I just grinned at her and said: "Okay, take it easy. Don't say anything harsh to your brother."

"Brother?"

"In law," I nodded, "as soon as we can get a parson to say the proper words over us. Where's Joe?"

"That's just what I was going to ask *you*," Jeanie said, "He was supposed to meet me at eleven tonight, but he didn't show up. I had an earlier engagement with a booking agent—business you know. Joe didn't seem to like the idea very much. I hope he's not angry."

"If he is," I said cheerfully, "he won't stay that way long. I've got a great idea. Let's all run over to our place and surprise him with the good news about Jane and me? Then we'll adjourn to Mike's Grill and celebrate the coming event with an armload of Martinis. Good thought?"

"Excellent," said Jane from the circle of my arm.

"Excellent," echoed Jean, "with a minor revision. We'll celebrate the coming events."

"Huh?"

"Well, one, then. But a *double* wedding. Darned if I'm going to let my own sister beat me to the orange-blossom and burned biscuit brigade. Let's go find Joe and advise him that he's just become engaged."

So we went to the apartment I shared with Joe. But no Joe. In the living-room, no Joe; in the bedroom, no Joe; in the kitchen, nothing but the remnants of a sandwich barely nibbled. I frowned at my lovely guests.

"This I don't get. Joe never goes out alone. As a matter of fact, he hardly ever went out at all until he met Jean. He spent most of his time working on his camera."

"Then maybe he's in the darkroom," suggested Jane.

"Possibly," I acknowledged. I went into the darkroom. And that's where I found Joe's farewell letter.

It wasn't really a letter. It was a note. A sad little note. It said:

> Mr. Ted, I'm sorry now I tricked you, but I guess it's better this way. I hope you and Jean will be very happy. I'll never come back to bother you, so please don't worry about me. Or try to find me.
>
> Yours, Joe Dorry.

I read it with a sense of frustrated incredulity. Joe had tricked me? How? And what was better *what* way? And why should he hope Jean and I would be happy? *Jane* was my heartthrob, not Jean. And Dorry knew nothing about Jane. So his note didn't make sense. Not a grain of sense. Until—

Until I happened to glance at the drying-racks, and found there the pictures that had caused Dorry's gloom when last I saw him, the pictures taken by an improved camera that finally *could* foresee the future, the devastating shots that had sent romantic Joe into his self-sacrifice act.

One of those pictures showed me at the telephone—as at ten o'clock the next morning I *was* seated—frantically calling anyone who might be able to help me catch Dorry and halt him in his headlong flight.

The second picture was the one with which Dorry had tricked me, the one which had previewed my activities at nine o'clock that evening. It showed me curled on the divan in an apartment familiar to Joe, ardently making up for lost time with a girl who was obviously enjoying herself as much as I was.

And the third picture—well, ma'am, that's why I'm here. Jane won't marry me till I get to Joe, explain matters, and bring him back to his brokenhearted Jean. I *know* it's hard to get a passport these days, but you've simply *got* to help me, because it means so much to all of us. And maybe to the United States Government, as well. Do you realize what that camera of Joe's can do now? It takes pictures of coming events. Think how the War Department could use *that!* A preview pipeline into the Kremlin's inner secrets—

Eh? What did that third picture show? I *told* you Joe was a romantic sort of goof, didn't I? Well, where do all moonstruck lovers go when their hearts are broken? Sure! I don't know how Joe managed to get there. But I've got to go there, too. Because that third picture, with its time selector set for *next week*, shows Joe Dorry lined up with a group of enlistees before a mustachioed recruiting officer of the French Foreign Legion! I've got to get to that Morocco outpost and stop him before he signs those papers or—

Oh, you will? Gee, that's swell. Thanks, ma.'am. I'll never forget— What's that? One more question? Of course. Anything you want to know.

Why did Joe think Jean and I— Why, didn't I *tell* you? You see, he thought Jane was Jean. Being sisters, they look a lot like each other. And of course they swap clothes sometimes. All he could see in the picture was the familiar background of an apartment he had often visited. Jane's face was obscured by mine. We were— well, pretty close when the picture was taken—

Ironic, isn't it? That two of the smartest cameramen who ever lived should come to grief because of a double exposure?

Yes, ma'am. This door? Thanks a million!

How do you do, Mr. Under-secretary.

Private Line to Tomorrow

ALL MY LIFE I'VE BEEN WANTING TO START A STORY *"Once upon a time,"* and at last I've got a chance.

Once upon a time there was a character by the name of Alexander Graham Bell and he put a lot of wires and things together and when he got through he didn't say *"What hath God wrought?"* or anything inspirational like that. He said to his assistant who was in another room, "Mr. Whoozit—please come quickly. I need you." And Mr. Whoozit heard him and what *he* said isn't in the history book and I'll bet money it isn't in the prayerbook either. But, anyhow, that was the beginning of the telephone. And ever since that time, anybody who uses a telephone very much uses pretty much the same kind of language I think Mr. Whoozit must have used.

Seventy-three years later there was another guy who—by a curious coincidence—was named Al Graham. His telephone wouldn't let him sleep. And that is the beginning of this story.

At 1:35 A.M. Al Graham, having finally finished compiling the estimates for his company's bid on the Nadir Construction Corporation housing project, sighed wearily and tumbled into bed. Three minutes later he was asleep. *Sound* asleep. The sound could be heard two city blocks away.

At 2:19 his telephone bell rang and a contrite voice said darling

45

it was sorry and could its honey-lovems ever, ever forgive her nasty old meany-pie? Al overcame his nausea with an effort, mumbled, "Wrong number!" and went to sleep again.

At 4:47 the phone bell rang again and this time a plaintive voice asked if the Keokuk Express were on schedule. Al said fretfully that he hadn't the faintest idea, hung up, and went back to sleep again.

At 6:03 the phone rang again and a hideously jovial voice informed him that if he could give the correct answer to this morning's Cheery-Kweery he would win from his friendly radio station's Rise-and-Shine Club one carboy of pine-scented window-cleaning fluid, a dozen lifetime desk calendars, and two passes to the American Goldfish Breeders' convention.

Al Graham didn't listen to the question. He slammed the phone into its cradle with a crash that punctured the announcer's eardrum. Then, with mayhem in his heart, he clambered from his bed.

He knew it would do no good simply to take the phone off the hook. Within a few minutes the operator would put a howler on the wire. But he had to have sleep. The telephone had to be cut off in some way.

Two screws held the faceplate on the wallbox. With a fingernail file Al removed these puny impediments, exposing a baffling maze of coils and wires. Al glared at these with a jaundiced, uncomprehending eye—then went to work. First he disconnected a red wire from a bronze screw and wound it neatly around a silver one. Then he tied a blue wire and a green one into a lovers'-knot, fastened both to a gadget that looked like a pair of Siamese spools. This caused complications. A spark danced between two terminals, a filament snake spat an irate, "Zzzt!" and Al tingled at the bite of its electric fangs.

Which made him all the angrier. By way of retribution he seized a double handful of wires, twisted them into a ball, and jammed them into the wallbox. Then he replaced the screws, kicked the box once for good luck, and contentedly crawled back into bed.

And that, he told himself, was that. Now he would sleep undisturbed until noon. Or later.

He was living in a fool's paradise. At 7:45 on the dot, the phone bell rang again . . .

At 7:45 the phone bell wakened him. Al answered it wearily, drowsily, with a sense of gaunt frustration, to hear the voice of

Longshot McGurk, a gentleman of some distinction in the world of books.

Longshot was lugubrious. He was also very gallant. In addition, he was cryptic. He said, "About that grand, Al. I ain't got it."

"Eh?" said Al, still half in the land of dreams.

"You wiped me good. I'll have to raise a stake."

"Ah?" said Al.

"But I'll pay off tomorrow if it's okay with you."

"Oh?" said Al.

"Only what I'd like to know," said Longshot McGurk plaintively, "is how you knew he was gonna win. That bag of oats ain't placed in the money since Moses was a corporal in the National Guard. How come you picked him on the nose? An inside tip?"

"I?" said Al.

"Okay," sighed McGurk. "I didn't think you'd tell me. Only —Boy Adjutant! Of all the nags—Boy Adjutant!" He sighed again and hung up.

Al said, "Good-by!" politely to the phone, began to hang up, then started violently as the double-take struck him. "Boy Adjutant!" he gasped. "Hey, Longshot—"

But Longshot was off the wire. Slowly Al cradled his phone, wide awake now, but still in a daze. Boy Adjutant? Al had bet his two bucks yesterday on a filly named Green Lady. He had never in his life heard of a horse named Boy Adjutant!

It's an unusual man who cannot rationalize himself into mild dishonesty where money is concerned. Especially a lush sum like a thousand dollars. Al Graham was by no means an unusual man. He was, in fact, a very commonplace guy with normal traits, reactions and acumen.

After all, he reasoned, it was not *his* fault Longshot had made a mistake. It was not his job to act as bookkeeper for a bookmaker. And besides, it was about time he collected a few bucks from McGurk. He had been contributing for some months, now, to that worthy's support.

With such arguments Al stilled the reproachful admonishments of that tiny inner voice called conscience. And being wide awake now, he showered, shaved and dressed.

Shortly after eight o'clock he recalled his labors of last night, his first duty of this morning. Noon of this very day was the deadline for submission of bids on that part of the Nadir Construction Corporation's housing project for which his company hoped to win the subcontract. It was Al's responsibility—his boss being out of town—to make certain that the bid reached Nadir headquarters before twelve.

He dialed Western Union, dictated his telegram to the receiving operator. As an afterthought he asked when the message would be delivered.

"Within two hours," was the reply.

"It is essential," Al said, "that this be delivered before noon today."

"It will be. Don't worry about that, sir."

"Okay," agreed Al. "I won't." He was feeling unusually cheerful. After all, it isn't every day a guy picks up a thousand beans on a hayburner he never heard of. With a pocketful of parsley pending, the Old Man vacationing, and all current obligations fulfilled, a celebration seemed to be in order. Al called Marcia.

"Morning, sweetcakes!" he greeted the object of his affections. "How's about lunch today?"

Marcia said a trifle acidly, "Lunch? Are you sure you want to eat with a stick-in-the-mud?"

"Huh?"

"After yesterday—" began Marcia. Then, being a woman, she changed her mind. And her tone. "We-e-ell," she conceded slowly, "if this is your idea of an apology—"

Al didn't get it. Offhand he could not recall anything which had happened yesterday that should inspire these icicles in Marcia's voice. Or call for an apology. It *could* be that she was registering belated protest at his rather ardent farewell caresses the night before. At the time she had seemed to reciprocate his feelings. But in the cool light of day, perhaps—

He said, "Special occasion, sugarlump. How about noon at the Samba Club?"

"The Samba!" Marcia had been wanting to lunch at the exclusive Samba Club for months now. "Not really, Al?"

"Absolutely! You'll be there?"

"Yes, indeed!"—enthusiastically; and then tremulously: "And— and about yesterday, Al. I'm sorry I mentioned it. It was—"

"Sure!" said Al. "That's all right. Twelve, eh? I'll be seeing you."

He made sickening sounds into the mouthpiece, hung up, and went down to his office.

The mail was light, routine duties could be handled by the secretarial staff, and the boss was out of town. Consequently, Al was working on the ring finger of his left hand when the phone rang. He laid down the nail file and answered politely, "Fosdyke Fixtures. Graham speaking."

Burton Fosdyke's bellow was undimmed by the distance between them. A note of agony was in his voice.

"Al! Did you finish those Nadir estimates?"

"Yes, sir. Got the bid off first thing this morning."

The bansheelike wailing was Fosdyke's vocalized despair. "Al, you've got to withdraw that bid!"

"What?"

"I made a mistake. A *terrible* mistake. Those production-cost figures I gave you were based on a fifty-family unit. The housing project is a one-hundred-family unit!"

"Oh, no!"

"Oh, *yes!* If our bid wins—and it's bound to be low—Fosdyke Fixtures will go broke fulfilling the terms of the contract. You've got to cancel that bid somehow, Al."

"But, boss, it's already wired. It—"

"I don't care what you do, but you must stop it somehow. Look, Al—if you can get me out of this, I'll give you a raise. Ten dollars a week."

"And if I can't?"

"Then you're out of a job," moaned Fosdyke hollowly. "We're all out of jobs—except me. I'll be making little ones out of big ones at the State Penitentiary! Al—get that bid nullified or canceled and, I'll raise you *fifteen* a week!"

"Okay. I'll do what I can," promised Al. When the boss had disconnected he dialed Western Union again. "About a telegram," he said. "Earlier this morning I sent a message to the Nadir Construction Corporation of White Plains—" He supplied the information about the message.

"Just a moment, please," said the operator. There was a lengthy pause, during which interval Al gnawed to shreds two of the fingernails he had so recently filed to immaculate perfection. Then the telegraph office clerk came back on the wire.

"I'm sorry, sir. We don't seem to have any record of that message."

Al's heart sank.

"You mean it's already been delivered?" he demanded hoarsely.

"No, sir. I mean, I can't find no record of its being filed through this office. Are you quite certain we accepted it?"

Al clutched his desk, which showed an unbelievable tendency to spin like a top. In a glad voice he cried, "The man who was on duty a little after eight—is he still there?"

"No sir. He's gone home. But I assure you, sir, he could not have made such a mistake. The employees of our organization are carefully trained—"

"Western Union," declared Al joyously, "I love you!"

"I beg your pardon, sir?"

"Granted! Call me up and let me make a mistake for *you* some time."

"Really, sir! Employees of this organization—"

Al cradled the phone and sank into a blissful reverie. How it had happened he did not know—but a miracle *had* happened. And because of it, beginning next Saturday he would be richer by fifteen dollars per week.

This, thought Al Graham, was beginning to look like his lucky day.

He was feeling very good indeed when at noon he stepped through the brilliant crimson-and-gold serape-draped portals of the exotic Samba Club. To the gaucho doorman who greeted him with a deferential flick of the quirt to flapping hatbrim Al said: "I'm expecting a young lady in a few minutes. If you have a nice table for two—"

"But surely, señor." The gaucho bowed him on to a grandee, who in turn passed him on to a matador, who seated him at a small table commanding a magnificent view of the entrance, the kitchen door, and another portal. Al ordered two daiquiris and settled back to wait for Marcia, complacently tapping one foot in time to the tantalizing rhythm of the dance from which the restaurant took its name.

Fifteen minutes later he decided he might as well drink the second daiquiri.

Thirty minutes later his foot was tired from beating out that stupid rhythm. His fingers started drumming on the table top.

Forty-five minutes later the matador attempted for the third time to take his order.

An hour later Al gave up. Signaling the matador to him he said: "I'm sorry. The young lady for whom I have been waiting has not come. May I have my check?"

The check, covering two daiquiris and two minimum charges, took Al's breath away. He started to complain, but when he considered the matador's truculence, the speculative appraisal of the grandee, and the way the gaucho was tapping the leaded butt of his riding-quirt in the palm of one horny paw, he thought better of it. He paid and stalked angrily out.

By the time he had reached the next street corner, however, his anger had given way to anxiety. It was not like Marcia to break a date. It was even less likely that Marcia should miss a long-awaited opportunity to lunch at the Samba Club. Al thought of traffic accidents. He thought of cops' whistles, screeching brakes, bodies hurtling through the air, clanging ambulances, and grave-faced surgeons sending out frenzied calls for blood donors. The cold hand of terror gripped his heart. He ducked into a drugstore on the corner and with trembling fingers he dialed Marcia's home phone.

"Is she all right?" he yammered when the connection went through. "Which hospital is she in? Will she live?"

"Al," said a cool, suspicious voice, "is that you? What on earth is the matter? Have you been drinking?"

"Only those two daiquiris. Yours and mine. Marcia, why didn't you come?"

"Come? Come where? And *what* daiquiris?"

"The ones I ordered at the Club. When you didn't show up I was sure you'd been killed. I could see you lying in the gutter, twisted and pale—"

"Alexander," said Marcia primly, "I am *not* in the habit of lying in gutters—pale or otherwise. What's more, I have no intention of talking to you while you're in this condition. I suggest that you go home and sleep it off!"

The receiver went *bang!* Something tinkled, and Al shook his head experimentally to make sure it was only his nickel dropping into the coin-box.

He emerged from the drugstore a sadly baffled man. Also a man with a headache. He decided that rather than go back to the office he would run over to his apartment and get an aspirin. He did so. He was standing at the kitchen sink gulping down the tablet when his phone rang. He answered it dispiritedly.

"Yes?"

"Al? It was Marcia's voice. "Is that you?"

The headache vanished abruptly.

"Marcia, baby! I'm *so* glad you called. I do hope my little honey lamb's not mad—"

"Don't baby *me*, you monster! And don't call me your honey lamb. After what you've done!"

"Huh? But, Marcia, I didn't do anything! I—"

"That's just it, you beast! I waited there for one solid hour, with that horrible little man with the knee-pants asking me every few minutes if I wanted to order, that nasty cowboy in the red bloomers staring at me—"

The descriptions were just too, too frightfully accurate. Al cried, "You waited *where*, darling?"

"At the Samba Club, of course. Where you said. Al Graham, I've never been so humiliated in all my life. If you think I'll ever forgive you for this—"

"Marcia, listen!" pleaded Al. "This is all a mistake. When I called you five minutes ago—"

"Don't lie to me. You never called me!"

"But I *did!* And you said I was drunk. That is, I told you *I'd* been waiting at the—" Al paused. "What I'm trying to say is—" Al frowned. "Marcia, where *are* you?"

"At home, of course."

"Stay there. I'm coming right over."

"Don't you dare! I never want to see you again."

"You've *got* to see me. There's something wrong. I can explain, though—I think," added Al.

"Well—" Marcia hesitated, and was lost.

"Dry those tears," said Al tenderly, "and put some powder on those pretty cheeks. I'll be at your place in ten minutes."

"Well—I don't know. Are you *sure* you love me?"

"Frantically. Will you wait?"

"All right. But don't disappoint me again.

"Never!" vowed Al. He picked up his hat and took off. There was a cab outside his door. Within the promised ten minutes he was pressing the doorbell of Marcia's apartment.

Youth is the happy time; youth is the joyous time; youth is the time of ignorance and naïveté. To all men comes the day of disillusion. This was the day on which Al Graham was fated to learn the Dreadful Truth about women.

When the door opened, he stood stock-still, frozen, benumbed. His first thought was: "Leprosy!" His second was, "Martian invasion!" Then the creature before him bleated and Al recognized Marcia's voice. Incredible as it might seem, this gray-faced, grinning mask surmounted by a crown of metal clothespins was his own, sweet, lovely Marcia!

Valiantly he strove to rally under the shock. His tongue struggled for expression, came up with the syllable, *Ulp!*"

And Marcia—if it were really Marcia beneath that muddy mask, and not a dreadful changeling—wailed: "Al! What are *you* doing here?"

Not without reason had Al won his Boy Scout merit badge for First Aid. He stepped manfully into the breach. He said crisply, calmly, confidently, "Don't get upset, baby. I'll take care of it. We'll call a doctor right away. Does it hurt?"

"Does *what* hurt? Al, what on earth made you—"

"Was it a burn? Or did somebody try to bury you alive? Let me feel your pulse."

"Al, you idiot!" Marcia tugged her wrist free and pulled away from him. "Let me alone! Go away! Oh, *why* did you have to walk in on me when I was having a hair-do and a facial?"

"Hair-do? F-facial?"

"Home permanent. Mudpack. Oh, I know I look perfectly *awful!*" wailed Marcia. "Al, you never should walk in on me like this without warning—"

"But, lamby, I *told* you I was coming over. I—"

"You never said anything of the sort. You called me up, drunk and talking wildly. I advised you to go home and sleep it off. Instead, you come here and—and stare at me as if I were some horrible monster!"

Enough is enough. In fact, there are times when enough is too much. Al leaped to his own defense.

"That's not true! I *did* call you up, after we had missed each other at the Club. But when I got home and you called me—"

"I called *you?*"

"Didn't you?"

"Of course not!"

Al took a deep breath. He said reasonably, "Look here, Marcia—I don't know what this is all about. Perhaps this is your way of telling me we're through. If so, I can take it. But what I cannot and will not take is your trying to lie to me and make *me* out the liar."

Marcia's eyes were widening slowly behind their grotesque mask. Now she backed away from him slowly, something like terror in her retreat.

"You're *not* drunk," she breathed.

"Of course not. I told you—"

"You're not drunk," repeated Marcia awedly. "You are insane! I was afraid this would happen some day."

"What? I'm—"

"Go-away!" cried Marcia. "Go away or I'll scream. *One, two—*"
"Marcia, listen—"
"*Three!*"
"Marcia, don't be—"
She screamed. Instantly there were voices raised in the building. Footsteps pattered to doorways.
"Oh, shut *up!*" howled Al. "I'm going. Good-by—you stick-in-the-mud!"

And he left. Hurriedly. Just in time. Angry and disillusioned. Vowing to himself that this was the last time he would ever see Marcia again. Or any woman. . . .

As he re-entered his apartment the phone bell was jangling. He picked it up, snarled a petulant, "Yes?" down its black throat. And then:

"Al Graham," said Marcia's voice, "I'm never going to speak to you again!"

"I gathered that," retorted Al bitterly, "when you threw me out of your apartment."

"What? Threw you out of where? That's what I'm calling about. Al Graham, what do you mean by telling me you would be here in ten minutes—and then never showing up?"

For the secnnd time that day, Al's surroundings did things like a top. This time a vertical-movement was added to the phenomenon. Al sat down suddenly. He said, "I . . . never showed up?"

"No. Al, this is going a little too far. First we had all that trouble yesterday. Then today you stand me up twice in a row. If you're going to be so difficult—"

"Just a minute, baby. *What* kind of trouble did we have yesterday?"

"I'd rather not talk about it," said Marcia coldly. "No girl likes to remember being embarrassed as I was. And under such circumstances."

A glimmer of light, vague and fantastic as foxfire, danced on the horizon of Al's mind. It didn't make sense—but neither did *any* of today's events make sense. Al said, "You mean—the mudpack?"

"Well, after all, everyone uses mudpacks. There's nothing wrong in that. If you don't want me to keep my skin fresh and lovely—"

Al hung up. He didn't do it roughly. He didn't do it nastily. He did it because it was the only thing he could do under the wacky circumstances. And because he had to have time to think this out—to think this business out . . .

The phone rang again. He sighed and picked it up, expecting

PRIVATE LINE TO TOMORROW 55

Marcia. It wasn't Marcia. It was Fosdyke calling from Oceanside. The old man's voice was gleeful.

"Well, Al, you did it! Congratulations, son!"

"Yeah," said Al dully. "I did it."

"Did you have to bribe somebody?"

"Huh? Oh—no. I just—" Al glanced at the wall box of his phone, and the proper answer came to his mind—"I just pulled a few wires. That's all."

"I see. Well, it was a swell job, boy! That raise I promised you goes through."

"Fine," replied Al mechanically. "Swell. Great." He was still muttering dazed incoherencies when Fosdyke hung up. An explanation had occurred to him; it was one he could not quite accept—yet. But all the evidence indicated it to be true. All calls this day, made or received on this phone, could be explained in only one fantastic fashion. The calls from Marcia, Fosdyke, McGurk . . .

"Longshot McGurk! Al started suddenly to his feet. There lay the proof of his theory. If Longshot had *not* made the mistake, a horse named Boy Adjutant should be running in a race *today!* Al hurried from the room.

At a nearby newsstand he bought a copy of today's Racing Form. Anxiously he flipped its pages, scanning the entries at the various tracks. Aqueduct . . . Pimlico . . . Havre de Grace.

He found what he was seeking in the fifth at Belmont Park. Boy Adjutant—listed with the field as a rank outsider. He hurried to the wall phone of the newsstand and dialed Longshot's number.

"Longshot," he croaked, "Al Graham. Got a little bet for you."

"Okay, pal—who'd you like today?"

"Boy Adjutant in the fifth at Belmont."

There was a brief silence, during which Al's heart skipped a dozen beats. Then McGurk chuckled.

"Cute, chum! Anything for a gag, eh? All right, I've had my laugh. Now, who do you *really* want?"

"Boy Adjutant," insisted Al, "in the fifth at Belmont. How are you booking him?"

"Are you serious?" Longshot snorted. "Al—we're friends. I wouldn't give you a licking. That plug hasn't got a chance. I've got him at a hundred to one—with no plungers."

"I'm a plunger," said Al. "I'll take ten on him."

The bookie sighed.

"Okay, bub. It's your funeral. But don't say I didn't warn you. Boy Adjutant!"

He was still laughing when he disconnected. Al wasn't. Al was wishing he could have bet a hundred. But he knew it was impossible. Because he *hadn't* bet a hundred.

It all made sense to him now—final, irrevocable sense. Without knowing how it had happened, he knew *what* had happened. Somehow—mysteriously, miraculously—when his angry hands had twisted the wires inside the wall box of his home phone, he had done something to connect that telephone to the circuits of *tomorrow.*

How this could be so, Al didn't know. He was not an electrical engineer. Indeed, even had he been one, he'd be not one whit wiser. For the top experts in the electrical field did not as yet dream that such a thing could be done. Only one man—so far—had shown that it *might* be done. Al made no pretense of understanding Einstein's unified-field theory, but be did know, vaguely, what it signified. Space and time—electricity and magnetism—gravitation and energy—all these were somehow curiously interwoven in the scheme of the universe.

If electricity and time were but diverse manifestations of a single phenomenon—and that not understood—it was no impossibility that an eccentric arrangement of electrical units should bring about an eccentric twist in time.

"Tomorrow!" whispered Al. "A private line to tomorrow!"

A sudden eagerness seized him. There were several things he wanted to do. He wanted to call Marcia from this phone and tell her not to be disturbed by anything unusual he might do tomorrow. But that could wait. He'd take his chances on squaring things with Marcia, once he had learned to capitalize on his fortunate discovery.

Right now he had to get back to his apartment and *get on that phone!* There were calls to be made—important calls. A call to the newspaper office, asking who had won today's games. A call to his stockbroker, asking for gains and losses on today's *tomorrow's!*—market. There were a hundred, a thousand, ways of using his unique telephone. The future loomed before him brightly rosy. Fame . . . wealth . . . power!

On a padding of pretty pink clouds, Al hurried to his apartment. He flung himself up the staircase to his floor, opened the door. . . .

A man in khaki grinned at him from the floor. His tool kit was open beside him. The wall box was open before him. He nodded and spoke cheerfully to Al.

"Telephone company," he said. "Janitor let me in. Your phone's been out of order all day, Mister. Busy signal whenever anybody called. So they sent me around. Efficient service, that's us. And boy, what a mess your phone was in! In all my days I've never seen anything like—Hey, Mister! Put down that vase! What do you think you're—"

The repairman dialed a number, backing away from Al. And into the mouthpiece of a phone in perfect condition he yelped a plea from the past: "Hey, Joe—come quick! I need you!"

The Castaway

THERE WAS AN AD IN THE CLASSIFIED COLUMNS OF THIS week's *Spaceways Weekly*. It asked for information concerning the whereabouts of one "Paul Moran, last known to have taken off from Long Island Spaceport for parts unlogged." Captain McNeally drew the notice to my attention. He said, "Look at this, Brait. Wasn't Moran the chap we picked up in the asteroids? It seems to me I remember—"

"You should," I told him. "You see his name twice every shuttle, engraved on cold steel. And you can be thankful for that. But I don't think he'll answer this ad. I don't think they'll ever hear from him."

"That," scoffed the Skipper, "is nonsense! Do you realize what this means, Brait? This ad was inserted by the Government Patent Office. There's a fortune waiting for Mr. Moran back on Earth when he sees this—"

"A fortune waiting," I said softly, "when and if he ever sees it. But I wonder, Skipper. I wonder."

We were about three thousand miles north, west and loft of Ceres when we first sighted him. I remember that well, because I was on the Bridge, and our Sparks, Toby Frisch, had just handed me a free clearance report from the space commander of that planetoid.

I read it and chuckled. I said, "Sparks, this bit of transcription is a masterpiece. Nobody expects a radioman to be goodlooking and have brains, but blue space above, man, your spelling and grammar—"

"Leave my relatives," said Sparks stiffly, "out of this. Is the message O.Q. or ain't it?"

"Yes," I told him, "with a light sprinkling of no. Sometimes I wish we had a good operator aboard the *Antigone*. Like one of those Donovan brothers, for instance."

"Them guys!" sniffed Sparks. "Too wise for their britches, both of 'em. I'm a bug-pounder, not a joke-book. If it's smart cracks you want, why don't you buy an audio?"

It was at this point that Lt. Russ Bartlett, First Mate of our ship, who had been shooting this azimuth through the perilens, turned and waved to me excitedly.

"Brait, take a look! Quick! There's a man down below! On one of the minor asteroids!"

I said, "A joke, Bartlett? You'd better check the alignment of that perilens. That's the Man in the Moon you see."

Gunner McCoy, Bartlett's staunchest friend and admirer, looked up from the rotor port, wrinkled his leathery, space-toughed cheeks into a frown, and squirted mekel-juice at a distant gobboon.

"Mebbe you better look, Mr. Brait," he said. "If Russ says there's a man there, then there's a man there."

So I looked. And to look was to act. I cut in my intercommunicating unit and bawled a stop hypo order to Chief Lester in the engine room below. Bartlett was right. There was a single, bulger-clad figure sprawled on the craggy rock of a tiny asteroid hurtling beneath us. A man who lay there quietly, did not rise, did not wave, gave no sign of noticing our approach even when I dropped the *Antigone* down toward the spatial island.

Bartlett, peering through the duplicate lens, said, "Dead, Brait. He must have cracked up. He's not moving."

But there was no wrecked spaceship anywhere around. I said, "We'll know in a few minutes." And then the Skipper burst into the bridge, startled and curious. "Something haywire, boys? Here, I'll take over."

He was a good man, Cap McNeally. A hardened spacehound, canny and wise to the ways of the void, always on deck in moments of emergency. That's why the IPS, the Corporation for which we work, had placed him in command of the *Antigone*, finest and fastest ship in the fleet.

But I calmed his rotors. "Everything O.Q., sir," I told him. "We're standing by to take on a space-wrecked sailor. I think."

My guess was right. A few minutes later we threw out a grapple, space-anchored the *Aunty*, and a rescue party landed on the asteroid. They brought back with them a sad looking specimen of the genus *Homo sapiens*. His cheeks were drained and sunken beneath a bristling, unkempt beard; his skin was blistered frightfully from long exposure to solars and cosmics; his limbs were so feeble that he couldn't walk unaided. He had to be carried.

Someone unscrewed his face-port for him. He drew a long, deep breath of the pure *Antigone* air. His wan eyes lighted dimly and he spoke in a voice that was a thin husk of sound.

"Thank you, gentlemen. I had hoped that at last I might—But you meant well, I suppose."

Which was, I thought at the time, a damned strange speech of gratitude. But I had no time to answer. For his knees suddenly buckled beneath him, his eyes closed. Had it not been for the friendly hands that supported him, he would have pitched forward on his face.

Cap McNeally snapped, "Sick-bay! Snap it up, you lubbers! The man's in bad shape. Out on his feet, cold!"

Sparks whispered, "Gosh, he looks like a corpus!" as the sailors bore our unexpected passenger away. I stared at him disgustedly.

"Corpse." I said.

"Huh?" said Sparks.

"Corpse!" I repeated. "Corpse!"

"You," suggested Sparks, "oughta take somethin' for that indigestion, Lootenant. My sister had it. It made her a physical reek."

It's against the rules for a Second Mate to punch a radioman. So I kicked him. There are limits.

That was our first meeting with the mysterious Paul Moran. We didn't know his name then, of course. We learned that several days later. After Doc Jurnegan, our medico, had coaxed, bulldozed and sulfanilamided him back off the brink of the dark and nasty.

Doc was the first to tag Moran with the adjective we all, eventually, accepted.

"It's the damnedest thing," he told me, "I've ever seen. Brait, I'll swear on a pile of prescriptions that he didn't have one chance in a million of pulling through. But he's still alive!

"By rights, he should have been dead two weeks before we found him. Do you know he was on that asteroid five solid weeks?

Without food. With only one container of water. With the oxygen reserve in his tank practically exhausted!

"And his condition—" Jurnegan shook his head uncomprehendingly. "Deplorable! He was dessicated, undernourished, fouled from weeks in a bulger. Acute cyanosis alone should have killed him. But—"

I said, "The will-to-live, Doc. It's the determining factor in many a borderline case. I've heard of men with holes in their heads you could drive a stratoplane through who simply refused to—"

"That's just it," said Jurnegan. "He *wants* to die! He refused to take food. I had to feed him intravenously and force him to drink. But in spite of his physical and mental condition, he still lives. It—it's mysterious, Brait!"

So I went in to visit our strange passenger.

He wasn't a bad looking chap, now that his whiskers had been plowed. Thin, of course; hollow of cheek and eye. His skin was sallow, faintly olive; the contours of his head long and narrow, short-indexed. He was a typical Mediterannean, if what my profs taught me is right. Medium stature, small-boned, thin, tapering fingers. Crisp, oily hair, black as space.

I said, "Well, you look like a new man!"—which he did, and, "You're looking fine!" I said—which he wasn't.

He turned his head slowly, studied me with grave, questioning eyes. His voice was faint, but low and pleasing.

"You are Mr. Brait, the Second Mate? I believe I have you to thank for having rescued me?"

"That's all right," I told him.

"Why," he interrupted gently, "did you do it?"

I said, "Oh, come now! You've got to perk up! You get a little flesh on your bones and you'll feel better."

But he went on, as though not hearing my words, "It was a chance. The best chance I've had for years—a thousand years—and you took it from me. Out there I might have found peace at last. The power cannot—it *must* not—extend into the depths of space."

His voice had risen; there was a light of madness, of strange, savage intensity in his eyes. I felt the little hairs on the back of my neck pringling. I knew, now, that the man had not come unscathed through his experience. He was space-crazy. Wildly, desperately so. I said, in what I hoped was a soothing voice,

"Now, take it easy, Mr.—er—Moran, isn't it?"

The ghost of a smile touched his lips, and his body became less tense. He said wearily, "Moran—yes. Or Ader. Or Cart—Oh, anything you choose. It hardly seems important any more. I've had so many, many names."

That wasn't exactly encouraging. But at least he was quieter now. And I had to know a few things about him to put in the ship's log. I asked, "How did you get on that asteroid, Moran? Were you space-wrecked? If so, what was the name of your craft? The authorities will want to know."

He answered, almost mockingly, "I was marooned."

"Marooned! But—but that's criminal! Who did it? We'll have them picked up and punished!"

"You'll do nothing of the sort. They marooned me on that asteroid because I deserved it, and I respect and thank them for it!" His voice was rising again; higher, shriller. "I thank them, do you hear? I bless them, a hundred, thousand, million times. Though their effort was in vain. I was, and am, a Jonah. A Jonah, Jonah, *Jonah!*"

He sat bolt upright in bed, screaming the word defiantly. Doc Jurnegan raced in, glanced at me reproachfully and took his patient in hand. "You'd better go, Brait," he suggested.

So I left. The sweat on my forehead was damp and cold. I needed a drink.

When I told Cap McNeally of my experience, he nodded soberly.

"I know, Brait. I saw him before you did. And he acted just as loony toward me. Warned me he was a Jonah—"

"I'm not superstitious," I interrupted, "but there *are* such things as Jonahs. Men whose very presence aboard a spaceship seems to cause trouble, dissention, disaster. You remember that Venusian blaster on the *Goddard III?* The survivors always swore he caused the crack-up."

"Moran's case," frowned the skipper, "is more than just superstition. He told me that he never wanted to see Earth again. When I told him that was too bad, that we were headed for Earth right now, he warned me solemnly that he'd do everything in his power to prevent our getting there. So what do you think of that?"

"I think," I said glumly, "he's nuts! And if we pay any attention to him, we'll all be nuts, too. Well, I've got to go, Cap. I've got to check the shield generators before we go busting into Earth's H-layer."

And I left.

Well, I was busy for the next four days on my job. It was a plenty important job, and had to be done carefully. The H-layer of the planets—the Kennelly-Heaviside layer—is a supertensioned field of force similar in composition to the corona of a star. A wide swath of ionized gas with high potential, serving as a shield against the murderous Q- and ultra-violet rays that emanate from solar bodies.

But the H-layer is a barrier as well as a shield. The first spaceflight experimenters learned that, and the knowledge cost them their lives. For their craft hit the H-layer unguarded; and where had been a glistening ship, now was pitted, blackened metal; where had been life, now there was charred carbon.

Now all spaceships were equipped with shield generators. They were "generators" by courtesy only; actually they were huge condensers fed by cable lines tied at intervals to the hull plates. The theory was that as the craft plunged into and through the H-layer, these condensers would absorb the excess potential, thus allowing the ship to pass through unharmed.

And it worked swell, most of the time. Oh, every year a few ships would get theirs—would blow out in a blue wreath of coruscating flame—but for the most part the trip was safe enough. Except, of course, when a condenser was in bad condition. Which was why I was giving ours a check and double check.

Still, I could never rid myself of a queasy moment when we hit that blanket of spark-happy ionization. Particularly when a planet was at aphelion as Earth was now. Because at such times the H-layer was more highly activated than usual.

And to tell the truth, I wasn't satisfied with the way my work was going. First I hit my thumb with a monkey-wrench. It didn't hurt the wrench, but the thumb turned pale mauve and throbbed like a sixteen-year-old kid's pulse on his first hayride.

Then I lost a brass collar off the hull-brace, and since we didn't carry a reserve stock I had to ask Chief Lester to make me one. By the time that was ready, I'd busted a .44 coil cable lock, and had to jerry-rig a substitute.

Oh, it was a headache! But I wasn't the only guy on board the *Aunty* who was having troubles. Slops raised a howl to high heaven because his stove went on the squeegee. Gunner McCoy stalked into the officer's mess one afternoon demanding what such-and-such so-and-so had stripped the gears of his pet rotor-gun. Sparks burned out three vacuum tubes in one day, breaking contact with all transmitting stations and almost causing us to crack up on a rogue asteroid. Even Cap McNeally was visited by the plague. He came wailing to me, on the bridge, that the refrigeration units in the No. 3 storage bin had broken down.

"—and we've lost a whole binfull of *clab*, Brait! Worth at least six thousand credits on Earth. The Corporation will be mad as hell."

"That's tough," I said, "but there's nothing we can do about it. It wasn't your fault."

He eyed me curiously. "Brait—" he said.

"Yes, Cap?"

"I've been wondering—do you think there could be anything in what Moran said? About him being a—a—"

"Jonah?" I'd been thinking the same thing myself. "I don't know, Skipper. I wouldn't say yes, and I wouldn't say no. But there's no doubt about it, things have been going haywire ever since we picked him up. I'll be glad when he lifts gravs off the *Aunty.*"

Cap said petulantly, "Of course it's just nonsense. Bad luck doesn't hang around one man like that. It's against the law of averages. Still, I wish you'd sort of keep an eye on him for the next three days, Brait. Till we land on Earth. I've got a notion—"

"So has Earth," I grinned. "Five of 'em. Atlantic, Pacific, Indian and the two Etceteras. What's yours?"

"It might," frowned the skipper, "be sabotage. He said he'd do everything in his power to prevent our reaching Earth. And he's up and around now."

"If you think that," I suggested, "why don't you shove him in the clink, just to make sure?"

"Can't do it. Because I've no *proof* he's responsible for these occurrences, and besides, a rescued passenger is entitled to the courtesy of the ship."

So that's how I assumed, in addition to the rest of my duties, the job of watch-dogging the mysterious Paul Moran. As Cap McNeally had said, Moran was up and about now. He had made what Doc Jurnegan claimed was the swiftest recovery in the annals of medicine. He still looked like a skeleton in search of a square meal. But there was sanity in his eyes. If not always in his speech. Like that afternoon in Sparks' radio turret, for instance.

We had been talking, Sparks and I, about space-flight. What a great thing it was. How, only in its infancy, it was already changing man's outlook, widening the borders of man's domain, creating a newer, greater universe.

"We got," Sparks said, "reason to be proud of ourselves. Gee, I was readin' in the library—"

"You," I interrupted wonderingly, "can read?"

"Comets to you, Lootenant!" sniffed Sparks. "As I was sayin' before I was so rudely ruptured, I was readin' in the library some old books from the Twentieth Century. Just about a hundred an' fifty years old, mind you! They had the craziest ideas about what men would find on other planets, if an' when they ever got there. Flame-men, an' robots, an' all sorts of things.

"Nothin' like what we actually found. 'Course, we shouldn't laugh at 'em too much. They had no way of knowin'. We're the first people ever traveled in space."

"No!" said Moran.

Sparks said patiently, "Well, I didn't mean us here in this room. Of course *we* ain't. But I mean the people in our time."

"And I still say," said Moran gravely, "no! Man in all ages is a creature of conceit, self-pride, self-glorification. There was space-flight long before you lived, Sparks. A race, long dead now, from a neighbor planet."

I said gently, "You're thinking of those pyramids found on Venus and Mars, Moran? I know that's a puzzler to modern science. And I've read several theories regarding their builders. But most authorities agree that their mere presence does not necessarily imply the existence of a single race of engineers. The pyramid is a fundamental structural form. Any intelligent race—"

"Man," said Moran almost sadly. "Man the dreamer; Man the doubter. No, Lieutenant, I am not speaking of theories, now. I am speaking of tales I've heard; accounts I've read in archives long molded into dust. At least three times in the past have civilized races spanned the void. It was the dying Martian race that first achieved space-flight. They found Venus a rank and stinking jungle, but on Earth certain of them set up their new abode." He smiled quietly. "And reverted to savagery, as is always the case when civilized men, removed from the source of their culture, find themselves face to face with stark reality.

"Then it was the Moon-creatures who fled their airless world, spanned the distance to nearby Earth."

I said, "That's an interesting thought, Moran. It explains the coloration of the races of man, doesn't it? I'd like to read that book you mentioned. Where can I get it?"

He shook his head sadly.

"You can't, Lt. Brait. The last copy of it was destroyed more than twelve centuries ago. Simon Magnus was the last man to read it as I remember. I loaned it to him—"

He stopped abruptly. But Sparks' eyes were plate-sized and incredulous. "—*You* loaned it to him?"

I spun on Sparks, angry. Jurnegan had told us to humor Moran, help him to a complete recovery. I didn't approve of this, not a little bit. I snapped, "That'll do, Sparks! Good Lord, man—What's the matter, Moran?"

For suddenly his face had paled, his eyes widened in horror, and he was backing away from me. He thrust out a trembling hand, gasped hoarsely, "Have a care, Brait! 'Thou shalt not take the name of the Lord, thy God, in vain—'!"

Then he fled; his running footsteps clattered down the ramp, and the echoes were strangely disturbing. Sparks stared after him, then made a circular motion at his temple.

"Nuts!" he said. "Crazy as a loon, Lootenant."

Oh, he was an odd one, that Moran. Those next days are somehow garbled in my mind. They were so full of incident that now, looking back upon them, I can hardly distinguish between that which actually *was*, and that which an active imagination conjured for me out of fancy.

This I do know—it was the worst trip I've ever experienced in the *Antigone* or any other ship. Something was always wrong. Lt. Russ Bartlett, whose mind is as accurate as the cogs of a computing machine, discovered to his dismay that he had made an error in calculation; that at our present rate of speed we would miss Earth entirely and plunge Sunward at a rate that would destroy us all. He discovered that by sheer accident, and just in time to scream a hasty, "Cut hypos!" to the engine room, else I wouldn't be here to tell it. Then there was that mysterious occurrence in the galley. Our cook had a pet cat, and if it weren't for his habit of feeding the pussy before he fed the crew, half of us would be stiff now. Because the cat slopped up its dinner and forthwith proceeded to give up all nine of its lives simultaneously. Ptomaine, from faulty food tins. The first time such a thing had happened in more than forty years!

You couldn't say Moran was behind either of these near-disasters. For I was dogging his footsteps; I'll take my oath he was not involved. Physically, that is. But they say a Jonah's curse works even though the Jonah takes no actual part.

Oh, he was an odd one, that Moran. For instance, the time Sparks' selenium plate blew out. It was Moran who got permission to use the machine shop, construct a substitute out of a uranoid-steel atmochamber. We used that freak audio throughout the trip, then replaced it with a standard one when we reached Earth. Like dopes! Because two years later that screwball First Mate of the

Saturn "invented" a uranium time-speech-trap exactly like the one Moran made us. He earned a quarter million credits from it. Imagine!

Then there was the time, as we were approaching the Lunar outpost, that our calculating machine jammed. Lieutenant Bartlett and Cap McNeally were in a dither trying to figure the approach velocity. It's a fifteen-minute job for the machine; a six-hour job for a man's brain. But Moran, who happened by, glanced casually at the declension chart, said, "Cut to forty-three at 3.05 Earth Standard, Captain. Maintain full speed for point three five parsecs, alter declension to north one, loft seven, fire fore jets twice—"

Having no better idea, McNeally did as Moran suggested. And we warped past the Moon oh-oh-oh on trajectory!

Which put us within scant hours of Earth's H-layer. And which also roused in me the realization that the mysterious Paul Moran was more than the ordinary space-sailor he pretended to be. Maybe I'm snoopy, I don't know. Anyway, I went to the radio room. I told Sparks grimly, "You and I are going to find out just who or what this Moran guy is. Send a message, Sparks. To Fred Bender, at Long Island Spaceport. Tell him to find out if there's a scientist missing who answers to this description. Five feet, seven and a half inches; a hundred and twenty-five pounds, dark hair, brown eyes—"

The relay of that description and the subsequent reply took longer than I had anticipated. That's why Sparks and I were among the last to learn of the new trouble. We didn't learn until, excited, we burst onto the bridge, confronted the skipper with our information.

"Look, Skipper!" I yelled. "No wonder 'Moran' was able to fix Sparks' radio and set your course! Do you—"

And the Captain raised haggard eyes to me.

"Brait, where have you been? I've been audioing all over the ship for you."

"In Sparks' cabin. Listen, though. Moran is—"

"I don't care," said the skipper wearily, "who he is. And in a little while, nobody else will, either. Your check-up, Mr. Brait, was a miserable failure! We are only an hour and a half out of the H-layer—and the shield generators refuse to function!"

I just stared at him for a minute. When I caught my breath, there was only enough of it for one word.

"Impossible!"

"Impossible, maybe," acknowledged the First Mate, "but unfortunately, Don, the Captain's right. Three lead-in cables are broken, the stripping is off the condenser."

"But—but everything was in perfect order an hour ago! I don't understand! Yes, I do! Moran! He said he'd destroy us all if he got a chance! Skipper, there's the answer. He's done it. The madman—"

Then there was a mirthful chuckle in the doorway, and Moran was standing there looking at us, his thin lips wide in a smile.

"You're right, Brait. I *did* do it. But I'm not a madman. I'm a happy man. The happiest man who ever lived!" His eyes lighted triumphantly; he stretched his arms above his head in a great, yearning gesture. "Soon will come freedom! The great, everlasting freedom of death."

"Get him!" said the Skipper succinctly. Gunner McCoy lumbered forward, his long, hairy arms encircled Moran's body. The Skipper pawed his graying thatch. "This is no time for reproaches, Mr. Brait. I told you to guard this man; for some reason you failed to do so. But now our problem is to repair the damage he has done. Or else—"

His pause was significant. But Moran's quiet, mocking laughter persisted.

"It is useless, Captain. Not in hours, no, not in weeks, will you repair the damage. Don't you see—" There was a feverish light in his eyes, a shuddering vibrancy in his voice. "Don't you see that I bring you the greatest of all boons known to man?

"Death! Wonderful, blissful death! Death that I have sought so long . . . so hopelessly."

Those were the last words I heard for some time. I dashed from the room, Bartlett, Sparks and McCoy at my heels. We picked up the Chief Engineer. We covered the *Antigone* from stem to stern. And our worst fears were realized. It was no use. The damage Moran had done was irreparable.

Russ Bartlett said, "There's only one way out. We mustn't try to penetrate the Heaviside layer. We must shift trajectory, pass Earth and remain in space until we get the shield generator operating again."

And Chief Lester said somberly, "Have you forgotten the trajectory you planned, Lieutenant Bartlett?"

"The trajectory?"

"I thought it was unusual," rumbled the engineer, "when you called it down to me. It's paper-thin, balanced on a knife-edge between counter-gravitations. If we try to shift course now, we'll tear the ship into shreds!"

I knew, now, why Moran had come up with such a ready answer when the computer failed. He had planned well. He had deliberately forced us into this trajectory from which there was no escape.

Back on the bridge, we found Captain McNeally pacing the deck like a caged cat. Moran was silent, watchful intent, with an unholy gleam of justification lighting his curious eyes. The skipper looked up hopefully as we entered.

"Well, gentlemen?"

Bartlett shook his head.

McNeally was silent for a long moment. His glance roved the smart, glistening interior of the *Antigone*'s control room. I knew exactly what he was thinking. It was too bad that this smooth perfection, this finest ship built by master craftsmen, should become a brief, winking flame in the atmospheric borders of Earth.

And it was tough that we must all go out together like this. Through no fault of our own. Through the machinations of a space-mad castaway. He turned to me. "Lieutenant Brait, you and Sparks will go to the radio turret. Send a complete report to the Earth authorities. Tell them—" He gulped. "Tell them why the— the *Antigone* will not come in."

I said, "Aye, aye, sir!" mechanically, and started for the door. But Sparks stopped me.

"Ain't you gonna tell 'em what we learned?"

"Eh?"

"About *him!*"

He jerked his head toward 'Moran'.

"It doesn't really make any difference now," I said. "But—" I suppose my voice was scornful. There was scorn and bitterness in my heart. "They might as well know that the man who has condemned us all to death is—or was—one of Earth's greatest scientists. Had he not become a raving lunatic his genius could have stemmed this disaster."

McNeally said, "What's that, Lieutenant? What do you mean?"

"I mean this man's name is not 'Paul Moran'—"

"Names," murmured Moran gently. "What difference does a name make? When one has had thousands of names."

"His name," I continued, "is John Cartaphilus!"

Bartlett said, "Cartaphilus!" In a leap he was at our strange guest's side, his voice eager. "Then be will—he *must*—help us!"

"Cartaphilus, listen to me! Of all men, only you have the genius to devise some way of escaping this peril! You've been mad, sir! Insane from your privations! But now I beg that you cast aside this madness, come to our rescue!"

Moran—or Cartaphilus—brushed his hand aside. A dreamy look was in his eyes.

"Death at last!" he whispered. "Oh, sweet boon of mankind —death! I who have suffered so long, waited such a long time—"

"Can't you hear me, man? Snap out of it! Time is growing short. In a half hour, maybe less, we'll nose into the H-layer. And then— Please, sir!"

But there was no reply. Captain McNeally looked at me uncertainly. "Are you sure, Brait?"

"Positive. I forwarded a description to Bender at L.I. He said Cartaphilus has been missing for a year and a half. He fled Earth because of a scandal. It seems—"

"Never mind that now." McNeally confronted the insane scientist. "Mr. Cartaphilus, you must help us out of this jam! We're not thinking only of ourselves, but of the mothers and children waiting for us on Earth. And of the future of space-travel. If the *Antigone*, the finest ship ever built, blows out in the H-layer, it will strike a heavy blow at all astronavigation. Help us, sir! For Heaven's sake—"

Cartaphilus spoke suddenly, sharply.

"Don't say that!"

"Only Heaven can save us now," said McNeally simply, "if you won't. It's our only hope. May the Lord help us if you—"

"Don't! The strange, thin man screamed the word. Suddenly he buried his face in his hands, and his words were an incoherent babble of torment. "Don't you see what you're doing? Man, have you no pity?"

He raised wide, tortured eyes. "The endlessness of time—" he whispered. "But I thought that, free of Earth, lost in the depths of space, I might at last find peace. But now you call upon me to save you in His name.

"I won't do it! I won't! The power cannot force me, here in the void. Two thousand years . . . No! No!"

McNeally stepped back, torn between dread and doubt. He shook his head at us. "It's no use. He's completely mad."

Then Russ Bartlett cried, "Wait! *Listen!*"

For Cartaphilus, his face worn and aged, had bowed his head as though surrendering to forces greater than his will-to-die. And he was droning in a drab, lack-lustre voice, "Tell the engineer to reverse the polarity of the alternate hypatomic motors. Transmit the counter electromotive force helically through the forward coils. Use full power. Keep all motors running at top speed. Cut out the intercommunicating and lighting systems; there must be no D.C. current in operation anywhere on the ship. The crosscurrents will—"

Chief Engineer Lester's face was a masque of blank dismay. He husked, "A hysteresis bloc! It might work. Nobody ever thought of it before."

"What do you mean?" That was Cap McNeally.

"His suggestion. Heterodyning the webcoils, so we'll counter the H-layer radiation with an alternating current of our own. It's just about one chance in a million!"

"Then take that chance!" cried the skipper. "Try it! Do as he says. And, for God's sake, man, *hurry!*"

Cartaphilus, his eyes drained of all expression, rose sluggishly. Once more he spoke, faintly. "It will work," he said. "It will work, and I have failed again. And all because I would not let Him rest . . ."

His voice broke in a great, wrenching sob. Then he lurched from the control room like a broken thing.

I never saw him again. No one aboard the *Antigone* ever saw him again. For the next hour we were in a turmoil, rearranging the electrical units of the ship as Cartaphilus had told us. We finished our task just in time; scant seconds after we had thrown on the power we nosed into the web-like field of force which is the H-layer.

It was a breathless moment. Despite our efforts, there was not a man of us but expected a brief, brilliant instant of horror—then oblivion. But we were as wrong as Cartaphilus had been right. There was a jolt as our forcefield met that of Earth's shield; the permalloy hull of the ship sang and hummed and glowed cherry-red under the impact of that terrific electro-motive strain, but we slipped through the barrier with greater ease than ever had any ship using the old style shield generators.

In our jubilation we quite forgot the mad scientist whose strange, last-minute change of mind had saved our lives. We landed. And sometime between the moment of landing and the moment when we remembered our passenger, he fled. Disappeared completely from the ship and from our lives.

Cap McNeally was nothing if not a square-shooter. He refused to take credit for the invention that had brought us through the

H-layer. The patent rights were taken out in the name of our deranged passenger. The "Moran H-penetrant" it is called. All spaceships used it until just recently; until Cap Hawkins of the *Andromeda* and the Venusian scientist, Jar Farges, discovered Ampies could be used as H-layer shields.

But afterward, Cap McNeally came to me, wondering.

"Why should he have wanted to die, Brait? I can't understand it. A man like John Cartaphilus; wealthy, intelligent, respected—was he really mad, do you think?"

I hesitated. I, too, had been wondering about that. I had gone so far as to look up the life history of the mad scientist. I had found several curious things. No man knew when, or where, John Cartaphilus had been born. All agreed that he was "remarkably youthful" in appearance. It was rumored that he had outlived a wife married in youth; that she had been an elderly woman when she died.

I said, "I told you there had been a scandal in his life, recently, Skipper. It concerned a friend of his, a worker in one of his shops.

"Cartaphilus was, and is, a genius, but he has a reputation for driving his men too hard. They say that on this occasion, seeking the answer to some problem that evaded him, he forced this assistant to labor for weeks, begrudging him even a few hours sleep each night.

"On the eve of the solution of the problem, this worker came to him, nervous, ragged, exhausted, begging for a brief respite. Claiming he was sick with overwork and fatigue. But John Cartaphilus insisted, impatiently, there was no time for rest. He ordered the man to get about his work.

"The job was completed. But the friend died. The doctors said it was a pure case of exhaustion. When he heard this, Cartaphilus' brain snapped. He blamed himself for the man's death, fled Earth. He became—or so we may believe—the wandering spaceman we found in the asteroids."

Cap McNeally frowned.

"Do you believe that story, Brait?"

I started to say no. I started to tell the skipper something else I had discovered while probing into the life history of John Cartaphilus. Something that, to my mind at least, more fully explained the oddness of our erstwhile passenger.

It was an old legend I had run across. The queer story of a man with many names ("I have had so many names," Moran had said) who wandered endlessly about the Earth, perhaps the universe now, simply because he had not let another rest for a moment on his doorsill.

Sometimes this man had been known as Carthaphilus. He had also been known as Juan Espera en Dios, as Ahasverus, and as Butta Deus. The Parisian gazette, "Turkish Spy," had in 1644 A.D. reported his presence in that city traveling under the name of "Paul Marrane." But men in general knew him by a more descriptive name. The Wandering Jew. The Eternal Jew . . .

But I did not tell Cap McNeally this. After all, it was a fanciful thought. And surely Moran or Marrane, or Carthaphilus—was mad when he claimed to have met and talked with Simon Magnus twelve hundred years ago?

Anyway, when we saw that ad in the classified columns of this week's *Spaceways Weekly*, and McNeally claimed Moran would return to claim his reward, it raised again the question in my mind.

Will he return? Or will he find, at last, whatever peace awaits him out there? In the vast emptiness of space, where the power cannot—must not—extend? I wonder . . .

The Message from the Void

THE COLD GLOBE PULSED UNEVENLY. IN ONE CORNER of the great vaulted chamber a fretful generator vibrated through an ever-rising tonic sequence to still itself in the silence of ultra-sound. A dim filament flared into a point of sparkling light, and Dor Jan nodded briefly to his assistant.

Silently the young mechanic pressed a button on the towering metal banks before him. Gears meshed. Wires, strung high above, hummed with an erratic vibration. Ozone crackled in the thin air, and a silent wave of power winged its way with the swiftness of light toward the pale green planet glowing in the darkness of the void. . . .

"Missing half your life. That's all there is to it!" declared the cheerful young man. "Nothing like a little home of your own with a plot of ground. 'Bring your friend out to dinner,' says my wife, 'we'll show him what real home life is.' Great girl, my wife. You'll like her. You say you've never been out to this section before?"

"Never," answered the other. With distaste he noted the tidy monotony of the small suburban community. Uniform stucco cottages; a thousand homes with a thousand similar tiny grass plots, a thousand cheery lights burning in a thousand windows for a

74

thousand husbands to "come home to." His nostrils twitched with the crisping odor of a thousand chops frying on a thousand "Little Genius" gas ranges. . . .

"Yes sir, nothing like it!" boasted his host again. "Marry and settle down is what I always say. You'll see for yourself in a minute. My house is just around the corner and past—"

"—the gas station," finished the visitor.

"What? What's that?" The proud young husband stared at his guest amazedly. "Hey, I thought you'd never been here before?"

"Why, I—I haven't!" stammered the visitor weakly. "I don't know *what* made me say that. I've never been to Highland Corners before. But all of a sudden, somehow I felt as though I'd seen this section a long, long time ago. . . ."

In the telescope chamber of the Flagstaff observatory, Sir Humphrey Wimpole, R.A., shook his head as he argued with his American friend and colleague.

"No, Wallace," he said didactically, "I'm afraid we must discard your fanciful theory of life on other planets. If you'll forgive my saying so, it smacks too much of the romantic. Like those incredible yarns one reads in the science-fiction magazines. Why, the atmospheric conditions, the lack of warmth and light, the shortage of oxygen—"

"But, Sir Humphrey," insisted Professor Wallace, "you must remember this. All life need not be exactly in the same form as ours. Different bodies, adapted to strange environments. A different form of reasoning, perhaps—"

"Tut, tut!" shrugged the British scientist impatiently. "All reasoning is based on the same fundamentals. You know as well as I do that the Milan Observatory has been attempting to communicate with other planets for more than thirty years.

"Twenty-four hours a day they broadcast a series of signals based on pure mathematics—the science which all logical creatures must recognize. The Law of the Squares. Two, followed by a four. Three, followed by a nine. Then a four—with a pause.

"Surely if there were intelligent creatures, say on Mars, they would understand the fundamental principle of this squaring factor —and send us a logical solution!"

He stopped abruptly and passed a bewildered hand over his broad face. The American leaped up.

"Sir Humphrey! What's wrong? Shall I get water?"

"No—nothing, thanks," faltered the visiting astronomer. "It's nothing at all. Just a peculiar sensation, such as we all experience occasionally. For an instant I felt that I had been through this same scene once . . . oh, a long time ago! And this is my first visit to America. Odd, isn't it?"

The magazine editor's look of amusement faded; gave way to a disturbed frown. He stared angrily at the manuscript in his hand, and pressed the buzzer on his desk.
"Miss Jenkins," he ordered, "send Murphy in here!"
Murphy entered, the broad grin on his face fading as he glimpsed the editor's expression.
"Murphy," growled the editor, "what in blazes is the idea of sending this story up here to me for reading?"
"Why—why, it's good!" stammered the first reader. "As a matter of fact, it's the best story I ever found in the unrush mail. And from an unknown, too. It shows a world of promise!"
"Good!" snorted the editor. "Of course it's good! It ought to be. It's the rankest kind of plagiarism. A direct steal from . . . from . . . well, I don't exactly remember where I read it before. But I did. I remember reading this story a long time ago. . . ."

The reciting student swayed suddenly; raised a hand to his forehead and shook his head. When he lowered it again the color had left his face. He stared at the professor with vaguely frightened eyes.
"Herr Toggman—" he whispered.
"Yes, Wilson?" The psychologist glanced at the boy curiously.
"I'm sorry," said the student, "but I've quite forgotten what question you asked me. I just had the most confused feeling. I felt as though I were suddenly repeating something I'd done a long, long time ago. Yet this is the first time we met in this classroom!"
The professor smiled gently.
"A very common sensation, Wilson. We will discuss it at greater length later in this course. It happens to all men at some time or other. Every psychologist recognizes it, and has some theory to explain it. Henri Bergson calls it, 'the memory of the present.'
"Humans walking down strange streets, talking with new acquaintances, often stop short—believing they have done the same thing some time before. Some people claim the sensation has some significance, but that is palpably absurd. It is an utterly meaningless—"

* * *

THE MESSAGE FROM THE VOID

In a control room more than 50,000,000 miles distant, Dor Jan removed the amplifying unit from his head. There was defeat in his large, many-faceted eyes as he gestured to his assistant. Once more a button was pressed. The crackling hum ceased. The generator whirred and died. The light of the pallid globe flickered wearily.

"Success, master?" The robot's assistant's thought came to the Martian astronomer's mind anxiously. Dor Jan grimaced.

"No. Failure again. I fear I must report to the Academy that the green planet definitely does *not* sustain life. I am certain that our signals reached there. Still, in more than 500 *rennai* of experiment we have received no answering signals from its cloudy obscurity.

"But surely . . . surely . . ." sighed the scientist, "if there were intelligent creatures, they would understand the fundamental principles of the Time-distortion factor—and send us the logical solution. . . ."

"Odds Without End"

Writing is fun!

If it were not fun we should not be doing it; we should be out playing some other kind of game, because life's too short that we should permit ourselves to become involved with tiresome, serious things!

In this section you will find not simply stories but auctorial playthings . . . one of the very few poems ever to appear in a science-fiction magazine . . . a story inspired by my venerable Smith-Corona in the good old days before word-processors and computers . . . stories based on my hobbies of fishing and chess . . . all admittedly odds created to the end that there should be food on the Bond dinner-table.

And wouldn't you think that after all these years I would have learned something? But apparently not, because as I prepare these tales for publication I discover to my mingled consternation and chagrin that there is little difference in length, style or quality between The Battle of Blue Trout Basin, *which appeared in Esquire in 1937, and* Proof of the Pudding *which appeared in Asimov's 62 years later.*

Ah, well a new millennium dawns. Perhaps there's still time for improvement? But come what may I'm still going to enjoy writing, because writing is and should be fun!

The Battle of Blue Trout Basin

FOR THE HUNDREDTH TIME MY LINE LOOPED OUT GRACEfully, knotted, backlashed, and fell a good six feet short of the mark for which I was casting. As I started to reel it in, grimly, I heard a sympathetic clucking from the fence that bordered on the roadside.

"Listen, guy," I said to the stranger watching me, "if you think you can do any better, come on in here and try it!"

With surprising alacrity he hopped the fence and took the rod from my hands. He balanced it daintily, lovingly, and nodded his head in approval.

"Very nice, sir," he said approvingly. "Very nice equipment, indeed. But if I might be permitted to show you—"

He cast. His movement was smooth, liquid, flowing. Like a coil of rippling light the line flew out in a beautiful arc . . . tip-poised for an instant over the distant mark . . . then slithered back toward where I stood gaping.

"Marvelous!" I gasped. "How—how do you do it?"

"The wrist. It's all in the wrist movement." He tapped my own aching member with a lean forefinger. "So many try to *snap* it here. You must *roll* it—that's the secret."

I tried it. Just as he had said, the secret lay in the proper roll and timing. My own cast flicked out—not so good as his, but good enough for me—and touched the corner of the mark.

"Well, I'll be damned!" I said. "Say—how would you like to come fishing with me some time? I could learn plenty from a master like you."

He sighed heavily. In the dusk I thought I saw two great tears well from his faded blue eyes. "I'm sorry, sir," he said, "but I really couldn't. You see—I don't fish any more."

"You don't *fish* any more!"

"Never," he said dolefully, "since I fished the wonderful Blue Trout Basin."

"Blue Trout Basin?" I repeated. "I never heard of it. But what—" An almost wistful expression on his face stopped me.

"It's a long story," he choked, "and a sad one. I used to love fishing—probably even more than you do. I went everywhere to try my hand and luck against finny warriors. I fished the backhills of Kentucky, the icy streams of Maine, the sluggish brooks of Pennsylvania. My name was on the lists of every major fishing club from Florida to Washington. I even had a fly named after me—never mind which one. There is no greater honor, sir for a true son of Izaak Walton.

"It was upon one of my trips that I discovered the Blue Trout Basin. Never mind which state I was in. Let us merely say that it is a land of trout and salmon. A fisherman's Mecca. And there, by chance, I came upon a pool hidden deep in a wooded dell. No local fisherman had ever mentioned it, so it was with the faintest hope of a kill that I cast out over its dark, sullen waters.

"Imagine my surprise, then, when my very first cast was greeted with a strike that shot up along my arm with an electric bolt! For an instant I was stupified—then instinct came to my rescue, and with all the caution and canniness that years of experience had taught me, I began to play what I was certain was a giant trout."

"And was it?" I asked eagerly.

The stranger gazed at me somberly. "I landed him," he said slowly, "in exactly two minutes!"

"*Two minutes!*" I exclaimed. "Why, that's impossible! Fifteen . . . twenty minutes . . ."

"I know," mourned the old man. "That's what I thought, too. But I was wrong. In two minutes I had landed my first trout in the Blue Trout Basin. Inside of half an hour my creel was groaning with a dozen more. In an hour's time I had two gaffs, a creel, and my lunch basket jammed with three dozen blue trout—none of them less than twelve inches long!

"Now that I look back on it, I wonder that I didn't see the truth immediately. At the time, all I could think was that I had inadvertently stumbled upon a fisherman's Paradise—that more luck was mine than any Waltonite deserves.

"I finally began to understand when I noticed that it was getting increasingly difficult to walk on the bottom of the little pool. The bottom, sir, was slippery. When I looked down to learn why, I saw that the pool was covered—absolutely covered—with layer upon layer of fish! And those fish, sir—*those fish were waiting in line to take my lures!*"

A sob broke the old stranger's voice.

"You may believe it or not, sir," he wailed, "but once I broke my leader in that accursed pool. When I drew in my line to replace it, I found a trout hanging on the end of the line with the cord drawn tight around his neck! That fish had deliberately hanged himself!"

My visitor pulled up one trouser leg, disclosing a jagged, semicircular scar on his calf.

"That," he whimpered, "is where one of those demon trout bit me. That was when I tried to get out of the pool. I had caught enough to satisfy even my inordinate lust for killing—but those trout wouldn't let me go. They built a bulwark of solid fish-flesh about my legs, hemming me in so I couldn't move an inch! Two of the larger and stronger ones jumped right into my haversack. I tried to throw away my rod, but three fish impaled themselves on it before it left my hand! And I found three large trout, later, in one of my bootlegs!"

"But listen—" I began angrily.

He wiped an arm across his streaming eyes. "You see, sir," he said piteously, "those fish wanted to be caught! They were weary of life and determined to commit suicide. That's why they called that pool the 'Blue Trout Basin.' Everybody in those parts knows about the fish, and won't go after them. So when a stranger gets in the pool, the trout just go crazy. They won't let him go until he catches *all* of them!"

"So you," I said scornfully, "caught them all, I suppose?"

He looked at me with pain-racked eyes. Slowly he backed away into the gathering darkness. His voice, aged and melancholy, floated back to me from the gloom of the roadside.

"No, sir!" he wailed. "I never did get away from those fish. By sheer weight of numbers they pulled me down. Up there in the Blue Trout Basin, sir—I drowned!"

I went in the house. Quickly.

The Unusual Romance of Ferdinand Pratt

THERE WAS A LITTLE MAN NAMED FERDINAND PRATT, and he was an undistinguished writer of romance fiction for the heart-throb magazines. He was small and quiet and very shy, and he had no bad habit whatsoever.

His life was uneventful except that he had a Secret Passion. Her name was Mabel Smythe, and she was his secretary. But he had never been able to summon up the nerve to tell her she was his you-know-what, so nothing had ever come of the affair.

Of course Mabel would have been a dope indeed had she not noticed by this time that Ferdinand's heroines were always blonde and petite and full-breasted, like herself, although the way Ferdinand always wrote it in his stories was "firm bosomed." But since he never said anything, neither did she, and you can't blame her.

Well, this day Ferdinand was walking down Fifth Avenue when suddenly the wind blew extra hard, and the skirts of the girl in front of him blew up, revealing a sizeable acreage of very nice limb, indeed. As might be expected, Ferdinand blushed and looked away, but he was both shocked and surprised to hear a low whistle of approval from a spot just beside him.

He turned to chide the person who had voiced such admiration, but all he could see was a large, black fog leaning against a lamp-post. At the base of this fog, he saw a silver stick. So he picked it up and said, "Excuse me, sir—but is this yours?"

For a moment there was silence, then a filmy appendage writhed out of the black fog and grabbed the stick from his hand. A thick, slightly muffled voice said, "Me wand! Geez, yeah! Gimme!"

The stick disappeared into the fog. Ferdinand was about to walk on when another black tendril twisted from the fog, twining about his wrist. It was dank and slimy and very disconcerting, as well as rather chilly.

"Wait a sec, bud!" said the voice. "How come you to see me? I'm invisible."

Ferdinand said politely, "Oh, I'm sorry. But you're not, really." And he explained that the black fog was *quite* visible. "Moreover," he added, "you're leaving a black stain on the sidewalk. If Mr. LaGuardia sees it, there's likely to be trouble."

The black fog bent to stare moodily at the mark. It said, in a disappointed voice, "Aw, geez! An' I t'ought dis time I had it down poifect. I guess me transreflex modifier musta got bawled up wid de supercoroner control!"

Ferdinand said, "That's too bad!" commiseratingly. "But I think I should be getting along—"

"Hold it," said the fog. "How come you wasn't surprised to see me, bud?"

Ferdinand explained that he was a writer of romantic fiction, and pointed out that in romantic fiction almost anything is more than likely to appear out of thin air, except maybe a pornographic phrase or Mr. Chamberlain's umbrella. The fog listened thoughtfully; meanwhile shifting from foot to foot as if worried about those inky stains it was leaving. Finally it said:

"Well, I guess it don't matter. I was kinda put out, on account of dis time I t'ought I really had it. I been woikin' on invisiblity for t'ree weeks, now, but I can't git to foist baste wid it. But seein' as how you done me a favor, I'll do *you* one. What would you like to have?"

Ferdinand looked mildly astonished. Thinking of Mable, he said, "Just anything at all, you mean?"

"You name it," said the fog proudly. "I'll do it." He sounded very pleased with himself. "You see, ever sinct I loined how to be a dejinn—"

"Gin," corrected Ferdinand. "Like the drink."

"Yeah? Geez, I t'ought you said de 'd' foist. Well, like I was sayin', I found dis ol' bottle in a junk shop over in de Bronx, where I live. An' when I opened it, I found out how to be a—a *gin!* So—" said the black fog triumphantly, "I been studyin' up ever sinct. Oney I can't seem to get de hang of dis invisibility stuff. I'll loin, though."

"I'm sure you will," Ferdinand assured him. "But now about my wish—"

"Just name it, pal. A million bucks? A Rolls-Rerce?"

Ferdinand said, "If you don't mind, I'd like a girl to fall in love with me."

"A goil!" said the Bronx djinn. "Say, bud, I t'ink you got somethin' dere. Why didn't I t'ink of dat meself?"

There was a fleeting glint of silver in the jet cloud, and suddenly Ferdinand had a horrible vision of himself being pursued up Fifth Avenue by a rapacious horde of assorted showgirls, shopgirls and debutantes. He cried, swiftly, "Oh, wait! not just *any* girl. One girl in particular, I mean!"

The djinn said disappointedly, "Just *one?*"

"That's all," said Ferdinand meekly. "My secretary."

The djinn sighed. "Pal, you're bein' a sucker, But if dat's what you want—" He waved the silver wand; muttered something that sounded like a Federal bureau. "Abracadabra—palegratyzsch—effish—locarnxy—make de guy's typewriter fall in love wid him—"

Ferdinand, a purist in spite of all, suggested, "Pardon me. Don't you mean *typist?*"

But he was talking to space. The black fog had suddenly whisked upward, and was now hovering before the third floor window of the Little Garmente Shoppe, Sol Greenstein & Sons, Props., peeking in at the Young Ladies' & Misses Ready-to-Wear Fitting Room. The wand was describing ecstatic undulations.

Ferdinand tut-tutted; then shrugged. It probably didn't matter how the djinn had phrased the command. So, with a disappoving frown toward the black fog, which was now perched with obvious enjoyment on the very window-sill, chuckling coarsely, Ferndinand hurried back to his office.

It was clear, however, that the command had not done anything to Miss Smythe so far. She was typing when Ferdinand entered, and she continued typing. Ferdinand searched her eyes hopefully for the love-light which should be glowing there, but found only a look of suspicious curiosity. So he blushed and hurried into his private office.

He sat down before his typewriter. He was disappointed. And

he had learned, in the past, that work was the best salve for disappointment. So he inserted a clean sheet of bond into the machine and began pecking at a new story.

It was most annoying. He had written for perhaps two minutes, when he chanced to glance at the sheet. It said:

"I LOVE YOU"
by
Ferdinand M. Pratt

"I love you. I love you. I love you, I love you. I love you. I—"

Ferdinand said, "Oh, my!" annoyedly. His mind must be woolgathering. The day's experience had upset him. He tore the sheet out of the machine swiftly. He ripped it into tiny shreds, and thrust them into his wastebasket. He was ashamed to think what Miss Smythe might think if she saw that stark revelation of his inner thoughts so clearly printed on that white sheet.

He reeled another sheet into the typewriter. This time he concentrated with extreme care. He was perfectly sure that his story started:

"She tripped lightly down the staircase; a vision of delight in a sapphire and gold evening gown. Her eyes—

But it didn't come out like that! Before Ferdinand's astonished gaze; plain, unashamed, on the sheet were the words:

"I love you. When are you going to stop ignoring me? If you but realized the depths of my pass—"

Ferdinand gasped, "Oh, my goodness!" and swept a hand experimentally over his forehead. It was a trifle feverish, he thought. He poured a drink from his desk carafé; gulped it. He mopped his brow. He wiped a hand across his eyes. He sat quietly in his seat a moment, staring at the typewriter. Then he started fingering the keys again. Deliberately. Carefully. He spelt his own name. He hit the F key, the E key, the R–D–I–N–A–N–D–

It came out—

I LOVE YOU!

Ferdinand fell back in his chair. He felt weak. He thought of calling Miss Smythe—then hesitated. He knew how sick men often raved their innermost thoughts. And he feared what he might say to her under this strange spell.

He got up and looked at himself in the tiny washstand mirror. As he was standing there, he heard the "plip-plip" of typewriter keys striking the platen roll. He wheeled swiftly. Just in time to see the carriage slam itself back!

He raced to the side of the machine. There was a new sentence.

It said, "Don't be afraid, Ferdinand, I have always loved you."

Ferdinand was terrified, but common sense told him it must be some horrible mistake. Some mechanical defect in the typewriter, maybe. He lifted the shield, peered curiously at the key-flanges. They looked all right. Everything seemed to be in order. But then, of course, he wasn't a mechanic—

He poked one of the inner parts experimentally. Then leaped back, startled. For the machine emitted a low, metallic giggle, and suddenly tapped out, "Don't! You tickle!"

For a moment, Ferdinand stood there, indecisive. He moved forward again; lifted the machine; looked under it. The clacking of the keys made him drop it to the desk. The thing had printed, in coy capitals, "NAUGHTY BOY!"

He lost his temper then. Actually! He gritted his teeth and up-ended the accursed machine, meaning to find once and for all the meaning of this incredible phenomenon. There was one spring that didn't look just right. He poked it—

"Ouch!" yelled Ferdinand. For the carriage, suddenly, had leaped back at his probing finger. The marks where the gears had nipped the flesh looked, for all the world, like wee *tooth*-marks! As he glared, the instrument started tapping. It pegged out, rebelliously.

"Really! What kind of a typewriter do you think I am?"

It was then that the truth of the whole terrible disaster dawned on Ferdinand. The djinn's command *had* come true! His typewriter had fallen in love with him!

It is best that we should draw a curtain of incurious charity over the strange romance of Ferdinand Pratt. Love is, at best, a dangerous toy. But love such as this—

During the next two weeks, things went from bad to worse. Ferdinand's typewriter, being an articulate creation, wanted to voice its affection. And did so, voluminously. Being a thing of low sensitivity, it lacked shame. It was, in short, a most persistently abandoned creature.

It wrote notes to Ferdinand. Wild notes. He tried to keep paper away from it, but it had a diabolic ingenuity at getting into desk drawers and cupboards. When Ferdinand came to his office each morning, he would find reams of correspondence, faithfully and lovingly tapped out by the impassioned machine during the night, neatly stacked on his desk. And the text of these notes was—well, uninhibited, to say the least. For Ferdinand had been a writer of romance fiction.

He *had* to get to the office first every morning. For if Miss Smythe should ever see one of those notes—He shuddered.

And the typewriter trustingly believed that his new habit of arriving early was a token of affection. As soon as he came in, it would tap a cheery, *"Good morning!"* Then like as not, it would hop off the desk onto his lap. It liked to sit on Ferdinand's lap and let him stroke its keyboard. It would tinkle its little bell, and tap out a slow, contented stream of little "mmmmmmmmm's."

To make matters worse, it was jealous of Miss Smythe. It wrote her notes; notes that Ferdinand carefully destroyed each morning when he came in. And the things it called her—well, Mable would have been outraged. Ferdinand was.

Ferdinand grew thin. He grew haggard. His nerves became as tense as a World's Fair mural. His eyes held a hunted look. His production diminished; finally stopped altogether.

Something had to be done. Finally, he thought of what he must do. Find the djinn. Make him repeal his command. So Ferdinand searched Fifth Avenue high and low. No djinn. He tried the Bronx. No djinn. And then, one day, inspiration came to him. One thing would bring the djinn. A girl show!

"I want it big, Miss Smythe," he said. "At least ten feet deep and thirty feet long. And make sure the advertisements are in all the papers."

Mable Smythe stared at her employer dubiously. He had been acting queerly, now, for almost three weeks. Quite unlike himself. He did not work. And she had several times seen letters around the office; letters obviously written to him by some woman. And such letters! Only a brazen hussy would dare to say the things that Mable had noticed—oh, just scanning, you understand!—on the last page.

And now, *this*—

She said, in what was intended to be a frigid tone, "I'm not certain, Mr. Pratt, that I should remain as your secretary. After all, I never expected to—"

"Oh, hush!" said Ferdinand petulantly. Which is an indication of the ragged condition of Ferdinand's nerves. He would never have dreamed of speaking to Mable in that tone a few weeks ago. "Just do as I say!" And he went out for a walk. The typewriter was waiting for him in the office. He didn't feel up to fondling its space bar for another single moment.

Miss Smythe got to her task thoughtfully. She was extremely disturbed. But she inserted the advertisement in the papers. She ordered the poster. It was a huge one, brightly lettered in red. It said, "SEE THE LIVING MODELS! COME ONE—COME ALL! 100 Beautiful Girls in Nothing Flat!"

It cost Ferdinand plenty. More than he could afford. But it was the only way he could think of to lure the Bronx djinn out of retirement.

By two-thirty the next afternoon, his office and those on either side of it were jammed to the portals with feminine pulchritude; the models Ferdinand had employed. There were all sizes and types of girls. Blondes, brunettes, redheads. Tall and short; slim and chubby. They had but one thing in common. Curves.

Mable Smythe looked at this bevy of beauties, and was shocked. This, she told herself, was the last straw! Of all persons in the world to turn—to turn *lecher!*—Mr. Pratt! And he must be perfectly horrible, you know, to do a thing like this! She had never before seen him in his true light. And these girls— Thoughtfully she smoothed her dress down in the front. And in the back; snugly over the hips. She sniffed. It was really rather insulting, in a way. That he should ignore her when planning such a—an *orgy* here in the office!

Ferdinand's typewriter was all aflutter. It tapped, over and over again, *"Why, Ferdinand, you perfect darling! And you're doing all this for poor little me!"*

The hours approached. Ferdinand walked to the window. The day was clear and warm. There was no sign of a cloud; not even a small, black one. He sighed. But he turned to his models.

"All right, girls," he said. "Get ready for the show. Try on the bathing suits given to you. And—take your time dressing."

One of the girls complained, "Mr. Pratt, there are no shades in the windows."

"You're on the fifth floor. It doesn't matter," said Ferdinand. But as he hurried out to the fire-escape he hoped it would matter. This whole thing, the huge canvas sign, the advertisements, the show, had been planned not for the gaping males gawking up from the streets below, but for the one person to whom height meant nothing. The djinn.

He sat down on the fire-escape and waited. For ten minutes. Fifteen. A half hour. Nothing happened. That is, nothing he was hoping for. Lots happened inside the offices. Girls undressed, leisurely; got into bathing suits and stood around talking.

They talked and laughed and posed. They compared suits audibly—and figures mentally.

But no black cloud appeared to perch on the window-sill. Another quarter hour passed. The girls inside were becoming restless. Ferdinand heard one of them say, "Well, this is the screwiest thing *I* ever did. If that funny little duck doesn't come back directly, and tell us what to do next, *I'm* going home."

And still no djinn. Ferdinand sighed. He started to rise. It was a failure. He might as well go back and pay the girls off; send them all home—

Then suddenly he gasped and started! For there, at the window, was one girl who was not being paid to model! And what a girl! Slowly pirouetting before the window and before Ferdinand's astounded gaze in the briefest, most daring of all the swimsuits Ferdinand had rented. It was—Mable Smythe!

And—

"Whew! Now, dere's w'at *I* call a real babe!" said a hoarse, familiar voice.

Ferdinand wheeled frantically. He saw nothing. But he cried, "You! Where are you? Djinn—"

"Right here," said a complacent voice at his elbow. "Geez, I been right here all along. You don't t'ink I was goin' to miss dis do you?" And, irrelevantly, "I finally got de invisibility down pat, see?"

Ferdinand clutched feverishly at empty space. He cried:

"I see! I mean, I don't see, so I must see. Listen, Mr. Djinn—you've got to repeal that order you gave! You made a mistake! You made my *typewriter* fall in love with me instead of my typist. It's been driving me crazy!"

"Geez," said the djinn regretfully, "I'm sorry, pal. I never stopped to think—" There was the faintest glint, and a swishing sound. "Cherawoeksivle—glapoo! Dere you are, bud. All fixed now! Hey, what's de rush?"

But this time it was he who spoke to empty air. Ferdinand was scrambling madly into the building, through the hall, to his office. He burst in, disregarding the affronted screams of semi-clad femininity. He raced to his desk; looked down at his typewriter—

Nothing happened. He touched it. Still nothing happened. Boldly, he picked it up; shook it. It was silent and immobile, as all good little typewriters should be. Ferdinand closed his eyes.

Angry hands plucked at his elbow. A shrill voice demanded, "Look here, what's this all about, wise guy? Do we get paid for this afternoon's work, or what?"

Ferdinand said nothing. Ferdinand had fainted!

Afterward, quite some time afterward, Ferdinand came to his

senses to feel soft, caressing hands on his forehead, and smell sweet, familiar perfume unfamiliarly near him.

He opened his eyes and looked into those of Mable Smythe. Everything came back to him. He stammered:

"The—the girls?"

"I paid them off," said Mable, "and sent them home." And reprovingly, "It wasn't very *nice* of you, you know! You shouldn't do things like that!"

Ferdinand blushed guiltily. He began, "Miss Smythe, I think you should know—"

"Mable," corrected the girl gently, "to you—Ferdinand. That is, if you *want* poor little me. But, of course, you will have to stop this dreadful philandering. I wouldn't want to marry a man who didn't stay home with his wife and—and—"

Ferdinand rose weakly. As he did so, a low, coarse voice chuckled in his ear, "Sorry I mixed it up, pal. But it looks like it's gonna woik dis way, anyhow, don't it?"

"Did you say something, dear?" said Mable. But it was a rhetorical question. Womanlike, there were several things she wanted to know. Most important of all—"Did you like me in that perfectly shocking swimsuit? I wouldn't *dare* wear it, of course, but still—"

Ferdinand, very wisely, said nothing.

The Ballad of Blaster Bill

When you're hurtling 'round the Sun
On the perihelion run
Through the asteroids from Jupiter to Mars,
You may chance to see a light
In the everlasting night,
An unwinking beacon sister to the stars.

Then each member of the crew
From the lowest wiper to
The Skipper on the bridge, a moment will
Drop all work and gravely, mute,
Raise his arm in full salute,
To the final resting place of Blaster Bill.

Afterward, if you are not
Just a nosey rankey-pot,*
And the thing that ticks within you isn't stone,
You may learn from spacemens' lips
Tales of ancient days and ships,
And why Bill the Blaster lies there all alone.

(* rankey-pot—Earthlubber; from the Venusian "renqui-pth")

II

Surly Jonathan McNeer
Was the Master Engineer
On the wallowing old freighter, *Dotty Sue*.
He was gruff, uncouth, unclean,
And his language was obscene,
But a better grease-pot never soared the blue.

He had nerves of tempered steel,
And without a squawk or squeal
He would plot a course to Hades for a thrill;
But his temper was like fire
And the man who drew his ire,
Who tried his patience most, was — Blaster Bill.

Bill the Blaster was a lazy,
Good-for-nothing (some said crazy),
Guy who didn't have a gray cell in his head.
He had muscle in his shoulders,
And his forearms were like boulders,
But his cranium and can were filled with lead.

Without ever even trying
He could make McNeer start crying
Down the wrath of Baal upon his hapless dome.
He and awkwardness were cousins,
He broke things by scores and dozens,
Just one look at him and tubes sang, "Ohm, sweet Ohm!"

On the *Dotty Sue*, his duty
Was to keep all tutti-frutti
The rocket-blasts, the motors and the rest
Of the intricate equipment
Which insures a speedy shipment
To the planets that are buttons on Sol's vest.

But McNeer's deserved objection
Was — Bill practiced vivisection
Every time he placed his thumbs (which numbered five)
On a section of machinery.
"He'd be better in a beanery!"
Was McNeer's complaint. "I'll skin the guy alive!"

"Now, there, Jonathan!" the Skipper
  Used to say. "Don't be a yipper.
I'm sure Bill does the best he can." But grief
  Etched gray, fretful lines and horrid
  On McNeer's space-weathered forehead.
"The best is none to good!" complained the Chief.

III

Two months out of Io City
  Everything was running pretty,
The asteroids were thirty hours away,
  When McNeer, to whom perfection
  Was a sort of predilection,
Said, "Bill, we'll take the hypos down today."

Well, the hypatomic motors
  Are the energy-plus rotors
That control a spaceship's motion in the void.
  When the ship is once free-wheeling
  'Neath the vast celestial ceiling.
Then's the time to clean the grit with which they're cloyed.

So Bill said, "Yup. Okey-dokey!"
  And with movements slow and pokey
Dismounted Number One and got to work.
  "Do a perfect job, you *globaar!**
  Or I'll crown you with a crow-bar!"
Warned McNeer—and then he vanished with a smirk.

(*globaar—shiftless person; Ionian term of reproach)

It was some two hours later
  As, upon his "sweet pertater"
The Chief Engineer was tootling *Venus Nell,*
  That the Second Mate, half witless,
  Out of breath and frightened spitless,
Burst in crying, "Chief, we're on our way to hell!"

"What, already?" drawled McNeer
  But the mate, pale green with fear,
Bawled, "Go get the hypos working, without fail!
  And go do it on the double,
  'Cause we're in a peck of trouble!
A rogue asteroid is riding on our tail!"

IV

Now, in case you don't remember,
A "rogue asteroid's" a member
Of the minor planet group that's slipped its cogs.
Wrenched by gravitational forces,
It careens about its courses
In an orbit not computable by logs.

Tons on tons of granite, metaled,
By the tug of Jove unsettled,
Weaving in, about, below its normal belt;
Is it any wonder why a
Spaceman fears this mad pariah?
Dreads the moment when its power may be felt?

With a single, sharp, explosive
Word that acted as corrosive
On the mate's embarrassed eardrums, raced McNeer
To the engine-room where, peaceful,
Happy, busy, very grease-full,
Labored Blaster Bill, with grins from ear to ear.

"Bill!" McNeer cried, voice all blurry,
"Get that hypo in a hurry—"
Then his order strangled as he stared, aghast.
"What is this?" he faltered weakly.
"What is this?" And Bill, quite meekly,
Said, "I thought I'd melt it down for a recast!"

His imagination racing
The Chief gazed upon the casing
Of the hypatomic motor Number Three,
Now a pool of molten metal
Bubbling gently in a kettle.
"Goddlemighty!" yelled McNeer. "This thing can't be!"

Bill asked, "Why the mad commotion?"
Then they glimpsed a sudden motion
And the Skipper's face was in the televise.
"Got the motors fixed, McNeer?"
And the Chief said, low and clear,
"No. Does someone know a prayer amongst you guys?"

THE BALLAD OF BLASTER BILL 97

"Why?" the Skipper roared, distrait;
The Chief let him have it straight.
"The hypatomic's melted into wax!
But before that rogue gets near,
I've a twelve pound hammer here
To warp across my blaster's parallax!"

"Wait!" the Captain cried, "Not yet!
We must cover every bet.
I'm commander of this freighter while she rolls.
We must somehow make a turn,
Shake that damn rogue off our stern.
Suppose you try the manual controls?"

McNeer sadly shook his head
As he saw the rusty red
Of the long neglected manuals, but yelled,
"Hop to it, Bill, you dope!
It's our last and only hope—"
And then he stopped and gulped, "Well, I'll be helled!"

With his back arched neck to heel,
Bill was straining at the wheel;
The year old rust was breaking off in flakes.
McNeer's eyes lit with joy,
He shouted, "Bill, my boy!
"She's yielding! See, there, lad? She gives! She shakes!"

And true enough, the screw
Of the gallant *Dotty Sue*
Was turning 'neath the blaster's mighty brawn.
The C. E.'s voice was thunder,
"We're getting out from under!
Just hold 'er, Bill; the danger will be gone!"

A moment, still as death,
While Bill the Blaster's breath
Rasped through the rocking room in tortured sobs.
Then from the bridge rang out
The Skipper's warning shout,
"Too late! Abandon ship. Chief! Don your lobs!"

McNeer said, "Too bad, Bill,
Just hold 'er there until

I get the lobs, and then we'll pull our freight."
  With firm, untrembling hands
  He took down from their stands
Two spacesuits, worn and old and out of date.

  But Bill the Blaster stood
  As motionless as wood;
His arms like knotted oak in cords of strain.
  He slowly shook his head
  And to the Chief he said,
"If all break ship, we'll not see Earth again."

  "I know—" began McNeer.
  But Bill roared out, "Stand clear!"
His arms upon the wheel were like a vise.
  "Break ship and wait outside.
  I'll make this baby ride!
I'll hold 'er till the devil skates on ice!"

  Then in the visiplate
  Appeared the Second Mate,
"All out below? Did you break ship, McNeer?"
  McNeer said, "Right away!
  Come on, Bill, don't delay!"
But Bill the Blaster panted, "Chief, stand clear!"

  "You fool, you're courting death!"
  Bill answered, "Save your breath."
And grinned, "You'll need that oxygen outside!"
  And stood like frozen steel
  Beside that bucking wheel,
McNeer, reluctant, hovered at his side. . . .

  Till Bill cried, "You damn fool!"
  And grabbed a handy tool
And slashed it 'cross his headpiece like a mace.
  There came a crashing roar,
  McNeer knew nothing more
Until he woke to find himself in space.

V

  About him, staff and crew
  Of the ill-starred *Dotty Sue*
Were huddled, bitter, grim, but unafraid.

A quarter mile away
The last scene of the fray
Tween Man and Asteroid was being played.

Her stern jets flaming white
Against the endless night
The bobbing ship was fighting, bolt and nail,
To curve from underneath
Those looming tons of death
That poised above her like a cosmic flail.

McNeer cried, "No, Bill! No!"
And then his audio
Clacked with the Skipper's thin, metallic voice,
"There's nothing we can do
But hope he pulls her through.
He made his choice, McNeer; a hero's choice."

As they watched tensely, all,
The spaceship seemed to crawl
An inch, a foot, a yard, another yard . . .
Meanwhile, the massive rock
Racked blindly toward the shock
With vast, colossal, cosmic disregard.

And nearer yet they drew,
To their strange *rendezvous*
In space; Fate's balance hovered fine and thin.
And then, "The Lord be praised!"
The crew a paean raised;
McNeer's white lips cracked in a nerveless grin.

Imponderable mass
And spaceship seemed to pass
Each other with a hair 'twixt hull and face;
But then, as every voice
Roused in a loud rejoice,
A single boulder slashed through empty space—

The spaceship buckled, bent;
A gaping, white-fanged rent
Split stern plates, and McNeer's voice cracked with fear.
"Board ship, all hands!" he cried!
"Bill's dying there inside!"
The wan sun watched the killer disappear.

McNeer was first to kneel
  Beside the shattered wheel
And Bill's pale, silent figure; gray with grief
  He cried, "He's breathing yet!
  Here, Skipper! Help me get—"
But Bill said, "No—don't try to lift me, Chief."

"I look all right on top
  But . . . better get . . . a mop . . .
My underneath part's not so good. . . . ." A chill
  Ran through his broken frame,
  But, to the last ditch game,
"I held 'er to 'er course—" said Blaster Bill.

VI

So—hurtling 'round the Sun
  On the perihelion run
Through the asteroids from Jupiter to Mars,
  You may chance to see a light
  In the everlasting night,
An unwinking beacon, sister to the stars.

And then, if you are not
  A lousy *rankey-pot*,
With the instincts of the back end of a horse,
  You'll stand a moment, mute,
  Arm raised in full salute
To Blaster Bill—who held 'er to 'er course.

Case History

"**C**ASE 139," SAID THE CHIEF OF STAFF. "JOHN WILSON, white, male, 45. He calls himself the man who solved the Flying Saucer secret. Listen carefully, please. When you have heard him, I'll ask for your suggestions."

He motioned to attendants, who ushered in a short, plump, balding man in beltless slacks and sandals without laces. The chief of staff greeted him gently.

"Mr. Wilson, these doctors are your friends. They want to help you. Will you be good enough to tell them your story?"

John Wilson nodded quietly, stepped to the rostrum and addressed the group.

"Sirs," he said, "I will not waste your time. I will tell you in simple, straightforward fashion how I solved the secret of the Flying Saucers. If there are any questions afterward, I will be glad to answer them.

"At the time I conceived my brilliant scheme I was a bank teller. An uninteresting occupation you will say—not one that calls for great imagination. Yet from my youth I was an imaginative man. An avid reader of fantasies and science-fiction, I had reached middle-age convinced that life is rich with unsolved mysteries. When an unusual circumstance presented itself I was not satisfied with a commonplace explanation. I preferred to seek beyond known facts for the unusual but possibly true solution which eluded the cautious minds of orthodox scientists.

"You are aware that a few years ago began a series of inexplicable appearances. In the skies were seen strange objects known as Flying Saucers. So many observations were forced to concede something unusual was happening. Commissions were appointed to investigate. These groups brought in reports. To their great shame, all claimed the Flying Saucers were merely optical illusions, known heavenly bodies, or runaway balloons.

"These explanations did not satisfy me. They were too pat, too simple. Studying the history of Flying Saucers I discovered that such objects had been sighted for over a hundred years. It became clear that Earth, for many decades, had been under observation by unearthly aliens. Who were these creatures, where they came from, or what they looked like, I had no idea. But I resolved to learn.

"I based my effort on two logical assumptions: that these visitors were intelligent, and that since observation was their purpose, they would be attracted by any unusual action. Obviously, if I could draw my quarry to watch *me* I could also see *them*. Therefore I determined to make myself uniquely, inescapably, conspicuous.

"Earth's most outstanding artificial landmark is the Empire State Building. I went to this structure, paying an admission fee like any visitor. But where others came to see, I came to be *seen*. To the tower I carried in a suitcase certain attention-compelling props: a crimson cloak similar to that worn by a cartoon character known as Superman; bells and horns of varied pitch and tone; an assortment of rocket flares. These last I selected in varied colors: red, green, purple, orange, not knowing which hues might be most visible to creatures of an alien world.

"I reached the observation tower on a fine, clear morning in midsummer. The sky was blue and cloudless; only a faint breeze stirred. Having reached my destination unchallenged, I committed the only act of violence of which I may be charged. At gunpoint I forced from the platform all others who were there—visitors and guards alike. Then I secured the doorway so I might be alone. I estimated that before I could be evicted from my eyrie I had about thirty minutes to attract those whose attention I sought.

"Alone on the tower, I sprang into action. Putting on the bizarre costume I have mentioned, I climbed from the platform to the tip of the metal spire which rises an additional hundred feet. To this I secured myself with a linesman's belt, then set into action my visible and audible apparatus. Bells rang, a siren howled, lights flashed about me, rockets flared; the sky was dyed with a dozen gorgeous hues as I made myself the center of a pyrotechnic display deliberately designed to gain attention.

"I attracted attention quickly enough. But not of those from whom I desired it. The city sprawled beneath me like a concrete web. Its street swarmed with a huddle of human ants, faces upturned. New York had turned out in mass to witness the suicidal swansong of a madman. But no unearthly visitors appeared.

"At such times as my siren was not wailing or I was not deafened by the clamor of my own bells I could hear men attempting to force the tower door. With battering at first. Then, when that had failed, I heard the hiss of a blowtorch as the door was seared from its hinges. This worried me, for I was well aware that if this attempt failed I would never get another.

"I can bridge the next ten minutes with one word—despair. My effort was in vain. In a moment of overzealous jangling I dropped my bells. I am sure they struck no one in the crowd below, for I saw a swift circle open in the ring of humanity packing the streets. For this I am grateful, since I had no wish to harm anyone.

"But my bells were gone, my siren battery finally failed, and eventually I exhausted my small stock of flares and Roman candles. I heard voices, and looking down discovered the tower door had been forced. Uniformed men were flooding onto the platform. A tense-jawed man—I presume a professional steeplejack—started climbing the spire toward me. He approached to within fifty feet, then thirty, twenty. As he moved upward he talked desperately, pleading with me to come down quietly and stop being, as he put it, a damned fool.

"Then, at the last minute, when all seemed hopeless—when I was about to unbuckle my belt and tell the advancing man I would follow him down—out of failure came triumph. Scudding across the sky appeared a Flying Saucer. The crowd below loosed a cry of amazement. I heard the gasp of my would-be rescuer, saw him hastily descend the spire, leaving me to my fate.

"But this I saw with only half an eye, for the Saucer was circling closer and closer, until at last I saw a portal open in its side. An alien figure appeared in this opening, gestured to me. I signalled my desire to speak to him. He nodded and drew closer still, bridging the gap between us to mere inches. I unfastened my safety belt, stepped into the Saucer, and—" John Wilson smiled—"you know the rest. I became the first Earthman to make contact with the occupants of a spaceship from the planet Tria of the star Aldebaran."

The speaker paused, glanced hesitantly at the chief of staff, who rose and nodded pleasantly.

"Thank you, Wilson. That will be all for now." To those who flanked Wilson he said, "Take him back to his cell."

When the man who solved the Flying Saucer secret was gone, the chief of staff turned again to his associates.

"I am sure," he said, "you have been interested by this narrative, the true case history of the first creature to be brought home to Tria alive from the planet Earth of the star Sol. As you see, theirs is a primitive civilization. But their planet is greatly to our liking. Now that we have successfully contacted one member of their race and can learn from him those things which we have been trying to discover over a period of decades, I believe we can proceed more swiftly toward our goal of occupation and conquest."

Herman and the Mermaid

THAT "ALL'S FAIR IN LOVE AND WAR" STUFF—THAT'S THE old malarkey. Any sap knows love is about as fair as a third called strike on a Dodger. And as for *war* . . .

You take Herman, for instance. When Uncle Sam starts pitching those Congressional Medals and Purple Hearts, who do you think's going to be behind the plate? Herman? Don't make me laugh! A bunch of guys named MacArthur and Doolittle, et cetera . . . they're the ones. Herman's only pay-off will be a comfortable feeling around his conscience and a twenty-five-per-cent profit on his war bonds.

Which goes to prove Sherman's point. Because, in his own small way, Herman McGonivan did as much to aid in the war effort as any officer with a sleeveful of braid. But no one will ever know Herman did any more to help Democracy's cause than boo at Hitler in the movies, because—

Well, it was like this:

Herman worked in a Bronx filling station, a duty he bore with stoic fortitude. Not all mortals are privileged to till the soil of Canaan for their daily bread. It was enough for Herman that when day was done he was free to return to that smallish segment of heaven bounded on the east by the Bay, on the west by the Dodgers, and on the north by Steve Brody's Bridge.

Herman came to work in the morning happy as a lark, the Dodgers having won two yesterday from the Reds. But his heart curdled within him at the sight of two immobile objects leaning against a Hi-Test pump. One of these was embellished with an angry, red face; the other with angry, red letters—No GAS!

"Phooey!" gulped Herman. "What does *that* mean?"

"Just what it says," said Al. "We aint got no gas."

"No gas?"

"Not a drop." Al glowered darkly and gestured at Herman with an indignant, stubby forefinger. "It's them submarines, that's what. Sinkin' our tankers if we don't keep 'em guarded. "Well,"—he scowled,—"no use of us both hangin' around. You might as well take the day off."

"With pay?" asked Herman hopefully.

"With," corrected Al, "my compliments. It's a swell day. Why don't you go to the ball game?"

"Ball game? They aint any. We're playin' in Chi."

"The Dodgers, maybe," sniffed Al. "The Yanks is home, though. Them an' Cleveland—"

"You," reproved Herman gently, "said a *ball* game." But he saw Al's point. For a few grease jobs and washes they need not both hold down the fort. "Well, see you later, then. Tomorrow, maybe?"

"Maybe," grunted Al. "Call me."

So Herman went to Coney. The decision required no long and sage deliberation. It was a fine, sunny day in late summer. He had a day off. He was a Brooklynite. A Brooklynite with a free afternoon on such a day has only two choices: Ebbets Field or Coney Island. The Dodgers were in Chicago. So Herman went to Coney.

Herman knew when he had reached the beach by a grittiness underfoot, but there was no sand in sight. The keen salt air was temptingly seasoned with the mingled aromas of chocolate, hot dogs, moth balls, lollipops, damp swim suits, salt-water taffy, suntan oil and kippered herring. A beach patrolman smiled at Herman companionably.

"Stick around, Mister," he said. "We're gonna start another layer in a few minutes."

But beyond a covey of damsels breathlessly clustered about a blasé mahogany god on a throne emblazoned LIFE-GUARD, Herman spied a miraculously untenanted swatch of green and toward this he set his course. A few moments later he was churning valiantly out to sea.

What happened next is not clear. Some witnesses contend Herman ventured out beyond his depth and was caught by an undertow. His cry for help, these say, could be heard plainly. Others point out that there *is* no undertow beyond the breakers. What's more, these argue, the cries preceding Herman's submersion were definitely the screams of a woman.

However the theories, the facts of the case are this:

Herman churned valiantly seaward, employing a variation of the Australian crawl not too accurately copied from J. Weissmuller's natatorial exhibitions in the *Tarzan* series. So pleasant was the water, so intent he on his endeavors, that he did not realize he had passed the buoys beyond which swimmers are not permitted, until from the shore sounded the petulant skirling of the lifeguard's whistle. Then he stopped, treading water, surprised and somewhat pleased to discover he had come so far in so short a time.

Being a law-abiding citizen with a wholesome respect for all forces of law and order save those myopic minions who hold forth on baseball diamonds, Herman was about to retrace his aqueous way when he heard the frightened screaming of a female. Whirling, he was shocked to discern, clawing frantically at a bobbing marker scarce twenty yards away—

"A girl!" gasped Herman—and he splashed to the rescue.

An instant later he was at her side. She was beating at the buoy with frantic hands. She wore no bathing-cap, but even the drenching waves could not straighten the natural curl of the gilt-copper hair tumbling to her waist. Her features were fine and even, though fear had mottled the soft whiteness of her flesh to a pale, greenish hue.

"Okay, sis," Herman cried. "You're all right now."

The girl, at sight of Herman, emitted a tiny bleat and began beating with redoubled vigor on the imperturbable buoy.

"Hey!" Herman called. "I told you everything was all right. What you so scared about? What's the matter with you?"

The girl stared at him bleakly for a moment. Then:

"I—I'm caught," she faltered. "In the buoy cable."

"Is *that* all?" snorted Herman. "I'll fix that."

He drew a deep breath and surface-dived. The greenish world beneath the waves was laced with bubbles, but he glimpsed the buoy halter twined, as the girl had said, about her nether parts. Herman loosed the snarled bight—and she was free.

Herman had a feeling he had seen something curiously wrong — but in the excitement of the moment he could not remember what it was. There was *something*, though.

Lungs straining with the length of his submergence, he shot upward, gaining the surface again with a gasp of relief. "There you are, sis," he spluttered. "Everything's okay now. Hey! watch what you're doing!"

For with a cry of gratitude the gilt-haired charmer has loosed her grip on the buoy, practically leaped at him, and was twining her arms around his neck with strangling enthusiasm.

"My hero!" she breathed. "How can I ever repay you?"

"Mostly," gasped Herman, fighting free, "by letting go my neck! What—"

"You," whispered the girl raptly, "must come home with me. Daddy will want to thank you for saving my life. Come!"

She grasped his hand. Herman grinned. This was something like! Sort of thing you see in moving pictures. Home to meet the old man, huh? Now if it turned out Papa was a big shot with a couple million in the bank and controlling interest in a synthetic rubber factory....

"Why, sure, baby," grinned Herman. "If you really want. But— hey! Where you goin'? You don't figure on swimmin' *under water* to the shore, do you?"

For his companion's tug had been directed not shoreward, but downward. Now she paused, staring at him oddly.

"Oh, of course! I almost forgot. You humans aren't accustomed to breathing under water, are you?"

"H-humans?" gulped Herman.

"How stupid of me. Here—I'll show you how."

And with a swift, flicking motion the girl was again at Herman's side, her cool shoulder close to his....

Flicking motion! *Girl?*

As his companion darted to his side, Herman saw once again that which, briefly glimpsed under water in a moment of confusion, had not registered upon his senses. It was no ordinary means of propulsion his newfound admirer used. Her cool, pale-green torso terminated not in legs, but in a glittering, scaly iridescence ... a *tail!*

Herman gasped.

"H-hey!" he stammed. "Y-you aint no girl!"

"W'y, of course not. I never said I was."

"You're a—a *mermaid!*"

"But, yes," rejoined the mermaid. "Didn't you know? Now, let's find Daddy. I simply won't take no for an answer."

"Look," lied Herman desperately, "I'd *like* to, but I just remembered I promised to meet a guy an hour ago—"

The mermaid smiled at him caressingly, and with deft fingers fluffed her coppery hair to a gleaming halo. "Why, I do believe," she pouted prettily, "you're afraid of me! Silly boy! *I'm* not afraid of *you*, am I? Now take my hand. I'll lead you."

Herman shuddered. "D-down *there*, you mean?"

"Certainly."

"B-but how about breathin'? I can't—"

"Oh, that? Just breathe like a fish—that's all."

"Like," repeated Herman dazedly, "a—a fish?"

"Of course. How do you usually breathe when you swim?"

"Why, in through the mouth and out through the nose—"

"Well, now, see?" laughed the mermaid. "No wonder! You should breathe like this—"

She demonstrated. It looked simple enough.

"Well," said Herman dubiously, "I don't know. But—"

He ducked his head under water and snuffed a tentative noseful. A second later, gasping, strangling, he was glaring at the girl with outraged indignation.

"What d'you—*whoosh*—mean by—*ga-wooosh*—"

"Oh, take a good *deep* breath!" scolded the mermaid. "There wasn't enough oxygen in that sniff to stiffen a jellyfish. Come on, now, try it again. A good, *deep* breath—"

Helpfully she twined her arms about Herman's neck, dragging him beneath the surface. Herman's eyes bulged. His chest contracted. He opened his mouth to protest—and water rushed in. He drew a deep breath to clear his lungs—and more water rushed in. Sea water roared in his ears. A black vertigo blinded him; a giddiness overwhelmed him. As in a dream he heard the hammering of surf against his eardrums, its dull threnody punctuated by a curiously insistent skirl fading farther and farther away ... dimmer and dimmer in the distance. . . .

And then:

"There!" said the mermaid. "That's better, isn't it?"

Herman opened his eyes. He was scudding through the amaranthine depths scant feet above sea-bottom. The malaise that had shaken him was gone. With a sort of wonderment he discovered he was breathing quite naturally, as the mermaid had advised.

Experimentally he drew a deep breath. The salt water tingled the membranes of his nose; otherwise the only sensation was one of revigoration. He stared at his companion delightedly.

"Why—why, it works!"

The girl—or half girl—smiled.

"Of course it does, silly. You don't think we could live down here if it didn't, do you?"

Herman asked, "You live down here all the time? You don't even go to the surface for fresh air once in a while?"

His new friend shuddered delicately. "Gracious, no! A few whiffs of that musty stuff you humans breathe is all we can stand at one time. That's why I was screaming for help. I was caught in the cable and couldn't get my head back under water. If you hadn't come when you did—"

"Aw," said Herman, embarrassed, "that wasn't nothing. Wh-what's your name, sis?"

"Myrtle."

"Mine's Herman," said Herman. "My friends call me Hermy."

"Do they—eh, Hermy?" whispered Myrtle softly. Herman wriggled. But his pleasure ended abruptly as at that instant the sandy bottom over which they had been whisking sheered off to a rocky chasm, and from this cleft swept a huge, streamlined figure at sight of which Herman trembled with horror.

"Beat it!" he cried. "Beat it, Myrtle! A shark!"

But Myrtle only pressed his hand reassuringly and flicked them forward to confront the sharp-nosed sea warrior.

"Hi Junior!" she called. "Daddy in the palace?"

The big piscine watchdog grumbled. "Yes, Princess. And restless as a squid, too. Where have you been?"

"I was tied up," said Myrtle. "It's a long tale."

"Well, I'm glad you're back safe." The shark's tiny eyes appraised Herman greedily. "What's that? Dinner?"

Herman said nervously, "Myrt, maybe I ought to be goin'. It's gettin' late, and—"

"Oh, don't mind *him!*" laughed Myrtle. "He's always kidding. See you later, Junior!"

And they whisked past the guardian into the abyss.

Now, where beneath them had rioted a seascape of lush jungle-land, Herman began to note increasing signs of intelligent organization. The whole sea-bottom looked neater, better-cared-for. Broad thoroughfares appeared, neatly paved with shells. Where previously such other denizens of the deep as they had passed had zigzagged about them in haphazard confusion, now their fellow travelers swam in definite levels and followed set routes.

Soon before Herman's eyes loomed a large signboard upon which a myriad of clinging barnacles formed the words:

You are Now Entering
FIDDLER'S GREEN
Pop: 2,389,574   Elevation—512
Speed Limit—12 Knots
(Snails Please Use Bivalve Pass 3A)

And beyond this signpost, rising from the depths of the abyss—
"A city!" croaked Herman. "It's a real city!"

Myrtle said impatiently, "Of course it's a real city! You didn't think we lived like—like lobsters, did you? Over there's the palace—" Herman gulped at beholding a magnificent edifice of latticed coral. It was by far the largest building in Fiddler's Green, and the most elaborate. "And there," cried Myrtle, "is Daddy! Oh, yoohoo! Daddy!"

And Herman gulped again. For the one to whom Myrtle called, a great, white-bearded giant who wore a golden crown and carried a trident, was none other than the fabled ruler of the undersea . . . old King Poseidon himself!

At sight of his daughter, the Emperor swished his monstrous tail and in one convulsive movement surged from a mossy balcony to greet them. The look of relief on his features became one of astonishment when he spied Herman.

In a voice like the rolling of storm-tossed seas he boomed, "Myrtle! Thank Chronos you're back! I've been worried seasick. But—but who is this!"

Myrtle beamed. "Herman, Daddy. Herman's a human."

Poseidon eyed Herman dubiously. "Now, Myrtle, I hope this isn't another of those flirtations—"

"Daddy!" breathed Myrtle reproachfully.

"But are you sure it's right for him to be here?"

"Of course, Daddy! I"—she siled at Herman affectionately—"I taught him how to breathe under water. Didn't I?"

"That's right," agreed Herman. "She did."

"Just the same," grumbled Poseidon, "we're not supposed to entertain humans here. If Davy were to learn about this—"

"But Herman," said Myrtle, "saved my life! I snarled myself in a buoy, and was going up for the third time when—"

"Really?" said Poseidon. "Well, in that case, maybe we can make an exception. But now that Herman's here, what are we going to do with him?"

"Why," said Myrtle simply, "I'm going to marry him."

"Marry!" exploded both males simultaneously.

"Why not?" demanded Myrtle.

Herman said, "Now, look, Myrt, you're sure you—"

And Poseidon growled, "Why *not*? Because it won't do, that's why. Our people won't stand for it."

This was a horse of a different color. Herman spun on the old ruler angrily. "What's that? Oh—I get it! Jealous of humans, eh? Sore because we live on land, and you're all wet—"

"Now, my boy," soothed Poseidon, "it's not that at all. It's just—well, in view of the current situation, my people are justifiably incensed at your race. They would never permit an alliance between my daughter and a representative of those ruthlessly destroying our cities."

Herman looked puzzled. "How's that? Destroying your cities? Why, we didn't even know you *had* cities!"

"Oh, no?" retorted Poseidon. "Then how about that?" He pointed his trident at a bulky adjunct to the palace's rococo architecture. Though red with rust and overgrown with a colony of small crustaceans, it was recognizable.

Herman cried, "Why—why, it's an oil tanker!"

"Smashed down on my palace," fumed Poseidon, "about three months ago. Completely destroyed the left wing. A fine how-de-do when you air-breathers haven't got anything better to occupy your time than chucking things like *that* down on us!"

Indignation suffused Herman. He snorted. "You don't think we did that on purpose, do you?"

"And those metal globes," complained Poseidon, "with warts. When we touch them they explode, killing our citizens. And those long black metal fish that spit bullets—"

"I tell you," stormed Herman, "it aint *us!* We hate them things even more than you do. We call them 'mines' and 'submarines.' An enemy of ours sends them to our coast. If you got any squawk to make, the ones to make it to—"

He stopped suddenly, an idea of such brilliance flashing into his mind that its daring tore a gasp from his lips.

"Golly! If *you* don't like them things, and *we* hate them, too—why don't we get together on the problem?"

"I'm afraid," frowned Poseidon, "I don't understand."

"Look," explained Herman eagerly, "up on top of the water our country's at war. You know what war is, don't you?"

Poseidon nodded. "Our people have been at war for over two thousand years with that Roman upstart, Neptune. A barbarian with the unmitigated gall to call himself 'King of the Sea,' whereas any fool knows *I*, Poseidon, am actually—"

"Why, gosh!" broke in Herman. "You're already at war with one of the nations America's at war with. That makes us allies! We ought to fight together."

"That sounds logical enough, my boy. But just how—"

"Easy," said Herman. "You got scouts and guards. Me and Myrt met one at the atoll gate. Don't those guys know the approximate location of where every mine is?"

Poseidon scowled. "Of course. For our national security—"

"Okay. And they know where the submarines are, too?"

"Certainly; but we can't prevent—"

"But you *can!* You've got to fight fire with fire!"

"What," demanded Poseidon curiously, "with what?"

"Skip it. I'll show you what I mean. You know where one of them subs is now?"

"Why—why, yes."

"And can you find me a mine?"

"Of course."

"Then," said Herman, "let's get going! I'll show you how, workin' together, our people can lick the common enemy!"

Within a matter of minutes a scout detail had located a submarine and Herman, astride a swordfish, had been conveyed with blinding speed to a bobbing mine planted by the Nazis in a lane commonly used by American freighters. This lethal globule Herman approached gingerly, explaining its mechanism as he did so.

"These here warts," he pointed out, "is what you call 'detonators.' This thing under here is the handling gear. Now, you—" He addressed his mount who, gills athrum with excitement, trembled from snout to sternplate—"you slip up on that bubble and push your sword through the ring easy-like, see?"

"Uh-huh," grunted the swordfish. "Then what?"

"Then," explained Herman, "lay the egg right smack over top of that submarine. When it tries to come up, it will blow itself to kingdom come! Get it?"

Poseidon brandished his trident with dangerous enthusiasm.

"By Cod!" he cried. "I believe it will work!"

"I know it will," said Herman. "All right—let's go!"

The mine was transferred to a spot slightly above and before the submarine, which was resting on the bottom, maintaining discreet silence until some tempting prize should happen by. As he worked, Herman was host to a second inspiration. Lest the mine float away from its intended prey, he bade his assistants secure it to the sub's conning-tower by a length of woven seaweed. Then he drew back and smiled at his handiwork, pleased.

"That," he approved, "ought to do it! Now, when that sub tries to rise—Well, you better warn everybody to steer clear of here, Posie, old boy. That's all I got to say!"

Poseidon stared at him with something like awe.

"Herman," he proclaimed, "you're a genius!"

"Aw," said Herman modestly, "in times like these, us peace-lovin' people got to stick together. . . . Hey! What's that?"

"That?" repeated Poseidon wonderingly.

"Voices," said Herman. "Hear 'em?"

"Now, darling," said Myrtle anxiously, "you're just a little excited. You've been working too hard—"

"But I *hear* them!" insisted Herman. *"Human* voices."

Poseidon stared at him with swiftly growing suspicion.

"What are those voices saying?"

"Crazy stuff," said Herman. "Double-talk. They say, *'Out goes the water; in comes the air. Out goes the water—'* "

"How horrible!" shuddered Myrtle. "What terrible sentiments. Out goes the—*ugh!* Isn't it loathsome, Daddy?"

But Poseidon was staring at his daughter grimly. And:

"Myrtle!" he thundered.

"I always say," pattered Myrtle frantically, "you never can tell *what* peculiar sounds you're going to hear under water. Now, for instance, those voices may have only—"

She stopped suddenly, a dull flush staining her sea-green features. In a thin, shaken voice—"Y-yes, Daddy?"

"You told me this young man was drowned!"

"Drowned!" gasped Herman. "Me—*drowned?"*

"Where," roared Poseidon, "did you leave him?"

"L-leave me?" piped Herman. "What do you mean, leave me? I'm right here, aint I? Or—*aint* I?"

He, too, fell silent, stricken by Myrtle's evasiveness. Her eyes lowered. In a meek, apologetic voice she said:

"At—at the buoy, Daddy."

"A fine how-de-do!" bellowed Poseidon. "We no sooner pledge ourselves allies to the humans than you, to gratify a silly, feminine whim— Herman, can you still hear those voices?"

Herman said, "Why—why, yes. Matter of fact, they're getting a little louder. *Ouch!* That hurt!"

"Hurt?" asked Myrtle. "What hurt, darling?"

"Somebody kicked me in the stummick!" And Herman glowered about him. "If any of you fishes want to start anything—"

"That settles it!" declared Poseidon. "Herman, you must return to the beach immediately. They're working on you. Not a minute to lose. All right, boys! Take him away!"

And before Herman could protest, two octopi writhed up behind him, slipping rubbery tentacles under his armpits. Bubbles churned as the trio whisked away. Poseidon cried, "Good luck, my boy! Don't worry about the submarines any more! We'll follow your plan and rid our homelands of the Nazi menace!"

But Myrtle, grief-stricken, was dabbing her eyes with the tip of her filmy tail. Between sobs she cried, "Good-by, Herman. I'll never forget you. C-come back . . . some day!"

"Myrt!" cried Herman. "Myrtle, my darling!"

His cry was drowned in the gathering thunder of surf. Blinding speed constrained his lungs. He choked and gasped, again experiencing that whirling moment of vertigo. Then the voices which had been a murmur in his ears strengthened. The stabbing pains in his ribs and back intensified. And:

"Out goes the water; in comes the air. Out goes the water; in comes—"

A voice was repeating the words with rhythmic monotony. With each spoken "water," a lancet of pain drove hard into Herman's midriff. Herman gasped and twisted to escape the pain. "Hey!" he cried. "Cut it out!"

Strange voices jabbered senseless syllables. *"He's coming to!"* . . . *"My, that artificial respiration is wonderful!"* . . . *"Here, old boy, take a sip of this!"*

Liquid fire scorched Herman's gullet. He strangled and fought himself to a sitting position. He was on the beach at Coney, center of a circle of fascinated faces, closest of which belonged to the lifeguard whose whistling was the last thing Herman remembered hearing before he and Myrtle descended to Fiddler's Green.

"The guard rose from Herman's side. "Okay, bud," he said. "Let that be a lesson to you to stay inside the buoys!"

"Who?" spluttered Herman weakly. "Me? Listen, I'm a good swimmer. They can't nothing happen to *me!*"

"Oh, no? Then why've I been working over you for the past ten minutes? G'wan, beat it before the beach cops run you in for violating the safety code."

Herman lurched to his feet. "I suppose," he wrangled, "*you* think I was drowned? Well, you're nuts! I was visiting my girl friend Myrtle and her old man, fixin' it up so—"

But he never got a chance to tell the diplomatic arrangement he had made with King Poseidon. The result of his *coup* was demonstrated before the words could leave his lips.

For somebody came up with the news that, well out at sea, an explosion had been seen by a patrol boat; a German sub had surfaced for a few seconds and then gone down for good. The most likely explanation was that the sub had been laying mines and hit one of its own.

"That," said Herman happily, "makes *one!*"

"Eh?" said the life-guard. "What's that you said?"

"That's one," repeated Herman. "But that's only the beginning. There'll be plenty more from now on. Because—"

But then, for the first, last, and perhaps only time in Herman McGonivan's life, common sense came to his rescue. That which he had been about to reveal was not only a truth so incredible that it would make him the laughingstock of all who heard. It was also a *very* important military secret! And Herman, who respected all authorities save those who serve as arbiters on baseball diamonds, paid heed to the admonitions of the "Keep Mum" placards he had seen in buses and in barrooms. So—

"Forget it!" said Herman. "I was just gabbin'. Bud, you aint happened to hear how the Dodgers made out this afternoon?"

Double, Double, Toil and Trouble

>Willow Road,
>Grove Park,
>Roanoke, Virginia,
>July 20, 1942

Mr. John W. Campbell, Jr.,
Street & Smith Publications, Inc.,
79 Seventh Avenue,
New York, New York.

Dear John:

Just a note to let you know I'm working on a new short story for Astounding, a neat little five-thousand-worder called "Test Case." The plot's quite different, and I'm sure you'll like it.

Oh, by the way—within a day or so I'm afraid you're going to receive a "crank letter" from a whackypot who lives here in Roanoke. Be a good chap and toss it in ye goode olde wastebasket, eh?

>Best regards,
>Nels Bond.

♦ ♦ ♦

> Willow Road,
> Roanoke, Virginia,
> July 21, 1942

Mr. John W. Campbell, Jr.,
Editor: Astounding Science-Fiction,
Street & Smith Publications, Inc.,
79 Seventh Avenue,
New York, New York.

My dear Mr. Campbell:

Within a few days you will receive the manuscript of my new story, a five-thousand worder entitled "Test Case."

Will you do me a great favor? If there should reach your office a manuscript by this name upon Page One of which is *not* marked a large red "X," will you please hold this manuscript for comparison with my own, which will be so marked? This is very important! The other story may be written under *my own name* by a faker and plagiarist now living in this town.

> Yours most sincerely,
> Nelson S. Bond.

♦ ♦ ♦

> Willow Road,
> Grove Park,
> Roanoke, Virginia,
> July 25, 1942

Dear John:

Here's that story I promised you. Hope you like it.

> Yours,
> Nels Bond.

♦ ♦ ♦

> Willow Road,
> Roanoke, Virginia,
> July 26, 1942

Dear Mr. Campbell:

Inclosed is the new short story, "Test Case" which I sincerely hope will meet with your approval.

> Very truly yours,
> Nelson S. Bond.

STREET & SMITH PUBLICATIONS, INC.
Astounding Science-Fiction
July 26, 1942

Mr. Nelson S. Bond,
Willow Road,
Grove Park,
Roanoke, Virginia.

Dear Nelson:

What on earth's the matter with you? Have you been writing too many fantasies? I've just read "Test Case," and it's a buy, but whatever possessed you to send me two copies? And what is the meaning of your recent letters?

Yours,

J. W. C.

♦ ♦ ♦

Willow Road,
Grove Park,
Roanoke, Virginia,
July 28, 1942

Dear John:

Glad "Test Case" is O.K. Thanks for the check. The letters? And the other manuscript? Why, I suppose they must be what I tried to warn you about. You see, there's a wingding living down the road from me a way—somehow or other he's got the idea he can knock off an easy living copying my stories and submitting them under my name. Just pay no attention to him; I'll straighten matters out somehow or other.

Ever thine,

Nels Bond.

♦ ♦ ♦

Willow Road,
Roanoke, Virginia,
July 30, 1942

Dear Mr. Campbell:

Did you receive my story, "Test Case"? The one marked with an "X"? Have heard no word from you.

Nelson S. Bond.

Willow Road,
Roanoke, Virginia,
August 3, 1942

Dear Mr. Campbell:

Did you receive my manuscript, "Test Case"? This is *vitally* important. Please answer immediately!

Nelson S. Bond.

♦ ♦ ♦

RKEVA: 815P842

MR. JOHN W. CAMPBELL, JR.,
ASTOUNDING SCIENCE-FICTION,
79 SEVENTH AVENUE,
NEW YORK, NEW YORK.

DID YOU RECEIVE MANUSCRIPT "TEST CASE"? TERRIBLY IMPORTANT. PLEASE WIRE REPLY MY EXPENSE.

NELSON S. BOND.

♦ ♦ ♦

NYCNY: 932A842

MR. NELSON S. BOND,
WILLOW ROAD,
ROANOKE, VIRGINIA.

OF COURSE RECEIVED MANUSCRIPT AND FORWARDED CHECK AS PER LETTER JULY 26TH. WHAT'S GOING ON? YOU'RE DRIVING ME NUTS. . . ?

JOHN W. CAMPBELL.

♦ ♦ ♦

Willow Road,
Roanoke, Virginia,
August 7, 1942

Dear Mr. Campbell:

I knew it! That dirty, sneaking scoundrel has done it again! Chiseled in on my brains—my work—and all because you did not pay any attention to my warning about the crayoned "X" on *my* manuscript.

He's been doing it for months, now. And there's not a thing I can do to stop him. I've been to the post office, and I've hired a lawyer, but everyone tells me it is his right to use the name "Nelson S. Bond," and so long as his stories reach you before mine—I mean they're both my stories, but—

I'd better start at the beginning. I am Nelson S. Bond—the Nelson S. Bond who started writing for Astounding Stories 'way back in 1937. I sold you "Down the Dimensions" and "The Einstein Inshoot" and a host of other stories.

Well, one day last year I was approached by a funny little old geezer who identified himself as a professor of mathematics at nearby Roanoke College. It seems his hobby was experimenting with time travel and knowing I was a science-fiction writer, he thought I might be interested in seeing a machine he was working on.

I went to his workshop and, sure enough! he had a machine. I can't tell you how it operated, because he wouldn't tell me. He can't tell either of us now, because he disappeared several months ago. Anyhow, to make a long story short, he demonstrated the instrument in my presence. I stepped onto a platform, and he pressed a couple of buttons— But why go into that? The same sort of things happened that have happened in a dozen of my yarns, as well as those of Binder, Wellman, del Rey and the rest of the gang.

Only the weird part was that when I stepped off the platform, I found myself facing not only the old scientist, but—*myself!*

What I believe is that when the old duck returned me to normal after my brief time flight, he missed his timing by a couple of minutes. So there we were, the two of us!

Well, naturally I insisted that this . . . this interloper should go through with the experiment, too, so we would become co-ordinated again. But he refused to do it. He said he had seen quite enough—"too damn much!" was his exact expression—and he pranced out of there before I could lay hands on him.

And that's when my troubles began. Ever since then, it seems my mind and that of the other Nelson S. Bond have been somehow *en rapport*. Only it works to my disdvantage. I think up story ideas and slave over 'em, but time after time, before I can get my manuscripts to your office or that of another magazine, he has stolen my idea, written and sold the story—in exactly the words I have concocted!

And that's not the half of it! He walked into my home, took it over as his own. He lives with *my* wife—plays with *my* baby—wears *my* clothes—eats the food *my* thoughts have provided—and I can't do a thing about it! Everyone in town believes what he has told them about me—that I am a faker trying to capitalize on a physical similarity to himself. I've lost all my friends. I've had to move to a dingy little dump at the other end of town. We both live on Willow Road, but *he* has my home in Grove Park, while I live down by the railroad yards.

Something must be done about this, Mr. Campbell! I can't think of any way to solve the problem, short of asking you to mail duplicate checks for every story he—I—we—send you. But that, I know, is impossible. Besides, there's my home and future to think of.

Won't you please ask some of your scientifically minded readers to help me out of this jam. And in the future, please don't pay for his manuscripts until you've read mine. I am slowly starving to death.

Desperately yours,

Nelson S. Bond.

P.S. I'm going to make one last try. I've got a new story idea—the best I've ever had. But I'm not going to tell anyone a thing about it. I'm going to keep it a secret until I can get it into your hands. Keep an eye out for it.

♦ ♦ ♦

Willow Road,
Grove Park,
Roanoke, Virginia,
August 7, 1942

Dear John:

I've got a new story idea—the best I've ever had. It's so good I'm not even going to tell you about it until I can get it into your hands. Keep an eye peeled for it.

Yours as ever,

Nels Bond.

Proof of
the Pudding

GEORGE TOWNSEND MADE A FORTUNE, THEN WENT MAD. Of course that term was not applied in his case. Only the poor are crazy. Persons of moderate means are mentally disturbed, while those of wealth are merely eccentric.

Nevertheless, George Townsend was insane. And the nature of his madness was that he believed the earth to be a hollow sphere. He claimed we live not *on* its surface but *within* it. At the drop of a hat (or without it) Townsend would defend his concept valiantly against all comers, meeting their arguments with rebuttals to him more reasonable than the evidence they offered.

"The sun," said adherents to orthodox science, "the moon, the planets, the distant stars. Aren't these proof that we look up and out to boundless space?"

"By no means," answered Townsend. "The bubble in which we live is quite large enough to contain the pinpoints which light our sky. Their alleged size and their distance is mere illusion. Astronomers measure with faulty instruments, that is all."

"And gravitation?" they asked him.

"Newton's error," said Townsend. "The force that binds us to earth is clearly centrifugal."

"But if you are right," they demanded, "what lies outside this hollow sphere?"

"That I do not know," conceded Townsend. "But I intend to find out. Talk is cheap, and empty barrels make the most noise. But actions speak louder than words. I will go out and see."

Thus, in a salvo of the timeworn clichés to which he was addicted, Townsand silenced his opponents and announced his plan. Townsend freely admitted his concept was not novel with himself; and that others had earlier advanced the same theory. But Townsend differed from his predecessors in that he was a multimillionaire. And as he was fond of saying, "Money makes the mare go." So he summoned engineers and told them what he wanted.

"I want you to build me a vehicle," he said. "A powerful machine that can drill completely through Earth's eggshell crust."

The engineers shook their heads. "We can create such a machine," they told him, "but it cannot do what you propose. Earth's heat increases as you travel toward its core. At a depth of ten miles you will die of suffocation. At forty the borer will dissolve in a sea of molten rock."

"Build the machine," said Townsend.

"Folly!" they warned him.

"Build the machine," said Townsend, "and call it Townsend's Folly, if you wish. Men may laugh, but I will go to Earth's outer surface. When I return I will laugh. And he who laughs last, laughs best."

They built the burrower. They did not call it Townsend's Folly, but the Earthworm. It was an ingenious vehicle, vermicular in form and operation. Massive atomic drills, like chomping jaws, gnawed a pathway before it, passed the detritus back through a cyclotron gizzard that digested its mineral diet and excreted its residue in the form of powdery ash, leaving in its wake a tunnel as smooth as if bored by an auger. And on a certain morning in mid-March, Townsend posed for news cameramen beside his metal worm.

"Many of you," he said, "have urged me to delay; to test; to ascertain the efficiency of this vehicle. But he who hesitates is lost, and there is no time like the present. I will go now, and when I return you will know the true nature of the world in which we dwell. And so you may share my great adventure, I will keep in touch with you by television. Thus you will actually *see* the outer world. And seeing–" added Townsend–"is believing."

Then he climbed into the Earthworm. Gears meshed, the giant jaws gnawed sandy soil, and he was gone.

* * *

At a depth (or height) of five miles, Townsend verified one prediction of the engineers. "It *is* hot here," he acknowledged. "About 400 degrees Fahrenheit. But the refrigerating unit is efficient, and I am comfortable."

At ten miles he reported, "The Earthworm is now boring through a stratum of solid ores. There is enough raw mineral here at this level to maintain mankind's industries for countless centuries."

At intervals of twenty miles and thirty his messages were in the same vein. Measurements of heat, pressure and composition in every way supported conventional theory. When at thirty-five miles his report was delayed, apprehension grew. Hasty pleas were transmitted.

"Come back, Townsend," begged his friends. "You have proved man can plumb the depths of Earth far deeper than was formerly believed. You have demonstrated the practicability of a new deep-drilling instrument. You have opened the way to undreamed resources, fabulous wealth. Come back and accept the plaudits of a grateful world."

"Not so," responded Townsend stubbornly. "I go on. Within the past half hour the temperature has dropped three hundred degrees. The matter about me now is less dense, more soil-like. According to my reckoning I am approaching the true surface of the earth. I will switch on the camera so you may see."

The screen, which had been blank, began to glow with flecks of mottled light. Viewers saw a tumbled sifting effect, as if great clots of soil were being churned from the mouth of a tunnel boring upward from great depths. At first there was more dark than light, then rapidly more light than dark, as the nose of Townsend's burrower emerged from Earth's hollow center to its outer shell.

Townsend rotated his camera. As its lens panned the horizon astonished viewers gazed upon a world of awesome beauty. A world of skies ablaze with countless suns; a world of vegetation wild and strange, amongst the towering fronds of which the Earthworm was no mighty mechanism but a tiny, wriggling mote.

Townsend's voice reached his listeners stridently, in triumph.

"I have succeeded!" proclaimed Townsend proudly. "Here is the true, the undreamed outer Earth. And I am the first to reach its surface.

"Proving," he gloated, "that where there's a will there's a way. And that fortune favors the brave—"

Abruptly the sun-strewn sky was overshadowed. The watchers

briefly glimpsed the swooping dive of a span of monstrous wings, saw the swift gaping of a tremendous beak that yawned to swallow everything . . . camera and Earthworm and Townsend . . . all in one gulp.

Then darkness fell.

George Townsend had proven his final adage: that the early bird catches the worm.

Pawns of Tomorrow

"**T**HE TROUBLE WITH BOTH OF YOU," SAID WEISSMANN, "is that you have too much imagination. In a world of stark reality you permit yourselves the luxury of being romanticists."

Deftly, as he spoke, he cleared from the chess table a litter of odds and ends: a clipping from a current periodical, a dregs-dappled highball glass, scraps of memo paper scored with hen-tracks to be incorporated into a monograph on which he was currently working, a crumpled cigarette pack, the program of last week's Philharmonic concert.

"Too much imagination."

Springer glanced at Tom Ross, who shrugged. *I won't argue with him,* said Tom's arched eyebrows. *I came here to play chess.* So Springer accepted the challenge.

"Isn't that natural?" he demanded. "Tom is an architect, I'm a writer. Imagination is our stock in trade."

Weissmann, taking from its plush-lined inlaid chest the exquisitely carven set of chessmen which was his proudest possession, smiled gently.

"I thought that would be your answer," he sighed. "Unfortunately it begs the issue. I accused you for what you *are*, not for what you do. As a means to an end one can, and should, employ the imaginative faculty to its fullest advantage. But you two are slaves to your own servant. Ross so depends on inspiration that he is lost without it. When his vagrant genius burns, he flames; when it fails, he is baffled and uncertain. He has so wholly surrendered to intuition that he has actually forgotten how to think."

"Just for that," announced Tom Ross, "I'll give you White and beat the socks off you."

"Accepted!" nodded Weissmann placidly. "I never refuse an advantage, my dear boy."

They started arranging their pieces. The thought occurred to Rufus Springer that Weissmann had deliberately tempted proffer of the White chessmen. But he rejected the notion. Weissmann needed no advantage over either Ross or himself. And his accusation had been hurled at both of them.

"How about me?" asked Springer.

Weissmann's eyes twinkled.

"You, Rufus? I hope *you're* not going to deny an excess of imagination? I know no one more hopelessly lost in the dream world than yourself."

"Is there anything wrong in wanting to make this world a better place?" demanded Springer. "*Someone* has to dream, to plan, to lay the groundwork—"

"Someone," conceded Weissman. "But you? Surely you don't delude yourself that *your* futile writings can alter that which must inevitably be?"

"Inevitably! Good Lord, Weissnann, don't tell me you've gone over to the predestinationists' camp?"

Weissmann winked drolly at Tom Ross. "You see?" he sighed. "Imaginative, yet inconsistent. He prefaces his tirade against religion with a sacerdotal invocation."

"Shut up, Rufe," said Ross. "Your move, Weissmann."

"Pawn to King's four," said Weissmann.

His strong, thick-knuckled hand—that of an artisan rather than an artist—advanced the pawn. Ross hesitated an instant, then pushed his King's pawn forward to meet it. The pieces of Weissmann's set were more than mere conventionalizations. The pawns were true foot-soldiers, just as the bishops were veritable ecclesiastics, mitered and gowned; the knights mounted horsemen, caparisoned for battle.

Springer persisted, "You say nothing we do can alter what is to be. Then you don't believe in free will?"

"'That man is the master of his fate, the captain of his soul?'"

chuckled Weissmann. "I fear not, Rufus. With all deference to the poet, I cannot credit foolish, fumbling Man with the power of controlling his own destiny."

"But that's ridiculous!" protested Springer. "I *do* make my own decisions. I *do* think."

"Shades of poor Descartes!" sighed Weissmann. "He, too, had too much imagination. You must one day read his dissertations on vortices and automatism. They shame the wildest fantasies of Verne.

"My boy, the mere existence of a thought within your brain does not prove you master of that thought. Or of the actions resulting from it. As well to say these gallant warriors—" Weissmann nodded at the chessman arraigned before him—"control the fate which is their destined lot. Doubtless they also love and hate, know fear and anger and an urge to make their world a better one."

"Now you *are* talking nonsense!" snorted Springer. "Chessmen who think, indeed!"

"And why not? What proof exists that Man alone can reason? Speech? There are talking birds. Writing? Beasts of burden have been taught to spell."

"But birds and beasts have life. Chessmen are bits of carven ivory."

"And who can say," parried Weissmann, "that bits of ivory may not think and talk, know life on a plane of existence incomprehensible to us? There are sounds we cannot hear, colors we cannot see. Can you not conceive of movement indiscernible to our eyes? Of speech inaudible to our senses? Of a mode of life so foreign to our own as to be a void in our awareness?"

"Frankly," said Springer, "no."

"Nor I!" laughed Ross. "Let's get on with the game, Weissmann."

"I can," persisted Weissmann imperturbably, "and do. I believe these chessmen *do* think. Just as I believe turnips scream in agony when they are pared and thrust into a boiling pot. As I believe flowers sing wild paeans to their god, the Sun. And that sluggish ores deep in bhe turgid caverns at Earth's heart dream slow unfathomable, metallic dreams."

"Oh, for Pete's sake!" jeered Springer. "Now who's got the surplus of imagination!"

The older man shrugged.

"You don't accept because there is no way to make you understand. Not unless I could force your awareness out of *this* world and into that of the chessmen—" He laughed softly, turning his deep, wise eyes upon Springer, holding the younger man's gaze intently. "Were I a mesmerist who could say, *'Sleep! Sleep, and in your dreaming walk with these other worldlings—'* "

"I'd do it," chuckled Springer. "Partly to prove you're wrong, and mostly because I'm dead tired, anyway. You guys don't mind if I snatch forty winks while you play?"

And he yawned, closing his eyes—annoyingly aware even as he did so that it was a ruse to escape the curiously potent compulsion of Weissmann's gaze. A strange character, Weissmann. Smart as a whip, but whacky in some ways. Mysterious, too. *"Sleep, and in your dreaming walk with these other worldlings—"*

And those eyes of his. Strange how deep they were. Like wells? No . . . the author in Springer rejected the cliché. Like high cliffs straining to a midnight sky. You could fall away and upward from such heights . . . fall outward to the cold and distant stars, alone and giddy in the emptiness of space.

As from far away he heard Tom's faintly acid voice. *"We're finally going to play, eh? Well, good! Your move, Weissmann."* The quilted whisper of a chessman in motion, and the older man's reply. *"Knight to King's Bishop three."* Then Ross, his bee-thin mirth a dwindling ghost of laughter in the void. *"So that's the plan? Bringing up the cavalry, eh?"*

Then the stars beckoned . . .

2.

"So that's the plan?" cried the Seneschal fiercely. "Bringing up the cavalry, eh? Bringing up the damned cavalry against our poor devils of foot soldiers!" He turned sharply from the battlement overlooking the plain and fastened irate eyes on his companion. "Well, sir?" he challenged, "What are you going to do about it?"

"Nothing," said Sir Rufus easily. "Nothing at all. What would you have me do, old grumbler?"

"What would I have you do?" grated the old warrior. "Why, you smirking young whippersnapper, I'd have you ride to the relief of those unhappy villains . . . that's what I'd have you do! And that's what you *would* do, too, were you a man and not a perfumed popinjay!"

"Without orders?" parried the young knight.

"Orders!" Sir Roderick spat contemptuously. "Name of God, who needs orders at a time like this? Any fool knows what must be done. They've attacked us, haven't they?"

"And the King dispatched a regiment to stop them."

"Aye! And now those men are threatened by superior forces. They must be protected."

Sir Rufus smiled lazily. "The trouble with you old timers is that you've never studied military tactics. Stop champing at the bit, old warhorse. The High Command knows best. There'll be action for all before this war is over."

"That there will," conceded the Seneschal gloomily. "Whole armies lost, and good men slain, and the plain burned bare with slaughter and destruction. Pox take them!" He exploded with sudden violence. "Will they never give us peace? Were ever a people plagued with neighbors so troublesome? Ten centuries of fruitless, bloody war . . . and still they attack. Ever *they* attack! Just once I'd like to see *our* armies seize the initiative, march against them and crush them into the muck from whence they sprang!"

Sir Rufus shook his head, his plumed casque waving feathery regret.

"That you will never see. We are a peaceful folk. We seek no trouble."

"Speak for yourself, coward!" blazed the older man. "*I* seek trouble. Give me the chance to meet them on the field of combat—"

"Coward, you said?" interrupted Sir Rufus softly. He slipped the knuckled gauntlet from his hand and creased it for the hurling. "Pardon, Sir Seneschal, but did I hear your words aright?"

Sir Roderick flushed. "Sorry, my boy," he grumbled contritely. "My old tongue needs a curb. I swallow the word; the thought I never had. You are young—yes. But when the time comes, you will prove yourself."

"And am I not mistaken," said Sir Rufus, satisfied, "the time comes now. See? Her Ladyship's messenger—"

Spurning cloudlets of dust, a courier gallped into the courtyard. He spied the men atop the battlement and cupped his hands.

"Sir Rufus? A message from Her Majesty the Queen. Repair at once to the aid of the King's guardsmen. All haste!"

"I hear and acknowledge!" shouted Sir Rufus. "Tell Her Majesty we take saddle at once." He whirled to face Sir Roderick, eyes shining. "Well, old timer, this is it!"

"The old plan," said Sir Roderick with satisfaction, "and the best. God shield you, lad. And—give them hell!"

His command consisted of two regiments: the mounted troop which he himself led, and an auxiliary force of pikemen captained by the Chevalier Rouget, and old cavalryman become too brittle of bone for mounted combat. Haste being of the essence, Sir Rufus ordered his mounted troops to press on ahead of the slower moving foot soldiers. Having reached the assigned position, he gave orders that the men rest, horses be watered and fed. Then, with a cadet lieutenant, he went to the top of a nearby rise to survey the terrain.

The subaltern, a fresh-cheeked youngster from the provinces, was frankly delighted with his first taste of action. He bubbled with schemes for sallies and campaigns—plans which Sir Rufus, trained under the stern tutelage of the War College, found fantastic and amusing.

"Why tarry here, Milord?" he pleaded eagerly. "We are fresh and strong. Another swift foray will bear us over the border into enemy territory—and they without an active force to block our way."

"Except," Sir Rufus reminded him wryly, "the enemy King's cavalry. Are you, then, so anxious to die young?"

"They wouldn't dare attack us!" persisted the cadet lieutenant. "With the foot regiment moving up to defend our flank, we'll outnumber them two to one."

"And what is to prevent them," laughed Sir Rufus, "from attacking the foot regiment instead of us?"

"Oh!" said the youngster bleakly. "I hadn't thought of that." Then his face brightened again. "But suppose they *do* turn against the border guard? I've heard you say yourself, Milord, that in a war of maneuver, men are expendable. We stand in position to thrust deep into the enemy's stronghold, before the Queen's cathedral. Let her stir a step and we lay seige at once to her bastion and to the King's own palace!"

Sir Rufus listened politely. He had no intention of shattering the youth's ardor with a gibe, a criticism. The lad was, at least, a thinker. From such as he were forged great leaders. Who could say but that from such wild dreaming might not one day come that which military strategists had been seeking for over ten centuries: the Perfect Campaign, the ideal counter-offensive which would lead inerrably to triumph? Still to this plan there was one obvious fault.

"The idea has merit," he acknowledged. "Indeed, it has been tried in other wars—though without success. But you forget one thing."

"Yes, Milord?"

"We may not press on immediately. Might not even if we willed. We must wait now to see what the enemy does."

The boy stared at him in bewilderment.

"And lose the initiative? But, Milord, *now* is the time to strike! Now, while they are unsettled and uncertain. Why wait for them to act? Every moment is precious."

"It is the Rules of War," shrugged Sir Rufus. "We *must* wait. To do otherwise would be unseemly."

"Rules of War! 'Swounds, Milord, war is no pastime played with bits on a wagering board! The single rule of war is to *win*, by whatever means available."

"Lieutenant!" Sir Rufus smiled tolerantly. "May I remind you we are knights and nobles met in honorable combat, not draymen brawling in a public house? It is a harsh game, certes, and a bloody one. But we play it by the rules."

The youngster's face was sullen. "Rules, pardee! Are we men, thinking for ourselves or puppets being dangled on the worn strings of tradition? Chivalry and gallantry are all very well, Milord, for noblemen. But how about the foot soldiers? Does it rest them easier in their graves to know they died in honorable combat? Does it sooth the aching of their widows' hearts to know the rules of war were well observed? You forget, Milord, that these little people also love and hate, know fear and anger and an urge to make their world a better one!"

"And you forget, Lieutenant," snapped Sir Rufus, "that you are talking to—" He stopped abruptly, a dazed look in his eyes—"What was that? What did you say?"

"I'm sorry, Milord. Perhaps too much."

"No, it's all right," said Sir Rufus, groping. "There is something in what you say. But the words . . . *'Fear and anger and an urge to make their world a better one.'* I seem to have heard them before. Elsewhere far away and long ago. But I cannot remember—"

He passed a gloved hand across his eyes, shaken by an emotion defying name or explanation. *Something,* he thought. *Or someone. A cone of yellow light in a vast, booklined room, and men like gods. A high hill yearning to the midnight sky, and the mocking thunder of celestial mirth . . .*

"You are all right, Milord?" asked the young cadet anxiously. "You are not unwell?"

Sir Rufus shook his head, with an effort clearing his brain of the inexplicable maggot.

"Yes, quite all right, thank you. A mood . . . a fleeting fancy. It does not matter."

"Shall we return to camp, Milord?"

"Good idea. There is much to—*Stay!*"

Sir Rufus hissed the final word, clutching the young man's arm, dragging him groundward beside him. The lad winced at the pressure but uttered not a sound. His eyes, following the gaze of Sir Rufus, widened at what they saw.

"Soldiers, Milord!" he whispered. "Enemy soldiers!"

"The Blanchard King's Crusaders," breathed Sir Rufus, identifying the approaching pennon. "Soldiers of the Church. But what are *they* doing out here at the border?"

"Milord," warned the lieutenant. "Behind us! Riding up from our lines—"

"The Queen's troops?"

"Nay, Milord. *More* Church warriors. And I think—nay, I *know* —they are His Majesty's priests. For, see, there rides his Bishop at the van!" The lieutenant's voice was hot with excitement. "This means a battle, Milord. They're certain to make contact at the border. Shall I haste back and sound the warning?"

4.

"No, wait!" bade Sir Rufus, tensing his grip on the cadet's arm. "Wait and watch. There is something here I do not understand. For, see—" A baffled and incredulous anger thickened his voice "they have met. And by the Saints, they meet in peace! They smile . . . greet each other like brothers. What devil's parley is this?"

The cadet said, "But the King's own confessor, Milord? Surly *he* would not conspire with the enemy in time of war?"

"Would he not? I don't trust him. I've *never* trusted him. Or his cunning kinsman, crouching slyly at Her Majesty's side, prating soft words of piety and peace, standing between the throne and the fighting men who would defend it."

"Peace?" echoed the other man hopefully. "Perhaps this is a parley? With the Churchmen serving as intermediary?"

"Possible," conceded Sir Rufus, "but unlikely. You don't know them as I do, lad. Strange creatures are these churchmen. They think and act obliquely, slanting off on tangents of their own. But stay—what do they now?"

For a stir had passed through the group assembled at the border. Brocaded pennons fluttered, the glinting beaks of lowered halberds titled suddenly aloft, the strident warning of a bugle shattered the silence of the plain. There was a bristling separation of the two forces, and that of His Majesty whirled abruptly to face the enemy's domain.

"Blanchard reinforcements!" cried the lieutenant. "A second army races to outflank them!"

"So that's it!" roared Sir Rufus. "Then it wasn't our churchmen who were guilty of treachery, but theirs! They violate a peace parley with a sneak attack? Come, lad!"

He sprang swiftly to his feet, started back toward camp. The cadet, racing beside him, panted, "What do we do, Milord? Haste to the King and warn him?"

"We do not! We ride forward. As soon as we take horse we ride to destroy their furtive rabble. If it be war they want, then they will have it!"

Now, behind them, rose the din of battle joined. Cries, and the clash of armor, the thud of mace and groan of denting shield. Sir Rufus bellowed furiously, "The fools! Why didn't they wait for us? This was *our* task."

The cadet ventured hopefully, "They seem to be doing well, Milord. They are pressing the enemy back."

"And if they do," growled the knight, "what gain? They should have let *us* meet the interlopers. We are mounted. We have the greater mobility. The High Command shall hear of this, pardee! A Church army crossing the border without one sign of plan, joining battle without orders . . . is it any wonder we lose wars?"

"But they're not losing, Milord, they're winning!" The cry ripped from the lieutenant's throat. "See, they have won! The varlets turn and flee. The field is ours. First victory for us!"

Sir Rufus slowed to a walk. No need to call his troops to horse. The careful strategy of the War College was undone, upset by the impetuous foray of a force that never should have taken the field. The Churchmen had won a battle, true. But . . .

"First blood," he conceded grudgingly. "And first victory. But who will win the last? That is what counts, Lieutenant. Who will win the last?"

5.

The encamped troops had heard the din of conflict, and like the action-hungry dogs of war they were had sent out scouts to learn what was going on. This was a minor breach of regulations for which Sir Rufus had not the heart to order punishment, knowing it was not mere curiosity that impelled them, but eagerness to be a part of any fighting within bow's reach.

There was disappointment when he told them of the ecclesiastics' clash with the flanking column, and that there would be no advance for the present. One of the squadron leaders suggested a deployment to the frontier, covering the Church army's flank, but Sir Rufus vetoed the suggestion on two counts. First, because no such orders had emanated from headquarters. Second, and more cagily, because he was not yet convinced the Crusaders could maintain firm footing in their newly-won terrain.

The soundness of this reasoning was soon proven. The scouts, returning, verified his fears. No sooner had the King's churchmen pitched camp than the enemy hurled a new column against them. Infantry battalions of the Blanchard Queen's Cross thrust forward to attack the freshly gained position. The Crusaders had scant choice of action. Either must they retreat homeward, or they must fall back to the border. The second was their chosen plan of action, much to the disdain of Sir Rufus.

"Had the idiots fallen back to support the King's infantry," he complained to his subalterns, "they would have freed *us* for action. As it is—"

He shrugged helplessly, and his battlewise warriors, scanning the field maps, saw what he meant. Far from being a mobile, roving force that could strike terror into the foe, they were becoming part of the tactical reserve, hemmed in on every side, unable to make a forward move, compelled to cover the flanks of two overextended advance units.

Even so, Sir Rufus yet could smile. It was a sorry enough war he was being forced to fight. But he was willing to wager that his impatience was a pallid fury compared to that of old Sir Roderick, chained to his tower, hopelessly distant from either sight or sound of action.

6.

Once in the night he woke, bemused and puzzled. Out of the depths of dreamless slumber came to him a voice, as from far away, but crystal clear, a voice that said, *"Rufus? Oh, Rufus?"* Then another voice, more quietly, *"He's sleeping, I believe. Let him rest."*

That, and no more. But the spectral conversation roused him from his pallet with a start, brought him bolt upright with cold sweat in his palms and a strange tingling of the small hairs at his nape.

"Who calls me?" he demanded. But there was no answer. Outside the tent a sentry paced his lonely watch. For to the east a cock crowed strident welcome to the dunlaced blue of dawn, and from nearby copse rang the clean bite of an axe as a scullery serf hacked fuel for the breakfast fire.

After a moment, Sir Rufus sank back to his cot. But he did not sleep again. He lay there listening to the sounds of a rousing camp:

the clank of metal, the hawk and spit of drowsy male animals reluctantly dragging themselves from the certain warmth of blankets to the possible cold of death before another nightfall, the conversations that began as muted whisperings and gathered to coarse cries and louder laughter as the moments passed. The nickering of horses, the crunch of post sentries, returned with leather boots on gravel, the bluster and complaint of outdawn to chafe blue wrists before the welcome fire. The good, familiar sounds of a wakening camp.

These things he heard and understood and loved, being one and a part of them. But this other thing? These occult voices whispering in the night. *"Rufus?"* Since his father's death a decade since, no man had called him by his Christian name. And that reply, *"He's sleeping, I believe."* Who believed? And why should there be doubt that he was sleeping?

There were those who claimed superstition was ignorance. But there were others, just as wise, who said superstitions were based on facts little comprehended but still true. And it was an antique superstition of the knighthood that when a man's time was upon him, when little longer would he walk the Plain, there came to him visions. Visions and sometimes voices.

Well, then? — Sir Rufus shrugged aside his covers — if he had an appointment with Destiny, there was no sense in dawdling here abed. No terror lay beyond the gates of death for a brave man; that he knew. Death was but a sleep and an awakening to tourneys ever joyous and triumphant.

Still . . . those voices? Voices unknown, yet frighteningly familiar. *A haze of fragrant smoke and tinkling glass. Grave, kindly eyes, and the brow of a windtorn hill.*

Rouget came from base camp to report on the night's events. He knew war, did Rouget. On this same plain, for more years than he cared to acknowledge, he had battled this same enemy. None knew the game of war better than this battleworn Chevalier.

He said abruptly, "Well, we're in for it now!"

"They moved during the night?" asked Sir Rufus.

Rouget nodded. "A fresh division. Forced march from the Queen's armory to the frontier. There were skirmishes between their men and the King's foot all night."

Sir Rufus studied the revised field maps, bit his lip thoughtfully. "You know what this means, of course."

"It could mean many things, Milord. The decision rests with the High Command. The King's Foot can attack them. Or we can. Or we can bring up our reserves. Or, best of all, the Crusaders can attack their line of supply. If—" His eyes reflected his doubt—"they have the courage."

"I think they have," said Sir Rufus thoughtfully. "I like Churchmen no more than you do, Chevalier. But I saw them fight yesterday, and this I will say for them: they don't know the meaning of fear. But—"

"But, Milord?"

"I doubt His Majesty will let them sacrifice themselves. He leans too much on the Bishop for guidance. He will not risk him. No, it will be the foot regiment, I'm sure."

"And then," said Rouget quietly, "their cavalry will come up. And we'll be in it by noon. I'll tell the men."

He started for the door of the tent, but fell back as the flaps parted suddenly, admitting Sir Rufus' lieutenant. The young cadet was vibrant with excitement.

"Have you heard the news, Milord? Great news!"

"Well?" cried Sir Rufus. "Well? We advance?"

"No need to advance, Milord! The King's Fusileers attacked the enemy at dawn—"

"As we guessed!" Sir Rufus tossed Rouget a swift, triumphant glance. "And then—?"

"You'll never guess what happened, Milord. Never!"

"They counter-attacked, of course."

"Nay, Milord. They did not. The miserable cowards fled. Their panic stricken King has left the capital and raced to the protection of his castle in the provinces!" The youngster laughed triumphantly. "The war is almost over, Milord—and we have won!"

7.

For a long moment Sir Rufus stared at the lad incredulously. Then: "Fled?" he choked eventually. "Their King fled? Incredible!"

"But true, Milord. He is gone, leaving the field to us."

The Chevalier Rouget groaned, twisting a balled fist in a cupped palm. "And we hemmed in, unable to stir a step! A murrain on those incense-swinging psalmists!"

"Even yet," blazed Sir Rufus, "they can atone. If they will attack the Blanchard supply line *now*, we'll cross the border behind them." His swift brain raced with the possibilities opened by the enemy's retreat. "Their cavalry must come out to defend the Queen's fortress. When it does, our infantry can slash them to ribbons!"

"Then Her Ladyship's reserve can come up," boomed Rouget, "and their whole frontier is broken."

"Come!" said Sir Rufus. "Let us see if I judged correctly. Let us learn if churchmen have courage or no."

He led the way from the tent. The three hurried to the watchtower flung up during the night and looked off across the dawn-hazed countryside to the neighboring camp of the Crusaders. It was a pleasant terrain, a land more suited to the soft pursuits of peace than to the bloody hazard of war. A fertile farmland, chequered with precise areas of crop and pastureland. Between the rows coursed tiny, purling brooks, and beyond the second of these natural barriers lay the camp of the King's churchmen.

There was a tense excitement in that camp, discernible even from this distance. Tents were being struck, pack animals hurriedly laden. Sir Rufus nodded, satisfied.

"Blow the assembly," he bade Rouget. "Bid the men strike camp. We move within the hour."

"Milord—" cried the cadet lieutenant.

"Later, Lieutenant!" snapped Sir Rufus. "Rouget, when you return to camp, send a message to the Queen. Bid her dispatch an advance guard—"

"Pardon, Milord," interrupted the lieutenant stridently, "but it is too late. Look! Across the border. The King's infantry—"

Sir Rufus turned, stared . . . then started violently. His voice cracked on his cry. "The fools! The everlasting damned fools! They'll destroy us all!"

Rouget asked fearfully, "What is it, Milord ? These weary old eyes of mine . . . I can't see as I used to."

"They're mad as hares," moaned Sir Rufus, "or drunk with victory! Without reserve or supplies, the idiots have pressed forward straight into the heart of the enemy's stronghold!"

8.

There was no doubt in the mind of Sir Rufus as to the enemy's next move. Clearly the Fusileers had dared too much and would suffer the consequence. True, the enemy King had fled. But his vixen consort—"The good Queen Blanche," thought Sir Rufus derisively, recalling the host of scandals evolving around the Amazon regent's name—had flying columns within easy march of the attackers. A swift foray . . .

Sir Rufus shrugged helplessly. Another Lost Battalion to have its name inscribed on the palace plaques with innumerable others.

And there was nothing he could do about it. Absolutely nothing. Nor at this late hour could the High Command dispatch relief to the over-aggressive footmen of the King.

So he chafed for a morning and a forenoon, waiting for the inevitable report of the advance guard's destruction. But when at weary last came word of the action going on, it was news of a startling nature. A messenger rode up from base headquarters. His face was wreathed in smiles. "How now, Sir Rufus? Ready for the fray?" was his greeting.

Sir Rufus said impatiently, "Fret not for us. We move at an instant's notice. How goes it with the battle?"

"Well," said the messenger complacently. "The enemy, methinks, has lost his cunning. This is one war he'll rue his brain's contriving."

"Aye," said Sir Rufus gloomily, "so we hope. But an army has been lost that never should have moved. The King's First Foot . . . did any escape the massacre?"

"Massacre, Milord?"

"You mean," demanded Sir Rufus, "the King's First Foot has not yet been attacked?"

"Not yet," chuckled the rider, "nor does the enemy seem to relish the prospect. The Queen refused battle. Instead, she deserted her palace and rode to her Bishop's camp."

"She *what!*" gasped Sir Rufus. "Show me!" Before the messenger he spread a campaign map. The rider pointed out the new positions of the enemy. Sir Rufus studied. And then: "There is more here," he said, "than meets the eye. I know their Queen, as ours, leans strongly on her Church advisors. But she did not seek them merely for conference. See, now, how their forces converge. Methinks she plans to thrust straightway to our capital."

The messenger grinned. "So thought *our* Queen, and moved her Elite Guard. Even now they stand before the West Gate. There'll be no attack, Sir Rufus, in *that* sector."

9.

"But the enemy King's infantry," frowned Sir Rufus, "stands within short march of the Queen's guard. If they advance, flanked by cavalry—"

There was respect in the messenger's eyes, respect infrequently accorded a field leader by one of the Intelligence corps.

"You have a nice eye for strategy, Sir Rufus," he conceded. "That is exactly what has already happened. Their infantry *did* come up. But—" He shrugged—"it was a gesture of no importance. Her Ladyship moved her forces to a previously prepared position a few miles away, a spot unassailable by any mere infantry detachment.

"And," he hinted broadly, "I might add that this move, also, was in accordance with plan. I am not permitted to say more . . . now. But since you're such a tactician—"

There he let the matter drop. Nor could further prodding by Sir Rufus draw another word from him. He left a while later, bearing with him Sir Rufus' formal request that the cavalry troop be permitted to attack the enemy advance guard. But even as he penned the request, Sir Rufus knew he was wasting his time. The High Command did not hearken to suggestions from the fighters on the field . . .

10. 11. 12.

So passed another weary afternoon, an evening, and a night. Which was, chafed Sir Rufus, the trouble with war. Things took so long to develop. If you could only pursue a plan while it was hot in your brain—But, no! the rules of war must be observed. And even if the enemy chose to dawdle and delay, there was nought to be done but wait, and wait some more.

It annoyed him to find himself reflecting the cadet lieutenant's thoughts. But Sir Rufus was a reasonable man. And there was, he conceded, much merit to the youth's complaining. The rules of war *were* a stifling inhibition to ingenuity. Sometimes a man felt as if he had no—

Free will? Once again, as yesterday, the casual employment of a phrase roused a strange reaction in his mind. It seemed to him that once, elsewhere, be had argued on that score. Someone, somewhere, had denied the existence of free will. *Deep leather chairs, and a box of carven pieces.* But that was madness. Certes, a man had free will . . . though of course there were commands to be obeyed, rules which must be followed.

During the night, the guardsmen of the provincial castle to which the enemy king had fled crept from their bastion to see what threat portended. But also in the darkness His Majesty's cavalry rode from their quarters to the King's court, clearing the way for the King to seek refuge should it finally become needful.

With dawn came news of further parley at the enemy Queen's camp. Her church army slipped forward to join the conference begun yesterday. What devil's broth was brewing Sir Rufus could not guess. But he did not now, nor had he ever, completely trusted churchmen. He sent for Rouget.

"You have courage, old friend," he said bluntly. "That has oft been proven. But have you also daring?"

Rouget asked simply, "What would you have me do, Milord?"

"The wind blows from the north," said Sir Rufus, "and I care not for its smell. My troops are frozen here, apparently forever . . . unless the stupid dolts at headquarters change their plan. We need information as to what Queen Blanche and her bishops conspire. Will you take your footmen forward to the border and observe them?"

"Is this a suggestion, Milord, or a command?"

"A suggestion only," admitted Sir Rufus. "And a mission fraught with peril."

The Chevalier said, "I am an old man, Milord, and a weary one. Life and death are one to me. We will advance."

At noon the Chevalier led his men past the encampment of their mounted allies. Then passed hours of brooding silence during which Sir Rufus, tent-bound, sat and gnawed his lips.

What he had done, he knew, was in violation of all regulations. The infantry was his to command, but only in accordance with orders emanating from headquarters. He had dared greatly in bidding Rouget advance his troops. If the plan succeeded there would be glory for all, possibly an Earldom for himself. But if it failed . . .

It failed. Late in the afternoon the slumbering pain shook to the thunder of battle. For hours the tumult raged. Sir Rufus paced the watchtower nervously, unable to tell from that great distance which side held the advantage. At evenfall he learned. A few stragglers, bloody and in rags, sifted back to camp as the sounds of conflict died. One stood before Sir Rufus wretchedly.

"We did our best, Milord. But we were outmanned ten to one. We were no match for the Queen's guard."

"How many escaped?" asked Sir Rufus.

"A score, perhaps, Milord. No more."

"The Chevalier Rouget?"

"He fought well," said the soldier simply. "The enemy dead lay in windrows about him."

"Very well," said Sir Rufus. "You may go." With a face like a carven mask he returned the man's salute and watched him a way. But a moment later, in the privacy of his tent, there were tears in his eyes. Tears of fury and despair at his own tremendous folly. And of regret for a gallant comrade lost forever.

How long he might have lingered there, berating himself and mourning Rouget, it is impossible to guess. He was roused from his brooding by a hoarse bellow in a familiar voice. "Rufus! Sir Rufus, there, young gamecock! What's going on? What's all this hellish pothering about?"

Sir Rufus sprang to the tent flaps. Stomping from his bastion at the head of his troops was Sir Roderick, red-faced and querulous, armed to the teeth and spoiling for a fight. He spied the younger man and shouted fretfully, "They tell me you lost your reserve. Is it true?"

Sir Rufus nodded glumly. "It is. I had a plan—"

"*You* had a plan! You mean you moved them without orders?"

"It was a good plan—" began the knight.

"Aye, maybe so. But they draw and quarter men for trying good plans that fail. What's to be done now?"

Sir Rufus said, "Nothing, I fear. You'd best get back to the castle. Even now their Queen advances on us—"

"Their Queen, is it?" bellowed Roderick. "Now, that I like! The quarrelsome, brawling wench. Let her show her face to me and I'll teach her a thing or two. Eh, lad?"

A spark of hope rekindled in Sir Rufus' despondent heart. Perhaps, he thought, the day might yet be saved. If he and Roderick joined forces . . .

"I'll back you up!" he cried.

"Good! Then we'll have at her!" roared the knight Seneschal. "Ho, messenger! A warning to that vixen scut who dares cross our frontier. Tell her an invitation to the battle waits . . . and we'll have her ears for breakfast!"

13. 14. 15. 16.

But it was no breakfast of queenly ears for Roderick that morning. After a cold night's waiting for reply to his challenge came with the dawn scouts from the outpost bearing news that under cover of night Queen Blanche had withdrawn her forces, retreating out of battle range to the safety of her own border.

Sir Roderick was furious. "A gallant bawd, indeed! Ventures forth to do battle with serfs . . . but when a noble shakes his banner, she lifts her easy skirts and vanishes like a doe. Fie on the round-heeled wench!

"And what is *this?*" he continued. "Who comes now to bar me from pursuing the pale-faced drab to her scented bedchamber?"

For blocked indeed he was from further action . . . because trooping back from the border came the Queen's Crusaders. To the site just across the river from Sir Rufus' camp they marched, and there halted. Sir Rufus frowned.

"I don't know what they're up to now," he said, "but I'll go find out. Hold tight, Sir Roderick."

In person he visited the churchmen's camp. His Grace the Bishop met him wreathed in smiles, soothing away all questions with deft movements of his soft, bejewelled hands.

"There, now, Sir Knight," he chided, "lose not in haste your wits. Retreat? Of course not. The Church defends the throne to the last man. We have but effected a strategic withdrawal to plan our new campaign."

"And what," demanded Rufus, "was the matter with the old one? If Your Grace had but attacked the enemy day before yesterday, we would not now be in this sorry plight."

"Those are harsh words," purred the Bishop dangerously, "for one whose reckless actions have already resulted in the loss of an entire regiment. Or perhaps the High Command ordered . . . No? Too bad. But if I can count on your support *now*, I might be able to return the favor if there should be—as of course we hope there will not—a court martial?"

Sir Rufus answered stiffly, "Your Grace cannot buy my connivance to private schemes. You realize, of course, that you waste time here? That the enemy's cavalry reserve has already started for the front?"

"We have heard some such rumor," smiled the Bishop languidly. "But we are not afraid. We are expecting our brother, the King's advisor, here for conference within the hour. *Private* conference. So if you will pardon me—?"

"Very well," grated Sir Rufus. "I shall go, Your Holiness. But mark you well—if there be from you or your psalter-smiting brother one false move—"

"Peace be upon you, my son," smiled the Bishop through clenched teeth. "Sergeant, his Lordship's horse."

So Sir Rufus left, even as the army of the other ecclesiastic moved in to hold converse with the first.

Meanwhile, Intelligence reported that the Blanchard cavalry reserve was on the move. Protected by the Home Guard, they had now advanced all the way to the border. What action this portended, Sir Rufus could not guess. But one thing was clear. With each passing hour the advance post held by the enemy's first infantry division—that which had crossed the border days ago—loomed more threatening. At all costs, this division must be isolated. His troops were in position to strike and strike hard. If Her Ladyship would back him up, Sir Rufus was eager to essay the task.

As if reading his desire, the Queen's regiment *did* move. And coincident with its advance came a message from headquarters:

> From: Base Headquarters
> To: Commander, His Majesty's First Cavalry
> Sir Captain:
> Her Majesty's Elite Guard has moved to the border in direct support of a campaign to suppress the invasion forces. Prepare to attack upon receipt of this order as prearranged by Defense Plan D. Long live the King!
> (signed) Thomas Viscount Ross
> *Commander-in-Chief*

It was a message which brought a thrill of pleasure to Sir Rufus. For more than one reason. First, it promised action to come. Second, by omission of any reference, it indicated that the High Command had decided—for the present, at least—to take no official cognizance of his recent impetuous action.

Perhaps the War Department had even found some way to make use of the tactical position his blunder had brought about. In that case, there might never be a court martial. Indeed, if the war were won—*when* the war was won, Sir Rufus corrected himself sharply—there might be a citation for "action in the field resulting in victory." Pleasant thought.

But this new Commander-in-Chief . . . Viscount Ross? His name was unfamiliar to Sir Rufus. Or . . . was it? Ross? Sir Rufus frowned. He had a vague recollection . . . someone he had met somewhere. But where? At court, perhaps?

A fretful face. Fingers drumming nervously on wood, and a mind that worked on impulse. A man victim to his own intuition . . . and the click of statuettes on a patterned board . . .

Sir Rufus shrugged. He knew no Viscount Ross.

Word came that the King's First Foot had finally been taken. Returning home from conference with their Queen, the enemy Crusaders had stumbled upon the camp of the Lost Battalion. The regiment had long been cut off from its line of supply; the men were gaunt with hunger, weak with despair. The result of the ensuing battle was a foregone conclusion.

Sir Rufus sighed to hear the news, but did not mourn. In war, men were expendable. And even in destruction the advance guard had given their fellow countrymen assistance. For by the rules of war, the Crusaders' conquest constituted an aggressive action, which meant the next move was that of the defenders. Sir Rufus bade his men strike camp and arm for battle, expecting momentarily an order to attack. The enemy *also* had an advance guard, a Lost Battalion of its own. An eye for an eye, a tooth for a tooth . . . a regiment for a regiment . . .

But the expected orders did not come. Instead, inexplicably, came a report from the scouts that in a sudden reversal of tactics the Queen's Elite, led by Her Ladyship herself, had whirled and raced along the border to a position opposite the enemy King's hide-away in the provinces!

Sir Rufus stood appalled at hearing this. He saw no reason for such headlong flight. It was insane, wastrel, mad! Or so, embittered by his disappointment, thought the knight. He was wrong. He was soon to learn the reason.

17. 18. 19. 20.

Sir Rufus had established a communication with his good friend, comrade in arms, and erstwhile classmate in the War College, Ippolytus Lord Quaestor, Knight Commander of His Majesty's Royal Cavalry. With other horsemen Sir Rufus felt more kinship than with any of his other associates . . . even than with old Sir Roderick who, like himself, was pledged to Her Ladyship's service. They thought and fought alike, he and good old Pol. And when the going was rough, there was nothing like mounted support to help one out of a fix.

It was from Sir Ippolytus he received direct news of the action coalescing on the western front. Pol sent his first alarum shortly before dawn. "Stand by," he warned, "for instant action. Enemy cavalry moving deeper into our territory. Expect flanking attack against Queen's Guard."

Even before Sir Rufus could acknowledge receipt of the warning, a second message followed. The squire bearing it was jubilant.

"They *did* attack, Sir Rufus," he explained, "even as Milord Ippolytus expected. But we repulsed them . . . cut them to ribbons. The threat is ended."

"Good!" said Sir Rufus. "And your infantry? They escaped unscathed?"

"Not quite, sir. In fact, they lost so many men that they are ineffective as a fighting force until they can be reconstituted. The enemy King's patrols advanced to rout our men from terrain briefly held, but—"

Sir Rufus exclaimed, "Then, idiot, Sir Ippolytus' camp is threatened? You told me all is well."

"And so it is, Milord," said the courier patiently. "The enemy attack has bogged down at our line of inner defense. And His Majesty's Home Guard has moved into position to support Her Ladyship's campaign."

"Her Ladyship's campaign?" repeated Sir Rufus wonderingly. He strode to the field maps and studied them. A dawning admiration gathered in his eyes. "Now, by the Sign, you are right! Our High Command is not the band of idiots I feared. A swift attack upon the enemy's cavalry, followed by destruction of their foot reserve, and their King will be trapped in his refuge!"

"Even so, Milord. Thus said Sir Ippolytus. Think you the war may end soon? A knight's rank," said the squire, "has been promised me with victory."

"Then," answered Sir Rufus, "I shall soon be calling you *Sir* Whatever-your-name-may-be. For unless the Blanchards move and move swiftly, the victory is ours. Any word as to their latest troop disposition?"

"Only that they are massing Home Guardsmen behind the lines. It is reported that their Queen's Seneschal has joined forces with the King's at the Queen's deserted palace."

Sir Rufus laughed. "*That* will not save them," he jeered. "The dolts gather strength where it is valueless. Return to your Lord Commander and tell him his friend Rufus stands to his support. Tell him also that we shall meet at the victory table to toast our earned success in this cam—Stay! What is that?"

For there came to his ears from outside the tent a sound of many voices. Triumphant voices lifting in mad clamor. Before he could reach the tent flaps, canvas parted, and his cadet lieutenant entered.

"Milord! Great news!"

"Yes, lad? What is it?"

"A victory surely won. Her Majesty's troops—"

"Have marched?"

"Have sped like the wind, Milord, in surprise attack. The cavalry guarding their King's hideout has been hacked to bits . . . and the Blanchard King lies helpless in his castle!"

* * *

Later, looking back upon the series of disastrous blows that struck with such sudden triphammer force, Sir Rufus was to wonder why at that moment he had been so blind, so blissfully confident of victory. When in those later hours scant breathing spells permitted him to review the whirling eddy of events, too late he realized that the enemy had taken into calculation even their foe's aggressive moves.

But at the time, it did not seem that way. For a brief, happy while Sir Rufus thought panic had engulfed the Blanchard command. Only thus could he account for the recklessness with which they started hurling men, whole troops and regiments, into what seemed a futile cause. In this hour when sanity would seem to dictate stern conservation of every available force, the enemy went berserk with an apparent lust for self-destruction. There came in the heat of noon a warning from Sir Ippolytus' camp.

"Sir Rufus, be on guard! Their Home Guard moves. They've crossed the border, are broaching my position!"

Sir Rufus sounded his men to horse instantly. The road was long and tortuous; be could not see what was going on ahead until he rounded the moat before His Majesty's palace. Then he discovered be had started not a moment too soon. Old Pol had not cried wolf; the enemy was attacking in force. Even as Rufus spurred his troops to greater speed the guidon fell from the hands of the last defiant knight in Ippolytus' command, and footmen from the Blanchard ranks began to storm the castle walls.

Like a whirlwind Rufus' horsemen struck from behind. The fray was brief but bloody. Men struck and struck again, cast shattered arms aside to ride full tilt into the crimson pikes of the interlopers. Sir Rufus hurled the bulk of his troops against the ring of foeman warriors girdling the palace grounds. With a picked handfull he dismounted and pursued their leaders into the very corridors of the palace. There in hand to hand combat they met and picked them off one by one—until at last the great stone walls echoed only to the panting sobs of men worn with combat, and the enemy invaders grinned in frozen death from the moat into which their bodies had been hurled.

Sir Rufus sought the regent in his quarters. The King was grateful for the battle won, but he was fretful, too.

"What now, Sir Knight," he demanded petulantly. "Is this the victory my Lord Commanders promised? Where is Her Ladyship, and what of the Plan they said she had?"

"The plan goes well, Sire," Rufus reassured him. "Her Majesty stands at the very gates of the enemy retreat. As for this attack of theirs ... it is the last defiance of a dying cause. They will try no more such futile forays."

The King, who had stalked to one of the windows, spun on him savagely, caustically.

"You're certain of that, Sir Knight?"

"As sure," said Rufus, "as of my name and honor."

"Then look to your honor," snarled the ruler, "and question your paternity. For *still* they attack, and in force! If I mistake me not, here come the troops of their vixen Queen herself!"

21. 22. 22.

In a stride Sir Rufus was at his ruler's side. A gasp escaped his lips. Fresh, strong, vigorous, the troops of the Blanchard Queen were pouring across the palace court in a silver flood. The regiment of guards at the postern gate delayed them scarce an instant; with pike and bow and spear they ripped the defenders to shreds. Into the palace grounds rode the hordes, and at their head rode the Amazon Queen Blanche.

Sir Rufus cried hoarsely, "Your Majesty—go! My troops are worn, exhausted. Even could I rally them, they could not set up a new defense line. Fly while there yet is time."

"Fly?" repeated His Majesty sternly. "And where is there to go, Sir Knight? Nay, Milord. I will show both you and they how a true King dies. Guard! To me, guard!"

So he strode forth ... to his foredestined doom.

All through the night the dreadful battle raged. How it went, Sir Rufus could not tell. From his own weary troops he dispatched every man able to bear arms, realizing as he did so that he risked swift destruction from behind should the Blanchard infantry detachment on his flank decide to attack. But when kingdoms tremble in the balance, there is small choice of action.

And then, with dawning, came the battle's end. A courier came crying, "Gird all! Gird all and rally to His Majesty the King!"

Sir Rufus clutched the bridle of the rider's steed, dragging him to a halt.

"How now?" he demanded. "What of the battle? Is it won or lost?"

"Both won *and* lost, Milord," replied the crier.

"Talk sense, varlet! Queen Blanche—?"

"Dead, Milord. Stricken in mortal combat by His Majesty himself."

"The worms feast poorly!" growled Sir Rufus. "But if she be

slain, why this tocsin of alarm? If we have met and killed their leader—"

"Because, Milord, still the damned Blanchards attack in ever increasing numbers. Their King's Crusaders have crossed the border. Not only that, but their dead Queen's Home Guard stands revealed in position to capture His Majesty if he does not flee at once."

Then his words were drowned in the thunder of hooves, and his Majesty's battered troops were pouring back into the court.

"Sir Rufus!" cried the King. "To me, Sir Rufus!"

"Aye, Sire?"

"I go to my palace. It is the last refuge. Do what you can to hold them. I have sent a messenger to Her Ladyship, begging instant aid."

"It shall be as you say, Sire," said Sir Rufus, and called his men to ranks.

But the foe had tasted blood, and there was no withstanding them now. Scarce had the King entered the palace than over the northern hilltops rose the cross-crowned emblem of the enemy Crusaders. With cries of challenge they hurled themselves across the plain, charging into the court by the very gate through which His Majesty had lately entered. The hooves of their plunging horses stirred crimson dust where moments before their own Queen's blood had been shed.

And they were strange ecclesiastics, these. There was little of the piety and mercy which they prated from their pulpits in this advance. For all their cross and candle, they were more like demons than priests as they thundered into the postern court screaming like madmen.

"Yield!" was their cry. "Yield or die!"

Sir Rufus held his men in readiness for orders. There was nothing he could do now but wait for the attack. Wait and hope the High Command could find some way out of this debacle.

What that way might be, he could not see. Far to the north, Her Ladyship was impotent to aid. His own troops were no match for those arrayed against them. And the King—no help might be expected from that quarter. For in his palace, the King, in utter panic, fled futilely from wing to threatened wing seeking a non-existent refuge.

24.

It was in the West Wing that His Majesty finally elected to make his last stand. That was the best hope . . . if best there was in hopeless situation . . . for at least there he had before him the knights of Sir Rufus' cavalry. And thus it was decided.

Sir Rufus told his men, "Their plan lies clear. That cursed regiment of foot—the regiment we should have finished long ago—lies on our flank. Undoubtedly they will attack. But we are stronger than they. If we fight well, there is still hope."

But it was not the infantry which, at the end, closed in for the kill. It was a force which Sir Rufus had ever distrusted, ever feared. Queen Blanche's churchmen, racing from their camp behind the border to avenge the death of their lady. It was they who smashed down upon the weary cavalrymen with all the strength and vigor of reserves well fed and rested.

There was no time for thought in that final conflict. Still in stark moments shreds of thought coursed through Sir Rufus' brain. As in a dream, he saw this war in its entirety; saw now and granted hatred-filled respect to the master plan of his foeman; saw, too, and loathed the treachery of those who had betrayed his liege lord's cause.

Those skulking churchmen. It was *they* whose machinations had brought disaster. They who from the first had conspired with the enemy to effect defeat. They who had refused to join battle earlier, when the contest teetered in the balance. They who had blocked Sir Roderick's eager troops from the fray when the weight of his armor might have tipped the balance from defeat to victory.

And now it was they who huddled in interminable "coherence" far on the eastern front, conserving two strong armies which, brought up in time, might have saved the day.

The Bishops, ever the Bishops! Soft-handed, lying rascals unworthy of the truth their rulers had reposed in them. Even as Sir Rufus fought, his right arm dragging with the weight of his slashing sword, there rose to his lips a last snarl of hatred.

"Now, by the Rood!" he swore, "may their name be damned forevermore. The traitors!"

And that was a strange thing, too. For even as he spoke there seemed a haze before his eyes. *Blue haze of oddly fragrant smoke, and bodies hunched across a patterned board.* And from a million miles, a million years away, came thin remembered voices. A taunting voice, yet kind, saying, *"You see? Imaginative yet inconsistent. He prefaces his tirade against religion with a sacerdotal invocation."*

But he did not stop fighting. Not when the enemy Crusaders

had cut their way across the court, forcing the horsemen to dismount and seek the refuge of the palace. Not when he saw his cadet lieutenant fall, strangling in a lungful of his own blood as his querulous fingers doubted the arrow that had found his breast. Not when, one of a scantling score, he took final refuge in the West Wing, before the very chamber where His Majesty awaited rescue . . . or death.

Even then he did not stop fighting. He was a Knight and a soldier of the Queen. That the campaign had been mishandled he knew well . . . but was not his to question these things. His but to fight, and keep on fighting, until death relieved him of his knightly vows.

And so it was that alone, he fell at last. Properly, it was to a peers blade he yielded. It was the Lord Captain of the Crusaders in person who slashed Sir Rufus' sword from his hands at the doorway to the King's chamber. And there was a warrior's admiration in his offer.

"You are the last of your men, Sir Knight," he cried. "You have fought a good fight, but it is finished. Will you yield now, and spare me the slaying of a brave man?"

In answer, Sir Rufus hurled himself forward. The sword in his foeman's hand might yet be wrested from him . . . and the fight prolonged another minute . . . second . . .

But the captain saw his purpose and stepped back. Then, with a sign, he stepped forward again, blade raised. Sir Rufus took it straight, and took it striking.

The world grew dim, and figures moved like trees. Sir Rufus coughed, and there was blood upon his lips. The splintering of wood was the crumbling of the King's last bastion. The sweat of battle ended; there was a cold, clear wind upon his brow. A high hill yearning to a midnight sky, and a soft reluctant voice whispering from afar as the captain stepped over his fallen body.

"*Well, now—I believe that's it . . .*"

"Well, now—I believe that's it," said Weissmann in a soft reluctant voice. He settled back to his leather chair, expelled a cloud of blue and fragrant smoke. "Checkmate, Tom."

Ross nodded grudgingly.

"That's it," he acknowledged. "Confound you! I'm one move from mate myself . . . and you spend men like pennies to bottle me up in my own back yard!"

Weissmann smiled gently, shrugged, and turned his curiously

gentle eyes on Springer, stirring in the chair beside the table. "Ah, there, lad . . . feel better?"

Rufus Springer passed a puzzled hand across his brow. He said uncertainly, "Game over? I must have slept."

There was a memory fleeting in his mind. Not recollection, truly, but the swift and scudding wisp of a fading dream. One he could not clutch for all his striving, elusive, growing dimmer with each instant. *Swords red with blood, and banners in the sun. Hoarse cries of pain, and the crash of a yielding door* . . .

"You were asleep," said Ross, "and missed seeing the sneakiest attack this cunning old rascal ever pulled on either of us!" He sighed and started rearranging the bits of carven ivory on the chessboard. "Ah, well, live and learn! Next time I'll watch my step when you start sacrificing men, Weissmann. If I'd trusted you less—"

"Or if you'd trusted your *Bishops* a little less, Tom," Springer said suddenly. "That's what destroyed you. The Bishops blocking out your Rook—"

He stopped abruptly, seized with the same wonder voiced by Ross.

"The Bishops? How in blazes do you know, Rufus? I thought you were asleep."

Rufus Springer said uncertainly, "I . . . I don't know how I knew, Tom. I—" He looked across the board at Weissmann. The older man was busy with his pipe, prodding its toothscored bit with a tar-stained cleaner. His eyes met Springer's, and in them was no answer. But there was a glint, a hint of mockery . . . or was it the reflection of the light on Weissmann's glasses? "I don't know," repeated Springer vaguely. "I honestly don't know."

"Ah, well," said Weissmann, "does it really matter? Our game next, Springer. That is, if you're ready to match wits with the old master?"

"I'm ready," said Springer, and slipped into the chair vacated by the disconsolate Ross. "My White?"

"If you wish," nodded Weissmann. Then, as he disposed the pieces, "Now, then, as I was saying before the game . . . about this matter of free will—"

"Good Lord!" sighed Ross. "There he goes again! Now we'll hear more about screaming and thinking chessmen!"

Rufus Springer said nothing. There rang in his ears the sound of distant battle, the nickering of horses and the screams of dying men. And suddenly he knew . . . *he knew!* And knowing, he was gripped with a terrible unease, a fear more strong than he had ever known.

Pawns like men . . . who fatuously dreamed that they were masters of their own fate, rulers of their own evitable destiny.

Then a chessman, he, on a patterned board so vast as to be inconceivable to his earthly mind? Even that idea he could accept and tolerate. Save for one thing . . .

By Whose hand was he moved? The swift and cunning hand of a Master Chessman? The sure hand of a supramundane Weissmann? Or the fumbling hand of an uncertain Ross?

For the benefit of those who would be interested in studying the game in which Rufus Springer participated as Queen's Knight, the following is offered:

	WHITE (Weissmann)	RED (Ross)
1.	P-K4	P-K4
2.	N-KB3	N-QB3
3.	B-B4	B-B4
4.	P-QN4	BxP
5.	P-B3	B-R4
6.	P-Q4	PxP
7.	0-0	P-Q6
8.	Q-N3	Q-B3
9.	P-K5	Q-N3
10.	R-K1	KN-K2
11.	B-R3	P-N4
12.	QxP	R-QN1
13.	Q-R4	B-N3
14.	QN-Q2	B-N2
15.	N-K4	Q-B4
16.	BxP	Q-R4
17.	N-B6ch	PxN
18.	PxP	R-N1
19.	QR-Q1	QxN
20.	RxNch	NxR
21.	QxPch	KxQ
22.	B-B5ch	K-K1
23.	B-Q7ch	K-moves
24.	BxN mate	

"Family Circle"

The offspring of a writer's imaginings are almost as near and dear to him as his flesh-and-blood children. To a certain sense he knows them even better *because whereas with age and experience his naturalborn kin develop personalities unlike his own, his fictional creations are* forever *mirror images of himself. As they are in his mind, he is in theirs; he experiences as his own their thoughts, their dreams and their desires . . . as well as their peculiarities.*

Thus if as their parent I am proud to claim the logical acumen of Horsesense Hank and the inventive ingenuity of Pat Pending, I must also confess to possessing the whimsy prankishness of the unpredictable Lobblies and the openly amoral avarice of Squaredeal Sam McGhee.

In the four stories that follow you will meet some of my dreamchildren whose lives became so closely associated with my own that I shared more than one of their adventures. Mag and Dave went on to appear in a half dozen stories, Pat Pending and Sam McGhee in more than a dozen each, Biggs' adventures became a complete book, and the Lobblies not ony appeared in magazine tales but as the central characters of a radio series, several TV shows, and a three-act stage play.

So, as I said, these offspring as almost *as near and dear to me as my two sons Lynn and Kit.*

But in that case, why don't they send me birthday presents?

Magic City

OUT OF THE SWEET, DARK EMPTINESS OF SLEEP THERE was a pressure on her arm and a voice whispering an urgent plea.

"Rise, O Mother! O Mother, rise and come quickly!"

Meg woke with a start. The little sleep-imp in her brain stirred fretfully, resentful of being thus rudely banished. He made one last effort to hold Meg captive, tossing a mist of slumber-dust into her eyes, but Meg shook her head resolutely. The sleep-imp, sulky, forced her lips open in a great gape, climbed from her mouth, and sped away.

Sullen shadows lingered in the corners of the *hoam,* but the windows were gray-limned with approaching dawn. Meg glanced at the cot beside her own, where Daiv, her mate, lay in undisturbed rest. His tawny mane was tousled, and on his lips hovered the memory of a smile. His face was curiously, endearingly boyish, but the bronzed arms and shoulders that lay exposed were the arms and shoulders of a fighting man.

"Quickly, O Mother—"

Meg said, "Peace, Jain; I come." She spoke calmly, gravely, as befitted the matriarch of the Jinnia Clan, but a thin, cold fear-thought touched her heart. So many were the duties of a Mother;

so many and so painful. Meg the Priestess had not guessed the troubles that lay beyond the days of her novitiate. Now the aged, kindly tribal Mother was dead; into Meg's firm, white hands had been placed the guidance of her clan's destiny. It was so great a task, and this—*this* was the hardest task of all.

She drew a deep breath. "Elnor?" she asked.

"Yes, Mother. Even now the Evil Ones circle about, seeking to steal the breath from her nostrils. He bides His time, but He is impatient. There is no time to waste."

"I come," said Meg. From a shelf she took a rattle made of a dry gourd wound with the tresses of a virgin; from another a fire-rock, a flaked piece of god-metal and a strip of parchment upon which a sacred stick, dipped into midnight water, had left its spoor of letters.

These things she touched with reverence, and Jain's eyes were great with awe. The worker captain shuddered, hid her face in her hands lest the sight of these holy mysteries blind her.

Dry fern rustled. Daiv, eyes heavy-lidded, propped himself up on one elbow.

"What is it, Golden One?"

"Elnor," replied Meg quietly. "He has come to take her. I must do what I can."

Impatience etched tiny lines on Daiv's forehead.

"With those things, Golden One? I've told you time and again, they won't bother Him—"

"Hush!" Meg made a swift, appeasing gesture lest He, hearing Daiv's impious words, take offense. Daiv's boldness often frightened Meg. He held the gods in so little awe it was a marvel they let him live. Of course he came from a sacred place himself, from the Land of the Escape. That might have something to do with it.

She said again, "I must do what I can, Daiv. Come, Jain."

They left the Mother's hoam, walked swiftly down the deserted walk-avenue. The morning symphony of the birds was in its tune-up stage. The sky was dim, gray, overcast. One hoam was lighted, that of the stricken worker, Elnor.

Meg opened the door, motioned Jain quickly inside, closed the door again behind her that no breath of foul outside air taint the hot, healthy closeness of the sickroom. She noted with approval that the windows had been closed and tightly sealed, that strong-scented ox-grease candles filled the room with their potent, demon-chasing odor.

Yet despite these precautions, the Evil Ones did—as Jain had told—vie for possession of Elnor's breath. On a narrow cot in the middle of the room lay the dying worker. Her breath choked, ragged and uneven as the song of the jay. Her cheeks, beneath their coat of tan, were bleached; her eyes were hot coals in murky pockets. Her flesh was dry and harsh; she tossed restlessly, eyes roving as if watching some unseen presence.

Jain said fearfully, "See, O Mother? She sees Him. He is here."

Meg nodded. Her jaw tightened. Two women and Bil, Elnor's mate, huddled about the sickbed. She motioned them away. "I will do battle with Him," she said grimly.

She poised a moment, tense for the conflict. Elnor moaned. Then Meg, with a great, reverberant cry, struck the sacred stones together, the bit of fire-rock and the rasp of god-metal. A shower of golden sparks leaped from her hands. Her watchers cried aloud their awe, fell back trembling.

Meg raised the gourd. Holding it high, shaking it, the scrap of parchment clenched in her right hand, she began chanting the magic syllables written thereon. She cried out reverently, for these were mighty words of healing power, no one knew how old, but they had been handed down through long ages. They were a rite of the Ancient Ones.

" 'I swear,' " she intoned. " 'by Apollo the physician and Aesculapius, and Health, and All-heal, and all the gods and goddesses, that, according to my ability and judgment, I will keep this Oath and stipulation—' "

The gourd challenged the demons who haunted Elnor. Meg crossed her eyes and crept widdershins three times about Elnor's cot.

" '—I will give no deadly med-sun to anyone—' "

The sonorous periods rolled and throbbed; sweat ran down Meg's cheeks and throat. Beneath her blankets, Elnor tossed. In the corner, Bil muttered fearfully.

" '—will not cut persons laboring under the Stone, but will leave this to be done by men who are practitioners of this work—' "

The candle guttered, and a drop of wax spilled on the floor as the door behind her opened, closed gently. Meg dared not glance at the newcomer, dared not risk halting the incantation. Some of the hectic color appeared to have left Elnor's cheeks. Perhaps, then, He was leaving? Without his prey?

" '—while I continue to keep this Oath unviolated, may it be granted to me—' "

Meg's voice swelled with hope. Oh, mighty was the magic of

the Ancient Ones! The spell was succeeding! In a vast, triumphant clamor of the gourd, tone shrill and joyful, she broke into the peroration.

" '—to enjoy life and the practice of the Art, respected by all—' "

A sudden, blood-chilling sound interrupted her. It was Elnor. A gasp of pain, a stifled cry, one lunging twist of a pain-racked body. And then—

"It is too late, Golden One," said Daiv. "Elnor is dead."

The women in the corner began keening a dirge. The man, Bil, ceased his muttering. He moved to the side of his dead mate, knelt there wordlessly, staring at Meg with mute, reproachful eyes.

Choking, Meg stammered the words required of her. " 'Aamé, the gods, have mercy on her soul.' " Then she fled from the hoam of sorrow. It was not permitted that anyone should see the Mother in tears.

Daiv followed her. Even in his arms, there was but little comfort—

Later, in their own hoam, Daiv sat watching in respectful silence as Meg performed the daily magic that was an obligation of the Mother.

Having offered a brief prayer to the gods, Meg took into her right hand a stick. This she let drink from a pool of midnight in a dish before her, then scratched it across a scroll of smooth, bleached calfskin. Where it moved it left its spoor, a spidery trail of black.

She finished, and Daiv gazed at her admiringly. He was proud of this mate of his who held the knowledge of many lost mysteries. He said, "It is done, Golden One? Read it. Let me hear the speech-without-words."

Meg read, somberly.

"Report of the fourteenth day of the month of June, 3485 A.D.

"Our work is going forward very well. Today Evalin returned from her visit to the Zurrie territory. There, she says, her message was received with astonishment and wonder, but for the most part with approval. There is some dissent, especially amongst the older women, but the Mother has heard the Revelation with understanding, and has given her promise that the Slooie Clan will immediately attempt to communicate peace and a knowledge of the new order to the Wild Ones.

"Our crops ripen, and soon Lima will have completed the new dam across the Ronoak River. We have now fourscore cattle, fifty horses, and our clan numbers three hundred and twenty-nine. All of our women are supplied with mates.

"We lost a most valuable worker today, when He came for Elnor, Loetent of the Field Coar. We could ill afford to lose her, but He would not be denied—"

Meg's voice broke. She stopped reading, tossed the scroll on a jumbled heap with countless others, some shining new, some yellow with age, written in the painstaking script of Mothers long dead and long forgotten.

Daiv said consolingly, "Do not grieve, Golden One. You tried to save her. But eventually He comes for each of us. The aged, the weak, the hurt—"

Meg cried, "Why, Daiv, why? Why should He come for Elnor? We know He takes the aged because in their weakness is His strength; He takes the wounded because he scents flowing blood from afar.

"But Elnor was young and strong and healthy. There were no wounds or sores upon her body. She did not taste of His berries in the fields, nor had she touched, at any time, a person already claimed by Him.

"Yet—she died! Why? Why, Daiv?"

"I do not know, Golden One. But I am curious. For I am Daiv, known as He-who-would-learn. There is a mystery here far greater than all your magic spells. Perhaps it is even greater than the wisdom of the Ancient Ones."

"I am afraid, Daiv. He is so ever-near; we are so weak. You know I have tried to be a good Mother. It was I who made a pilgrimage to the Place of the Gods, learned the secret that the gods were men, and established a new order, that men and women should live together again, as it was in the old days.

"I have worked to spread this knowledge throughout the world, through all of Tizathy. One day we will reclaim all the Wild Ones of the forests, bring them into our camps and together we and they will rebuild the world.

"Only one stands in our way. Him! He who strikes down our warriors with an invisible sword, reaps an endless harvest amongst our workers. He is our arch-foe. A grim, mocking, unseen enemy, against whom we are powerless."

Daiv grunted. There were small, hard lines on his forehead, between his eyes. His lips were not upcurved in their usual happy look.

He said, "You are right, Meg. He, alone, destroys more of us each year than the forest beasts or our occasional invaders. Could we but find and kill Him our people would increase in knowledge and power swiftly."

He shook his head. "But we do not know where to seek Him, Golden One."

Meg drew a swift, deep breath. Her eyes glinted, suddenly excited.

"*I know,* Daiv!"

"You know where He lives, Golden One?"

"Yes. The old Mother told me, many years ago when I was a student priestess. She spoke and warned me against a forbidden city to the north and eastward—the city known as the City of Death! That is, must be, His lair!"

There was a moment of strident silence.

Then Daiv said, tightly, "Can you tell me how to reach this spot, Meg? Can you draw me a marker-of-places that will enable me to find it?"

"I can! It lies where the great creet highways of the Ancient Ones meet with a river and an island at a vast, salt sea. But . . . but why, Daiv?"

Daiv said, "Draw me the marker-of-places, Meg. He must be destroyed. I will go to His city to find Him."

"No!" It was not Meg the priestess who cried out; it was Meg the woman. "No, Daiv! It is an accursed city. I cannot let you go!"

"You cannot stop me, Golden One."

"But you know no spells, no incantations. He will destroy you—"

"I will destroy Him, first." The happy look clung to the corners of Daiv's lips. He drew Meg into his bronze arms, woke fire in her veins with the touching-of-mouths he had taught her. "My arm is strong, Meg; my sword keen. He must feel its bite if we are to live and prosper. You cannot change my mind."

Then Meg decided.

"Very well, Daiv. You shall go. But I will make you no marker-of-places."

"Come now, Golden One! Without it I shall not be able to find—"

Meg's voice was firm, unequivocal. "Because I shall go with you! Together we shall seek and destroy—Him!"

II.

So started Meg and Daiv for the City of Death. It was not a happy parting, theirs with the men and women of the Jinnia Clan. There were tears and lamentations and sad mutterings, for all knew the law that the eastern cities of the Ancient Ones were forbidden.

There was bravery, too, and loyalty. Stern-jawed Lora, Captain of the Warriors, confronted Meg at the gate. She was clad for battle; her leathern plates and buckler were newly refurbished, her sword hung at her side. Behind her stood a squad of picked warriors, packed for trek.

"We are ready, O Mother!" said Lora succinctly.

Meg smiled, a sweet, proud smile. She knew only too well the mental terror, the physical qualms of fear these women had overcome to thus offer themselves. Her heart lifted within her, but she leaned forward and with her own fingers unbuckled Lora's scabbard.

"You are needed here, my daughter," she said. "You must guard the clan till I return. And"—she faltered an instant, continued swiftly—"and if it is the will of the gods I return not, then you must continue to see that the law is obeyed until the young priestess, Haizl, is finished her novitiate and can assume leadership.

"Peace be with you all!" She pressed her lips to Lora's forehead lightly. It seemed strange to none of them that she should call the harsh-visaged chieftain, many years her senior, "My daughter." For she was the Mother, and the Mother was ageless and of all time.

Others came forward then, each in their turn to ask a farewell blessing, to offer silent prayers to the gods for Meg's safe return. Young Haizl, the clear-eyed, inquisitive twelve-year-old maiden whom Meg had selected to succeed her as matriarch of the Jinnia Clan, whispered: "Be strong, O Mother, but not too daring. Return safely, for never can I take your place."

"But you can, my daughter. Study diligently, learn the speech-without-words and the magic of the numbers. Keep the law and learn the rituals."

"I try, O Mother. But the little pain-demons dwell in my head, behind my eyes. They dance and make the letters move strangely."

"Pursue your course and they will go away."

Came 'Ana, who had been a breeding-mother before the Revelation, and who was now a happily wedded mate. Her eyes were red with weeping and she could not speak. Came Izbel, strongest of the workers, who with her bare hands had crushed the life from a mountain cat. But there was no strength in her hands now; they trembled as they touched Meg's doeskin boots. Also came Bil, eyes smoldering with hot demand.

"I would go with you to destroy Him, O Mother! It is my right. You cannot refuse me!"

"But I can and do, Bil."

Bil said rebelliously, "I am a man, strong, brave. I fought beside Daiv when the Japcans attacked. Ask him if I am not a great fighter."

"That I know without asking. But now we fight an invisible foe. Of all the clan, only Daiv and I can stand before Him. I am a Mother, inviolate; Daiv is sprung of an ancient, sacred tribe. The Kirki tribe, dwelling in the Land of the Escape.

"And now—farewell—"

But after they had left the town, Daiv repeated his objections, voiced many times in the hours preceding this.

"Go back, Golden One! This is a man's task. He is a potent enemy. Go back to the clan, wait for my return—"

Meg said, as if not hearing him, "See, the road lies before us. The broken creet road of the Ancient Ones."

It was not a long journey. Only eight days' march, according to Meg's calculations. Scarce one fifth of the distance she had covered in her pilgrimage to the Place of the Gods in 'Kota territory a year before. And Daiv was an experienced traveler; alone, he had wandered through most of Tizathy from sun-parched 'Vadah to bleak Wyomin, from the lush jungles of Flarduh to the snow-crested mountains of Orgen. Only this one path he had never trod, for all tribes in wide Tizathy knew the law, that the east was forbidden.

So their journey was one filled with many wonders. It was difficult walking on the crumbled creet highways of the Ancient Ones, so Meg and Daiv walked in the fields but kept the white rock roadbed in sight. They passed through an abandoned village named Lextun or Veémi—the old name for it was confused in the records—and another known as Stantn. Only by the intersections of the roads could they tell these towns had once been. No hoams stood: grass ran riot where once had been fertile fields and pasture land.

On the morning of the fourth day they took a wrong turning, departed from the high plateau and climbed eastward into a blue and smoky ridge of mountain. Here they found a great marvel. High in the hills they came upon the broken walls of an ancient shrine, stone heaped upon stone, creet holding the blocks together. Spiked with god-metal on one wall was a green-molded square. Daiv, scraping this out of curiosity, uncovered oddly shaped letters in the language. The letters read:

URAY CAVER
–dmss – – – –One dol–

Beyond the shrine was a huge hole, leading deep into the bowels of the earth. Daiv would have gone into it, seeking a fuller explanation of this wonder, but cold dampness seeped from the vent, and the stir of his footsteps at the entrance roused a myriad of loathsome bats from below.

Meg understood, then, and dragged Daiv from the accursed spot hastily.

"This is the abode of one of their Evil Gods," she explained. "The bats are the souls of his worshippers. We must not tarry here."

And they fled, retracing their steps to the point at which they had made the wrong turning. But as they ran, Meg, to be on the safe side, made a brief, apologetic prayer to the dark god, Uray Caver.

Oh, many were the wonders of that journey. Perhaps most wondrous of all—at least most unexpected of all—was their discovery of a clan living far to the north and east, near the end of their sixth day's travel.

It was Daiv who first noted signs of human habitation. They had crossed a narrow strip of land which, from a rusted place of god-metal Meg identified as part of the Maerlun territory, when Daiv suddenly halted his priestess with a silencing gesture.

"Golden One—a fire! A campfire!"

Meg looked, and a slow, shuddering apprehension ran through her veins. He was right in all save one thing. It could not be a *campfire*. Flame there was, and smoke. But in this forbidden territory smoke and flame could mean only—a charnel fire! For they were nearing His abode. Meg's nostrils sought the air delicately, half-afraid of the scent that might reach them.

Then, surprisingly, a happy sound was breaking from Daiv's throat, he was propelling her forward.

"They are men, Golden One! Men and women living in peace and harmony! The message of the Revelation must somehow have penetrated even these forbidden regions. Come!"

But a great disappointment awaited them. For when they met the strange clanspeople, they found themselves completely unable to converse with them. Only one thing could Meg and Daiv learn. That they called their village Lankstr. Their tribal name they never revealed, though Daiv believed they called themselves Nikvars. Meg was bitterly chagrined.

"If they could only speak the language, Daiv, they could tell us something about His city. They live so near. But perhaps—" She looked doubtful. "Do you think maybe they worship—Him?"

Daiv shook his head.

"No, Golden One. These Nikvars speak a coarse, animal tongue, but I think they are a kindly folk. They have never received the Revelation, yet they live together in the fashion of the Ancient Ones. They plow the fields and raise livestock. They have sheltered and fed us, offered us fresh clothing. They cannot be His disciples. This is another of the many, many mysteries of Tizathy. One that we must some day solve."

And the next morning they left the camp of their odd hosts. They bore with them friendly gifts of salt and bacca, and a damp-pouch filled with a strange food, krowt. And with the quaint Nikvar farewell ringing in their ears, "Veedzain! O Veedzain!", they continued their way east into a territory avoided and feared for thrice five centuries.

Through Lebnun and Alntun, skirting a huge pile of masonry that Meg's marker-of-places indicated as "Lizbeth," up the salt-swept marshes of the Joysy flatlands. The salt air stung their inland nostrils strangely, and the flatland air oppressed Meg's mountain-bred lungs, but she forgot her physical discomforts in the marvels to be seen.

And then, on the morning of the tenth day, the red lance of the dawning sun shattered itself on a weird, light-reflecting dreadfulness a scant ten miles away. Something so strange, so unnatural, so absolutely incredible that it took Meg's breath away, and she could only clutch her mate's arm, gasping and pointing.

Hoams! But such hoams! Great, towering buildings that groped sharded fingers into the very bosom of the sky; hoams of god-metal and creet—red with water-hurt, true—but still intact. Some of them —Meg closed her eyes, then opened them again and found it was still so—must have been every bit of two hundred, three hundred feet in height!

And as from afar, she heard Daiv's voice repeating the ancient description.

" 'It lies where the great creet highways of the Ancient Ones meet with a river and an island at a vast, salt sea.' This is it, Meg! We have found it, my Golden One!"

The sun lifted higher, spilling its blood upon the forbidden village. There was ominous portent in that color, and for the first time fear crept from its secret lurking place in Meg's heart, ran on panicky feet to her brain. She faltered, "It . . . it is His city, Daiv. See, even the hoams are bleached skeletons from which He has stripped the flesh. Think you, we should go on?"

Daiv made a happy sound deep in his throat. Still it was not altogether a happy sound; there was anger in it, and courage, and defiance.

He said, "We go on, Golden One! Mv sword thirsts for His defeat!"

And swiftly, eagerly, he pressed onward. Thus came Meg and Daiv to the City of Death.

III.

It was not so easy to effect entry into the city as Meg had expected. According to the old marker-of-places she had brought, the city was connected with the road by a tunl. Meg did not know what a tunl was, but clearly it had to be some sort of bridge or roadway.

There was nothing such here. The road ended abruptly at a great hole in the ground, similar to that which they had seen at the shrine of Uray Caver, except that this one was begemmed with glistening creet platters, and everywhere about it were queer oblongs of god-metal scored with cryptic runes. Prayers. "O Left Tur," said one; "O Parki," another.

Daiv glanced at Meg querulously, but she shook her head. These were—or appeared to be—in the language, but their meanings were lost in the mists of time. Lost, too, was the significance of that gigantic magic spell carven in solid stone at the mouth of the hole—

N. Y –MCMXXVII–N. J.

Discouraged but undaunted, Meg and Daiv turned away from the hole. Fortunately this was uncivilized territory; the forest ran right down to the water's edge. It eased the task of hewing small trees, building a raft with which they might cross the river.

This they did in the daytime, working with muffled axes lest He hear, investigate, and thwart their plans to invade His domain.

At night they crept back into the forest to build a camp. While Daiv went out and caught game, a fat young wild pig, Meg baked fresh biscuit, boiled maters she found growing wild in a nearby glade, and brewed cawfee from their rapidly dwindling store of that fragrant bean.

The next day they worked again on their craft, and the day after that. And at last the job was completed, Daiv looked upon it and pronounced it good. So at dusk they pushed it into the water. And when the icy moon invaded the sky, forcing the tender sun to flee before its barrage of silver hoar-shakings, they set out for the opposite shore.

Without incident, they attained their goal. Behind a thicket, Daiv moored their rough craft; each committed the location to memory. Then they climbed the stone-rubbled bank, and stood at last in the City of Death, on the very portals of His lair.

Nor was there any doubt that this *was* Death's city. So far as the eye could see or the ear hear, there was no token of life. Harsh, jumbled blocks of creet scraped tender their soles, and there was no blade of grass to soften that moon-frozen severity. About and around and before them were countless aged hoams; their doors were gasping mouths, their shutterless windows like vast, blank eyes. They moved blindly forward, but no hare sprang, startled, from an unseen warren before them; no night bird broke the tomblike silence with a melancholy cry.

Only the faint breath of the wind, stirring through the great avenues of emptiness, whispered them caution in a strange, sad sigh.

A great unease weighted Meg's mind, and in the gloom her hand caught that of Daiv as they pressed ever forward into the heart of Death's citadel. High corridors abutted them on either side; by instinct, rather than sense, they pursued a northward path.

A thousand questions filled Meg's heart, but in this hallowed place she could not stir her lips to motion. But as she walked, she wondered, marveled, at the Ancient Ones who, it was told, had built and lived in this great stone village.

Perhaps the creet roadbed on which they walked had once been smooth, as the legends told, though Meg doubted it. Surely not even the ages could have so torn creet into jagged boulders, deep-pitted and sore. And why should the Ancient Ones have deliberately pockmarked their roads with holes, and at the bottom of these holes placed broken tubes of red god-metal?

Why, too, should the Ancient Ones have built hoams that, probing the sky, still were roofless, and had in many places had their façades stripped away so that beneath the exterior showed little square cubicles, like rooms? Or why should the Ancient Ones have placed long laths of metal in the middle of their walk-avenues? Was it, Meg wondered, because they feared the demons? And had placed these bars to fend them off? All demons, Meg knew, feared god-metal, and would not cross it—

How long they trod those deserted thoroughfares Meg could not tell. Their path was generally northward, but it was a devious one because Daiv, great-eyed with wonder, was ever moved to explore some mysterious alley. Once, even, he braved destruction by creeping furtively into the entrance of a hoam consecrated to a god with a harsh-sounding foreign name, Mcmxl, but from there Meg begged him to withdraw, lest He somehow divine their presence.

Yet it was Daiv's insatiable curiosity that found a good omen for them. Well within the depths of the city, he stumbled across the first patch of life they had found. It was a tiny square of green, surmounted on all sides by bleak desolation. Yet from its breast of high, rank jungle grass soared a dozen mighty trees, defiantly quick in the city of the dead. Meg dropped to her knees at this spot, kissed the earth and made a prayer to the familiar gods of her clan.

And she told Daiv, "Remember well this spot. It is a refuge, a sanctuary. Perhaps, then, even He is not invulnerable, if life persists in His fortress. Should we ever be parted, let us meet here."

She marked the spot on her marker-of-places. From a plaque of the Ancient Ones, she learned its name. It was called Madinsqua.

Through the long night they trod the city streets, but when the first faint edge of gray lifted night's shadow in the east, Daiv strangled in his throat and made a tired mouth. Then Meg, suddenly aware of her own fatigue, remembered they must not meet their powerful foe in this state.

"We must rest, Daiv. We must be strong and alert when we come face to face with Him."

Daiv demanded, "But where, Golden One? You will not enter one of the hoams—"

"The hoams are taboo," said Meg piously, "but there are many temples. Behold, there lies a great one before us now. I am a Priestess and a Mother; all temples are refuge to me. We shall go there."

So they went into the mighty, colonnaded building. And it was, indeed, a temple. Through a long corridor they passed, down many steps, and at last into the towering vault of the sacristan.

Here, once, on the high niches about the walls, there had stood statues of the gods. Now most of these had been dislodged, their shards lay upon the cracked tiles beneath. Yet a few stood, and beneath centuries of dust and dirt the adventurers could still see the faded hues of ancient paint.

The floor of the sacristan was one, vast crater; a wall had crashed to earth and covered the confessionals of the priests. But above their heads was suspended an awesome object—a huge, round face around the rim of which appeared symbols familiar to Meg.

Daiv's eyes asked Meg for an answer.

"It is a holy sign," Meg told him. "Those are the numbers that make and take away. I had to learn them when I was a priestess. There is great magic in them." And while Daiv stood silent and respectful, she chanted them as it was ordained, "One—two—three—"

The size of this temple wakened greater awe in Meg than anything she had heretofore seen. She knew, now, that it must have been a great and holy race that lived here before the Great Disaster, for thousands could stand in the sacristan alone without crowding; in addition, there were a dozen smaller halls and prayer rooms, many of which had once been provided with seats. The western wall of the cathedral was lined with barred gates; on these depended metal placards designating the various sects who were permitted to worship here. One such, more legible than the rest, bore the names of communities vaguely familiar to Meg.

THE SPORTSMAN—12:01
Newark
Philadelphia
Washington
Cincinnati

This was, of course, the ancient language, but Meg thought she could detect some similarity to names of present-day clans. She and Daiv had, themselves, come through a town called Noork on their way here, and the elder legends told of a Fideffia, the City of Endless Sleep, and a Sinnaty, where once had ruled a great people known as the Reds.

But it would have been sacrilege to sleep in these hallowed halls. At Meg's advice they sought refuge in one of the smaller rooms flanking the corridor through which they had entered the temple. There were many of these, and one was admirably adapted to their purpose; it was the tiny prayer room of a forgotten god, Ited-Ciga. There was, in this room, a miraculously undamaged dais on which they could sleep.

They had eaten, but had not slaked their thirst in many hours. Daiv was overjoyed to find a black drink-fountain set into one of the walls, complete with a mouthpiece and a curiously shaped cup, but try as he might, he could not force the spring to flow.

It, too, was magic; at its base was a dial of god-metal marked with the numbers and letters of the language. Meg made an incantation over it, and when the water refused to come, Daiv, impatient, beat upon the mouth part. Rotten wood split from the wall, the entire fountain broke from its foundation and tumbled to the door, disclosing a nest of inexplicable wires and metal fragments.

As it fell, from somewhere within it tumbled many circles of stained metal, large and small. Meg, seeing one of these, prayed the gods to forgive Daiv's impatience.

"The fountain would not flow," she explained, "because you did not make the fitting sacrifice. See? These are the tributes of the Ancient Ones. White pieces, carven with the faces of the gods: the Red god, the buffalo god"—her voice deepened with awe—"even great Taamuz, himself! I remember his face from the Place of the Gods.

"Aie, Daiv, but they were a humble and god-fearing race, the Ancient Ones!"

And there, in the massive pantheon of Ylvania Stat, they slept—

Meg started from slumber suddenly, some inner awareness rousing her to a sense of indefinable malease. The sun was high in the heavens, the night-damp had passed. But as she sat up, her keen ears caught again the sound that had awakened her, and fear clutched her kidneys.

Daiv, too, had been awakened by the sound. Beside her he sat upright, motioning her to silence. His lips made voiceless whisper.

"Footsteps!" Meg answered, fearfully, "His footsteps?"

Daiv slipped to the doorway, disappeared. Minutes passed, and continued to pass until Meg, no longer able to await his return, followed him. He was crouched behind the doorway of the temple, staring down the avenue up which they had marched the preceding night. He felt her breath on his shoulder, pointed silently.

It was not Him. But it was someone almost as dangerous. A little band of His worshipers—all men. It was obvious that they were His followers, for in addition to the usual breechclout and sandals worn by all clansmen, these wore a gruesome decoration—

necklaces of human bone! Each of them — and there must have been six or seven — carried as a weapon His traditional arm, a razor-edged sword, curved in the shape of a scythe!

They had halted beside the entrance to a hooded cavern, similar to dozens such which Meg and Daiv had passed the night before, but had not dared investigate. Now two of them ducked suddenly into the cavernous depths. After a brief period of time, two sounds split the air simultaneously. The triumphant cry of masculine voices, and the high, shrill scream of a woman!

And from the cave mouth, their lips drawn back from their teeth in evil happy looks, emerged the raiders. Behind them they dragged the fighting, clawing figure of a woman.

Meg gasped, her thoughts churned into confusion by a dozen conflicting emotions. Amazement that in this City of Death should be found living humans. The ghouls, His followers, she could understand. But not the fact that this woman seemed as normal as her own Jinnians.

Second, a frightful anger that anyone, *anything*, should thus dare lay forceful hands upon a woman. Meg was of the emancipated younger generation; she had accepted the new principle that men were women's equals. But, still —

Her desire to do something labored with her fright. But before either could gain control of her muscles, action quickened the tableau. There came loud cries from below the ground, the sound of clanking harness, the surge of racing feet. And from the cavern's gorge charged the warriors of this stranger clan, full-panoplied, enraged, to the rescue of their comrade.

The invaders were ready for them. One had taken a position at each side of the entrance, another had leaped to its metallic roof. As the first warrior burst from the cave mouth, three scythe swords swung as one. Blood spurted. A headless torso lurched forward a shambling pace, pitched to earth, lay still. Again the scythes lifted.

Daiv could stand no more. A rage-choked roar broke from his lips, his swift motion upset Meg. And on feet that flew, sword drawn, clenched in his right fist, bellowing his wrath, he charged forward into the unequal fray!

IV.

Nor was Meg far behind him. She was a Priestess and a Mother, but in her veins, as in the veins of all Jinnians, flowed ever the quick-silver battle lust. Her cry was as loud as his, her charge as swift. Like twin lances of vengeance they bore down upon the invaders from the rear.

The minions of Death spun, startled. For an instant stark incredulity stunned them to quiescence; that immobility cost their leader his life. For even as his scattered wits reassembled, his lips framed commands to his followers, Daiv was upon him.

It was no hooked and awkward scythe Daiv wielded; it was a long sword, keen and true. Its gleaming blade flashed in the sunlight, struck at the leader's breast like the fang of a water viper—and when it met sunlight again, its gleam was crimson.

Now Daiv's sword parried an enemy hook; his foeman, weaponless and mad with fright, screamed aloud and tried to stave off the dripping edge of doom. His bare hands gripped Daiv's blade in blind, inchoate defense. The edge bit deep, grotesque-angled fingers fell to the ground like bloodworms crawling, bright ribbons of blood spurted from severed palms.

All this in the single beat of a pulse. Then Meg, too, was upon the invaders; her sword thirsted and drank beside that of her mate. And the battle was over almost before it began. Even as the vanguard of clanswomen, taking heart at this unexpected relief, came surging from the cave mouth, a half dozen bodies lay motionless on the creet, their blood enscarleting its drab. But one remained, and he, eyes wide, mouth slack in awestruck fear, turned and fled down the long avenue on feet lent wings by terror.

Then rose the woman whom the invaders had attempted to linber; in her eyes was a vast respect. She stared first at Daiv, uncertain, unbelieving. Then she turned to Meg and made low obeisance.

"Greeting and thanks, O Woman from Nowhere! Emma, Gard of the Be-Empty, pledges now her life and hand, which are truly yours."

She knelt to kiss Meg's hand. Then deepened her surprise, for she gasped:

"But . . . but you are a Mother! You wear the Mother's ring!"

Meg said quietly, "Yes, my daughter. I am Meg, the Mother of the Jinnia Clan, newly come to the City of Death."

"Jinnia Clan!" It was the foremost of the rescuers who spoke now; by her trappings Meg knew her to be a lootent of her tribe. "What is this Jinnia Clan, O Mother? Whence come you, and how—"

Meg said, "Peace, woman! It is not fitting that a clanswoman should make queries of a Mother. But lead me to your Mother. With her I would speak."

The lootent flushed. Apologetically, "Forgive me, Mother. Swiftly shall I lead you to our Mother, Alis. But what—" She glanced curiously at Daiv who, the battle over, was now methodically wiping his stained blade on the hem of his clout. "But what shall I do with this man-thing? It is surely not a breeding-male; it fights and acts like a Wild One."

Meg smiled.

"He is not a man-thing, my child. He is a man—a true man. Take me to your Mother, and to her I will explain this mystery."

Thus it was that, shortly after, Meg and Daiv spoke with Alis in her private chamber deep in the bowels of the earth beneath the City of Death. There was great wonder in the Mother's eyes and voice, but there was respect, too, and understanding in the ear she lent Meg's words.

Meg told her the tale of the Revelation. Of how she, when yet Meg the Priestess, had made pilgrimage, as was the custom of her clan, to the far-off Place of the Gods.

"Through blue-sworded Tucky and Zurrie I traveled, O Alis; many days I walked through the flat fields of Braska territory. In this journey was I accompanied by Daiv, then a stranger, now my mate, who had rescued me from a Wild One. And at last I reached the desolate grottoes of distant 'Kota, and there, with my own eyes, looked upon the carven stone faces of the gods of the Ancient Ones. Grim Jarg, the sad-eyed Ibrim, ringleted Taamuz, and farseeing Tedhi, He who laughs—"

Alis made a holy sign.

"You speak a mighty wonder, O Meg. These are gods of our clan, too, though none made your pilgrimage. But we worship still another god, whose temple lies not far away. The mighty god, Granstoom. But—this secret you learned?"

"Hearken well, Alis, and believe," said Meg, "for I tell you truth. The gods of the Ancient Ones—were *men!*"

"Men!" Alis half rose from her seat. Her hands trembled. "But surely, Meg, you are mistaken—"

"No. The mistake occurred centuries ago, Mother of another clan. Daiv, who comes from the sacred Land of the Escape, has taught me the story.

"Long, long ago, all Tizathy was ruled by the great Ancient

Ones. Mighty were they, and skilled in forgotten magics. They could run on the ground with the speed of the woodland doe; great, wheeled horses they built for this purpose. They could fly in the air on birds made of-god-metal. Their hoams probed the clouds, they never labored except on the play-field; their life was one of gay amusement, spent in chanting into boxes that carried their voices everywhere and looking at pictures-that-ran.

"But in another world across the salt water from Tizathy were still other men and women. Amongst them were evil ones, restless, impatient, fretful, greedy. These, in an attempt to rule the world, created a great war. We cannot conceive the war of the Ancient Ones. They brought all their magics into play.

"The men met on gigantic battlefields, killed each other with smoke and flame and acid and smell-winds. And at hoam, the women—in secret magic-chambers called labteries—made for them sticks-that-spit-fire and great eggs that hatched death."

"It is hard to believe, O Meg," breathed Alis, "but I do believe. I have read certain cryptic records of the Ancient Ones—but go on."

"Came at last the day," continued Meg, "when Tizathy itself entered this war. But when their mates and children had gone to Him by the scores of scores of scores, the women rebelled. They banded together, exiled all men forevermore, set up the matriarchal form of government, keeping only a few weak and infant males as breeders.

"When they could no longer get the fire-eggs or the spit-sticks, the men came back to Tizathy. Then ensued years of another great war between the sexes—but in the end, the women were triumphant.

"The rest you know. The men, disorganized, became Wild Ones, roving the jungles in search of food, managing to recreate themselves with what few clanswomen they linberred from time to time. Our civilization persisted, but many of the old legends and most of the old learning was gone. We finally came to believe that *never* had the men ruled; that it was right and proper for women to rule; that the very gods were women.

"But this," said Meg stanchly, "is not so. For I have brought back from the Place of the Gods the Revelation. Now I spread the word. It is the duty of all clans to bring the Wild Ones out of the forests, make them their mates, so our people may one day reclaim our deserved heritage."

There was a long silence.

Then asked Alis, "I must think deeply on this, O Meg. But you spoke of the Land of the Escape. What is that?"

"It is the hot lands to the south. Daiv comes from there. It is a sacred place, for from there—from the heart of Zoni—long ago a Wise One named Renn foresaw the end of the civilization of the Ancient Ones.

"In the bowels of a monstrous bird, he and a chosen few escaped Earth itself, flying to the evening star. They have never been heard of since. But some day they will come back. We must prepare for their coming; such is the law."

Alis nodded somberly.

"I hear and understand, O Mother to whom the truth has been revealed. But . . . but I fear that never can we make peace with the Wild Ones of Loalnyawk. You have seen them, fought them. You know they are vicious and untamed."

Meg had been so engrossed in spreading the news of the Revelation, she had almost forgotten her true mission. Now it flooded back upon her like an ominous pall. And she nodded.

"Loalnyawk? Is that what you call the City of Him? Perhaps you are right, Mother Alis. It would be impossible to mate with the children who worship Death as a master."

"Death?" Alis' bead lifted sharply. "Death, Meg? I do not understand. They do not worship Death, but Death's mistress. They worship the grim and savage warrior goddess, the fearful goddess, Salibbidy."

"Her," said Meg dubiously, "I never heard of. But you speak words unhappy to my ear, O Alis. A long way have Daiv and I come to do battle with Him who nips the fairest buds of our clan. Now you tell me this is not His city—"

"Aie, but you must be mistaken! Of a certainty it is His city. His tumbled desolation reigns everywhere."

Alis made a thought-mouth.

"You force me to wonder, Meg. Perhaps He is here. Of a truth, He takes many of us to whom He has no right. A moon ago He claimed the Priestess Kait who was young, happy, in wondrous good health.

"A sweet and holy girl, inspired by the gods. Only the day before had she been in commune with them; her tender young body atremble with ecstasy, her eyes rapt, her lips wet with the froth of their knowledge. Oft did she experience these sacred spells, and I had planned a great future for her. But—" Alis sighed and shook her head. "He came and took her even as she communed with the gods. It was a foul deed and brutal."

Daiv said grimly, "And by that we know that this *is* His city, indeed. For where else would He be so powerful and so daring?"

"Yes," said Alis, "the more I think on it, the more I believe you are right. Above ground must be His domains. We have not guessed the truth, because for countless ages we have dwelt in the tiled corridors of Be-Empty."

"Tell us more," demanded Daiv, He-who-would-learn, "about the halls of Be-Empty. Why are they called that?"

"I know not, Daiv. It is the ancient name, yet the corridors are *not* empty. They are a vast network of underground passages, built by the Ancient Ones for mystic rites we no longer know. Great wonders are here, as I will later show you.

"These corridors are tiled with shining creet, and upon their roadbeds lie parallels of god-metal, red and worn. Aie, and there is a greater wonder still! From place to place I can show you ancient hoams, with doors and many windows and seats. These hoams were tied together with rods of god-metal, and whensoever the Ancient Ones would move, they had but to push their hoams along the parallels to a new location!

"Once we were not all one clan, but many. There were the Women of the In-Deeps, and there were the Aiyartees. But we were the strongest and we welded all the livers-underground into one strong clan.

"We have many villages, wide creet plateaus built on the sunken roadways of the Ancient Ones. Each village has its entrance to the city above, forbidden Loalnyawk, but we use these only when urgency presses. For there are openings aplenty to the sun, there are streams of fresh water. Safe from the Wild Ones above, we raise our vegetables and a few meat-animals.

"Yet," continued Alis proudly, "there is no spot in all Loalnyawk to which we have not ready access should it be necessary to get there. Above ground there are many shrines like that of great Granstoom and the fallen tower of Arciay. There is also the Citadel of Clumby to the north, and not far from where we now sit could I show you the Temple of Shoobut, where each year the Ancient Ones sacrificed a thousand virgins to their gods. There is the forbidden altar of Slukes—"

The Mother's mouth stayed in midsentence. Her eyes widened.

"Slukes!" she repeated awfully.

"Well?" Meg and Daiv leaned forward, intent.

"That must be it! In the ancient legends it tells that there was where He visited most often. That must be His present lair and hiding place!"

"Then there," proclaimed Daiv, "we must go!"

V.

Meg stumbled on a sharp stone, lurched against Daiv and steadied herself on his reassuring presence. Her eyes had become somewhat accustomed to the endless gloom, now, though they ached and burned with the concentration of peering into murky blackness, then having the blackness lighted from time to time, unexpectedly, by a shaft of golden sunlight flooding into the corridors of Be-Empty from the city above.

Her feet, though, thought Meg disconsolately, would never accustom themselves to this jagged, uneven roadbed. She had been told to walk between the parallels of god-metal, for that was the best, driest, safest walking. Maybe it was. But it was treacherous. For there were creet crossties on which her doeskin-clad feet bruised themselves, and ever and again there were rocks and boulders lying unsuspectedly in the road.

How far they had come, Meg had no way of guessing. It must have been many miles. They had passed, easily, twoscore tiny, raised villages of the Be-Empty Clan. At each of these they had tarried a moment while the warrior lootent, under whose guidance Alis had dispatched a small foray party at Meg's disposal, made known herself and her mission.

Meg panted, hating the heavy, stuffy air her lungs labored to suck in, fuming at the slowness of their march, eager only to reach their destination. It did not improve her temper to slip on a round rock, submerge one foot to the ankle in a stream of sluggish water. Of the lootent she demanded, "How much farther, my daughter?"

"We are nearly there, O Mother."

Daiv grunted. It was a think-grunt. Meg tried to see him, but in the darkness his face was a white blur.

"Yes, Daiv?"

"There's more to this than meets the eye, Golden One. These passageways are not the purposeless corridors Alis thought. I was wondering—"

"Yes?"

"Well—it sounds ridiculous. But do you remember those hoams on wheels? The ones with the windows? Suppose the Ancient Ones had the magic power to make them run like horses along these parallels?"

Meg shrugged.

"But why should they, Daiv? When it would have been so much

simpler to make them run on top of the earth? These grottoes were built for some sacred purpose, my mate."

"I suppose you're right," acknowledged Daiv. But he didn't sound convinced. Sometimes Meg grew a little impatient with Daiv. He was, like all men, such a hard creature to convince. He couldn't reason things out in the cold, clear logical fashion of a woman; he kept insisting that his "masculine intuition" told him otherwise.

Much time had passed. They had broken fast at the hoam of the Mother, and had eaten a midday meal here in the depths of Be-Empty. The last opening under which they had passed revealed that the sun was being swallowed by the westward clouds; for twelve hours it would pass through the belly of the sky, then miraculously, tomorrow, a new sun would be reborn in the east.

So it was almost night when the lootent halted at a tiny, deserted creet platform, turned and touched her forehead to Meg.

"This is it, O Mother."

"This?" Meg glanced about. There was nothing unusual about this location.

"Above this spot lies the forbidden altar of Slukes. I . . . I fear—" The lootent's eyes were troubled. "I fear I dare take you no farther, O Mother. You and your man are inviolate; I and my warriors are but humble women. That which lies above would be destruction for us to gaze upon."

Meg nodded complacently.

"So be it, my daughter. We shall leave you now, go to dare Him in His den."

The lootent said, "We shall wait, Mother—"

"Wait not, my child. Return to your village."

"Very well, Mother. Your blessing ere we leave?"

Meg gave it, touching her fingers to the lips and the forehead of the kneeling lootent, chanting the hallowed phrases of the Ancient Ones' blessing. " 'My country, Tizathy; sweet land of liberty—' " Then there were stifled footsteps in the gloom and Meg and Daiv were alone.

Only briefly did Meg consider the possibility of entering His temple at this time—and then she abandoned the project. It would be suicidal. Everyone knew He was strongest at night. His powers waned with the waxing sun. So she and Daiv built a tiny fire in the quarters of a long-vanished warrior named Private Keepout, and there huddled together through the long, dank, fearsome night.

* * *

They awakened with the sum, broke their fast with unleavened biscuit given them by Alis. Daiv, who was expert at such matters, then examined with painstaking care their swords and hurling-leathers, He approved these. And as if feeling within his own breast an echo of the dread that fluttered in Meg's, he pressed his lips hard against hers in a touching-of-mouths. Then, hand in hand, they climbed a long flight of steps, into the sunlight, forward to the threshold of his stronghold.

It was a majestic building.

How many footsteps long and wide it was, Meg could not even conceive. It reached half as far as the eye would reach in one direction; in the other, it branched into many smaller buildings. And it was pine-high. An awe-inspiring sight.

Daiv, standing beside her, stared dubiously at the main portal. He said, "This may not be the place, Meg. Alis said the name of the temple was Slukes, didn't she? This is called—" He glanced again at the weather-worn carving atop the doorway. "This is called Stlukes."

Again, as oft before, Meg felt swift pride at her mate's intelligence. Daiv was a living proof that men were the equals—or almost, anyway—of women. It had taken her many, many summers to learn the art of reading the speech-without-words; he had assimilated the knowledge from her in a tenth the time.

"It is the right place, Daiv," she whispered. "The Ancient Ones were often careless in putting down the language. But can you not *feel* that this is His abode?"

For she could. Those grim, gray walls breathed an atmosphere of death and decay. The bleached walls were like the picked bones of a skeleton lying in some forgotten field. And the great, gaping vents of windows, the sagging lintels, the way one portion of roof had fallen in—there were marks of His dominance. Meg did not even need the omen of the red-throated carrion buzzard wheeling lazily ever and ever about the horrid altar of Slukes.

"Come," she said, "let us enter."

Daiv held back. There were anxious lines about his eyes. "He does not speak, Meg?"

"No one has ever heard His voice, Daiv. Why?"

"I thought I heard voices. But I must have made a mistake. Well"—he shrugged—"it does not matter."

Thus they entered the secret hiding place of Death.

* * *

All the great courts lay silent.

What Meg had expected to see, she did not rightly know. Perhaps a charnel house of human bodies, dismembered and gory, raw with frightful cicatrices, oozing filth from sick and rotting sores. Or perhaps that even more dreadful thing, chambers in which were imprisoned the mournful souls of the dead. Against flesh and blood, no matter how frightful, Meg knew her courage would hold. But she did not know whether her nerves would stand before the dim restlessness of the gray unalive.

She found neither of these in the temple of Slukes. She found only floors and walls and ceilings which had once been shining white, but were now gray with ages of floating dust. She found her footsteps muffled beneath her upon a mat of substance, now crumbling, but still resilient to the soles. She found silence, silence, silence that beat upon her eardrums until it was a tangible, terrifying sound.

And finding that, she took comfort in Daiv's keen, questing, ever-forward search for Him.

Down a long hallway they strode on catlike feet; a chamber they passed in which heaped dust outlined the seats and stools of Ancient Ones. Past a god-metal counter they walked, and saw within its confines not one but a half-dozen water fountains like that Daiv had wrenched from the wall of Ited-Ciga's shrine.

Above their heads, from time to time, they glimpsed strange, magic pendants of green and red god-metal; beneath one of these was a greater marvel still—a pear-shaped ball with wire seeds coiled within. Transparent was the skin of this fruit, and slippery to the touch. Daiv tried to split it, hungering for a taste of its newness, but it exploded in his hands with a fearful *pop!*—and there was nothing but its stem and seeds!

The fruit itself had vanished, but the skin, as if angered, had bit Daiv's palm until the blood flowed.

Meg blessed the wound, and begged forgiveness in a swift prayer to the gods of the harvest at having destroyed the magic pear.

And they went on.

Either side of the corridor through which they moved was lined with doorways. Into one of these they looked, believing He might have hid there, but the rooms were vacant except for strange, four-legged god-metal objects humped in the middle, on which reposed parasitic coils and twists of metal twined inextricably together. Dust lay over all, and in one room more carefully shuttered, barred and sealed than the others, they saw tatters of something like homespun covering the coils. But when Meg attempted to touch this, the wind from her motion swept the gossamer cloth into nothingness.

Aie, but it was a mighty and mysterious place, this altar of Slukes, where dwelt Him who steals away the breath! There were rooms in which reposed great urns and pans of god-metal; these rooms held, also, huge metal boxes with handles on the front, and their platters were crusted with flaked and ancient grease. Meg shuddered. "Here," she whispered to Daiv, "He burnt the flesh of them He took." In the same room was a massive white box with a door. Daiv opened this, and they saw within neat metal racks. "And here," whispered Meg, "must He have stored the dwindled souls until again He hungered. But now He does not use this closet. I wonder why?"

And they went on.

Until at last, having climbed many flights of steps, Meg and Daiv came at last to the chamber they had been seeking. It lay on the story nearest the roof. Oh, but He was a methodical destroyer. The compartments in which he imprisoned His victims were all carefully labeled in the language. Contagious Ward, Infants' Ward, Maternity Ward—all these Meg saw and read, and shuddered to recognize. And this, his holy of holies, was symbolized as His workroom by the sign, Operating Room.

Once it had been a high, lofted chamber; now it wore the roof of infinity, for some antique cataclysm had opened it to the skies. Crumbled plaster and shards of brick heaped the floor.

But in its center, beneath a gigantic weapon defying description or understanding, was His bed. It could be nothing else, for even now, upon it, lay the lately-slain body of a woman. Her face was a mask of frozen agony; His touch had drawn taut her throat muscles and arched her back in the final paroxysm. Her lifeless fingers gripped the sides of the bed in unrelaxing fervor.

And the room bore, amidst its clutter and confusion, unmistakable signs of recent habitation! The trappings of the newly slaughtered woman had been tossed carelessly into a corner, along with countless others. Feet, many feet, had beaten firm the rubble on the floor; in one corner, not too long since, had been a fire. And the blood that had gushed from the dead woman when her heart had been roughly hewn from her bosom still clotted the floor!

Meg cried, a little cry of terror and dismay.

"He is here, Daiv!"

Then all things happened at once. Her cry wakened ominous echoes in chambers adjacent to this. Daiv's arm was about her, pulling her away. There came the patter of footsteps, voices lifted, and the door at the farther end of the room jerked open.

And Daiv cried, "Not only He, but His ghouls! Behind me, Golden One!"

Then the deluge. A horde of Wild Ones of the same tribe as those whom they had fought two days before, charged into the room.

VI.

There was no taint of cowardice in the heart of Meg the Mother. Had she any fault, it was that of excess bravery. Oft before had she proven this, to her own peril. This time, Daiv's speed left her no opportunity to become a courageous sacrifice to His minions.

His quick eye measured the number of their adversaries, his battle-trained judgment worked instinctively. For an instant he hesitated, just long enough to strike down with flailing long sword the foremost of their attackers. Then he swept Meg backward with his mighty right arm, thrust her irresistibly toward a doorway at the other end of the room.

"Flee, Golden One!"

Meg had no choice. For Daiv was on her heels; his body a bulwark of defense against hers and a battering-ram of force. They reached the door, crashed it shut in the face of the charging ghouls. Daiv braced himself against it staunchly, his eyes sweeping the small chamber in which they found themselves.

"That!" he commanded. "And that other, Golden One. And that!"

His nods designated objects of furniture within the room; heavy, solid braces of god-metal. Meg bent to the task, and before Daiv's strength could fail under the now clamorous pounding on the doorway, the portal was braced and secured with the massive frames that once had been chairs, a desk, a cabinet.

Now there was time for breathing and inspection of their refuge. And Meg's soul sickened, seeing the trap into which they had let themselves.

"But, Daiv—there is no way out! There is but one door to the room. The one through which we entered!"

Daiv said, "There is a window—" and strode to it. She saw the swift, dazed shock that creased his brows, moved to his side and peered from the window.

It was an eagle's aerie in which they stood! Down, down, down, far feet below, was the sun-lit courtyard of this building. But the wall was sheer and smooth as the jowls of lean youth; no crawling insect could have dared that descent.

Daiv looked at her somberly, and his arm crept about her.

"Since we cannot flee, we must outwait them, Golden One. If we cannot get out, they, at least, cannot get in."

He did not mention the thought uppermost in his mind and in hers. That their food pouches lay far below them, in the murky grotto of Be-Empty; that they had no water. And that the shortest of sieges would render them impotent before their adversaries.

For he was Daiv, known as He-who-would-learn. And even in this moment when things looked darkest, he was roused to curiosity by the chamber in which they were immured.

It was a small and cluttered room. More dusty than most, and that was odd, because it was not open to the dust-laden air.

But Daiv, questing, discovered the reason for this. The floor was gray not with rock dust, but with the fragments of things which—which—

"This is a great mystery, Meg. What are, or were, these things?"

Meg, too, had been staring about her. A faint suspicion was growing in her mind. She remembered a word she had heard but once in her life, and that when she was but a young girl, neophyte priestess under the former Mother.

"Shelves," she whispered. "Many long shelves, all of water-hurt god-metal. Desks. And crumbled fragments of parchment.

"Daiv, long ago the Ancient Ones had houses, rooms, in which they kept, pressed flat between cloth and boards, parchment marked with the speech-without-words. These they called—" She cudgeled her brain for the elusive word. "These they called 'lyberries.' The flat scrolls were known as 'books.' This room must have been the lyberry of Slukes."

"And in these books," said Daiv in hallowed tones, "they kept their records?"

"Aie, more than that. In them they kept all their secret knowledge. The story of their spells and magic, and of their foretelling-of-dreams."

Daiv groaned in pain as an unhappy-imp prodded his heart.

"We stand at the heart of their mysteries, but He who withers all has ripped their parchment into motes! Meg, it is a sad and bitter thing."

He saw, now, that she spoke truth. For he pawed through the

piles of rotted debris; in one spot he found a frayed leather oblong from which, as he lifted it, granules of charred black sifted. Once, again, he found a single bit of parchment marked with the language, but it fell into ten million bits at the touch of his fingers.

"There have been fire and flame in this room," Meg said. "Water-hurt, and the winds of the ages. That is why no books remain. It must have happened in the wars, when the fire-eggs fell upon the building. Daiv! What are you doing?"

For Daiv, still pawing the ruins, had uncovered a large, metal cabinet deep-set in the wall. This alone seemed to have escaped, unhurt, whatever holocaust had destroyed all else. With a swift grunt of satisfaction, he was tearing at the handle of this cabinet.

"Don't open it, Daiv! It is a forbidden thing! It may be a trick of the Ancient Ones. Of Him—"

But Meg's warning was futile. For Daiv's fumbling fingers had solved the secret of the antique lock; creaking in protest, the door swung open to reveal, in an unlighted chamber from which a faint, musty breath of wind stirred—*books!*

Books! Books as Meg had described them. Books as Meg had learned of them from the lips of the elder Mother. Books, still encased in jackets of cloth and leather, unhurt through thrice five centuries of time, preserved, by a whim of the gods, in a locked and airless cabinet!

And again it became Meg's lot to save Daiv's life and soul, for he, manlike, impatient, paused not to placate the gods, but groped instantly for the nearest of the forbidden volumes.

Fervent were the prayers Meg made then, and swiftly, that the gods destroy him not for his eagerness. And she was rewarded graciously, for Daiv did not fall, mortally stricken, as he knelt there muttering over his find.

"Behold, Meg—the secrets of the Ancient Ones! Ah, Golden One, hurry—read to me! This speech-without-words is too mighty for my powers; only the knowledge of a Mother can tell its meaning. But, lo! here are drawings! Look, Golden One! Here is a man like me! But, behold, this is a mystery! The flesh has been stripped from his body, disclosing hordes of tiny red worms covering his carcass—but he still stands erect!

"And, see, Meg—here is a woman with white sheets of bandage about her head. What means this? And behold this man's head! It lays open from front to back, but Meg, there is no village of tiny pain-imps, and like-imps and hate-imps dwelling within! Only red worms and blue, and inside his nostrils a sponge—"

Meg took the book with trembling hands. It was as Daiv said. Here were drawings without number of men and women who, their bodies dismembered horribly, still smiled and stood erect. Little arrows pierced them, and at the end of the arrows were feathers of the language, saying magic words. *Serratus magnus— Poupart's ligament—transplyoric plane.*

And the name of the book was "Fundamental Anatomy."

In their moment of wild excitement, both Meg and Daiv had quite forgotten the danger of their situation. Now they were rudely reawakened to a memory of that danger. For the sounds outside the door of the lyberry, which had never quite ceased, now sharpened in tone. There came the sound of a voice raised in command, cries of labor redoubled, and with an echoing crash, something struck the door of their refuge!

The door trembled; the braces gave a fraction of an inch. And again the crash, the creak, the strain.

"A ram! Daiv, they are forcing the door!"

Daiv the dreamer became, swiftly, Daiv the man of action. With a single bound he was on his feet, his sword in hand. His brows were anxious.

"Take you the right side of the door, Golden One; I will guard the other. When these ghouls burst in upon us, we shall split them like pea pods—"

But a great idea had been born to Meg.

Her face glowing with a sudden happy look, she spun to face her mate.

"No, Daiv. Open the door!"

"What? Golden One, has fear softened your brain?"

"Not my brain nor my heart, beloved! But do as I say! Look you! I am a Mother and a Priestess, is it not so?"

"Yes. but—"

"And I have just discovered a mighty secret. The secret of the knowledge of the Ancient Ones."

"Still—" said Daiv.

"Would not even the underlings of him," cried Meg, "pay greatly for this knowledge? Open the door for them, my mate! We will parley with them or with Death, Himself, for an exchange. Our lives in payment for the sharing of this secret!" Daiv might have withstood her logic, but he could not refuse the eager demand of her eyes. Like a man bedazed, he moved to the door, started, scraping the bulwark away even as the horde outside continued their assault.

When he had almost completed, the door shook before imminent collapse—

"Stand you out of sight, Daiv. I would meet them face to face."

And she took her post squarely before the door. In the hollow of her left arm she cradled the Book of Secrets. On her face was the smile of triumph, and a look of exalted glory. The door trembled; this time it split away from its hinges. Once more, now! Came the final crash, and—

"*Hold!*" cried Meg, the Priestess.

Through the oblong of the door, faces frightful with fury and blood lust, tumbled the ghouls of Death. Their hook-shaped scythes swung ready in their hands; a scream of triumph hovered on their lips. Hovered there—then trembled—then died!

And of a sudden, a miracle occurred. For the flame died from their eyes, their sword-arms fell, and as one man the attackers tumbled to their knees, groverling before Meg. A low muttering arose, was carried from man to man as the breath of the night wind is passed through the forest by the sad and whispering pines.

It was a murmur, then a cry, of fear and adoration.

"Mercy, O Goddess! Slay not your children, O Everlasting. O Goddess—great Goddess Salibbidy!"

VII.

Not in her most hopeful moment had Meg expected so sudden and complete a victory as this.

For her plan she had entertained great hopes, true, but she had wagered her life and Daiv's on the balance of an exchange. But here, suddenly, inexplicably, was utter capitulation. Surrender so complete that the leader of His warriors dared not even lift his eyes to meet hers as he slobbered his worship at her feet.

She glanced swiftly at Daiv, but for once Daiv had no knowledge in his eyes; they were as blank and questioning as her own.

Still, Meg was a Priestess and a Mother. She was a woman, too, and an opportunist. And instinct governed her actions.

She stepped to the leader's side, touched his brow with cool fingers.

"Rise, O Man! Your Goddess gives you grace."

The ghoul rose, shaken and fearful. His voice was the winnowed chaff of hope.

"Be merciful unto us, O Goddess. We did not know—we did not dream—we dared not hope for a Visitation."

Meg chose her words carefully, delivered them as a Mother

intones a sacred chant, in a tone calculated to inspire dreadful awe in the hearts of her listeners.

"You have sinned mightily, O Man! You have laid seige to the holy refuge of the Goddess. You have linberred and slain women of the Be-Empty Clan, a grevious deed. You have forgotten the Faith, and have bowed down in worship before Him, the arch-enemy, Death—"

"No, O Goddess!" The contradiction was humble but sincere. "These other sins we confess, but not this last! Never have we worshiped Him! Never!"

"You dwell in His citadel."

"His citadel!" There was horror in the Wild One's voice. "We did not know it was His, O sweet Salibbidy! We live many places as we journey through Loalnyawk. Today we rested here because we had a sacrifice to make unto thee; a woman unfit for mating whom we linberred last night." His eyes pleaded with Meg's. "Was the sacrifice unpleasing to thee, gracious Salibbidy?"

"It was foul in my nostrils," said Meg sternly. "Her blood is a wound upon my heart. This is the law from this time henceforward! There shall be no more linberring or slaying of women. Instead, there shall be a new order. You shall go to the women and make peace. They will receive you with singing and soft hands, for unto them I have given the law.

"Together, you shall form a new city. They shall come out of the caverns of Be-Empty. You and they shall reclaim the hoams of the Ancient Ones. When again I visit the village of Loalnyawk. I shall expect to see men and women living together in peace and harmony as it was in the days of old.

"Do you understand the law?"

"Yes, mighty Goddess!" The cry rose from each man.

"You will obey it?"

"We will obey it, sweet Salibbidy."

"Then go in peace, and sin no more."

The vanquished worshipers, intoning prayers of thanksgiving, crawled backward from the chamber. When they last had disappeared, and they were again alone, Meg turned to her mate. His strong arms soothed the belated trembling of her body.

"Fear not, Golden One," he whispered. "Today have you performed a miracle. In bloodless victory you have borne the Revelation to the last outpost. To the accursed and forbidden city of the Ancient Ones. To the stronghold of Him."

"But they said they did not worship Him, Daiv! And they dared not lie, believing me their Goddess. If He does not rule them, if He reigns not here, then where is He, Daiv? And why did they accept me as their Goddess? Why?"

Daiv shook his head. This was unimportant now, he thought. It was sufficient that the enemy had been overcome. There were great things to do. He returned to his cabinet, and drew from it its precious store of books—

Afterward, in the hoam of Alis, Meg learned part of the answer to her questions. When she had told Alis what had happened, and received the Mother's pledge to accept the Wild Ones' envoys in peace and good will, she told again of their sudden surrender.

"I sought but to parley with them, Mother Alis. At the door I stood, and thus I stood, waiting calmly—"

She struck the pose. Book cradled in her arm, the other arm lifted high above her head, chin lifted proudly.

And then Alis nodded. But in her eyes, too, came unexpectedly a worship-look, and she whispered brokenly, "Now I understand, O Goddess who chooses to call herself Meg, the Mother. From the beginning I felt your sanctity. I should have known then—"

She rose, led Meg to the surface above. Be-Empty, now no longer forbidden territory to the women. Once there had been many and great buildings here, but ancient strife had stricken them as the whirlwind hews a path through solid woodland.

Far to the southward, where the green ocean waters met the creet shores of Loalnyawk there was a figure, dimly visible. But not so dimly visible that Meg and Daiv could not recognize it.

"There is thy image; sweet Salibbidy," whispered the Mother, Alis. "Still it stands, as it did in the days of the Ancient Ones. Forever will it stand, and you remain the Goddess of broad Tizathy."

Meg cried petulantly, "Alis, do not call me by this name, Salibbidy! I am Meg, Mother of the Jinnia Clan. Like yourself, a woman—"

A smile of mysterious understanding touched Alis' lips.

"As you will—Mother Meg," she said.

But it was strange that her head should still be bowed—

Thus it was, that with the breaking of the new dawn over the creet walls of Loalnyawk, Meg and Daiv said farewell to these friends and converts, and turned their faces south and west to the remembered green hills of Jinnia.

Nor was this a sad parting. An envoy of the men had come this morning; long had he and the Mother parleyed, and an understanding had been reached. As ever, there were women who demurred, and women who disapproved—but Meg had seen a young maiden looking with gentle, speculative eyes upon the envoy. And a grim warrior had spoken with unusually gentle warmth to one of the envoy's guards—a bristle-jowled man of fighting mold.

These things would take care of themselves, thought Meg. The new order would come about, inevitably, because the men and women, both, would wish it so—

Then the last farewell had been spoken, the final blessing given. And once more Meg and Daiv were striding the long highway to Jinnia.

Daiv was strangely silent. And strangely inattentive, too, for he was attempting a difficult task. Trying to march without watching the road before him. His eyes were in one of the many books he had brought with him; the others he wore like a huge hump on his back. He stumbled for the hundredth time, and while Meg helped him reset the pack on his shoulders she said, ruefully:

"There is but one thing I regret, Daiv! Much we accomplished, but not that one thing we came to do. We found not Him, nor destroyed Him, as we willed. And our problem is still great, for ever and again will He pluck the ripest from our harvest of living."

But Daiv shook his head.

"Not so, Golden One."

"No?"

"No, my Priestess. It has come to me that we have more than fulfilled our mission. For you see—"

Daiv looked at the sky and the trees and the clouds that floated above. He took a deep breath, and the air was sweet. Life flowed strongly and true in his veins, and the knowledge he was eking, laboriously, from the magical books was potent liquid in his brain.

"You see, Golden One, we were wrong. He does not, nor ever did, live in Loalnyawk. He has no hoam, for He is everywhere, waiting to claim those who violate His barriers."

Meg cried bitterly, "Then, Daiv, we are forever at His mercy! If He cannot be found and destroyed—"

"He cannot be slain, Meg—and that is well. Else the crippled, the sick, the mad, would live forever in endless torment. But He can be fought—and in these books it tells the ways in which to do battle with Him.

"They are not the ways of magic, Golden One. Or of any magic you know. These are new ways we must study. These magics are called by strange names—serum, and vaccination, and physic. But the way of each is told in these books. One day we shall understand all the mysteries, and Death's hand will be stayed.

"Boiled water He fears, and fresh air, and cleanliness. We shall not fight Him with swords and stones, but with sunshine and fresh water and the soap of boiled fats. For so it was in the old days—"

And a great vision was in Daiv's eyes; a vision Meg saw there, and, seeing, read with wonder. Of a day to come when men and women, hand in hand, should some day climb again to assail the very heights lost by the madness of the Ancient Ones.

His shoulder touched hers, and the day was warm and the road long. Meg was afire with impatience to get back to Jinnia, to bring this new knowledge to her clan. But there was other fire within her, too, and the message could wait a little while if she and Daiv tarried in the cool of a leafy tree.

Her hands met his and clung, and she turned her lips to his in the touching-of-mouths. She was Meg, and he was Daiv, and they were man and woman. And the grass was soft and cool.

So, too, it was in the old days—

The Masked Marvel

"ONE THING LEADS TO ANOTHER," SAID SQUAREDEAL Sam McGhee. "We started out by talkin' about horses; then somethin' was said about stud, an' the first thing you know me an' this feller was havin' a little game o' poker."

I recognized the gamit to a touch. But Sam's preambles are always disastrously alluring. I nodded toward the box of cigars; Sam selected a handful, lighted one, and sprawled back in his chair, emanating smoke and satisfaction.

"But this unfortunate 'feller'," I guessed, "apparently didn't know you used to deal three-card monte with a carny?"

"I don't never discuss backgrounds with strangers," said Sam with simple dignity. "It might embarrass them—not to mention *vicey-versy*. Besides, this feller could afford to lose. His name was Pat Pending. He was a great inventor—"

"Already the tale sounds incredible," I said. "But go ahead."

Well (Squaredeal Sam began), I met this here Pending at the Sportsman's Club. He was a big ugly red-headed mick an' he talked funny. He played poker likewise. He stayed in on three-card flushes, drew to middle straights, an' his idea of good clean fun was to raise into a loaded hand.

Under them circumstances, what could I do? He give me his

cash in the first hour, his war bonds in the next, an' I could've had his shirt if it had fit me. Naturally, he was gettin' worrieder an' worrieder by the minute. Finally on my deal I bust out a new deck for luck, an' dole him a king in the hole with two more kings an' a pair of aces on top: kings full. I had two aces an' a pair o' queens showin'.

"Aces an' bulls" I said, "is high. Your bet."

He studied the hands, his buckteeth hangin' out; then he wriggled like a housewife with ants in her pantry.

"Mr. McGhee," he bleated, "I *want* to bet this hand, but you've won all my money. Would you be willing to bet all my losses so far against my latest inventulation?"

That was the way he talked, y'understand. Whenever he got excited he run the King's English through the mangler. I eyed him thoughtful.

"That depends," I told him. "What is it?"

"Come with me," he said, "and I'll show you. We'll seal these hands and leave them with Hodgins till you decide. But I'm sure you'll agree. My inventulation is stupendicly importulant. One of the greatest things ever discoverized by man. It hasn't even been patentated yet. Well?"

"Okay," I said. "I'll take a look."

So we sealed the two hands an' left them in care of Hodgins, the club steward. Then we grabbed a cab, but not to Pending's apartment, like I figgered. We went to the Lakeview Country Club. Pending parked me at the first tee.

"You wait here," he said. "I'll be right back with him."

"*Him?*" I ast.

"It," said Pending, an' disappeared into the lockerroom.

I was still standin' there wonderin' if he ought to be salted an' served with beer, when back he come, draggin' in tow the strangest-lookin' jasper I ever clamped glims on. My poker-playin' sucker—I mean, friend—wasn't exactly what you might call a beauty-contest winner hisself, but he was a pin-up compared to this newcomer.

The guy was built all right—sort of slim an' tall an' whippy, like an athlete—but he walked like a mamma duck with arthritis; jerky an' stiff, you know, like his knees was sayin' "You let me past this time an' I'll let you past next time."

An' his face! Well, did you ever see a rough model of a zombie's death-mask in clay? This guy looked like that. His flesh was the color of a parboiled parsnip, and had about as much rise-an'-shine.

If they was any sparkle in his eyes, you couldn't see it nohow, on account of he was wearing big black sunglasses. He was a beaut, all right!

Pending said: "Mr. McGhee, this is Homer . . . Homer, shake hands with Mr. McGhee."

He patted his friend on the back real affectionate-like, an' this Homer lurched toward me like a cow on a pogostick. I ignored his outstretched flipper an' glared at Pending.

"Say, what's the gag? You brung me out here to see some kind of invention."

"Shortly . . . Shortly," soothed the redhead. "First I thought you might like to see Homer play a few holes of golf. He's *very* good."

"Now, look here!" I began. Then I stopped. Homer was apparently a man with a one-track mind. Despite the fact I wasn't payin' him no heed, he'd grabbed my mitt, and with that pale anemic-lookin' flipper of his wet an' cold as the inside of an old rubber boot, he was practically yankin' it off at the wrist. *"Hey!"* I yelled. *"Leggo!"*

Pending said hastily, "Er—that'll do Homer!" and patted his pal on the back again. Homer let loose an' backed away without sayin' a word.

Pending said apologetically: "He doesn't know his own strength, Mr. McGhee. I'm very sorry."

"You're sorry! I growled. "What's the matter with your buddy? Can't he beg his own pardon?"

Pat said, "Well, you see, Mr. McGhee, Homer doesn' know he hurt you."

"Well, I'm tellin' him!"

"Er—yes. But he can't hear you."

Came the dawn. "Oh!" I said. "I see. Deef, eh?"

"That's right. And he can't apologize for himself, because he can't talk. But he *can* play golf. Watch!" An' Pending pushed a wooden tee into the ground, placed a ball on it, an' crossed to Homer's side. He picked a club out of the bag he's brung with him, handed it to his friend, an' prodded Homer forward with pats on the back an' a runnin' fire of encouragin' comment.

"Show Mr. McGhee what a good golfer you are, Homer. Address the ball . . . There, that's right! Now, let's see—the green's about four hundred and twenty-five yards dead ahead. Ready? Very well—"

"If he's deaf," I said, "how come you talk to him?"

Pat just smiled.

"Very well, Homer," he said. Then: "Swing!"

Homer swung. That is, I suppose he swung. Because somethin' went *swoosh* an' somethin' went *splat!* . . . An' when I stopped blinkin' the ball an' tee had vanished, an' Homer was standin' there motionless. Whether he had actually moved was somethin' I couldn't swear to; all I'd seen was a brief blur.

But he must've hit that ball, because there it was rollin' down the fairway, dead center—onto the apron of the green *four hundred yards away!*

Squaredeal Sam paused to break the ash of his cigar into the cuff of his trousers. "Good for the moths," he said thoughtfully.

"Good for them, your Aunt Tillie!" I retorted. "It kills them!" And I stared at him in some pique. "Look here, Sam, are you trying to tell me this Homer person drove a golf ball four hundred yards?"

"I aint just tryin'," said Sam. "I'm tellin'."

"But that's incredible!" I protested. "It can't be done! The record is—"

"Six hundred an' thirty-seven," supplied Sam. "Jim Braid done it, 'way back when. I looked it up."

"But that was on ice," I said, "in the winter. And he had a stiff tailwind."

"This Homer was a cool customer, too," said Sam.

Nevertheless (so Sam continued), I don't much blame you for doubtin' me. I didn't believe my own eyes when I seen it happen. But Pending yelled, "Nice shot, Homer. Oh, a *lovely* shot!" He banged his pal on the back, clutched my elbow, an' before I could say anything we was walkin' down the fairway.

The ball was on the very edge of the green. It was a slopim' green—one o' those things where if you don't play strong enough you're short o' the cup, an' if you play it too strong you overrun the hole about ten feet . . . A nasty putt.

Cluckin' an' chirrupin' like a bird in a hedge, Pat guided his morgue-meat friend to the ball an' shovin' a putter into his hands, he said, "About twenty-four feet, I'd say—wouldn' you, Mr. McGhee? Go ahead, Homer. Putt!"

Homer putted. But none o' that crouchin' an' sizin-up the layout like you see most golfers do, none o' that testin' the wind, or fingerin' the grass to get the run of it. Homer just putted. The ball rolled up the slope, not too fast, not too slow, an' curled into the can for an eagle two!

An eagle! Imagine that! Two under par on the very first hole! An' that was just the beginnin'. We went to the second tee. Again

Pending squirmed an' fidgeted an' beat his buddy on the back, an' again Homer busted one down the middle o' the fairway. This time he had bad luck, though. His ball kicked into a bunker about two hundred yards from the green.

I said, "Tough luck, Homer! You'll have to waste a niblick shot gettin' out o' there."

"He can't hear you, Mr. McGhee."

"Well, then maybe he can feel me bein' sorry," said I. "Bein' a golfer myself—"

"Oh, then you play?"

"A little. I aint so good."

"No? What seems to be the trouble?"

"Well—distance, mostly. I stand too close to the ball after I hit it. I got a few other faults, such as not bein' able to use the woods or the irons—"

Pat said shrewdly: "You'd *like* to be a good golfer, wouldn't you?"

"Sure. An' I'd like to be Frank Sinatra, too, only it makes me nervous to hear women scream. So what?"

"So," said Pending, "would you like to take lessons from the finest golfer in the world?"

"Oh!" I said flatly. "So that's it? The invention gag was just a trick to get me out here an' sell me a bill o' goods on takin' golf lessons from this here friend of yours?" I turned toward the clubhouse. "Well, thanks for the mummery—but I aint havin' none. Poker's my athaletic exercise."

Pat grabbed my arm. "Wait!" he said. "Watch Homer make this shot, will you?" We had reached the bunker, where the ball was half hid under a clump o' dried grass. Pending took the Number 7 iron out of his bag, handed it to Homer. "About two hundred yards, Homer. Take plenty of turf." He massaged his buddy's dorsal fins as usual. "All set? Then—*swing!*"

This time I seen Homer swing. That is, part of it. A cloud of dirt an' shredded grass blotted out the grand finale, as Homer, obeyin' orders, took plenty of turf.

But the result was what counted. An' the result—when the dust-clouds rolled away—was that the ball eased to a lazy, rollin' stop eight feet from the pin!

"Wonderful!" yelped Pat Pending. "Oh, certainaceously marvulular, don't you agree, Mr. McGhee?"

"It—it's not bad," I admitted. "Only I still say I didn' comerhere to watch a golf exhibition. I come to see an invention—"

"Well, beemed Pending, "you've seen it!"

I stared at him. "Huh?"

"Homer," said Pat.

"Homer? I don't get you. What—"

"Look!" grinned the inventor, an' scurried to where our pile-drivin' companion stood motionless. "You've noticed the way I touch Homer's back everytime he's getting ready to make a shot, haven't you?"

"Yes," I said, "come to think of it."

"Well," chuckled Pending, "while I was doing that I adjusted the dials for the proper distance and power. On his back, you see, is—"

He lifted his pal Homer's shirt, an' I sat down, sudden an' hard, on the nearest bunker. Because his golf-playin' friend didn't have no back. Leastwise, no back like you an' me got, with skin, an' floatin' ribs, an' vertigris an' the like.

No, his southern exposure was nothin' but one big panel full of dials, buttons, an' levers atween his shoulderblades. Homer was a robot!

Squaredeal Sam paused, with a hopeful glance toward the decanters on my bookcase. "Hot!" he hinted. Funny how dry your mouth gets—"

"Help yourself," I told him, and watched admiringly as he drained at a gulp two jiggers of water diluted with one glass of rye. Then: "A *robot*, Sam?" I repeated. "You mean a mechanical man?"

Sam nodded. "Exactly! A walkin' creature of metal an' plastic an' some kind o' rubber composition. Electricity for a ticker, an' a calculatin' machine for a brain—"

"But a golfing robot!" I protested. "That's almost impossible! How would he—it—know how hard to hit a ball, or which club to use?"

"Them gadgets on his back, like I told you. An' he had somethin' like range-finders for eyes. It didn't make no difference to him how many rolls they was on a green; he just lined up his putt, the addin'-machine inside him measured the angles, an' *zowie!*—in the bucket! Homer couldn't miss. He didn't have no nerves to get jangly, or emotions to get upset. He was steady—steady like a rock.

"Why, all the sports-writers said he was the perfect golfer. Better'n Bob Jones, even. When he won the Greenview Open—"

"Greenview Open!" I interrupted. "Hold everything, Sam! Stanislaus Steele won the Greenview Open—the one they called the Masked Marvel. You don't mean to tell me—"

"Sam nodded slowly. "That was him," he said. . . .

Yes, Homer was the Masked Marvel (repeated Sam sorrowfully). After I won my bet with Pending. I become Homer's new manager an' owner. Bein' a good businessman, I right away reckonized the possibilities Pending hadn't saw. His only idea had been to rent Homer out as golf-instructor. I seen immediate how we could mop up a little filthy sugar in the big tournaments.

"You an' me'll be pardners," I told Pending. "I'll cut you in for twenty per cent. You keep Homer in good repair an' I'll handle the finances. Incidently, what makes Homer work?"

"Why," explained Pending, "the accumulizing of ohmical electriculosity impignates on the rheostats I built in him. That causes him to respondulate with the mathemaceous calcularity when the proper buttons are pressed—"

That's what I mean about Pending. His language was okay except when he got escited, or was tryin' to explain one of his inventulations.

"Never mind," I said, "you service him. I'll take care o' the finances. Now, the first thing we'll do is put a mask on him."

"Mask?" repeated Pending. "But why?"

"Because he's got a mesh flesh with a green sheen," I said, "which sooner or later somebody's going to figure out he's as phoney as an executive's desk unless we hide his face under something. Anyhow, it'll be good publicity: The first golfer in hist'ry to cover his grins on the greens."

"You're not going to try to pass him off as a human?" asked Pat dubiously.

"Why not? He fooled me, didn't he?"

"So much the better. That'll make him all the more mysterious. All the golfers I ever met up with had hoof-an' mouth disease—hoof all day an' mouth all night. They won't understand his silence, an' that'll unnerve his opponents."

"We-e-ell," said Pat, "it doesn't sound quite ethical to me. Honesty is the best policy—"

"Yeah, but policies don't pay off till you're dead. Now, you just leave everything to me. I know what I'm doin'. We'll start off by enterin' him in the Greenville Open; that's next week. You can be his caddy. That'll give you an opportunity to set his controls for each shot. Okay?"

"I don't like it," sighed Pending. "But if you say so, okay."

An' there we left it.

* * *

Well, since you read about that tournament, I won't keep you on tenderhooks about what happened.

My intention was to enter Homer as the "Masked Marvel," an' let it go at that. But Pending, who filled out the entry card, was suddenly taken ethical an' in the space where it said *Birthplace* he wrote: "Stainless Steel Works." Luckily, Pending's handwriting was as bad as his poker, an' the Greens Committee thought it said "Stanislaus Steele, Warsaw." That's how Homer come to be knowed as the "Poundin' Pole."

We played that whole tournament cagey. It wasn't a big one, an' my idea was just to find out how good Pending could control the robot under actual playin' conditions, to pick up a few bucks on the side bets, an' to win Homer a bit of a reputation so's he'd be invited to enter the National Open—which same I done, all of them.

"Excuse me a minute, Sam," I interrupted. "National Open? Isn't that being played right now?"

"You are so right," sighed Squaredeal Sam. And he continued:

The Greenview Open made Homer's name. I should say it made "Stanislaus Steele's" name. We eased him along, only turnin' on the heat when we had to, just takin' each opponent by enough margin to win, but not enough to discourage anybody or make anybody suspicious.

We took the first match three-and-two, the second two-and-one, an' the quarter-finals on the first extry hole. Pending pulled only one boner in the entire tournament. In the semi-final match, on the ninth tee he twisted the dial a trifle too far. It was a 368-yard hole. Homer not only reached; he overdrove it. Seein' as how the wind was in his face, people talked about this.

As we walked down the fairway, Pending whispered to me, "I'm sorry, Mr. McGhee. I didn't mean to twist that dial so far."

"That's okay," I told him. "It's good publicity—once. But don't let it happen again."

So he didn't, an though Homer never come near duplicatin' that drive again, the sports-writers gleefully tagged him with the title, "Poundin' Pole," an' a star was born when we won the tournament on the last hole, one up.

After that, just like I'd expected, they give Homer an invite to enter the National Open. An' the stage was ripe for the kill . . .

Squaredeal Sam paused, shaking his head slowly from side to side.

I grinned.

"When better metaphors are mixed, Sammy, you'll mix them. But I'm afraid I'm getting sort of confused here. The National Open is being played right now—this weekend. It's been on for three days. Didn't Homer enter?"

"Enter!" snorted Sam. " 'Course he entered! What's anxious to back the ex-Yankee outfielder two yards' worth."

That brung us into the quarter finals. We had some trouble in that round—yestiddy morning that was, by the way—because our opponent was off his game, an' he was all over the course like crabgrass. I told Pat, "Stick with him. If Homer whips him too bad, we won't be able to *buy* a bet around here."

Pending nodded an' pounded Homer's back approvingly as the robot stepped up to the tee. Homer's drive was like a bullet, as usual, but smack into the woods, like Pat had meant it to be. From then on we had a wildcat scramble—the other guy hookin' an' slicin' an' missin' putts; an' Homer matchin' him muff for muff, top for rop, to keep the contest somewhere near even up to the last hole. Which same, at my nod, we won with a birdie three to take the match.

Since that was the morning round, all the wise guys figgered Homer was a soft touch for a licking in the P.M., so I wrapped up a neat bundle when he hammered out a snappy four under par to go into the finals.

Well, if you'd been readin' the papers, or at least the sports pages, like you ought, you'd know we met "Ironman" Wilksen in the showdown. He got his nickname because he's an expert with the irons, an' because he's such a steady golfer. The playoff match was thirty-six holes, eighteen this morning an' eighteen in the afternoon.

They was a lot of excitement when we turned up this morning at the clubhouse. A big gallery was gathered at five bucks per head, newspaper reporters an' cameramen was out for stories, pitchers an' free drinks, contact-men was there from all the big golf-equipment manufacturin' companies to sign up the winner for advertisin' purposes.

The reporters was particularly troublesome, because they kept beggin' for a few words with Homer. "Just a word," they kept sayin'. We've got to get a statement, Mr. McGhee, in case he wins—"

"I've told you boys," I repeated for maybe the hundreth time, Stanislaus is deef an' dumb. *I* do his talkin'. If you'll come back after the match—"

"Then how about letting him slip off his mask, just for us? Why does he play in a mask, anyway? Who is he? Let us have one picture of him without the mask—"

I finally shooed them out o' there, explainin' that Homer had to dress. Pending was worried; he said: "It's not so good, Mr. McGhee. People are starting to get curious. We better win quick, and blow before they—"

"Nonsense!" I snorted. "We'll play it like I planned it and make a killing. Let Homer lose this morning—"

"Lose!"

You heard me. Let him go into the afternoon round about three down. That'll build up the odds. I've won seven hundred on him already, in this an' the Greenville tournament. I'll get three-to-one at lunch, lay it all on his nose—"

"And then?" asked Pat.

"And then," I told him, "we lift scalps!"

Well, Pat done like I said. He got quite a chuckle from the audience, the way he chattered to Homer, encouragin' him with pats on the back—but them back-pats did the trick.

With a fluff here an' a short putt here, we managed to get three down on the morning eighteen. That's it was when we went to lunch. Pat ate. I didn't. I was busy hunting up fat rolls to cover my lean one. I found them, too. I ended up with an average of almost four-to-one—about twenty-five hundred we stood to collect when Homer come hammerin' home a winner.

"An' that not countin' the prize money," I told Pat cheerfully. "It's all over but the shoutin' now, son."

Pat nodded. "Yes, I suppose so, Mr. McGhee. But I still don't think its ethical."

"Pooh!" I said.

"And it looks like rain," said Pending.

"So let it!" I sniffed. "That'll hurt Wilksen more than it will Homer. He could get distance in a blizzard."

"Yes," said Pat, "But if it rains—"

"You'll get wet an' ruin your clothes?" I chuckled. "So what? We'll be able to buy out the best tailor in town, soon as we win. Come on."

Homer took the hole with par figures. My advice to Pat was get even as quick as possible without letin' Homer do anything unusual. Wilksen's drive found a sand-trap, an' since I was part of the gallery that reached there before he did, somebody stepped on the ball and squashed it in the grit before he got there.

The second hole bein' a short par three, with the green in plain sight of the tee, was a break-even. Both players was on in one, an' it would of looked bad for Homer to sink a thirty-five-foot putt this early in the game. So Pat let him play an approach—which incidentally give me the time to get across to the third fairway, right over the rise where Wilksen's drive had fell on the morning round.

It landed in practically the same spot again. This time, though, when I strolled over to take a look at it I saw it was in a cuppy lie. Bein' a good sportsman, I fluffed the grass around it to sort of give Wilksen a break—an' I guess I must have fluffed it too much, because when he addressed it the ball wobbled off the turf an' rolled five inches, costin' Wilksen a stroke . . .

A tough break.

We won that hole, leavin' Homer one down.

The fourth and fifth holes was push, but Homer took the sixth when Wilksen lost his ball an' conceded. With golf balls as scarce as they is, it was a shame to lose that there one. . . . Brand new it was, without a mark.

So the match was even up again, with only twelve to play.

It was right about that time it started raining—a slow drizzle, hardly enough to hurt the course. But I didn't want to stay out in the rain all afternoon if I could help it, so I give Pat the nod. And then's when he turned on the heat—an' I do mean heat!

Homer won the par four seventh with a birdie three. Wilksen blew on the eighth, an' Homer's par was good enough. Pat had to sink a long, curly 40-footer to win the ninth—which he did, with the aid of Homer's telescopic optics. And Wilksen, who'd started this final round three up, was now that many down.

The tenth hole, a pitch-an'-putt shot, was push. A 225-yard brassie dead to the pin give Homer the eleventh, an' put the other so-called "Ironman" four down. And on the twelfth hole, Homer pitched a Number 6 iron shot to within four feet of the cup, dropped the putt for an eagle three, an' put Wilksen five down, with five holes to play. Dormie five.

On the way to the thirteenth tee I sauntered past Pat and give him the business out of the corner of my mouth.

"Now," I said. "It's startin' to rain harder; take this hole an' we'll go home."

"Yes, Mr. McGhee," he said. Then: *Homer! Careful where you're going!*" He hurried to the robot's side, grabbed him and pawed at his back just in time to keep pal Homer from taking a header into a sand-trap. "Over *that* way, Homer." "I'm sorry, Mr. McGhee. Must have pushed the wrong button—"

"Well, push the right ones about three times more," I told him, "and the game's over. Meet you at the clubhouse. I'll have the money."

An' because it was starting to pour down in buckets by now, I pulled my coat-collar up around my ears an' lit out for a dry shelter and a wet refreshment. . . .

I should've known better than to leave. I began to get curious about ten minutes after I'd reached the clubhouse porch, an' still nobody else had follyed me in off the links. I'd been expectin' the gallery, soakin' wet, to come back any minute. But they didn't.

Another five minutes, and I wasn't curious any more—I was anxious. An'with reason! For just then one of the newspaper reporters came runnin' in all excited. He grabbed the phone and dialed a number.

"Hey, Chief!" he bawled. "Kill that lead about the Masked Marvel winning! The match has gone haywire. Call you as soon as I get the results!"

He hung up and started out again. I caught him an' yelled: "What do you mean haywire? What's happened?"

"Plenty! The Marvel's blown sky high and Wilksen's taken the last three holes. They're playing the seventeenth now and he's only one down!" He paused and pointed. "No! See? The hole's finished, and they're walking to the eighteenth tee! Wilksen won that one, too, and it's even up! What a match! What a match!"

Both players got off their drives while I was on my way to Homer an' Pending. Wilksen's was the kind the duffers dream about . . . two hundred seventy-five right down the middle of the fairway.

Homer outdrove him by eighty yards, but the trouble was his was a low, slanting slice that ducked into the jungle and would've been out-of-bounds if I hadn't been the first to reach it. As it was, I just barely had time to locate it an' hand-mashie it over the fence when the gallery headed by Pat an' Homer, tromped into the forest.

I grabbed Pat's arm and ast him: "What in blazes is goin' on? You aint gone conscientious at the last minute. I hope!"

Pending said worriedly, "No, Mr. McGhee. It—it's Homer. The rain—"

"What about Homer? And what about the rain?"

"It—it got into him!" whispered Pending bleakly. "The water

soaked in through some of his joints. He's short-circuited! That's why he's driving the ball all over the course! His controls don't work right!"

"They've *got* to work right!" I hissed. "We've got thirty-five hundred dollars dangling on the next couple of shots, Pat!"

"I'm doing my best," moaned the inventor. "But—"

He shrugged and moved to Homer's side, placed a Number 3 wood in the robot's hands. The ball was settin' up on a nice tuft o' grass, and we was about two hundred-odd yards off the green. Wilksen had already shot, an' his iron was about fifteen yards off the apron.

"About two-ten," clucked Pending, paddling Homer's back. "A high spoon shot right over those trees. *Swing!*"

Home *swooshed* an' the gallery gasped as the ball lashed off the head of his club like a bullet out of a pistol.

Then I seen what Pending meant: Because that ball was still rising when it topped the trees. It was at the top of its rise when it reached the green. That drive was on its way for at least four hundred or five hundred yards!

I groaned. When an' if that ball ever come down, we still had as long a shot to the green as we'd started with—

"And then we got a break. The ball hit the roof of the caddyhouse, bounced fifty feet in the air, hit the limb of a tree, bounced off the fender of a parked automobile, an' rolled down the incline to the green—less than two feet from the pin!

Well, I'll say one thing for Wilksen. He was game. He didn't bat an eyelash at seein' Homer's lucky break sew up the old ball game. He crouched over his Number 8 iron, approached, an' run his ball up to within inches of the pin. It was a concede—an' with the consent of Pending, the other caddy tossed the ball back to Wilksen.

This left only one final act to the drayma. Homer had to sink a two-foot putt to win the match.

The newspaper cameramen was all around, forcused to record the title-winnin' putt for the newsreels. The gallery circled the green, hardly breathin', as Pat urged Homer forward.

"Easy now, Homer!" I heard him whisperin' hoarsely. "Just one teensy-weensy putt and it's all over. A straight one, about twenty-two inches. Ready. All right—*putt!*"

There was dead silence for a moment. I glanced at Squaredeal Sam, who sat steeped in gloomy reverie, staring at the decanters again.

"Well, Sam?" I asked. "Did he sink it?"

Sam groaned.

"Would I be here now if he had've? No, he didn't sink it. Instead of puttin', that darn fool robot *swung!* He r'ared back on his plastic heels and sloughed into that ball with all his might!

"I don't know where that ball landed. "What's more, I don't think *anybody's* every goin' to know where that ball landed. He was facin' east when he swung. The ball was just really beginnin' to rise when it cleared the clubhouse roof, three hundred yards away, by at least a good fifty feet.

"We watched it—me an' Pat an' the gallery—with open mouths until it turned into a dark speck in the sky, an' disappeared. We seen an airyplane suddenly shift its course a couple minutes later; we aint sure, o' course, but we *think* the pilot was duckin' out o' the way of what he must've thought was ack-ack fire . . . so the match was lost—an' all my bets with it."

"And that," I said as Sam paused, "is why you're here? Well—how much this time Sam?"

"A hundred will do it, I think," said Sam.

"You mean repair him so he can play again?" I shook my head. "I'm afraid not, Sam. By this time, everyone must know the Masked Marvel was a robot."

Sam nodded. "That's right, they do. I already made my apologies to the greens committee for enterin' him under false pretenses. Told 'em it was just a joke—a sort of a publicity stunt. They been right nice about it—"

"Well, then what earthly reason—"

"That's just it—an *earthly* reason! 'Cause, you see, Homer didn't *stop* swingin' after that last, match-losin' poke. He kept right on. He swung again . . . an' again . . . an' again. Pat can't get near him to turn him off, on account he's likely to get his head chopped off. With each shot, Homer digs up another bucketload o' dirt. When I left the club two hours ago, he was standin' at the bottom of a hole thirty feet deep—an' still goin' strong?

"I figger that for a hundred bucks we can take that putter out of his hands, equip him with a shovel . . . an' rent him to the United States Government. At the rate he's goin' now, he ought to have a hole dug deep enough for a land invasion o' Japan inside another month!"

I surrendered meekly. I always surrender to Sam's touches.

Silently I handed him the needed hundred, confident I would hear from neither it, nor Sam, until the dire finger of fate again intervened in my yarn-spinning friends' affairs.

But as he rose to go, a final thought struck me.

"There's just one more thing, Sam." I said. "You said you won Homer from this Pending chap in a poker game?"

"That's right."

"But you said Pending had kings full over aces. You had a pair of aces and a pair of queens showing. What could you possibly have had to beat him?"

"Oh, that!" said Squaredeal Sam. "Another ace o' course. Didn't I tell you we was playin' dealer's choice? It was my deal—an' I chose to play with a pinochle deck."

The Scientific Pioneer Returns

THIS SOUNDS SILLY. AT HALF PAST THREE ON A TUESDAY afternoon, in broad daylight, Professor Hallowell of the Midland University physics department left Jurnegan Hall, walked down a campus path clogged to the gutters with students—and disappeared into thin air.

This sounds even sillier. At nine-fifteen the next Friday morning, Travis Tomkins, chief technician of Midland's new observatory, stepped to the platform of Old Main to speak before an attentive crowd of twelve hundred undergraduates—and vanished before their eyes!

But this sounds silliest. H. Logan MacDowell, fat, fifty, feverish, and president of our institute of (alleged) learning, came to *me* about it! He came on the run. That is, he came at a brisk, lurching shamble. Which is, to him, the equivalent of a Cunningham four-minute mile. He collapsed on my studio couch, gasped and panted like the White King for a minute, then wheezed out a strangled plea.

"Blakeson, you—you've got to do something!"

I looked at his gaping mouth and bulging eyes, and nodded.

"Right!" I remembered. "I've got to rewind my bass rod and see that the reel is oiled. They'll be running in a week or so."

"No, you impertinent young snippet! I mean, you've got to do something about these mysterious disappearances."

I laughed right out loud. I bared my arms frankly.

I said, "Grab a look, Prexy! Nothing up the right sleeve; nothing up the left sleeve. I didn't snatch your pedagogues. After all, just because certain members of the faculty find it expedient to take a powder—"

"A what?"

"Powder," I repeated. "Can't you understand plain English? To lift one's feet. Scram. Blow. Take it on the lam. Sweet whistleberries, Doc, I'm not something from the 'FOLLOW THAT MAN!' advertisements. I'm just the publicity expert for this football-team-with-a-campus. If you want to learn what happened to Hallowell and Tomkins, why don't you get a dick?"

His jowls sagged to his breastbone. He said in an anguished tone,

"I suppose that means a detective? I did hire one."

"Well? And what did he find out? Aside from the well-known facts that Hallowell was carrying the torch for a red-headed senior, and Tomkins was up to his zipper in debt? Did he dig up any clues? Footprints? Blunt instruments, or ashes with rare cigarettes dangling on the end of them?"

"He didn't," said H. Logan in a hollow voice, "find anything, Blakeson. *He* disappeared, too!"

I said, "Oh-oh!" Which was inadequate, but it was all I could think of at the moment. "That's bad. It must be contagious. But where do I fit into the picture? Why ask me to do something?"

H. Logan wrestled with his scruples for a long and difficult moment. Then, suddenly,

"Cleaver!" he blurted. "Where is that man?"

Merely saying the name cost him an effort. And why not? Hank Cleaver was the one soul whose amiable meanderings, crossing the life-path of H. Logan MacDowell, had interrupted the smooth flow of traffic along that broad highway, torn up the roadbed, and sprinkled tar and gravel along the right-of-way.

The common-sense genius of Hank Cleaver had made MacDowell look like a cross between a baboon and a stuffed shirt, with the baboon getting the worst of the bargain.

Then, to cap the climax, Hank had handed Prexy's daughter the jilt, leaving sweet Helen high and dry at the altar when he returned to his beloved cabbage patch on his farm.

To say that MacDowell was unfond of Cleaver would be like saying that nice people disapprove of *Herr* Hitler.

About the campus it was commonly rumored that the president of Midland had a little China doll into which, each midnight, he jabbed many red hot needles.

The plaything wore coveralls and bulldog shoes, just like Hank Cleaver!

I said, "So you're going to call in 'Horse-sense' Hank."*

"Don't talk about him!" growled MacDowell savagely. "Find him! If we don't solve this mystery soon, we're going to have F.B.I. men romping all over our campus. The reputation of glorious Midland will be ruined. Our noble banners, heretofore untouched by the faintest breath of scandal—"

"Okay!" I said hastily. "Save that for the Alumni Banquet. I'll see what I can do, Doc."

He left, making noises like a sizzling steak. And I got on the phone.

But the results were strictly stinko. I grabbed a blank on my first call. The local operator at Westville intoned,

"No, puh-lease! Sor-ree, puh-lease! There is no telephone listed under the name of 'Gleeber'—"

"Back up," I snorted, "and start over. Look, Sis! 'C' as in cuckoo; 'l' as in lunkhead, 'e' as in—"

"Oh, is that you, Mr. Blakeson?" she chirruped. "I knew you by the description." Ouch! "I'm sorry I can't connect you with Mr. Cleaver. Do you want to talk to Mr. Hawkins?"

"Yeah," I said. "Gimme."

Hawkins was the amateur star-gazer working in Westville as a lay member of the Midland observatory staff. He owed his reputation to Hank and his income to me.

But he turned out to be a perfect bust, and I don't mean the Venus de Milo.

He said "Hank Cleaver? No, Jim, I haven't seen him for—oh, several days. I don't know where he is. But why do you want him? What's the matter? Is anything wrong?"

"Is anything," I countered, "right? Look, Hawkins, take a run out to his farm. Find Hank and tell him I've got to see him immedi— Who's there?"

"Nobody," said Hawkins querulously, "but our party-line subscribers. They're always listening in. What's ailing you, Jim?"

---

* Horse-sense Hank Cleaver, one of the best-known characters in modern science fiction. Hank, a dirt farmer never subjected to education, has an amazing ability to fix things of a mechanical nature when they go wrong, make infinitely accurate mathematical calculations and, above all, foretell the future in his own homely and intimate fashion.—*Ed.*

"I wasn't talking to you. There's somebody at the door of my apartment. Who's there?" I bawled again.

No answer. So I said to Hawkins,

"Well—do what I say. Find Cleaver. Tell him I've got to see him immediately, if not sooner. And let me know the minute you find him. So long—Oh, *wait* a minute, can't you?"

I hung up and stormed to the door, my foot itching to bury itself in the southern exposure of a salesman facing north. I flung it open, yelled,

"No, I don't want some! Go peddle your damn junk somewhere else—"

And then my jaw hit the top button of my vest.

"Hank!"

"Hyah, Jim!" said Horse-sense Hank.

Big as life and twice as natural.

There's only one Horse-sense Hank Cleaver. When they poured him, they laughed so hard they dropped the mold and broke it. Tall and gangly, so thin of cheek that the cud which constantly caresses his bicuspids sticks out like a cue-ball; tow-colored ravelings of hair waving experimentally in all directions; raw-boned of wrist; eyes mild and incurious as those of a heifer—that is my pal, Hank Cleaver.

I clapped him on the back and dragged him, by main force, into my apartment.

"Golly, guy, I'm glad to see you! You're looking a million. Do you know, I've been slaving like a census-taker to find you? I've called Westville, and—"

"I figgered," said Hank mildly, "as how you might be."

The wind whooshed out of my sails.

"You," I gulped, "did?"

"Mmm-hmm. Heard a feller say as how there'd been funny goin's-on down thisaway. Thought to myself, 'Well, now, Hank, 'pears like fust thing you know, ol' Jim'll be needin' a mite o' help, so you better hump along an' give him a lift.' So I come, and—" He beamed. "Here I am!"

"Yes," I said weakly. "Here you are."

Dammit, I don't know why I should have been surprised. Especially after having lived under the same roof as this gawky genius for three solid months. But as ever, it utterly confounded me to realize that Hank's thought processes were so simple, so altogether down-to-earth and natural, that he invariably did the right thing at the right time.

I said, "And a mighty good thing you came, too. But your turnips, Hank? How—"

He shook his head dolefully. Turnip growing was Hank's one and only obsession.

"Turnips," he grimaced, "is hell. It don't matter how you plant 'em, or where, or when, or what you do—they don't never act like you'd expect 'em to. I plant 'em wide, I plant 'em close; I plant 'em in cuts an' slips an' seeds; I plant 'em yeller, white an' mottled. I water 'em an' potash 'em an' treat 'em like babies—an' I *still* can't make 'em behave!"

He wedged a bulldog-tipped toe into the rug and looked at me from under his bushy brows.

"Helen?" he asked. "How's Helen?"

"Iroquois!" I told him grimly.

"Come again?"

"After your scalp. Didn't you ever hear the adage about Satan's old homestead having no fury like a woman left out on the limb? If you bump into Helen MacDowell, pal, you better fly, not run, to the nearest cavern."

Hank cracked his knuckles in misery.

"Couldn't do nothin' else, Jim. Couldn't marry her. 'Twarn't logical."*

"So," I reminded him, "aren't females. But never mind that, Hank. Let's get down to brass tacks. The reason I wanted to see you—"

"I know. About the way them men's been disappearin'," he said. He rose and walked to my radio set. " 'Pears like you oughta have this turned on. With all the trouble, seems like you'd be listenin' for news bulletins."

"It's busted," I said. "It hasn't worked for weeks."

"No?" He shifted it around, peered into the maze of coils, tubes, wires and utter incomprehensibles that comprise a modern radio set.

"Hmm. Never see'd the innards o' one o' these things afore. Interestin', ain't it?"

His lean fingers began weaving among the gleaming entrails. A tiny crease appeared over his right eye. He muttered as he pushed and jiggled and explored.

---

* In "The Scientific Pioneer," *Amazing Stories* for March, 1940 Horse-sense Hank refused to marry Helen MacDowell because, with his uncanny power to foretell the future, Hank knew their baby would be a chorus girl when it grew up. Hank is allergic to chorines.—*Ed.*

"This one goes there; that one goes *there*. 'Pears like— Well, I'll be durned!"

Something clicked, and his fingers made a twisting motion. He grinned at me.

"How d'you make 'er talk, Jim?"

"She doesn't. She's a deaf mute. But that vernier on the left—"

He turned it. My long-silent radio went, *"Phweeee-gwobble-gwobble!"*—and became coherent. Strains of hot jive assaulted my eardrums. I moaned.

"Hank, do you know everything? The repairman who looked at it said it would never work again. He said—"

"He jest wanted to sell you a new one," consoled my friend. "I kinda figgered as how adjustin' that little hunk o' metal would fix it. You see—"

But I never got to see. For at that moment my eyes went wobbly all of a sudden. Out of nowhere came a brilliant light, flooding the room with blinding intensity. There was no sound; just that sharp, bright glare—and my arms tingled with a sort of electric vibration.

And as I blinked, the light coalesced into a form! It was, roughly, the form of a man—and from where its head should be there came a strange, strained, hollow voice.

"Ombiggs!"

Then the light flickered, and was gone, and with it was gone the voice and the last vestige of my self-control. I let loose one squawk —out loud!—and dived for the darkness and comparative security of the region under the couch!

Not so Hank. He stood stockstill in the middle of the floor. I yelled at him,

"Hank, did *you* do that? Did you touch something on the radio?"

There was a faint, puzzled look on his face.

"Nope, Jim. I didn't do nothin'. Did you see him, too?"

"I saw him. Whoever he was. But who—how?"

"I dunno." Slowly. "Leastwise, the only thing I can think of is so durn unlikely— Hey, listen!"

The radio music had stopped suddenly. The voice of the announcer was clear, crisp, ominous.

"Ladies and gentlemen, we interrupt this program of dance music to bring you a special bulletin. *Flash!* Midland University campus. Dr. H. Logan MacDowell, president of this institution, vanished suddenly five minutes ago from the midst of a group of friends gathered at his home to discuss two similar occurrences at Midland within the past week.

"Police efforts to solve the mystery were hampered by the ensuing panic. A diabolic plot against the persons of eminent American educators is feared by observers—"

The rest was lost to us. Frenzied footsteps beat a tappity-tappity path to the door of my apartment, and nervous hands beat wooden panels. A sweet, familiar voice, now high-pitched in fright, cried,

"Jim! Jim Blakeson! Quick—"

The door and sheer courage were all that sustained her. As I opened the first, the second gave out. And Helen MacDowell moaned gently and collapsed into my arms!

CHAPTER II
Unexpected Journey

I yelled, "Get some water, Hank! And some brandy!"

I carried her to the studio lounge. Hank came back with two glasses. I gulped the brandy swiftly, and held the water to her lips. Pretty soon she spluttered, pushed the glass away, and opened her eyes.

"Oh, Jim! The most dreadful thing has happened to daddy. We— *You!*"

Hank swallowed convulsively and essayed a grin.

" 'Lo, Helen."

Helen MacDowell's fingers made motions like shears on a rampage. Her eyes roved. She asked thoughtfully,

"Jim, where's that paperknife you used to have? The long one? I'm going to stab somebody in the back!"

"Look, sugar," I pleaded, "Hank's come to help us. We have more important things to worry about now than your injured ego. After we've cleared up this trouble, you can have him alone in a dark room for ten minutes—"

"Is that," she demanded fretfully, "a promise?"

But her bitterness subsided; anxiety rekindled in her eyes. That, and the recollection of a shocking moment.

"Daddy disappeared, Jim! Right from the middle of a group. He was standing at my side; his shoulder was almost touching mine. Then all of a sudden—he was gone! Like that!"

Under any other circumstances, I would have guessed that the old windbag had finally blown up and drifted away. But there was precedent now for his Houdini act. One with sinister overtones. Three men and an animated gumshoe detective had vanished.

But I said, in a voice that I hoped wouldn't sound too much like a dish of unchilled tapioca,

"Now, don't worry, Helen. Everything's going to be all right. There must be a logical explanation for this. Hank's just the man to—"

And then—there it was again!

A blinding flash of light. A weird vibrancy tingling my body, drawing taut the tiny hairs of my forearms and neck. Light motes dancing giddily before my eyes, coalescing to form the figure of a man. A wavering, mobile figure, from the uppermost nebulosity of which emanated a piteous, hollow voice.

"Skleeva! Skleeva—"

Then a swift, dulled paling of the light. Burning white tarnished into red-ochre, red-ochre brazened, the green palpitated to a deep blue-indigo. The figure before my eyes took on form and substance. I saw with a sense of stark disbelief it was tall and lanky as Hank himself, that it wore a uniform of some sort, that its eyes were not unfriendly, but haggard and despairing. And then,

"Ombiggs!" wailed our impossible visitor. *"Ombiggs! Skleeva?"*
And vanished!

I stood still. Very, very still. It was not courage. It was rivets in the soles of my feet. My brain clamored,

"Go, boys, go!" But my knees were clattering and banging like the fenders of a T-model Ford.

Helen wasn't much better off. Her eyes looked like a pair of sealed-beam headlights, and the most intelligent sound she could summon was a faint, plaintive,

"Oooooh!"

Only Hank retained an iota of self-control. And to tell the truth, his comment was far from enlightening.

"Well!" he said. "So *that's* it!"

"What's what?" I asked him shakily. My paralysis was slipping away, and I prepared to do ditto. "Friends, did you see what I saw. Or has the little brown jug finally done what the Temperance Society told me it would do some day?"

Hank said, "Now, Jim! It ain't like you to act so. 'Specially when we've reached what you might call a crooshul moment.

Hmm! Now, lemme see. You folks seen him most plain when he was what color? Blue?"

"Sort of. Bluish-green."

Helen said, "Greenish-blue."

"That's near enough," mused Hank. "That'd be—mmm!——'bout .0005 millimetres. I'll tell him that when he comes back—"

"*When he comes back?*"

"Why sure!" Hank stared at me amiably. "He'll be back any minute now. He done a lot better this time than the first, don't you think? Next time he'll probably get what he wants."

"And," I faltered, "and I suppose you know what that is?"

"Reckon I do," said Hank complacently. "He wants *me.*"

I gave up trying. My brain was in a muddle, anyway.

I said, "All right, Hank. You win. Now get down to straight facts. Who *is* he, *where* did he come from, *why* does he want you, *how* do you know he does, and *what* is this all about?"

Hank shifted uncomfortably.

"Well, now, Jim, that's a powerful lot of questions at one lump. Dunno's I can answer 'em all—yet. Hafta talk to him first, o' course, but as near as I can figger, here's the set-up.

"That guy ain't from our time. He's from some time which ain't come yet. The future, so to speak. I don't know his name, 'cause he didn't speak very clear, but I know who he wants 'cause he said me."

Helen said dazedly, "He *said—*"

" 'Where's Cleaver?' " explained Hank. "Oh, it wasn't very clear. He was all excited. But that's what he meant, I reckon."

I swallowed hard and wished the goose pimples would get off my hide.

"You mean," I said, "he's coming back out of future time to talk to you?"

"Seems as if. More like, he'll want to take me with him," Hank said calmly.

"What! But, Hank, that would be awful! You mustn't allow anything like that—"

Hank said bluntly, "You want I should find out where Helen's old man is, don't you? And them two puffessors? Way I figger, Jim, there must be somethin' awful drastic goin' on there in the future. Somethin' so bad, it's got 'em all upset an' they're back-draggin' the past for me. By accident, they musta got Hallowell an' Tomkins an' Helen's pop. I've got to get over there an' find out what's the trouble— Here it is!"

For an instant there had flickered again that ray of light. Hank warned hastily,

"You two stand back out o' the way! Keep calm an' don't worry. I'll be back directly."

He stepped into the middle of the room as the bright, golden light suddenly flamed anew. He lifted his voice.

"Point oh-oh-oh-five, friend. Or thereabout—"

And the light changed. Slid swiftly down the wavelengths again to that hue most favorable. The figure appeared, this time firm, unwavering. It was the face and figure of a man remarkably like Hank Cleaver himself; a young man, serious-eyed, hopeful of voice.

"Cleaver?" he cried. "You Cleaver?"

Hank nodded "Mmm-hmm. I'm him."

"Come!" said the young man. "Come, Hank Cleaver."

He held out his hand. And Hank stepped forward into the blaze of pallid, green-blue light.

Which was just one too many for Helen MacDowell. A tiny groan escaped her lips. She tottered, pitched forward to Hank's shoulder. Hank turned worried eyes to me.

"Grab her, Jim! Get her back before—"

And I, too, leaped forward. I got my hands on Helen, started to pull her from that color-field. I was aware of the distant throbbing of some unknown machine, then of a swift, sudden shock. Great forces wrenched at my body. I felt as if I were being racked in a titanic tug-o'-war. There was an instant of frightful cold, another of giddy nausea, a sensation of wild, hurtling motion.

Then blackness, soft, warm and impenetrable . . .

No, not impenetrable. For there was a light in my eyes, and my head was no longer swimming, and I was lying on something comfortable, and a friendly voice was saying,

"Here you are, Buster. Drink this!"

So why look a gift drink in the bottle? I drank it, and immediately felt warmer inside. And more confident, too. Until I lifted my head and looked about me. Then I let loose a howl that stretched from here to there, with reverberations.

"Great galloping saints, where am I? No, don't say it! Let me guess. World's Fair?"

My young companion looked puzzled. He was a decent-looking chap, except for that wild costume he was wearing. A sort of uniform, but it reminded me painfully of a Buck Rogers serial.

Loose tunic and slacks, sky-blue, with a Sam Browne belt and a gun holster into which was jammed a weird-appearing weapon, all knobs and studs and buttons.

"How?" he said.

I said, "My—my friends? Where are they?"

"They're up and around. You're the only fader."

He grinned. "You must be allergic to electricity, huh?"

I was still staring about me. The room was a humdinger. All metal and plastic and glass; a small cubicle about six by ten, with a single bunk (that on which I now sat, poised for flight) a desk, chair, porthole—

Porthole!

"So that's it!" I yipped. "Shang-haied!"

I made a dive for the porthole, pressed my nose to it, hoping that across the bounding blue I might see at least one faint ribbon of good old terra firma.

But there was no land. There was no bounding blue. There weren't even any clouds or sky! There was—just gray. Wan, dismal gray that seemed to stretch into infinity!

It was plain that I needed either one less drink or one more. I settled for the latter. A long, straight one. It snapped me hurriedly out of my speechlessness.

"Not that it's any of my business," I said, "but it looks to me like there's nothing outside that porthole but a lot of gray emptiness."

My companion nodded dolefully.

"Yeah," he said, "I know. I've looked—and looked."

"Where I come from, space usually has things stuffed inside it. So apparently I'm not there. Which being the case, would you mind telling me where the hell I *am?*" I demanded.

He shook his head. "That's just it, Buster. We don't know."

"You," I told him, "are a big help. Pass the bottle. Do you happen to know your own name?"

"Yeah," he said. "Mud. It used to be Bert Donovan. I'm the radio operator aboard this ship."

"Ship?" He was beginning to talk sense now.

"Lugger, I should say. This is the *Saturn,* friend. IPS freight lugger, operating on the Earth-Mars shuttle. Or, anyhow, we *used* to. *Till* he got monkeying around with that new power drive of his—"

"IPS?" I strangled. "Earth-Mars? *He?*"

"Take it easy, friend. IPS—interplanetary space ship. Earth-

Mars— round-trip route, originally. Navigator, Lancelot Biggs, the first mate.* Didn't you know—"

"Omigod!" I bleated. "Don't tell me, but I—we—all of us are in the *future!*"

Donovan caught me as I was about to collapse and clapped me heartily on the back. I think it did more harm than good, but at least it brought me out of the fog.

"Correct," he said unhappily. "We're off in the future—hmm—maybe two-three hundred years. Myself, I don't understand how the hell it happened, but—"

At that moment a bell sounded. We turned to a hunk of square glass set in a side wall. It lighted, and a crusty-looking face scowled down at us, eyed me appraisingly.

"Ah, so you've recovered, young man? Fine! Your friends are waiting here in the control turret. Sparks, come along up here. Mr. Biggs has called a general conference."

The light dimmed. Sparks grinned at me languidly.

"That's the Old Man. Cap Hanson. Well, let's go, Buster. The fireworks are about to begin."

"The name," I told him, "is Blakeson. And how come the fireworks? Me no savvy."

"You heard him say L. Biggs was in the control turret, no? That's the tip-off, Bust—"

"Blakeson!" I said firmly.

"Blakeson," he corrected. "Okay, Buster. Come on!"

CHAPTER III

Lancelot Biggs' $\sqrt{-1}$

Things moved so swiftly then that the series of surprises I received was practically one continuous blow. The walk through the *Saturn* was a revelation in itself. Like the cabin in which I had awakened, the ship was all metal, glass and plastic. And a funny metal at that.

---

* Author Nelson S. Bond first introduced Lancelot Biggs, space navigator and jack-of-all-trades, in the November, 1939 issue of *Fantastic Adventures,* our companion magazine, under the title "F.O.B. Venus." The second mate aboard the *Saturn,* space freighter plying between Earth and other colonized planets under the somewhat bilious leadership of Cap Hanson, Lancelot Biggs got himself promoted to first mate after getting the space freighter out of a bad fix. Author Bond, now one of the top-notchers in popular fiction, has in this story combined two of his best-liked scientifictional characters—Lancelot Biggs and Horse-sense Hank.—*Ed.*

It was hard, but it looked soft, if you know what I mean. Which I'm sure *I* don't! The name of the metal, Donovan told me, was "permalloy." It was a special, non-conductive, something-or-other resistant alloy.

"—invented," said Sparks, "around the end of the twentieth century." And he looked at me curiously. "Oh. I forgot. You wouldn't know about that, would you?"

"Look," I said desperately. "Let me know when we get to the Psychopathic Ward, will you?"

But he didn't get it. We walked down one ramp and up another, through an observation room, climbed a ladder, and finally ended in the room the skipper had called the "control turret." And what a place *that* was!

It looked like an overgrown cyclotron with a purpose. Huge, banked panels with studs on them, cryptic plates, coiled thingamajigs, mechanical what nots and doolollies all over. More guys in sky-blue uniforms. Bells tingling, television screens popping on and off at intervals . . .

"Interestin'," said a voice at my elbow, "ain't it?"

And it was Hank, gulping and grinning and shaking my hand.

"Kinda worried about you, Jim. You shouldn't ought to have allowed yourself to be drawed into the power-field."

But seeing Hank had made me think of Helen; and now, looking for Helen, I found something that completed my mental collapse. Helen was standing shoulder to shoulder with—none other than her old man, himself, in person! And right behind H. Logan MacDowell stood the missing professors, Hallowell and Tomkins. And lurking behind them, looking more baffled—if possible—than myself, was an exceedingly disgruntled individual in a hard hat. The vanishing detective.

I answered their nods weakly. Then I turned to Hank.

"I give up, pal. What is it? The after-world? Or Old Home Week?"

Hank said seriously, "Well, reckon as how you might call it the after-world, Jim. In a way. It's the world which is to be. But here comes the feller that can explain everything."

For the door had opened, and in walked the chap whom we had seen thrice in my apartment, the effervescent spirit of electricity, the blue-green mystic, the first mate of the *Saturn*—Lancelot Biggs!

Did I say "walked?" Excuse it, please. What he did with his feet could never, by the wildest stretch of the imagination, be called walking. Oh, he progressed forward, yes—but there are no words to describe his locomotion. Think of a polar bear on a pogo stick. Or a secretary bird on skates. A two-footed octopus, even.

His gait was a combination of the worst features of all three. He lurched and shambled, his bony knees protruding as if acknowledging introductions at each passage. A sort of, "You let me by this time, and I'll let you by next time!" deal.

But the peculiarities of Signor Biggs did not end at that point. He had others. I have said that he looked a bit like Hank Cleaver. That is true. They shared lean lankiness of build. Each was blessed—or cursed—with a mop of faded-yellow hair; their eyes were alike in that they mirrored soft curiosity. But Biggs had an appendage Hank lacked.

Matter of fact, no man ever had an Adam's-apple like that before or since. It hung in his scrawny throat like an unswallowed cud; and when he smiled—which was often—or talked, it woggled up and down like a runaway elevator.

To Sparks, beside me, I said dreamily,

"I see it, but I don't believe it. Is it alive?"

And then Biggs addressed us.

"First of all, I must apologize to you, Mr. Cleaver, and to Miss MacDowell and Mr. Blakeson for this rude infringement upon your personal privacy. It was an unwarranted step I took, intruding on your lives this way, but I hope that you'll agree it was not unforgivable.

"I have already explained to these gentlemen"—he bobbed his head toward the pedagogues and the shamus—"the urgency of our situation. To clarify in your minds the how and where of your present location—"

Hank Cleaver *harrumphed!* and interrupted.

"Reckon as how you can skip that, Lootenant," he said. "It's purty clear. You bridged the time gap from *your* time to *ours* by means of an ultra-wave temporal aberrant. Brought us up a couple o' centuries t 'bout the—well, 'bout the twenty-third century."

Lancelot Biggs tried hard to swallow the billiard ball under his chin.

"How—how did you know that, Mr. Cleaver?"

Hank scratched his head, and into his eyes came the old, baffled look that always came there when he was asked how he knew anything.

"Well," he confessed, "I don't 'zackly know how I know, but I do. Just stands to reason, that's all. When you come slidin' down the visible waves to hunt for us, an' when we woke to find ourselves on a space ship—an' as for the time element, well, I alluz 'lowed as how it'd take people 'bout fifty years, more or less, to make the first successful space flight, an' another two hundred to git it workin' proper—"

Lancelot Biggs' eyes lighted with a great joy.

"Mr. Cleaver, I touch my rocket to you! The ancient records do not lie. You are indeed a remarkable man. *Now*"—he turned to his fellow officers triumphantly—"now I *know* we shall win free of our difficulties. With your assistance."

Hank flushed, and squirmed a bulldog toe.

"Mebbe you better explain these here difficulties."

It was Biggs' turn to flush.

"I'm afraid," be said miserably, "it's all my fault. Six days ago, Earth Standard time, we lifted gravs from Long Island space port for Mars Central. This was to be my final shuttle before getting married to the skipper's daughter, Diane. Consequently I was a trifle—well, impatient. But I'm sure you understand, Mr. Cleaver."

Hank said hastily, "You better git on, Lootenant." He didn't look at Helen, which was a good thing.

"For some time," continued Biggs, "I have been experimenting with a new device, designed to increase the speed of our vessel. It seemed particularly appropriate that this shuttle should be the test period. So with Captain Hanson's permission I installed my new velocity intensifier on the hypatomics. After we cleared Lunar III, I switched it on—"

Biggs stopped. His eyes were haunted.

Horse-sense Hank said, "Yeah?"

"There was a moment of frightful acceleration, then a sharp explosion, and when order was resumed—here we were!"

Nobody spoke, which seemed silly.

"That," I said, "doesn't make sense. Here you were. So *where* were you?"

"That," said Biggs dejectedly, "is just what we don't know! Ah, that sounds ridiculous to you, gentlemen? Believe me, if you knew space, as we who shuttle back and forth within it in our daily toil, you would recognize by merely glancing through the quartzite viewpanes that we are nowhere within the confines of man's studied universe!

"Space is an ebon, eternal night, pricked by a myriad glowing sparks. The stars wheel in their courses. Comets scream through the infinitude. The planets, firmly shining in the reflected glory of their several suns are colored gems upon a velvet pall. But about us now we see nothing but a dull, endless gray. There are no cosmic clouds, no meteor mists, no stars; neither light nor dark. Only nothingness, complete and unresponsive to our best instruments!"

"Huh!" broke in Hank. "Whazzat you say?"

"Apparently," explained the young lieutenant, "our delicate instruments were broken during the explosion. That is the factor making more perilous our position. We are not able to orient ourselves, discover into what portion of the universe our moment of wild flight flung us.

"I have studied and worked and thought on the problem, but to no avail. That is why, Mr. Cleaver, I undertook to find *you.*"

Cleaver looked at the youngster admiringly.

"Smart feller!" he said. "Time travel, huh? Alluz thought it could be made to work. Mighta tried it myself if it hadn't been I was so durn busy on them turnips—"

"It was an accidental discovery, sir. I chanced upon it several months ago while inventing a new type of uranium speech condenser. It turned out to be a time-speech trap."*

"Nevertheless," insisted Hank, "you done a good job. Findin' a way to transport your body across time. An' pickin' me up outa 1940, bringin' me here. Like to talk to you about that later. But right now—" He frowned severely. "You say them instruments o' your'n won't work?"

"No, sir."

"Not *a*-tall?"

Biggs swallowed with difficulty.

"The truth is, Mr. Cleaver—"

"Hank's good enough."

"Well, Hank, the truth is—the instruments *do* work! But they work so dad-blamed funny—"

"Let's," suggested Horse-sense Hank mildly, "have a look."

That was all the invitation the young lieutenant needed. Without so much as a backward glance at the rest of us, he led Hank to the control banks of the space freighter. They began to talk in undertones. Biggs pushed buttons and explained things. I heard snatches about, "tensor alleviators," "orbital velocity adjusters," and a bunch of terms even less comprehensible, and gave it up as a bad job.

It was Hank's party. And his headache.

---

* "The Madness of Lancelot Biggs," *Fantastic Adventures*, April, 1940.—*Ed.*

I turned to my self-appointed guide, the radioman, Bert Donovan.

"Do you understand what they're talking about?"

He grinned. "Buster, I've been listening to Lancelot Biggs talk for almost a year now. And I have yet to understand the first thing he tells me."

"Then in that case," I said, "it looks to me like a drink is indicated. Right?"

Right is might, and shall prevail.

I don't know how long later it was that we wandered back to the control turret. It must have been quite a while, for Sparks had shown me through the entire ship. When we got back, Cap Hanson and Doc Hallowell were playing a game of high-low, and the *Saturn*'s skipper was giving Hallowell a good old-fashioned, twenty-third century going over.

Tomkins and MacDowell were napping quietly. The second mate, a guy named Todd, was making motions at guiding the ship's flight through nothing, and also making a mild play for Helen MacDowell. And not getting very far with either job.

Biggs and Cleaver had finished inspecting the instrument panels, and were in earnest confab by the plot charts. Hank seemed to be summarizing their decisions.

"—your new gadget was supposed to eliminate every speck of energy waste, huh?"

"That's right. And thus conserve fuel, at the same time giving tremendous speed," Biggs nodded.

"An' when you plugged the switch, it gave one whoop an' holler, the *Saturn* went like a bat out o' hell for a few seconds—"

"—and then," finished Biggs, "we found ourselves here. That's the story, Hank. The whole story, so help me. But if, from those few facts and what I've shown you, you can explain in what part of the universe we are, you're an even greater genius than history says you were— I mean, are."

Hank cocked a quizzical eye. "That's funny, ain't it?" he mused. "I was, but I still am. Time's tricky, Lanse. But, listen, you made one mistake."

"Yes?"

"In sayin' 'what part o' the universe.' Way I see it that ain't the explanation a-tall. Way I see it, there's two kinds o' universes. The *is* an' the *ain't*. An' we're in the other one."

"I—I beg your pardon?" faltered Biggs.

"Put it this way. You draw a graph, an' you cross two lines. The block at the upper right intersection o' them two lines is the *is* universe. The one we live in. Ain't that right?"

Biggs nodded. "That's a simple way of graphing existence, yes. The horizontal line would represent existence in space, the vertical line existence in time. At any given moment, a man's position in space and time is coordinated in the positive sector. But—"

He stopped abruptly, looking at Hank with startled eyes.

"But you don't mean, Hank, we're in the *bottom* sector of the graph!"

Hank sighed. " 'Fraid that's 'zackly what I do mean, Lanse. It's no wonder nuthin' looked natcheral to you. We done bust plumb out o' space an' time as we ordinarily know it. We're in the imaginary sector o' space-time! The coördinate of where we are now ain't even positive numbers. They're all based on a negative factor—the square root o' minus one!"

CHAPTER IV
Danger Ahead

I looked at Bert Donovan and he looked at me. Judging by the faces of our two screwball intellectuals, there was something smelly on the *Saturn*. But it was all a deep and dark mystery to me.

I said, "Hank, for old times' sake, would you brush that off again lightly for me? In words of one syllable, what has the little letter i got to do with space flight, gray skies and time-travel?"

But Hank ignored me. On the right track at last, he was developing his arguments.

"Reckon you know more 'bout energy-mass relationships than I do, Lanse. 'Spect you'll remember, then, the transformations cooked up by a guy from our time, feller by the name o' Lorentz? Him an' a couple other guys named Einstein an' Planck fiddled around with hyper-spatial mechanics an' discovered some interestin' things. Includin' the fact that mass is altered when it travels at high velocities.

"Whut I figger musta happened is this. The gadget you invented worked even better'n you expected. It worked so durn well that it give the *Saturn* one whale of a kick in the pants. Made it accelerate at a speed *greater than that of light!*

"So then what? Why, then the *plus* universe warn't big enough to hold the *Saturn* any more! That wild minute or two you talked about was when you exceeded the limitin' velocity. An' then here you was in the minus universe! Which is, so to speak, the negative matrix of the normal *plus* universe we ordinarily live in."

It didn't make sense to me, but apparently it did to Lieutenant Biggs. He passed a damp palm across a sweating forehead.

"You're right, Cleaver! You must be right, because your argument agrees with all the known theories and observed facts. The incredible readings on our instruments, the weird surroundings in which we find ourselves—" He stared at my friend sombrely. "But what are we going to do? How shall we get out of here?"

Hank said, "Same way we come in. We blast out."

"But I've tried that, Hank," Biggs defended. "Before I realized the full extent of our situation. And nothing happened. There's something strange in the response of the motors. Don't ask me what. It's hard to say, when the *Saturn* is plunging into beaconless, starless nothing. But stepped-up acceleration is just a waste of fuel."

"Yeah?" mused Hank. "That's queer. Now, I wonder why—"

At that instant came a most unexpected interruption. Todd, who had been quietly tending his controls, suddenly came to life with a startled cry.

"Well, I'll be— Biggs! Captain Hanson!"

"Yes?" Both men answered at once.

"There—there's a large body before us!"

He pressed a button. A glassy pane above the panel glowed into life. As if a portion of the *Saturn*'s prow had been sheared away, I was looking at the vista before us. But it was no longer empty as, according to Biggs, it had been ever since the moment of the "accident." The stark, gray loneliness was relieved now by a monstrous pockmark in space. A giant sphere, imponderably distant, but definitely on our trajectory!

Hanson was a man of action, I learned. He leaped to the intercommunicating system.

"Chief Garrity! Large body for'rd! Reverse hypes and apply drag instantly. Todd, plot a course revision! Man! What a monster! Biggs, get out the charts. Something solid at last. Maybe we've busted back into our own universe!"

Biggs said, "Yes, sir! Right away, sir!" His eyes questioned Hank. But Cleaver shook his head.

"Nope, I don't think so. It ain't logical. That's a phenom—a phenom—a pee-culiarity o' the cockeyed universe we're in— Hey! What's goin' on here?"

The constant hum of the hypatomic motors below, one I

hardly noticed until suddenly it no longer throbbed in my ears, had subtlely altered. A brief instant of silence, a jarring concussion—and a deeper, more resonant sound.

Biggs explained, "That's the hypatomics being thrown into reverse. Antigrav units are activated in the nose of the ship, then when we get the course variation we swing around our objective. Common space practice, Hank."

"That's what," said Hank dubiously, "I figgered. Is it common space practice to make a beeline for danger, though, like Billy-be-damned?"

And he pointed to the visiplate. Biggs' eyes followed his finger—and Biggs gasped.

"Great whirling comets! It's got us caught!"

For despite the mounting clamor of the reversed engines, despite the antigravitational units of which Biggs had boasted, despite the swiftly redoubled orders and efforts of a shocked Captain Hanson—the *Saturn*'s speed had definitely increased!

The figure in the plate was looming larger moment by moment, and even to my untrained eye it was plain that we were slam-banging, hell-for-leather, toward a crackup!

Don't ask me what happened in the next few minutes. I wouldn't know. It's all one whirling blind spot in my memory. Up till now, this entire affair had partaken of the nature of a dream. Amusing, not unpleasant, but quite remote and faintly incredible.

Now, suddenly, I realized it was not a dream. But that I, Jim Blakeson, publicity representative of Midland U., had somehow been dragged out of the normal routine of everyday life and thrust into a wild, impossible adventure in a world three centuries beyond my time.

It was a disturbing awakening. It didn't make matters a bit better to realize that I was now—along with five other twentieth century exiles—in imminent peril of being slapped out of existence by a gigantic planet that shouldn't be in a dull, gray universe that didn't exist!

About me, frantic figures boiled and churned. The skipper of the *Saturn* was bouncing about the control room like a bipedal gadfly, jerking switches, bellowing orders, pawing through charts that—to me at least—were a complete mystery.

Dick Todd still sat, tense and grim-jawed, in his bucket-shaped pilot's chair. His fingers played the banked controls before him as the fingers of an accomplished organist seek stops, but so far as I could see, his movements availed nothing. For the object in the visiplate loomed larger and ever larger.

Lancelot Biggs had wasted very little time scanning charts. Despairing of finding any record of this cosmic visitor, he had grabbed paper and pencil, and was now scrawling hasty calculations. Hank Cleaver was watching him. I glanced at Helen. She was watching Hank. Rather hopefully, I thought.

Hank said, "What's it show, Lanse?"

Biggs looked up at him haggardly.

"The mass of that planet must be terrific. It has a heavy gravitational attraction. We're accelerating by leaps and bounds. At our present rate of acceleration, only about twenty minutes remain before we—we—"

He paused, glancing helplessly at Helen MacDowell. There was a strange longing in his eyes. I remembered, all of a sudden, a fact he had mentioned. That somewhere back on Earth, a girl waited for him. A girl who had promised to be his wife. His next words showed that he shared my thought.

"I don't mind checking out," he said quietly. "We who dare the spaceways risk that hazard always. But I wish I could have seen her once more before—"

It was then that Hallowell pushed forward. He was scared, and plenty scared. So scared that his voice was a thin, bleating yammer.

"Lieutenant, you can at least send us back to our proper time! You can't let us die like this! Without a chance—like trapped rats!"

"Rats!" I said scornfully. "Speak for yourself, Hallowell!" But Lancelot Biggs nodded.

"He's right. We still have twenty minutes. It is not right that you of another age should share our fate. We must get the temporal deflector into operation, send all of you back—"

Hank cried sharply, "Just us? Why not everybody, Lanse? Let's *all* escape to the twentieth century. The whole kit an' kiboodle!"

But Biggs shook his head.

"I'm afraid that is impossible, Hank. There are limitations to temporal transmission. You and your friends can enter *our* time because there is no natural barrier, but *we* cannot violate the established world-line of things that have been. We never were in your time, therefore we cannot now go there. But, wait—"

He spun swiftly to a wall-audio, spoke to the engine room below.

"Get the deflector ready. We're sending our guests back!" Then, nodding to all of us, "If you will come with me—"

We started for the door. But we had taken just a few steps when the audio buzzed. Biggs answered its call, listened for a moment, cried out,

"But Garrity, are you absolutely sure? It can't be! It mustn't be!"

The clacking voice was regretful but positive. I felt a thin, cold edge running up and down my spine. Now I look back upon it, I think I guessed what Garrity was saying even before Biggs turned to us, his eyes wide with sympathy and sorrow.

"My friends," he said in a choked voice, "forgive me for what I must say. Your lot is irrevocably cast with ours. The strain on the motors has burnt out several vital units. There is not time enough now to repair them. The temporal deflector is—useless!"

That was a jolt. The way my several comrades took the message was the measure of their characters. Hallowell cried out sharply, began to scream protests in a frightened voice until Prexy—fat, staid, stuffy old H. Logan, himself—silenced him with a back-hander across the mouth.

"That will do, Hallowell!" snapped MacDowell. And he seemed to grow three inches. It was a mile in my estimation. "I think, Lieutenant Biggs," he said, "we need no further apologies. We are not afraid to die with you."

I forgot to dislike the old guy then. I loved him a little bit for that. And I liked Tomkins' reaction, too. The little observatory technician sighed wistfully.

"It's too bad, though. I should have liked to take back to our time a knowledge of some of the marvels we have seen here."

The detective said nothing. He still didn't seem to know what the hell it was all about. But Helen MacDowell was as game as her old man.

She said, "We're not licked yet. I still think Hank—I mean, Mr. Cleaver—will find a way out of this."

Biggs said gently, "I'm afraid not, Mrs. Cleaver. This is the end for all of us."

Helen's eyes darkened suddenly.

"*Mrs.* Cleaver! My dear lieutenant! I'll thank you not to couple my name with that of this—this person! What ever made you think I was his wife? I wouldn't marry him if he were the last man on earth—"

And then Lancelot Biggs did a strange thing! For a startled moment he stared at Helen MacDowell incredulously. Then he loosed a terrific whoop. And I don't mean whisper.

"*Eeee-yow!*" he howled. "You and Hank aren't married?"

"Why, of course not!"

"You—you haven't any children?"

Helen turned, brick-red.

"After *all*, Lieutenant—" she began stiffly. "But, *really!*"

I don't think Biggs heard her. For he had leaped to Cleaver's side, was pounding him enthusiastically upon the back and shoulders.

"It's all right, then! You understand—it's all right! Get those brain-cells to work, Hank; old boy! It's in the bag! *Eeee-yowee!*"

And Hank Cleaver, from the depths of a brown study, said suddenly,

"Say, looka here—I been thinkin'—"

CHAPTER V
Minus Math

Lancelot Biggs said feverishly, "Don't think, Hank—act! Anything you say is all right by me. You're in command here! Give your orders!"

Hank said hesitantly, "Well, if you say so—" and moved to the audio. With his unerring sense of assurance, he selected the right button, contacted the engine room. Chief Engineer Garrity's grizzled face appeared in the plate.

"Yes, sorr?"

"Chief, turn off them there reverse engines right away," said Hank hesitantly. "An' disconnect them anti—er—anti-grav doogummies."

Garrity's jaw fell open. He said, "I—I beg your pardon, sorr!" and looked around the room for verification of the orders. Cap Hanson, too, had heard the command, and was turning a violent mauve. But Lancelot Biggs nodded.

"Do as Mr. Cleaver says, Chief."

"—an' when you git done doin' them things," Hank persisted gravely, "I want you should git up steam. An' push for'rd as hard an' as fast as you can. With—" He swallowed hard. "With the auxil'ry use o' that new speed gadget Lootenant Biggs invented."

Garrity almost strangled, but he got the words out.

"Yes . . . sorr!" Then he faded from the plate. Biggs stared at Hank.

"You—you're sure you know what you're doing, Cleaver?"

"I think I do," said Horse-sense Hank. "It's the only thing makes sense. I figgered an' figgered, and it looks to me like there's only one logical way to act. We'll know in a minute if I'm right."

He dug his toe into the carpet, sort of grunted, coughed, glanced at Biggs.

"Got a mite excited about me not bein' married, son. I been thinkin' that over. You mean to say—"

Biggs, looking confused, said,

"But you see, Hank—"

"Yeah. Reckon I do. An' you—an' you—"

"Yes, sir," said Lancelot Biggs.

I stared at Donovan.

I said, "What makes with the brain trust? Double talk?"

He said, "Don't ask me, Buster. I just work here. Or used to. It's even money whether I continue working or learn to play a harp. What with that screwy command your friend Hank gave—"

Then he, and I and everyone in the room stopped speaking. For again there had come, remotely, a different tone-value from the engine room. Hank's orders were being obeyed! And all eyes centered painfully on the visiplate in which, almost blotting the entire frame now, was mirrored the on-rushing planet. . . .

Can I explain my feelings to you? I doubt it. All I can think of is to say that I felt like a very tiny fly on a wall, watching helplessly, wingless, unable to escape, as a gigantic flyswatter smashed down at frightful speed upon me. The *Saturn* was a huge craft, yes, but it was a speck of dry dust compared to the colossal sphere toward which it plunged.

At this velocity there could be but one result to a collision. Death, swift, crushing, horrible, for all of us. A moment, I thought, of incredible pain. A torrent of madness beating at the eardrums, the fires of hell flaming before the eyes—then oblivion.

Nearer came the planet. I could see now that it was as mad and wild as the unspawned negative universe in which it floated. No life. No thin film of atmosphere to blue the sharp definition of its raw terrain. A weird, dead world in a universe that could not be.

I was aware of Donovan at my side, breathing hard. I glanced across the room at Lancelot Biggs. His eyes were strained, the muscles of his jaw white. His lips were half parted. Perhaps it was imagination, but I thought I caught the whisper of a name.

"Diane!"

And then a stranger thing happened. There came a sudden, tender little cry from Helen MacDowell. A flurry of movement. And then she was across the room, was in the arms of Hank Cleaver! And she didn't seem to care that her words carried to all of us.

"You've failed, Hank! But I don't care. I don't care. It's too late to pretend now that I hate you. For I don't. I love you, Hank . . ."

Then everything happened at once. My eyes leaped back from the Helen-Hank tableau to the visiplate, as abruptly there came a crashing explosion from the bowels of the ship. I saw the planet before us now within—it seemed—but inches! There was a high, tortured screaming in my ears. The grind of motors, the pounding of massive drums, a scream ripping from the throat of Hallowell, a muffled curse from Cap Hanson—

Then a horrible, wrenching shock. I felt my body lifting, floating, hurtling across the floor! Something fell sprawling upon me, glass splintered, a dozen voices cried out at once.

And everything was black, and there was a dead and sickly pressure across my body—

—from the center of which came a muffled voice. The voice of Bert Donovan.

"Well, I'll be triple and everlastingly damned to a fare-you-well!"

I kicked, and he wriggled. I kicked again and he moved.

I said, "If you'll get off my head, you damned fool, maybe I can see what's going on!"

He got up. And so did I. All about the control room, men were picking themselves up, lifting their voices in astonishment, staring at a visiplate from which had disappeared that gigantic, threatening orb.

A visiplate in which was now depicted sweet, jet depths of darkness, pin-pricked with glowing points of light!

Cap Hanson's voice was a paean of joy.

"We're home again! Home in our own universe! By God—in our own solar system! For there's Io, the pretty little devil!"

Helen was crying, "Then you didn't fail, Hank! It worked! We're saved!"

And Biggs, only sane man in a roomful of delight-maddened lunatics, was ambling to the audio, face wreathed in a seraphic grin.

"Garrity?" he called down to the chief engineer. "Take a look out the viewpanes if you want to holler with joy. And then—set course for home! And, oh, yes, Garrity—set men to work immediately on the repairing of the temporal deflector."

So that was that. We took time off to recuperate. Some hours later we were standing in the *Saturn* before a large, cylindrical, glass-walled machine, Lancelot Biggs' "time-travel" gadget which had absorbed us up here into the future. That is most of us were still standing here in the *Saturn*.

Professor Hallowell had already been projected back to our

time. So had Travis Tomkins, Midland's observatory expert, his arms loaded with books from the ship's library describing the great inventions of, as on the *Saturn*, the last two centuries—or, to us of 1940, the inventions of the *next* two hundred years.

"Which books," commented Lancelot Biggs wryly, "will do Tomkins a lot of good—I don't think! They won't arrive with him, you know—because in his time they weren't even written! I hope both those fellows will return to their original places on Earth. Rather amazing, wouldn't it be," he chuckled, "if something went wrong with the machine and Hallowell appeared suddenly on the campus of Midland University with some gadget from the future—*his* future-which fell into his pocket in his transit through space and time!"

"Campus?" exclaimed H. Logan MacDowell. "Don't tell me that time-travel thing of yours will actually set us down in our own time!"

"If it doesn't," grinned Lancelot Biggs, "a lot of faces are going to be very red indeed."

He motioned to the second mate, Lt. Dick Todd. Todd set himself at the controls. Then he nodded to the detective.

With unseemly haste the gumshoe scrambled into the time machine.

"Contact!" Biggs ordered.

The second mate pressed the button that sent the snooper back to Midland campus. That lug! I don't think he ever did figure out what it was all about! In fact a week later, when I met him skulking along a corridor, I asked him how he liked his round trip through space.

"I'm trying not to think about it," he groaned. "Confidentially, in another ten days I'll be able to believe it never happened *a*-tall, no sir!"

"Brother," I said to myself, "if imagination was a baby chick, you couldn't scratch yourself out of an eggshell."

But I'm getting ahead of the story. After we got rid of the gumshoe, there was Prexy H. Logan MacDowell to be considered.

"You are next, sir," Lancelot Biggs said courteously. "And a pleasant journey."

"Harrumph!" growled his academic nibs. "This is a damnable outrage!"

Biggs bowed him into the time-traveling contraption.

"I think you've got something there," he grinned—and signalled to Dick Todd. One second later H. Logan was flitting through space back home.

And now it was time for last farewells. But Biggs asked, in gripping Hank's hand, the question I'd been dying to ask myself, but hadn't dared.

"You should tell me, Hank, how you struck on the solution. We may get in a jam like that again, some day. And if we do—"

"Send for me," grinned Hank. "I like this period o' your'n okay, Bud. But you won't get in no more messes like that. Not if you tone down the speed o' that gadget o' your'n, like I told you to.

"My figgerin'? Why, it was just plain, dumb hosslogic, that's all. The tip-off come when we started whiskin' faster an' faster by the moment toward that there planet in our path.

"Y'see, we was in a negative universe. We decided that. But whut we overlooked was the simple, logical fact that in a negative universe all natcheral physical laws ought to operate in reverse!

"Way I see it, we just happened across that planet by accident. An' had we been content to let well enough alone, we'd never have come anywhere near it! It would have shunted us off on its own account!"

I said, "What? How do you figure—"

Biggs exclaimed, "*I* see! In our positive universe, it is axiomatic that all objects attract each other in direct ratio to their masses. But in a *negative* universe—"

"They'd repel each other," nodded Hank. "Right. I guess we was dumb, though. We done the *one* thing we shouldn't have ever done. Put out antigravs and repellor-beams against the upstart planet! Which was the one thing calc'lated to drag us to it! In this backward universe, mathematics an' physics worked in reverse. Antigravitational beams attracted, and propellors repelled!"

Biggs sighed. "And I've always considered myself a logical man! What you did was turn on every available ounce of energy and thrust the *Saturn* at full speed toward the planet, realizing that for every action there is an equal and opposite reaction, and that the planet's terrific repelling force would throw us completely back out of negative space—is that it?"

Hank gazed at him admiringly.

"I reckon," he said softly, "that's about it. But you sure explain it purty . . ."

So why go on? We got into the machine, then. Hank and Helen

and I. And again things began flickering. And at the last minute, I remembered there was something I wanted to ask Biggs, but it was too late then, for there came another moment of giddy spinning, fireworks in my eyes and butterflies in my tummy, and then—

We were back in my apartment. And it was broad daylight, but my radio was still on, as I had left it, and already it was blatting a news item about how Prof. Hallowell had inexplicably returned. There'd be other flashes later, I knew. And a lot of explaining to be done to an unbelieving public . . .

Then I said, "Damn!"

"Yeah?" said Hank. "Why for, Jim?"

"Something I meant to ask Biggs and forgot. But you can tell me, I guess. One thing I never did understand, was why Biggs got so excited when he found out you and Helen were not married. What difference did *that* make? Why did that cause him to show such great confidence that we were going to pull out of our jam?"

Hank flushed. "Well, you see—" he hesitated.

"I don't. But I'm listening."

"Well, it was this way. Soon as Lanse learned me an' Helen wasn't hitched, he couldn't help knowin' everything was gonna be all right. On account of it warn't logical her an' me should git kilt *before* we was married an'—an' had a youngster . . ."

His face was flaming. But I was inexorable.

"I still don't get it. Why not? Why wasn't it logical?"

"Aw, durn, Jim—don't you see? Because Biggs knew that much o' my 'history.' That is, my future, to me, is my *past* to him. He knew who I'd married, and that me an' my wife had a youngster, an' consequently if them things hadn't happened yet, we was bound to live an' make 'em happen!"

So it finally sank in.

I said, "Golly! You're right—as usual! But wasn't it a lucky break that Lancelot Biggs happened to know something about your history, Hank? Your name must be pretty well known to the men of the future—"

Hank writhed in embarrassment.

"Well, now, I wouldn't 'zackly say that, Jim. Lanse knew about me, yes. But then, he'd be likely to. Him an' me bein' related, so to speak—"

"Related!"

"Yeah. Spoke to him 'bout it later. Y'see, Lanse is a sort of grandson o' mine, with a lot o' great-greats on the front of it—" He gulped and looked at Helen miserably. "I—I'm afeared they ain't nothin' we can do 'bout it, Helen. Lanse says you was his great-great-grandmammy!"

And then Helen MacDowell—smiled! And it was the kind of smile I hope to see some time on the lips of a woman looking at me. And she said, very softly,

"There's no sense in fighting fate, is there, Hank? What must be, must be. And there *is* something we can do—to make the future happier . . ."

Aw, hell! I promised Helen she could have him alone in a dark room, didn't I? So I said good-by.

I don't think either of them heard me. In fact, I'm sure of it!

Miracles Made Easy

WHAT I ALWAYS SAY IS, DON'T COUNT YOUR BRIDGES until you've crossed them. After I'd scored that subway accident beat for the dear old *World-News* and finagled a five-hundred-buck bonus, plus my old job back, plus a paid vacation out of the Great Stone Heart who is my boss, I thought everything was going to be pretty.

Henry Mergenthwirker and his lobblies had moved into my apartment, and—except for the fact that both Japheth and Henry were practical jokers—we were getting along fine. We were all having breakfast together one noon when the doorbell rang. I went to the door and stared smack into the homely pan of Bill Maguire.

He was loaded to the gunwales with the paraphernalia of his trade, which is snapping news photos. He said, "Hyah, Len!"

"He's not here," I said. "And we don't want any today. Goom-bye!"

"That doorstop," said Bill, "you're closing the door on is my foot. Think twice before you throw that, pal. I've got the password."

"Lobblies!" said Maguire boldly.

I gulped and stared at him. Or maybe I stared first, then gulped. My heart did a sudden, sickening flip-flop, and I reversed my engines. "C-come in, old chum, old chum! Come on in and have a bit of breakfast! You remember Mr. Mergenthwirker?"

Bill entered, dumping his gadgets on the floor. "Sure," he said cheerfully. "I remember Mr. Moigenthwoiker?" How are you, Hank?"

Mergie flushed, and twiddled his fingers. He was a nervous little twerp, five foot one—or possibly two—inches of concentrated energy. From the top of his sand-colored head to the tips of his 5A shoes he was always on the move; fidgeting, fumbling at imaginary lint on his coat lapels, shuffling from foot to foot.

He said, "Mergenthwirker, Mr. Maguire. *Henry* Mergenthwirker."

"That's what I said," grinned Bill, "Moigenthwoiker *Ah-haaa!*" He jabbed in my ribs with a gleeful elbow "Life in the old boy yet, ain't they, Len? Trot 'em out, palsy; let's have a look at 'em!"

"Them?" I repeated wonderingly.

"Don't worry about me," reassured Bill. "I'm a clam. But I can add. Two and two make four. There's only you two in sight, but there's four coffee cups on the table. Which adds up to—" he winked lasciviously—"dames!"

Mergy gasped and drew himself up to his full height. For the first time in my life, I saw color in the tiny man's cheeks. His tawny eyes sparked indignantly.

"Well, *really!* I'll have you know Mr. Maguire. I'm a clean, Christian gentleman!"

"Sure!" chuckled Maguire. "And Hitler's a shy, retiring artist— *Ouch!* Who flang that!"

Mergy's anger faded. He turned and shook a reproving finger toward what looked to me like a large hunk of ozone at the tableside. "Now Japheth!" he scolded. "How many times must I tell you never to throw things at people? What? Yes, I know he was calling names, but—" He turned to Bill apologetically. "I'm sorry, Mr. Maguire. Japheth promises he won't do it again."

Most of Maguire's cocksureness had oozed out of him when that breakfast bun caught him on the nose. Now he stared at me dazedly and groped for the nearest chair. "Len, who's he talking to? And who heaved that?"

He started again, this time violently, as Henry Mergenthwirker suddenly grasped his shoulder.

"Oh, do be careful, Mr. Maguire! Not in *that* chair! You'll sit on Henry!"

Maguire's lips looked sort of green. He licked them and

demanded in a quavering voice, "H-henry? J-japbeth? Am I nuts, Len, or is he? Who—"

I felt a lot better now, I said. "Mergy, how about asking the boys to leave the room for a few minutes? Apparently Mr. Maguire doesn't know as much as he pretended to when he forced his way in here. I think we should have a little chat."

"All right, Mr. Hawley," said Mergy. He turned once more to stark emptiness. "Japheth . . . Henry . . . you heard what Mr. Hawley said? Now run along and play like good lobblies. We won't be long."

He cocked his head to one side as if listening to an answer, smiled and nodded. Bill and I, both watching. both listening, heard nothing. But suddenly, across the room, the door opened, hung ajar for a few moments—then closed.

Bill shuddered.

He revived somewhat a few minutes later, after I had poured a cup of coffee into him. But he still kept twisting his head around nervously from time to time. Which suited me fine. I lighted a cigarette, pointed it at him accusingly.

"Now, Maguire," I said sternly, "you used the word 'lobblies' to get in here. What did you mean by that?"

All the starch had wilted out of Bill's spinal column now. He was meekly supplicative.

"To tell you the truth, Len—I don't know. I ain't what you might call one of them mental whizzers. But like I said before, I can add two and two. Which I done—and come up with a funny answer.

"Such as this, for instance"—he ticked his mental arithmetic off on acid-browned fingers—"a couple weeks ago you was plain old Len Hawley of the *News*. Meaning no offense, you wasn't no world-beater—just a commonplace guy, no better and no worse than any.

"Then all of a sudden, one day this Moigenthwoiker, here—"

"Mergenthwirker!" said Henry.

"This Moigenthwoiker comes and visits you, and all of a sudden you start acting queer. You ask questions about a hammer-killing which ain't even happened while you're asking. Then a couple of days later you call the turn on that First National holdup, and the *World-News* scores a beat on it because you was Johnny-on-the-spot. Just like last week again, when you and Moigenthwoiker and me covered the Eighth Avenue subway smashup.

"All of them times this little guy was mixed up in it. And the other day I heard him saying something about a couple of 'lobblies'. So I figure you and him got something good, and I want in on it. Only now I'm more confused than before. What I want to know is—what are *lobblies?*"

"Why, Henry and Japheth!" said Mr. Mergenthwirker promptly.

"I guessed that," nodded Maguire. "But what are Henry and Japheth?"

"Why, they're lobblies!" Mergy told him triumphantly.

By the glassiness in Bill's eyes I could tell he was getting nowhere fast. "Wait a minute, Mergy," I said. "Let me handle this."

I had been thinking swiftly. Now I decided Maguire wouldn't be a bad guy to let in on our little secret. He was just dumb enough to keep his yap shut, and just smart enough to be useful. And it stood to reason that from time to time we'd be needing the services of a photographer. Maguire was one of the best in town.

"It's this way, Bill," I explained. "Mr. Mergenthwirker has a very unusual—er—gift. He is accompanied everywhere he goes by two invisible companions—"

"Excuse me, Mr. Hawley," interrupted Mergy stubbornly. "Henry and Japheth are *not* invisible!"

"By two companions," I amended, "invisible to anyone but himself. They are creatures known as 'lobblies'. Their names are Japheth and Henry."

"The little one is named after me," said Mergy proudly.

"And they have the amazing ability," I continued, "to predict unerringly what is going to happen in the future."

"Holy Ike!" gasped Bill. "So that's how—"

I nodded. "Exactly. For perfectly obvious reasons, Mergy and I do not wish to share this knowledge with the whole world. He has had these—er—companions for years. But it never occurred to him that they were of inestimable value until he met me. Then I pointed out—"

"Don't tell me!" babbled Bill. "I know! They could make us all rich! Stinking rich! All they have to do is tell us which nag is going to romp home at Sarasota . . . which ball club will win the pennant . . . which stocks are going to rise . . . what number to play in the daily drawing—" He stopped abruptly. "Len, you're kidding."

Mergy twidgeted excitedly. "No, he's not. It's the truth, Mr. Maguire."

"But they can't nobody tell what's going to happen in the future," said Bill. "Nobody!"

"Henry and Japheth can," Mergy assured him. "Wait! I'll prove it. Oh, boys!" He raised his voice. Immediately the door swung open. Though I had known about and lived with the lobblies for almost two months, now, it still gave me the creepy-crawlies to witness that mute testimony of their presence.

"Boys, Mr. Maguire, here, doesn't believe you can tell what is going to happen in the future. Will you prove— What did you say, Henry? Oh, you knew he was to doubt your ability. You prepared a proof? Under your plate?"

He turned to us shyly. "Henry has already written us a note describing exactly what was to take place in this room this morning. It is under his plate."

Bill and I dived for it at the same time. It was a folded sheet of notepaper, covered with neat, precise script. I read it aloud. It was painstakingly, you might almost say photographically, accurate. It even anticipated the look on Maguire's face at this moment.

"You see?" said Mr. Mergenthwirker. "They can!"

"Wait a minute!" yelled Bill. "Maybe they can tell the future about some things. But they pulled a boner here! Look at this, Hawley! It says: 'At exactly 12:43 o'clock, Mr. Maguire will be given the hotfoot.' Well, that's what it is now, and I ain't been given no—*Ooowww!*"

His protest ended in a howl of pain. Like a whirling dervish he went dancing around the room on one foot, roaring and scorching his fingers as he tried to jerk the burning matchstick from between the instep and sole of his shoe. I glanced at my watch. It was exactly 12:43 o'clock.

"Henry!" Mr. Mergenthwirker was wailing like a grieved parent. "Japheth! Was that a nice thing to do to our guest?"

After things had quieted down, I set the proposition bluntly before Maguire. "We'll cut you in on the gravy-train," I told him, "if you'll play ball. Which means keeping a lock on your lips. We've got something in the lobblies, so long as the world isn't in on it.

"Otherwise we'll be pestered to death with scientists and doctors trying to find out where they came from and what makes them tick. Maybe the government will take them over as a defense measure, even. Well?"

"A little while ago," said Bill, "I told you I was a clam. I was wrong. Clams are talkative compared to me."

"Then that's settled," I said. "Now, the first thing we must do is—"

"Oh, my golly!"

"What's wrong?"

"The first thing we got to do," gasped Maguire, "is grab a taxicab to Baker Field. I clean forgot; me and you's supposed to cover the Columbia-State football game today!"

"What!" I snorted. "But I'm on vacation!"

"The boss said an outing would be good for you. He also said your vacation would be a million years long if you didn't do it."

Mr. Mergenthwirker coughed gently. "I think it would be very nice, Mr. Hawley. It should be a close game. And I'm sure Henry and Japheth would enjoy it very much. Wouldn't you, boys?"

Bill snapped his fingers. "And listen—what's wrong with us makin' a little pocket money while we're at it? Moigy, ask the boys who's going to win. We'll make a few bets."

"Why, that's a marvelous idea! Henry, you heard Mr. Maguire. Do you know who's going to win the game?" He listened for a moment, then turned to us beaming. "Henry says of course he knows. They both know."

"Well, which?"

"Which, Henry? Mr. Hawley wants to know— What did you say? You don't believe in—not in favor of— Oh!"

We stared at him anxiously as his face fell.

"What is it?" I demanded.

Mr. Mergenthwirker turned troubled eyes to us. "Henry says," he relayed, "that he and Japheth don't believe in gambling. They say it would only encourage us to bad habits if they told us the result."

Bill Maguire moaned. "I knew it! I knew there was a hitch in it somewhere. Moigy, where are them lobblies? Let me at 'em!"

I grabbed him as he started cocking fists at empty air. "But, Mergy," I wailed, "won't they help us at all? I have a story to write. Tell them it will help me a lot."

Again Mergy listened. This time he smiled.

"Japheth says," he transmitted, "that he and Henry are very fond of you. You were nice to them while I was in the hospital, therefore he will give you a couple of hints. But you must figure the rest out for yourself."

"That's swell," I said hoarsely. "Just a couple of hints like what color the winning team will be wearing—"

"Japheth says to tell you," Mergy went on, "that there will be only three touchdowns in the final score. And the winning team will be the team which has the greatest number of men on the field. And now"—the little man smiled beatifically—"shall we go to the game?"

* * *

We went. We had to go. All the way out to Columbia's stadium, Bill Maguire expressed his opinion of lobblies in no uncertain terms.

"Most men on the field!" he growled. "Them lobblies is nuts! It don't even make sense!"

I had been thinking it over. Now I said, "I think it does make sense, Bill. I'll show you what they meant in just a few minutes."

I showed him as soon as we were seated. We arrived a few minutes late, but the game had just started. I pointed to the players' benches on either side of the field.

"That's what Japheth meant. The number of players on each squad. State only brought about twenty-five men down here to this game; the Lions have forty-five men in uniform. So Columbia will win the game."

"But all them guys ain't on the field!"

"No, but most of them will he. As replacements," I told him. "Furthermore, properly speaking, everything below us is part of the 'field'. Japheth didn't mean the gridiron only. Bill, you know where to lay a few bets?"

"Yes, but—"

"Then go make some. I'll take a hundred for myself. Mergy? You want some?"

"I'll take ten, Mr. Hawley."

"And I'll take," snorted Maguire, "nothing! You're off your button, Len. Maybe the Lions have got the most men. But State is the favorite. They got an all-America end—"

"And we've got," I told him serenely, "lobblies! I'm so sure Japheth is right that I've got half a notion to 'phone my lead in to the office right now, and then sit back and enjoy the game!"

I didn't go quite that far. But at the end of the third quarter, the Lions tallied the touchdown that made the score Columbia 13, State 7. That was enough for me. I stood up. "That settles it," I said. "The lobblies had the right dope. They said three touchdowns and that's the third. I'm going to shoot the score in to the office."

"Don't look now," said Maguire moodily, "but there's fifteen minutes left to play. Moigy, stop that!"

"I'm sorry, Mr. Maguire. I didn't do any—Japheth! You mustn't throw peanut shells down Mr. Maguire's neck! Oh, is that it?" Mergy smiled shamefacedly. "He says he'll stop when you stop criticizing him and Henry."

"Be back in a minute," I said, and left them.

New York, as you know, goes football-crazy in autumn. It's a cold sellout for the paper that hits the street first with the scores. So it would be a feather in my shako to steal the march on the boys.

"Columbia wins," I reported, "13 to 7. There's your screamer, Joe. I'll bring in the play-by-play directly."

Joe Foster said, "Columbia, 13-7, right! Game over so soon, Len? Hell, I thought—"

"See you later," I said hastily and hung up. The booth from which I had called was under the stands. On my way back up the ramp, I heard a terrific burst of noise.

I hurried to see what was going on. It *was* a sight. Some nutsack —a Barleycorned fan in a tweed suit and battered derby—had lurched out onto the field to do his bit for dear old Columbia. He wasn't a student: he was just an over-charged rooter. But there he was in the Lions' lineup, spitting on his hands, crouching.

It didn't last long. A couple of cops came out and hauled him away. The officials rallied the players into the game again. They were sort of messed up and confused; I saw the Columbia captain squawking about something. But finally they got straightened out, and the game went on from there.

But *how* it went on!

State gained a yard on a line buck. But then came the blow-off! On the next play, State risked a desperation measure—heaved a fourth-down forward. And it worked! All the way to Columbia's twelve-yard line.

After that, things happened so swiftly that I can't tell it right. All I know is that within seconds, Columbia stopped being the kingpin in the ball game. The stands went wild. State went wild. The lobblies predictions went hogwild! State shoved the ball across the goal line, kicked the precious point—and the score was State 14, Columbia 13.

What I should have done, I suppose, was charge back to the telephone and call Joe Foster. But somehow that never occurred to me. All I could think of was my hundred smackers, and that I had to see Mergenthwirker & Co.—but quick!

That's where I wasted time. Because the stands were jammed with standing rooters; it was all I could do to force my way back to the section where I had left the others. When I finally got there, Mergy was gone. Maguire was waiting for me, his jowls as limp as a pair of plush curtains.

"Wh-where are they?" I howled.

"They went," said Bill, "a couple of minutes ago. The lobblies got tired watching. They said it wasn't no fun when they knew what was going to happen."

"They *knew!*" I yammered. "Then they deliberately lied to me! I guess they thought they were being funny. So their little joke cost me one hundred bones!"

"A hundred," corrected Bill, "and fifty. You was so sure that I hiked the ante a little for myself. Only I made the bet in your name, on account of I'm broke."

I think I would have wrung his neck right then, only that I suddenly remembered what I should have done before. I gasped.

"Great cow! And the *World-News* is going out with a phoney result! Come on, Bill! Quick!"

We had to climb over backs and shoulders to get down to the telephone booth again. The game must have been thrilling; I wouldn't know about that. I didn't care. No matter who won or lost, now, the score I had phoned it would be wrong. I had to change it.

I dialed Joe Foster so fast it made my fingers spin. "Joe" I hollered. "About that State-Columbia game! I wanted to tell you—"

"That you, Len? Say, hurry in here with your play-by-play, will you? I want to get it into the second edition."

My heart sank.

"Th-the *second?*" I echoed haggardly.

"Yep! The sporting extra is already rolling. It'll be on the streets in three minutes. Hey, Len? Len?"

I hung up, turned to Bill.

"I don't know what you're going to do," I said, "but I'm going out and get very, very drunk!"

The rest of the evening is very fuzzy in my memory. I dimly remember developing a Charley-horse in my right knee from lifting it to so many brass-rails. I also recall sobbing on Bill Maguire's shoulder and assuring him that he was the "beshfrennamaneverhad!" I remember singing in close harmony with a bartender and his identical twin; that was somewhat confusing inasmuch as they were two separate people with only one voice.

Then I seem to recollect a slight altercation with a man in a blue uniform who said, "Shure, an' I'll l'arn ye to call Patrick O'Reilly an Eye-talian spy!" After which I went for a long, dizzying ride in a closed car with a siren.

I don't remember anything more until the next morning, when I woke to find myself in the hoosegow with a dusty-carpet taste in my mouth. A policeman was prodding me. He said, "You been tried and fined, now your fine's been paid. Beat it! There's a little man waitin' for you outside who's a better friend than a good-for-nothin' drunk like you deserves!"

So of course it was Mergy. One look at him and the whole sad story came back to me. I closed my eyes.

"Go 'way!" I bade him feebly. "Disappear like your lobblies! I never want to lay eyes on you again!"

Mr. Mergenthwirker looked startled.

"Oh, gracious me, Mr. Hawley" he said. "I had no idea you were so upset. You must come right home and have a hot cup of coffee. Japheth and Henry told me you were down here, so I came right away."

"Japheth!" I spat. "Henry! Don't ever mention them to me again! After what they did to me. Lost me a hundred and fifty dollars . . . probably cost me my job."

"I—I'm afraid I don't understand, Mr. Hawley?"

"The game, stupid," I moaned. "They said *Columbia* would win."

"But, Columbia *did* win!" said Mr. Mergenthwirker. "That last State touchdown didn't count. Oh, goodness, no! It wasn't legal you know. The referee made a mistake. He admitted he got confused when that—er—intoxicated gentleman ran out on the field. He allowed the State team *five* downs instead of four. And after the game, State refused to accept their illegal touchdown, so the score reverted to the earlier count." He smiled pleasedly. "Henry says he thinks it was very sporting of the State team."

I stared at him aghast. "Then—then I was *right?*"

"You were the only sportswriter at the game," said Mergy, "who was right. All the others printed the erroneous score in their papers. Your boss called up this morning to congratulate you. He said it was a very fine piece of reporting, and he's going to see that you get a bonus for it."

"That's swell," I muttered dazedly. "Swell!" Then the double-take struck me. "Reporting! What reporting? I didn't turn in any story!"

Mergy smiled shyly. "I know. But I did, Mr. Hawley. I wrote the whole story and signed your name to it. You see, Henry and Japheth explained what was going to happen."

"In Uffish Thought"

> *'And as he stood in uffish thought*
> *The Jabberwock, with eyes of flame,*
> *Came wiffling through the tulgy wood*
> *And burbled as it came."*

    I've never been threatened by a Jabberwock, but like all the writers I have spent many hours in uffish thought.
    "All writers?" you ask. But of course! John Steinbeck acknowledged this as his source of inspiration when he titled a novel Uf Mice and Men, Somerset Maugham when he penned Uf Human Bondage . . . and surely you have both read and viewed L. Frank Baum's classic fantasy, The Wizard Uf Oz.
    Uffish thought produces uncommon results. In the pages hereafter you will encounter characters with personalities quite unlike those of your everyday acquaintance. They think strange thoughts and do unlikely things. But that is to be expected. For they have stood longtime in uffish thought, and their adventures are such stuff as dreams are made uf.

The Amazing Invention of Wilberforce Weems

WILBERFORCE TOOK ONE LAST, LINGERING, HOPELESS look at the page before him, then resolutely closed the book over a pudgy forefinger. He shut his eyes; knit his brows. Doggedly he began to repeat the text.

"Although repossession values are included in the total Used Car Department gross loss, they should *not* be included when ascertaining the cause of the—the—"

The furrows deepened. The tight web of tiny, white lines about his eyes relaxed. His fingers twitched, and the book slipped open . . . just the tiniest bit. Wilberforce opened one eye . . . just the tiniest bit. Then, blushing, he hurried on, "The total loss directly applicable to Buying, Reconditioning and Selling of used cars. The income—"

From the adjacent room rose a familiar squall.

"*Unkie!*"

Wilberforce's straining memory faltered, stalled, and ground to a four-wheel stop. He sighed. He answered.

"Yes, Herbie?"

"I wanna dinka water, Unkie!"

Wilberforce said patiently, "You just *had* a drink of water, Herbie. Now, go to sleep. It's getting late."

"I wanna *nother* dinka water!" insisted the plaintive voice.

Wilberforce glanced at the clock as he rose wearily. Had anyone told him, three hours ago, that within the space of one hundred and eighty short minutes a man could grow to abhor the sound of a single word, Wilberforce would have laughed in derision. But not now. For between the hours of seven-thirty and ten-thirty, he had learned to loathe and despise one word. The word which meant himself. "Unkie!" As emitted at regular intervals by the four year old towhead in the adjoining room.

Wilberforce filled the glass in the bathroom, letting the water run for a minute to "get cold." Then he walked into the nursery; snapped on the light. Herbie was standing up in his crib, wide awake as he had been when Wilberforce had undressed him and put him to bed three hours ago.

"Here's your water, Herbie!" said Wilberforce. "Now, I want you to go right to sleep!" He hoped his voice sounded acceptably stern and avuncular. This was the first time he had ever "watched house" for his sister and brother-in-law. And he meant it to be the last.

Herbie said, "Fank you, Unkie!" in a meek voice. He took a sparrowlike sip of water; handed back the glass. Then he smiled disarmingly. "Tell me a story, Unkie?"

Wilberforce said, "No! It's 'way past your bedtime. What will Mama and Papa say if they come home and find you're still awake? Goodnight."

He went out and turned off the light. He listened outside the door for a moment, hoping to hear a small body lie down. He didn't. With forebodings of trouble yet to come, he returned to his studies.

Wilberforce Weems was an automobile salesman. He was not a particularly good one. He knew the selling points of his product. That it had Quintri-Coil Springing, Y-Membered Frame, 93 H.P. Savo-Gas Master Engine with Rifle-Geared Lubrication. He knew it had Streak-Lined Hunter Body Frame, with Crashproof Glass and Multiple-Center-Steering-Control, but—

He couldn't tell it! For despite his long legs, athletes' body, lanky handsomeness—Wilberforce was dreadfully shy!

Every time he got a prospect into a demonstrator, he froze in sudden panic. Embarrassment may have had something to do with it, for Wilberforce always had trouble getting into a car. Especially, a coupe, in which he had to push the Adjusto-Seat-Slide all the way back before he could even squeeze under the wheel. By the time he got the car in motion, Wilberforce had forgotten all the selling points be had ever learned. He forgot to point out the great improvement of the Flood-Wash Lubrication system over the old-fashioned Duplex-Splatter. He forgot to draw the customer's attention to the Permatone finish of the dashboard. He forget—well, he forgot everything, and just sat there stuttering and stammering like a vociferous blimp!

The Company had a remedy for that situation. They provided their salesmen with manuals which had only to be memorized. But Wilberforce had been studying his manual, now, for more than two months. And was getting nowhere with it—fast! He had hoped that tonight, alone in his sister's home, he might be able to memorize the section dealing with Used Car Trade-in Allowances, but—

"Unkie!"

Wilberforce groaned. There it was again! The reason he was making no headway. The reason why, tomorrow, old Sour-Puss Petersen would call him on the carpet and give him his walking papers!

But he said, "Yes, Herbie?"

"I wanna go to the bathroom!"

Wilberforce called impatiently, "Now, Herbie, that's not necessary. You—"

Then he stopped, suddenly remembering the number of times Herbie had demanded a "dinka water." He said,

"Very well. But then I want you to go right to sleep, do you understand?"

"Yes, Unkie." Meekly.

The trip was safely negotiated. Herbie was tucked in for the tenth or twelfth time—Wilberforce had lost count—and again there was quiet. Wilberforce began again,

"Although repossession values are included—"

"Unkie!"

Wilberforce groaned. His fingers tightened on the book in a spasm of despair. He yelled, "Yes, yes! *Now* what do you want?"

"You fordot to give me my medicine!" prompted young Herbie.

Wilberforce, a broken man, appeared at the doorway. He glared down at his nephew.

"Medicine?" he said. "What kind of medicine?"

"For my tummy," said Herbie. "An' for my head, an' for my footses, an' for my—"

"Oh, all right!" choked Wilberforce. "I'll give it to you. Be quiet!"

He went into the bathroom and opened the cabinet.

A gleaming array of bottles confronted him. Some were liquid, some were powder, some were powdery-liquid. He stared bewilderedly at this galaxy of nostrums. It never occurred to him to doubt Herbie's need of bedtime medicines. This was Wilberforce's first experience as a child-nurse; and he didn't know the depths of infant strategy.

He pawed over the panaceas. He found one labeled, "Headache," and ladled out the proper child dosage. He took down the one marked, "Stomach pains," and poured the proper amount in a glass. There was one for the feet, and one—

"Aaah!" said Wilberforce. He poured into the glass a generous dose from a bottle labeled, "Slocum's Syrup for Sleepless Souls."

Wilberforce was not a doctor. He was an automobile salesman and not a very good one, at that. His methods were—well, unorthodox, to say the least. He poured all of the liquids into the same glass. He dissolved in them the two or three powders that seemed necessary. He added a touch of glycerine to make the potion smooth; and a little cherry cough-syrup to lend it flavor. He carried the glass to Herbie.

"Here!" he said.

Herbie looked at the glass dubiously. He had not bargained for this. He said, feebly. "I—I feel all right, now, Unkie. I—"

"Drink it!" said Wilberforce, his patience exhausted. "Drink it, or by golly, I'll—"

Herbie drank. Two mouthfuls. Then he gasped. His eyes bulged. His little body jerked. He said, "Oo-wah!"

Wilberforce said, "How do you feel now?" He put the glass of medicine on the night table; picked up the text-book from which he had been studying; prepared to go back to the other room.

"Oo-wah!" said Herbie. His little eyes had a glassy look. Wilberforce got worried. Herbie choked. He began to turn a brilliant pink. . . .

"Hey!" shouted Wilberforce. He reached out to touch Herbie. He still had the book in his hand, and in his haste he hit Herbie's forehead with it. Not exactly hard, but not exactly easy, either. Herbie bounced down on the cot. His breath came in sobbing gulps.

Wilberforce went into a panic. He yelled, "Herbie, Unkie didn't mean it! Are you all right? Are you—"

Then the spasm passed, and Herbie sat bolt upright in bed. He said, plainly, distinctly, "Unkie!"
"Yes, Herbie?"
"Although repossession values are included in the total Used Car Department gross loss, they should *not* be included when ascertaining the cause of the total loss directly applicable to Buying, Reconditioning and Selling of used cars. The income of Reserve Credits from—"

Wilberforce started! Word for word, the infant was repeating the text which *he* had been struggling to memorize all evening. He gulped,

"Herbie—where did you learn that?"

"—if you will assume," continued Herbie placidly, "a standard quota evaluation equal and equivalent to the past year's rationalization value on stock turnover—"

Wilberforce knew what that passage was. It was the section on Overhead Computations, which so far he had not had time to study! He looked at Herbie; then at the book in his hand. A sudden thought struck him. He said,"Herbie, wait!"

He rushed downstairs; pawed wildly through the bookcase. He was looking for something light; something a child *should* read. He found a copy of "Alice in Wonderland." He raced upstairs with it. Gently this time, he raised the book; tapped it against Herbie's forehead. Then, fearfully, he said,

"Herbie—recite 'Jabberwocky'!"

Obediently, the child began,

> " ' 'Twas brillig, and the slithy toves,
> Did gyre and gimble in the wabe,
> All mimsy were the borogroves,
> And the mome raths—' "

"Stop!" cried Wilberforce. "I—I mean, that will do, Herbie. *Ohhhh!*"

He tottered. His wild hunch was right. Somehow—through some strange, unsuspected chemistry, his admixturing of medicines had brought about this fantastic result. Knowledge, transferable by the simple application of any book to the forehead!

Herbie suddenly yawned. He said, "Unkie, I fink go to sleep now—" and forthwith proceeded to do so. Wilberforce looked at him lying there for a moment, leaned over and felt his pulse. It was normal. As a matter of fact, everything was normal, now, about Herbie except—except—

Then Wilberforce Weems' eyes lighted. He came to a great resolve. He picked up the glass from the night table, tilted back his head, and took three *great, big swallows!*

The doorbell rang. Wilberforce put the glass down hastily, guiltily, and ran down to answer it. He hadn't expected Myra and Sam home this soon—

But it wasn't Myra and Sam! It was none other than Old Sourpuss—Josiah B. Petersen himself! Wilberforce's boss. And his face was a thundercloud. He seemed about to explode with righteous wrath. He shook his fist in Wilberforce's face.

"So here you are, you young rapscallion! They told me I'd find you here! Well—"

Wilberforce gulped uneasily. He said,

"Wo-won't you come in?"

Petersen stamped in, muttering heavily. He reopened the attack as soon as they reached the living room.

"I suppose you realize, Weems, that it's an exceptional thing that brings me out of my house at this hour of the night. Well, it may interest you to know that I've just been talking over the telephone to—*Mr. Townsend!*"

He shot the name at Wilberforce. Wilberforce winced. He said, weakly, "M-Mr. Townsend?"

"You heard me! Wilberforce Weems, do you know that this afternoon you almost cost our company a profit amounting to fourteen thousands of dollars? By your sheer ignorance and inability to sell the best car on the market. Mr. Townsend is the buyer for the Green-and-Gold Taxicab Company. He was all ready to order our Deluxe Omnibus model until you—you—"

He spluttered and choked. Wilberforce said, "I—I'm sorry, Mr. Petersen. I—"

"Sorry! Why, confound you! You ought to be sorry. Had I not called Townsend up by chance, and learned what had happened—" The boss finally lost his temper entirely. He grabbed a book off the living room table. "But that's not the reason I came here tonight. I came to tell you not to come in tomorrow morning. You're through! Done! Washed up! Fired!"

And with the last word, as a mark of emphasis, he shied the volume at Wilberforce. Wilberforce ducked—but not in time. The book hit him a glancing blow over the temple, shooting a galaxy of stars before his eyes, momentarily stunning him. Then he came out of it. And when he came out of it, be was a new man. A voice, strangely like his own voice, but deeper, more resonant, more assured, cried out,

"Just a moment, Sourpuss!"

Petersen, halfway to the door, wheeled, shocked. His face turned crimson.

"What? What did you call me?"

Something stronger than himself impelled Wilberforce forward. He stopped, finally, with his jutting jaw mere inches from Petersen's frightened face. His voice was the roar of an enraged lion.

"I called you 'Sourpuss'—because that's just what you are! Why, you insignificant little squirt, I ought to put you across my knee and spank you—"

Wilberforce made a lunge for Petersen. But the boss squealed and dove for the safety of an armchair. Wilberforce stopped.

"On second thought," he mused aloud, "I won't bother you after all. You're not worth it. Anyone who is so stupid as to not recognize my superior intelligence, my sterling character, my deep potentialities—"

"Stupid!" squawked Petersen. "What do you mean? *I'm* stupid?"

"Of course, you dope!" roared Wilberforce. "Why else would you have me—*me*—" he repeated loudly, "working as a common, ordinary, everyday *salesman*. When, by all rights, I should be at least sales manager—and maybe even a vice-president of the company!"

Petersen's sense of humor overcome his judgment. He emitted a snort of derision.

"You a vice-president!" he chortled. "Or even sales manager! Why, you don't even know the sales quota expectancy in our region and zone. How could *you*—"

Wilberforce said, "Oh, is that so! Well, just wait here a minute!"

He ducked into an adjoining room; searched feverishly through his sales portfolio. Finally he found what he was looking for. A *precis* of automobile sales in the United States for the period embracing 1920–1939. He grabbed the book; tapped it lightly against his forehead. Instantly things began to swirl before his eyes, but when the moment of vertigo had passed—

"See here, Sourpuss!" he yelled, stalking back to confront Petersen. *"You're* the stupid one! You can't even take advantage of the figures when you know them. Now, last year our company sold 687 cars in this area. Year before that, it was 713. Our total sales represent oh-point-two per cent of the total sales throughout the country. But the year we increased our newspaper advertising by seven-point-four per cent, our sales increased nineteen-point-four-four! In other words, just because you're too miserly, and too much of a skinflint to spend a little money on advertising—"

Petersen's mouth dropped open. He gulped,

"W-weems—how did you know all that?"

Wilberforce said airily, "It's my business to know such things. You've been making a mistake, Sourpuss. I'm not just a salesman—I'm exceptionally gifted at organization."

Petersen's head bobbed. He said, weakly, "I—I am beginning to think you're right, Wilberforce. Perhaps I have misjudged you—"

Just then there was a sound at the door, and Sam and Myra came in. They stared at Wilberforce, then at Petersen. Wilberforce's brother-in-law said, "Hyah, folks!"

"Myra," said Wilberforce mechanically, "Sam—I want you to meet my employer, Mr. Petersen."

"Glad to know you, pal," said Sam. Then, curiously, "What's up, Willie? You gettin' the can tied to—"

"Samuel!" interrupted Myra. She smiled, meanwhile planting a French heel on her husband's instep. "Well, we'll be running along upstairs, Wilberforce. Was Herbie a good boy tonight?"

Wilberforce said, vaguely, "Oh, yes. Quite good."

He waited until their footsteps had reached the top of the stairwell. Then, to Petersen,

"So you're coming around, eh, Sourpuss?"

"*Don't* call me Sourpuss!" snapped Petersen irately. "I—I'm not sure about you yet, Wilberforce. There's something awfully fishy about the way you're acting. I don't—"

Wilberforce smiled complacently. He said, "Now, look here, Petersen, I'm beginning to get tired of this stalling. I don't like people to underestimate my abilities. I'm a well educated man. Oh, maybe I didn't have much schooling, in a formal way, but—"

He strode to the bookcase.

"Just as an example, choose any subject you can think of. I'll show you why I am so unusual."

Petersen said suspiciously, "Well—all right. But no tricks, now. Let's see. How about—er—*Drosophila?*"

Wilberforce said, "Dro—" then stopped. He had been about to ask how to spell it. Already Petersen was staring at him dubiously. He said, "Oh, yes! You shouldn't *mutter* your words like that, Chief. Dro—here we are! Now you look it up in the Encyclopedia while I—"

He took the DEN-EFI volume from the bookcase. As he did so, he contrived to stumble slightly. The book jounced up and bumped his forehead. Again there was a moment of giddiness; a fresh, flooding rush of new knowledge. . . .

"Did you hurt yourself?" cried Petersen.

"No. Nothing at all," smiled Wilberforce. "Now, you were asking about *Drosophila?* Well, let me see. The *Drosophila* is a genus containing the common fruit fly, *Drosophila melanogaster*, used extensively in breeding experiments to study inheritance of characteristics and the mechanism of heredity. FitzLawrence O'Hara discovered in 1874—"

"Amazing!" cried Petersen. "Astounding! Incomprehensible! My dear boy, you have a memory that is nothing short of incredible! Do you realize that you were repeating the Encyclopedia *word for word?* Why, you must have literally pored over this to—"

Wilberforce smiled.

"It's nothing, really," he said coyly. "I—well, just absorbed it, that's all!"

"And to think," continued Petersen, "I've been holding back a man of your genius in the sales force! Wilberforce, I apologize for all the mean things I've ever said to you. In the morning, when you come in, I shall attempt to prove I mean it—" He smiled companionably. "You will find your name newly printed—on the door of the office next to mine!"

"That's fine," said Wilberforce heartily. "Goodnight, Sou—I mean, Mr. Petersen!"

Petersen left. Wilberforce picked up the book which Petersen had thrown at him, and which had remained, ever since, lying on the floor. As he did so he noted with approval, its title. *"Wake Up and Assert Yourself!"*

He was feeling quite pleased with himself when he went upstairs. And why not? But he felt somewhat less pleased a few minutes later when both Sam and Myra confronted him. Sam was holding the now-empty glass in which Wilberforce had mixed his curious concoction. Myra was staring at him wrathily.

"And what," she demanded, hands on her hips, "might this have been?"

Wilberforce tried to smile. It came out sour. He stammered, "W-what happened to the rest of it?"

"Unfortunately," stormed Sam, "we both tasted to see what hideous mixture you were forcing on our child! What sort of an uncle are you, Wilberforce, to give a wee tot a draught like this? Why, I ought to—"

He stepped forward angrily. Wilberforce retreated. He said, "Sam—Myra—Look, it's all right—"

"All right!" stormed Myra. "Why, you might have killed him! Look how soundly he's sleeping. I don't know what you mixed into this—" She sniffed the concoction suspiciously. "—but it smells awful!"

Wilberforce said, "Myra—you know the trouble you've always had memorizing recipes?"

"Yes. But what has *that* to do with—"

"Just a minute!" Wilberforce ducked out of the room. He returned with the Homemaker's Recipe Guide; strode to his sister's side and tapped the book gently against her forehead. She cried out in sudden fright; reeled dizzily. Wilberforce steadied her. Sam yelled, "Why, you brute! Attacking Myra, my wife!" and made a lunge for Wilberforce. Myra rallied out of the fog. She demanded, "What's the big idea! What do you mean by hitting me with that cook-book!"

"Myra," stammered Wilberforce, "How would you go about making a *bouillabaisse New Orléans?*"

Myra said promptly, "Why, you take ½ cup of oil, 2 chopped onions, 1½ pounds of haddock, 1½ pounds of cod, 2 slices of lemon, one boiled lobster—"

Sam stared. He said, dazedly, "Myra!"

There was a look of amazed elation in Myra's eyes. She said excitedly, "Sam—I've just remembered the recipe for Boiled Cider Pie! You take ⅓ cup of rich, boiled cider, a teaspoon of butter, ⅓ cup of grated maple sugar, 2 eggs, ½ cup of seeded raisins—"

Sam stammered, "W-what does this mean?"

"Nothing," said Wilberforce complacently, "except that we three—and little Herbie—now have it within our power to become the world's most intelligent people. Sam, you've always been interested in astronomy, haven't you?"

"Y-yes. But I never could memorize—"

"You can now." Wilberforce produced the second volume he had brought from the bookcase. It was "Star Secrets," by Professor J. Climpton Flubb, R.R.G. He tapped it against Sam's forehead. Sam staggered. Then—

"What are the names," demanded Wilberforce, "of the satellites of Saturn?"

Mechanically, Sam began, "Why, anybody knows that. Mimas, Enceladus, Tethys, Dione, Rhea, Titan—"

"Hah!" said Wilberforce.

The eyes of his sister and brother-in-law were great as saucers. They stared at him mutely. Finally Sam ventured, "The—the medicine, Wilberforce?"

Wilberforce nodded. "My own invention," he boasted. "It heightens the receptivity of the mind. You can memorize anything you want to, merely by tapping printed matter against your forehead. It immediately transfers its learning to you."

A sound from the crib turned them all. Little Herbie had awakened, and was rubbing his eyes sleepily. He said,

"Morning, Mama an' Papa. Morning, Unkie."

"It's not morning, honey," said Myra. "Go to sleep."

"I wanna dinka water," protested Herbie.

Myra lifted him; carried him out of the room. Sam turned to Wilberforce.

"Wilby," he said in hallowed tones, "it looks like you've hit the jackpot! Will this work on anyone?"

Wilberforce started, "I believe so. It—" Then a cry from the other room stopped him. Myra came racing back to confront her husband angrily. Her voice was quivering with rage.

"Samuel, you—you unspeakable brute! How often have I told you to stop buying those sexy humor magazines? You should be ashamed of yourself! Now, see what you've done—"

Sam said, "But, I didn't do anything, honey? What—"

"He stumbled!" sobbed Myra. "And bumped his head on one of your nasty old magazines—"

Little Herbie appeared in the doorway. He was smiling cherubically. He was saying, "Papa, did you hear the one about the traveling salesman who had to stay overnight on a farm—"

The next morning, Wilberforce woke with a dull headache. For a moment, the mad experiences of last night seemed like the fantasy of a nightmare—then he remembered everything that had happened; the angry recriminations of Sam and Myra, the way they had finally soothed little Herbie to sleep after permitting him to tell three perfectly awful stories; the way Sam had acted after he had tapped himself on the pate with a copy of *Mein Kampfe* and expressed a determination to *drang nach Osten* into their next door neighbor's house; Myra's insistence that the two men allow her to prepare them a full-course dinner at that unrighteous hour of the morning. It was only a brilliant inspiration on Wilberforce's part that had permitted any sleep at all. Surreptitiously, be had tapped Myra, Sam and himself with a copy of the popular ballad, "Ain't

Ya Kinda Drowsy, Dear?"—which had acted as a soporific on all of them.

He didn't feel up to another session with his relatives, so he stole away from the house, had a bit of breakfast in town, then went to the office. There he found factual evidence that last night had not been sheer fantasy. He found workmen busily engaged in painting, on the glass pane of the office next to Old Sour—Mr. Petersen's—his name. To his unbiased eye, the legend, "Wilberforce Weems, General Manager," looked very, very good.

Josiah Petersen rubbed his hands gleefully as Wilberforce entered.

"Well, good morning, Wilberforce," he said genially. "Let's get right down to work! The first thing I want you to consider is the question of our new advertising appropriation. What newspapers and magazines do you recommend?"

Wilberforce said, "Why—er—uh—"

Petersen frowned.

"Well, speak up, man! You appeared to have sterling ideas on the subject last night!"

"Er—let me get my notebook," said Wilberforce. "I never—er—move hastily, or without consulting my notes."

He lumbered from the room; went into the outer office. There he pawed hastily through a desk for a copy of *Standard Rate & Data*. It was a bulky volume. He lifted it; punched it smartly against his forehead. Through the familiar moment of reeling inequilibrium he heard the secretary's astonished voice crying, "Why, Mr. Weems!" But be didn't bother answering. He had the information he wanted. He returned to Petersen's sanctum.

"I would suggest," he said, with perfect assurance, pretending to read from his small pocket notebook, "the *Star*, because of its urban coverage; the *Times-Call*, because of its low milline rate; the *Borough News*, because of its rural readers; the *Gazette*—"

Petersen smiled broadly.

"Remarkable!" he said. "Wonderful! Just the papers *I* had decided on, after a long study of the question. My decision appears to be justified, Wilberforce." He stretched out an eager hand. "May I see your notebook? It is marvelous to think that a man who, yesterday, was a common salesman has kept such careful notes—"

Wilberforce backed away hastily. He said,

"If—if you don't mind, Mr. Petersen, there are lots of things in here which are rather—"

Petersen smiled again.

"I understand, Wilberforce. Private, eh? Very well, I respect your privacy. And now, about our Used Car problem?"

After all, Wilberforce had absorbed the entire sales manual the night before. They talked for an hour, at the end of which time, Petersen said,

"Oh, by the way, Wilberforce, I enjoyed meeting your relatives last night. I'd like to know them better. Perhaps if I could come out to dinner some time—say, tonight—"

Wilberforce froze. He thought, suddenly, of Sam's devouring of *Mein Kampfe*, of little Herbie's prattled bawdy jokes. He stammered, "But, Mr. Petersen—"

"Tut-tut, son! I'm used to taking pot luck. We'll call it a date, then. About seven-thirty?"

Wilberforce nodded miserably. He said, "Yes sir!"

He didn't work well the rest of the day. Fortunately, little was expected of him, since his new private office was in the process of being renovated. He amused himself—tried to rid himself of the thought of impending disaster, rather—by strolling over to the public library.

He strolled moodily down the long lanes of books, brushing up on knowledge that heretofore he had always considered too deep for him. He started out by catching up on the latest fiction, but stopped after the first two or three volumes, feeling faintly sick at the stomach. He made a stab at *"Gone With the Wind,"* but only managed to absorb the first thousand pages with his first wallop, and didn't feel that the rest of it was worth the effort. Since he had previously tapped himself with *"Vanity Fair,"* he felt he was just running over the same ground for the second time.

He had a good time, however, with the *World Year Book*, some encyclopediae, and a folio of back issues of the *Readers' Digest*. At last, feeling sufficiently well informed on news, he searched out the answer to a problem which had been bothering him considerably. He had to literally beat his forehead black and blue with musty tomes—but ultimately he got it.

Then, with a thoughtful expression, he soothed his troubled feelings with a few anthologies of poetry. Later he managed, with the aid of a musical score, to comprehend for the first time the depth and scope of a Wagnerian opera.

But eventually he had to turn his steps homeward. He had telephoned Myra and informed her of Petersen's impending visit. The news sent her into ecstasies. She immediately set about preparing an elaborate dinner . . . though she did advise Wilberforce, somewhat wanly, that Sam had not gone to work.

"He's out at Locarno racetrack," she said. "He spent all morning hitting himself with old form sheets. Now he says he has a system."

"And little Herbie?" asked Wilberforce.

"Inventing a space-ship," said Myra disconsolately. "He fell out of his crib this morning onto a pile of Sam's old copies of *Fantastic Adventures!*"

So Wilberforce went home, still apprehensive but hopeful that the recent acquisition of a science-fiction background might have driven from little Herbie's mind the story he had related with such gusto last night. The one about the Republican who met an old maid on the golf course. . . .

At dinner, Petersen appeared to be charmed with Wilberforce's relatives. Everything had gone off smoothly since his arrival. Little Herbie, temporarily diverted with an innocent copy of "Buster Bunny and the Magic Turnip" behaved perfectly. Sam, who had, miraculously hit the daily double, paying $673 on a $2 ticket, was in rare good humor. Myra's satisfaction with her elaborate banquet expressed itself in a glowing smile.

Dinner ended, and the two men repaired to the living room for cigars and conversation. Since Myra wished to keep a watchful eye on the maid's handling of her best china, wee Herbie was sent in with the men. Contentedly puffing on his cigar, Petersen congratulated Wilberforce.

"It's an inspiration to me," he said, "to see a man whose home life is really contented. There's nothing I like better, especially in these parlous times—"

Trouble struck. "That reminds me," interrupted the voice of little Herbie. "Did I tell you the one about—?"

"*Herbie!*" said Wilberforce and Sam in one breath.

"Tut-tut!" reproved Petersen. "Let the child have his say. Never curb youth. I don't believe in—"

Sam's jaw jutted strangely. A lock of hair tumbled down over his forehead, and Wilberforce remembered with a burst of horror, Sam's reading *Mein Kampfe*. Sam rose; stood belligerently confronting Petersen.

"*You* don't believe!" he roared harshly. "And who might *you* be to tell me how to raise my own child?"

"Now, Sam—" interpolated Wilberforce weakly.

"Silence!" bellowed Sam. He wheeled on the pop-eyed businessman. "You—you individualist! Your mind is tuned to the false ideology of democratic principles. The hour is near when we will force the world to recognize the virtues of the dominant races! The Aryans will arise! The spawn of the Mediterranean will be liquidated—"

Petersen stared. He stammered, "I—I don't understand—"

"Hello, hello, everybody!" chirruped a voice from the doorway. Wilberforce turned—and gasped. It was Myra. And she clutched, in dainty fingers, a current copy of the *Sane Health* magazine. "Haven't we all been silly this evening? Sitting around like this, when every sane and normal person realizes that *nudism* is the only intelligent cult?" And as Wilberforce stared, helpless, she began to slip out of her gown!

Petersen turned crimson. He bellowed. "Have you all gone mad? Wilberforce, what does this mean!"

"—the Republican," piped little Herbie, "said, 'If you ask me, sister, Roosevelt's going to have us—' "

"The time will come," barked Sam, "when the totalitarian states will assume their rightful place—"

"—nothing shameful," continued Myra blithely, "in a beautiful body, shamelessly exposed to the sun—"

"Stop it!" roared Petersen. "Stop it, I say! This is too much! Wilberforce, I take it all back. You're fired! How I was ever deluded into believing—"

Wilberforce felt sick. Suddenly, swiftly, completely sick. He groaned and pressed his hands to his head. It felt as though a thousand demons were somewhere inside, pounding at it with a thousand tiny, red hammers. He struggled desperately to speak. He choked out, "I—I—"

Then suddenly he realized he was talking to silence. He forced back his own weakness; stared at his relatives. Like himself, all of them were pressing fevered hands to their foreheads. Sam was groaning. Little Herbie had begun to cry. Myra, with a little bleat of embarrassment, had picked up her discarded evening gown and was racing to another room.

Little Herbie stopped crying. He said, "Papa, I wanna dinka water."

Sam said, in a normal, quiet tone of parental resignation, "All right, sonny. Come with Papa." And they left the room.

"Wilberforce's face sagged with chagrin. His voice was tremulous. He said, "Mr. Petersen, I hope you're not offended—"

But, amazingly, Petersen was smiling.

"Tut-tut, Wilberforce. It was so unexpected, that I didn't realize you were just kidding me at first. But I have as keen a sense of humor as the next man." He chuckled. "I declare, your family is delightful. That brother of yours sure can take off Hitler, can't he? And your sister—didn't she make those nudist enthusiasts look like idiots?"

He bellowed his amusement.

"And that youngster," choked Petersen, "is a little whiz! Of course, I don't approve of teaching innocent children such jokes, but—Hah!—I'll have to remember that one about the Republican—"

Then he stopped chuckling; eyed Wilberforce with approbation.

"Yes, Wilberforce, I'm more than ever pleased with you. You combine good business sense with a gift for providing pleasure. Now, when we take up that matter of dividends with the Board tomorrow—I suppose you have your views on the question?"

Wilberforce shook his head. He knew where he could study up on the matter. In the Organization Stock Reports in the office. But just now—

"I—I'm afraid I don't know much about it, Chief."

Petersen looked pleased.

"I'm glad to hear you say that, Wilberforce," he said. "I was beginning to fear you were a little bit of a showoff. The way you always had figures at your fingertips. There's always opportunity for a man to learn, my boy."

"Yes, sir," said Wilberforce humbly.

Petersen chuckled and rose.

"It's been a pleasant evening, Wilberforce. Now I must be going. If I could have my hat and coat—" And at the door he waggled a finger admonishingly. "See you at eight, my boy. I expect my General Manager to always be on time!"

After he had left, genial and patting Wilberforce on the back not once but many times, Wilberforce groped his way upstairs. He found Sam staring at the collection of bottles in the bathroom. Sam said dully, "I—I've lost my knowledge, Wilby."

"I know. We all have."

"But why?"

Wilberforce strained to remember. He said, "I tried to learn the reason today, in the library. It's all pretty vague now. But it has something to do with the conversion of electricity and thought.

"You see, some scientists believe thought is only a hyperelectrical phenomenon. And even when thoughts are put in print, they retain the electric pattern that generated them.

"When we read, we absorb some of this electrical pattern through the senses. It stimulates the brain and creates new thought-patterns in our minds."

"And—and the drink you invented?"

"All I can figure," confessed Wilberforce, "is that somehow my mixture heightened the chemical receptivity of the brain, so that the *touch* sense, rather than the visual or auditory, was sufficient to describe a new thought-pattern on the brain. Frankly, I don't know. But if I can ever get back that ability, I'll study and learn why . . . and how. . . ."

He pushed Sam aside. He began to lift bottles from the cabinet. He descended to the basement.

"Make way for a genius!" said Wilberforce Weems.

Brother Michel

THE REAL PRESS CLUB IN MANHATTAN IS NOT BEHIND that sober brownstone front and shining brass plate you pass on 42nd Street. That's just a front maintained by the boys to impress the general public and visiting firemen with their respectability. The *real* Press Club is up one block and two to the right and down a short flight of steps to a green-curtained spa which calls itself simply, *Al's Place.*

That's where the gentlemen of the working press congregate. Don't make the mistake of going there hoping to make the acquaintance of some word-slinger whose byline is familiar to you. You won't be welcomed. If you're not escorted by one of the boys in the know, a roar of disapproval will greet your entrance. And even if you're thick-skinned enough to ignore that concerted "Get out!", you'll discover when you place your order at the bar that Al is fresh out of whatever brand of alcoholic refreshment you call for.

Al's Place is strictly for shareholders in the Fourth Estate. No laymen, sob-sisters, long-hairs, or persons who call themselves "journalists" are solicited. Al is loyal to the newspaper men. He maintains for them a strictly private establishment; the true, unofficial Press Club. And they, appreciatively, maintain Al in a style to which a thousand less fortunate barmen would like to become accustomed.

We were sitting there one night, giving this cockeyed world the good old double-oh, taking busman's holiday as newsmen will, discussing beats we'd made and missed in our daily tussle with Old Man Deadline. Pinky Crockett of the *Intelligencer* was in reminiscent mood.

"My favorite story of all time," he said, "is the one about the cub who—"

"I'm empty again," interrupted Bud Callison of the *Blade*. "Who'll have another of the same? All around? Al!"

"The cub who was sent to Harlan, Kentucky," persisted Pinky, "during the coal strike—"

"You see what Peg said this morning?" asked Jerry Travers, the *Clarion* city man. "He gave John L. fits for that defense tie-up in Indiana. Damn good thing, too."

"This cub," continued Crockett doggedly, "got a rush of words to the brain and started shoving mellerdrammer over the wire to his city editor. You know how cubs write, anyhow. Perpetual emotion. He started off something like, 'God sits brooding tonight on a little hill overlooking Harlan—'"

Ordinarily Pinky would have been allowed to finish his story, ancient as it was. But tonight he was in disgrace. We were giving him the quick-freeze treatment for having yesterday failed to cover for a buddy who was suddenly taken drunk.

Phil Grogan of the *Times-Star* yawned ostentatiously. "Yeah, we know. So the C.E. wired back, 'The hell with Harlan; interview God!' Put these on my chit, Al. Okay, boys—down the hatch!"

Crockett gave up and swallowed his drink in contrite silence. I guess we all felt a little bit sorry for him, then, because conversation languished until Grayson took the ball: He said thoughtfully, "That was a typical cub boner. But you know, I think I can almost understand how that kid felt when he started filing his epic. There are some stories that are just too damn big to play down. They seem to scream for dramatic presentation. Of course, you can't write them that way, so you don't write them at all. And the world loses a story that might—mind I say *might*—be of tremendous importance."

We looked at him in some astonishment. Grayson was just three days in by clipper from Lisbon, which haven of safety he had reached just one hop-skip-and-jump ahead of a bunch of Gestapolecats who wanted most desperately to create an international incident with Grayson as the *cause celebré.*

Grayson's stories out of the Low Countries, then out of *blitzed* Paris and occupied France were Pulitzer Award stuff, but they hadn't endeared him to the Reich official news fabricators. They were harsh and cold and brutal and devastatingly revealing. Grayson wrote that way. Thus it was astounding to hear him defend a dramatic style of presentation. Callison shook his head. "A gag, Grayson?" he ventured. "I don't get it."

"It's no gag," said Grayson soberly, "it's the God's honest truth." He wrapped his long fingers around his highball glass, stared at, through, and beyond us. "Once—" he said, "perhaps only once in a newspaperman's career, he stumbles upon the perfect story. The story that has everything. Plot, incident, drama, and—more important than all these things—significance. When such a story comes, it should be written as befits its importance. And yet—"

He paused. Travers said, "You're holding out, Grayson. Have you found such a story? Then why the hell don't you write it, man? Use any style you damn well please. Write it in Choctaw or Sanscrit if it's that good."

"It's better," said Grayson simply, "but I won't write it. There's no use. Because, you see, no paper would print it. There are limits to what the public will believe. A story like this—"

I said, "But you can tell us, can't you, Grayson? Off the record, if you like."

He smiled wanly. "Off or on, Len, it doesn't make any difference. It still wouldn't be believed. But I *would* like to tell you. If you'd be interested—"

"We're all," I told him, "agog."

"Well," he said, "after Paris I went to Tours . . ."

After Paris he went to Tours. That was not so easy as it sounded. Only two hundred and forty kilos separated the two cities. A month ago it was possible to negotiate the distance in a trifle over three hours. That was before the grim, clanking line of mechanized Nazi soldiery scythed the frightened populace out of its homes and onto the narrow roadways of France. Now the four hundred mile stretch of road between Paris and Bordeaux was packed solidly with a sluggish stream of refugees. Dazed little people, hurt children of a toppling empire who did not yet clearly understand what had happened. Whose only urge was to keep moving, ever south, away from the pain and noise and confusion that had uprooted them.

Grayson was the last of the American newsmen to leave Paris. He could have gone almost a week before with Ted Downs of the INS, or a couple of days ago with Reynolds, but had turned down both offers of a lift. Some said Paris was to be conceded without a struggle, but there were counter-rumors that not so easily would the pleasure capital of the world be taken. Grayson conceived it his duty as a newspaperman to be on hand if something should happen. Until Billy Wallace of Universal talked turkey to him.

"You're getting out of here, Stu—but fast! It's only a matter of days, hours maybe, before the Germans march in. It's all right for a few dopes like me to stick around. Our noses are clean. But Herr Goebbels has your name written on his black list in capital letters. If they come in and find you here, it's going to be just too bad!"

Grayson said, "I'm sticking. They won't dare touch me. I'm an accredited press man from a neutral country—"

"So was Webb," pointed out Wallace. "But they got him. And in London, of all places. You can't tell *me* he just up and fell off that platform. He had cat-eyes. Now, look, chum—I've got a Baby Austin downstairs I've been saving to get buried in. It's no good to me, 'cause when the Nazis get here they're going to empty the town of petrol. But it has a full tank now. So you hop in it, point your nose south—then follow your nose like a bat out of hell!"

So now Stu Grayson was in Tours. But already Tours was not the place where he should be. For the Nazi bombers had come with the monotonous regularity of passenger trains at home—every hour on the hour—and dropped their flame-spewing, death-dealing visiting cards on the ancient city.

The government had fled again; this time to Bordeaux. The news correspondents had followed them, and all France, it seemed, clogged the southward road.

There was only one thing for Grayson to do. Keep moving. Of the details of his flight he was never afterwards certain. There are certain boundaries of horror beyond which the human mind refuses to take cognizance. Later, Grayson discovered that upon his mind's retina had been imprinted sights and scenes that at the time of their occurrence made no impression on him.

The strafing of civilian-packed highways by swastika-marked pursuit planes which swooped down upon the roads, machine guns chattering leaden death into the defenseless fugitives. The sprawling, grotesque bodies in their wake. The scores upon endless scores of derelict motor vehicles abandoned by the roadside as the way grew longer and the petrol supplies shorter. The faces of the fugitives. ("Their faces," said Grayson. "At night I see their faces and their eyes. Not wracked with pain or fear or anger, but blank with bewilderment. They were numb with the shock of their betrayal.")

Grayson never reached Bordeaux. He was in Angoulême when the incredible rumor filtered through the fugitive column that the Renaud cabinet had resigned; that in Petain's withered hands now rested the fate and future of France. An uglier rumor came concurrently. There was talk of a separate peace. The bistro attendant from whom Grayson heard these things discounted his own words.

"So one hears without authority, m'sieu," he said cautiously. "But surely it cannot be of the truth. Petain of Verdun would never surrender to *les Boches.*"

But the rumor was verified, sickeningly, the next day. The octogenarian Marshal was no longer the same Petain whose *On ne passe pas* had emblazoned a watchword of valor and defiance into French history a quarter century before. His humble capitulation, his call to the French soldiers to lay down their arms, his plea to the Reich for an armistice were the last, crushing humiliation to an already spiritless people.

Grayson heard the news with a sense of quickening fear. Billy Wallace's warning now assumed new meaning. His name *was* on the Gestapo black list. If, as most assuredly they would, the Nazis occupied France or most of it, in the resultant upheaval and confusion the disappearance of one small American news correspondent would pass almost unnoticed.

It was madness to continue into Bordeaux. His only chance of safety lay in flight to Spain, or—Grayson snapped his fingers—or better still, Marseille. He had friends in Marseille. Also if there were an occupation of that *Provencal* port it would probably be by the junior partners of the Axis. And the Italians were disposed to be friendly to Americans; particularly American newspapermen.

So Grayson shifted his course southeastward through Brive and Figeac, following secondary highways to expose himself as infrequently as possible to curious local officials. Past Rodez and Le Vigan, where it was easier to get gas but harder to get information. Then down the Rhone valley into St. Remy and Salon. It was there he met Frère Michel.

He reached Salon in the dark of night, a phrase that was particularly apt since the town was, like every other in stricken France, swaddled beneath the mantle of a complete blackout. Grayson could not help thinking that this total absence of light represented Marianna's mourning. Yet the blackout was more than mere symbolism; it was stark necessity as well. For although there was a well-confirmed rumor that Petain had already met the new Attila with the operabouffé moustache in the historic railway car at Compeigne and signed armistice terms, the cessation of hostilities was yet a night, a day, and another night in the offing.

This was a small but typical indication of the victor's vindictiveness. The vanquished had been ordered to lay down their arms immediately, yet still the planes of the conquerors swarmed over all of France bombing, burning, destroying, in the hectic last hours of pseudo-truce. Particularly was this true in southern France where, the waspish Morannes having been grounded, the Italian airmen were free to make a final, braggart display of their prowess.

So Grayson reached Salon in the dead of night, winding cautiously into the village through groves fragrant of olive and almond, past a dim-jutting wall built twenty centuries before by legionnaires whose fasces had been surmounted with the emblem SPQR.

He was nearly into the village proper when overhead he heard the high, thrumming drone of motors. Then the spiralling scream of falling death, then before him—so near that his tires rocked crazily on the shuddering earth, and the steering wheel struggled against his grip—the darkness bursting suddenly asunder in a pillar of crimson flame.

Instinctively Grayson stepped on the brakes. He had no fear of night bombing. He had for it, rather, the contempt of long familiarity. His only recognizable emotions were anger at thus being hindered in his flight and a fierce scorn for such an obvious and useless exhibition of terrorism on the part of the Italian airforce. He knew, as they must also know, that the lazy village of Salon concealed no military objectives more important than the ancient, ravaged fortifications of the 15th Century. The canal of Craponne was a mere irrigation ditch.

But furious or not, he was under fire. And dangerously so. He heard cries before him, and the jet streets were illuminated with a blaze that etched his surroundings in stark relief. Beside him loomed a massive, Gothic building. Its ramparts of staunch stone offered refuge. He abandoned his car and raced for the wall, seeking an entrance.

He could find none. He felt his way blindly, helplessly, along the wall as the motors droned overhead, as the bombing increased in fury and the whole village trembled beneath thudding shocks.

Then suddenly, startlingly, there was a quiet voice calling to him.

"*Messire! Viens-tu, messire!*"

The call came from a shadowy figure in an arched niche. Grayson lurched gratefully toward the gateway.

"Thanks, friend," he panted. "Tony's really making things hot, no? Where's the shelter?"

"*Tu es ung Anglaise?*" His accoster seemed faintly surprised. "*A bas, messire.*"

He led the way through a short, walled corridor, down a stone staircase mildewed with age, into a slab-lined cell so closely joined that it seemed to have been hewn of solid rock. Grayson heaved a sigh of relief. This was more than safety; it was sanctuary. When his companion closed the huge metal door behind them, engulfing silence stifled even the pounding reverberations of the holocaust above.

Some inner chamber of Grayson's consciousness had recognized an abnormality about the *Provencal* stranger with whom he was now closeted. But in the haste and excitement of their meeting his mind had not found time to analyze his reaction. Now the man spoke again.

"*Dictes-moy—*" he said softly, "Tell me, my son, whence comest thou?"

And Grayson knew what it was that had struck him as unusual. The stranger not only addressed him in the familiar *tu* form, but he spoke in a *patois* so awkward and heavy as to seem almost archaic.

It was not the typical tongue of the district. Grayson had spent so much time in the Midi and was familiar with the strong, resonant accent of the *Provencalese*, the heavy vowels and rolling r's. This was more like—Grayson strained for recognition that eluded him—more like the French *patois* spoken by the Canucks of New Brunswick and Nova Scotia. An antique French derived from the tone of Ronsard and Villon.

He was thankful, now, for his many salmon killing trips to the Gaspé. He answered slowly, choosing his words with care. "From Paris. I was on my way to Marseille, whence I hope to find a ship to England. My name is Grayson. Stuart Grayson."

His companion lighted, now, a stub of candle, placed it in a shallow wall sconce. By its guttering flare Grayson saw an older man, sturdily built, whose heavy beard was faintly salted with gray. A man lofty of brow and deep of eye, garmented in a long black robe that might be either a cassock or a scholar's grown. That, thought Grayson, explained his use of the familiar "thee." Priests customarily used it, as did masters addressing their pupils.

The older man nodded quietly. "I am called," he said, "Michel. Michel de—"

He gave the place name of a small cathedral town in northern France. But Grayson was only half listening. He was glancing curiously about the chamber in which they stood. "*Ou sommes-nous, m'sieu?* Where are we? This is no new bomb shelter."

"No, my son, we are in the vault below the church of St. Laurent."

"Below?" Grayson studied his surroundings with new understanding. "Then these are—"

"The crypts, yes. The birds of death spew flame and violence above us, but here we are safe in the company of the imperishable dead. I, myself," said the old man, "shall some time rest here. Yea, shall and in thy day, do."

His words, thought Grayson, were vague and more than a little confusing. But recent events had addled the brains of men more important than this small town monk or sage. So he didn't press the question. He asked instead, "How long do you think this will last? I must get away from here tonight to make Marseille by morning. Tomorrow's probably the last day I'll be able to get out of the country. Before the Fascists march in."

The old man shook his head. "You can judge better of that than I, my son. I cannot say. But—" A curious eagerness lighted his eyes. "But you spoke of Paris. What has happened there? Why do you flee?"

Grayson answered shortly, "Don't tell me you haven't heard? Paris has fallen. France has surrendered. Tomorrow she becomes an occupied country like Poland and Norway and the rest. But you must know these things. Where have you been, anyway?"

"I have been—" The old man hesitated, "—traveling, my son. I am but newly come here. What you tell me is unexpected. So France bleeds again! Will she never find peace?"

"Not while there's a Hitler," said Grayson grimly. "Or a Nazi party." A long pent anger burst within him. "The tragedy is we should have seen this coming long ago. The handwriting was on the wall if we'd only had sense enough to read it. The sects and creeds that sprang up in post-war Germany. The Neo-paganism trend. We thought it was an escape valve. Actually it was the forging of a new national philosophy that despised death, gold, honor—everything but the domination of the world."

His companion studied him appraisingly. "Thus it was, my son?"

"That's how it was," said Grayson bitterly. "I was as blind as the rest of them. Yet it's supposed to be my job to see things coming. I'm a newspaperman."

"And your country, England, is also in this war?"

"England is, yes. But that's not my country. I'm an American," Grayson told him.

"I see. An American writer. I, too, am a writer, my son. A—a poet, of sorts. Perhaps you know my verses?"

Grayson shook his head. "I'm afraid—"

The old man sighed. "I had hoped my work might be familiar to you. It is a history. A history in verse. Each new day, each new journey, adds another chapter. That which you have just told me is worthy of a stanza—

"En germanie," he said, "naistront diverse sectes S'approchant fort de l'heureux paganisme . . ."

> *"In Germany will spring up different sects,*
> *Closely approaching a careless paganism . . .*
> *A new sect of philosophers*
> *Despising death, gold, honor, and riches—"*

It was, thought Grayson, pretty lousy verse. Not only that, but it was in damn bad taste. Years hence, when this was all over and men could look back upon what was now happening with a detached analytical view, there would be histories of the period. But they would not, he felt sure, be poorly rhymed histories written in a jumbled, archaic *patois* by a dingy *maitre*—for so by now Grayson had decided his companion to be—from an obscure village.

Still, you couldn't tell a man who had befriended you and possibly saved your life that his verse was bad and he was half cracked. Grayson turned toward the door, opened it. "It's quiet, now. They must have gone. Shall we go up?"

"As you wish, my son. But tell me first—this Hitler you spoke of? Has he gained many followers?"

"Too many. His own countrymen, the Italians; even the newspapers thought for a while he was a good thing for Germany. He was restoring a nation in chaos, they said. He had admirers here and in England. They saw the National Socialistic state as a buffer between the democracies and Soviet Russia, But when the chips went down they discovered that Socialism and Nazism were one and the same. The democracies were caught in the middle. Well—"

They had reached the great arched gateway by now. The bombers had gone, leaving part of the little town ablaze behind them. The streets of Salon were a wild confusion, but Grayson felt that was an advantage to him rather than a hindrance. He held out his hand.

"Well, goodbye, sir. And thank you for your help."

"Go thou in peace, my son," said the old man.

And Grayson turned to the spot where he had left his car. Only to pull up with a cry. The Austin no longer existed save as a heap of twisted metal. A crater yawned in the street where it had stood; fused at the bottom of the crater lay the ruins of the vehicle be had hoped would bear him to safety.

His cry brought Michel to his shoulder. "What is it?"

"My car," choked Grayson. "Smashed to smithereens. I doubt if there's another one in town. I wouldn't dare look for it anyway. And if I'm not in Marseille by morning—"

It was at that moment, in midsentence, that the sun and Grayson's world collided. Stars roared hurtling to earth in a crash of tumultuous thunder. He was aware of a dreadful concussion plucking him from his feet, tossing him bodily back through the arch into the corridor beyond . . . of the taste of hot salt blood in his mouth and pain that lanced his body with agony . . . then a crushing earth, and darkness surging up to meet him . . .

Grayson said, "Al—" Al, who had been listening from behind the bar, started violently. "Set 'em up, Al. Same thing all around."

Al said, "Yessir, right away, Mr. Grayson."

Phil Grogan said, "Wait a minute, Stu. This round's on me."

"Me," corrected Grayson. "I owe you all one for having listened to me thus far. I'm sorry I ever started. It's a whacky story. And it gets even whackier."

"Put it away," said Grogan. "Your money's no good in this joint."

Grayson shrugged. "Well, O.K. But you see, now, what I meant when I said this was a story no newspaper could print. I'm convinced that it's the greatest, most important, most significant thing that ever happened to me, and possibly that ever happened to any living soul. But I can't prove it. Because, you see, I was injured in the delayed explosion of that time bomb.

"You—I suppose you know how I got to Lisbon?"

"By boat," said Callison. "Wasn't it by boat?"

"That's what I told them," said Grayson, "to explain my presence there. But I don't know. I don't *think* so, but I honestly don't know.

"After I'd been there a few days and come to my senses a bit, I covered the waterfront like a bloodhound looking for some skipper who remembered having had me as a passenger. I found none. Still, that doesn't signify, for ships were constantly shuttling in and out of Portugal in those hectic days.

"So here starts the hair-thin line, on the one side of which lies fact, and the other side fancy. Perhaps what I am about to tell you really happened to me. I think it did. On the other hand, you must remember that I was injured and possibly delirious. The while thing may have been a wild fantasy, born of the night and the crypt and the horror and the strange old sage who spoke in a Villonesque *patois*."

"Suppose," I suggested, "you get on with the story?"

"Well—" said Grayson . . .

Grayson's wakening was like the rising of a diver from a dark, swirling depth into a weirdly unfamiliar world. It was not that he suffered bodily pain. By some miracle he had escaped all injury except a few bruises. But the fierce, close explosion of the delayed bomb had dealt his nervous system a violent blow. It was shell-shock, though he didn't know it then. He didn't know anything at the time of his awakening. Not his name, nor where he was, nor what he was doing here, or above all who might be the bearded stranger bending over him.

He pushed himself up on one elbow and moaned as a myriad of tiny cogs in his brain seemed to shriek rebellion at the movement. "Where am I?" he asked.

"Peace, my son," his companion soothed him gently. "You are safe now."

Wisps of recollection seeped back upon Grayson. A once-heard name eluded him. He grasped at it . . . caught it. "You are—Father Michel."

"*Brother* Michel, my son," corrected the old man. "Now rest, and be still. All will be well soon."

"And this is the crypt," murmured Grayson. "No, it is not the crypt!" His eyes widened as he scanned his surroundings. They were neither on the open streets of Salon nor the underground refuge where they had taken temporary shelter. They were in what seemed to be a sort of metal cubicle. The interior of their room or conveyance—Grayson could not tell which, though a faint, almost imperceptible swaying motion led him to believe it was the latter—was Spartan in its simplicity. Only on one wall were set several levers and a dial, the purpose of which Grayson could not remotely hazard.

"No, we are no longer in the crypt," said Frère Michel.

"Then, where—?" asked Grayson confusedly.

Brother Michel's voice was calm and his hands were deft as they moved the levers on the forward wall. "It was needful that you be brought away, my son. You were hurt and in danger. Only thus could I bear thee to a friendlier spot." His brows contracted into a mild frown. "I had not meant that any save myself should ever look upon this conveyance. But surely it cannot be of harm if one single time I concern myself in affairs that are to be. And who knows but it was thus planned, by He who ordains all?"

His meaning was obscure, his actions even more so. And it pained Grayson to try to concentrate. His thought processes were thick and sluggish, as though stifled beneath a comforter of down. He did not understand. Never during that weird voyage did he clearly understand what was transpiring about him. It was as though he drifted in a febrile dream peopled with strange sights and scenes.

Brother Michel was speaking again, but Grayson heard his words only fitfully. "Let us go up the stream a little way, my friend. I would learn what is to come of that which we have seen. Shortly I shall return thee to thy proper place."

He tugged yet another of the intricately wrought levers, and it seemed to Grayson that the floor beneath him shuddered for a moment in impatient flight. Then;

"This should be—far enough," said Brother Michel. "Let us see what now transpires."

What window or portal he opened, Grayson could not say. But where had been shadowy darkness, now warm sunlight flooded the chamber, and it seemed they looked down upon the fields of France from towering heights. ("It was as though," said Grayson, "we were in a plane. But it wasn't that. Even in my dazed condition I'm sure I would have recognized the drone of airplane motors.

And besides, did you ever know a plane to stop and hover over a single spot, motionless? That's what we did.")

So they looked down upon the fields of France. But these were not the lazy, quiet fields through which Grayson had driven in his pellmell flight from Paris. This *champs* was abustle with activity. Widespread upon the great plain, so far as the eye could see, were massed men and troops and armament. Westward lay the rolling sea. Ships lay in the harbor; grim, gaunt dogs of war. Armed barges lined the beach. A clouded instinct for news stirred Grayson. Forgetting to be astonished that so swiftly could the occupation of France have been accomplished, he cried, "Invasion! They're preparing for an invasion of Britain!"

The old man shook his head, smiling sagely. "Nay, my son. That attempt I saw thwarted while you slept. Not yet shall England admit a foe. Look again at the banners of the warriors."

And Grayson, looking again, saw that he had indeed misjudged the nationality of those assembled on the seacoast plain. Their uniforms were not the gray-green of the Nazi troops. There were blue uniforms and khaki, olive, and even plaid. And Grayson marked at different points throughout the camp banners he recognized. The tricolor of France; the St. George's cross of England. The flags of Poland and Norway and Belgium, the Netherlands and tiny Portugal.

He turned to his companion confusedly. "But I don't understand. This is an army of the Allies—on French soil! But France has fallen. And the English were driven out at Dunkirk."

"Time passes swiftly, my son," said Brother Michel, "and with its passage many changes are wrought. Hear! Even now the bugle sounds! The army of exiled and vanquished sets forth to reclaim its own. Let us see what shall come of it."

As suddenly as light had blossomed in the small conveyance, it faded. Once again they were walled in foursquare metal. There was that sensation of flight. Then Brother Michel's pronouncement.

"This should be Rome—shortly hence."

And where he had seen below him the army of the Allies Grayson found himself looking down upon the Seven Hills of the ancient city. But it was a fearful scene upon which he gazed. A scene of flame and ruin, fire and death and desolation. Sky-searing tongues of flame swept avenues that once charmed a world with their beauty. Great craters yawned where had stood milestones of a glorious elder culture. The charred, abandoned hulk of one once magnificent edifice brought a cry of horror to Grayson's lips.

"The Heart of Rome! Even this great capital destroyed!"

Said Frère Michel. "Even so, my son. Thus ends the folly of the second pretentious Caesar.

"Romaine pouvoir," he said, as though committing a verse to mind aganist some future setting down, *"sera de tout a bas . . .*

> *"Roman power will be completely brought low*
> *O Great Rome, thy ruin approaches,*
> *Not only of thy walls but of thy blood*
> *and substance . . ."*

It was then that something of Grayson's dull-witted acceptance slipped from him. His slow mind began to comprehend that which he had seen, and a great, incredulous wonder gripped him. He turned to his companion feverishly.

"What magic is this Frère Michel? Where are we? What are we doing? How are we seeing these things? These events cannot be!" He pounded his temples as an effort toward coherent thought drove bright hammers of pain through him. Logic supplied but one answer. "Am I—" he demanded fearfully, "Am I insane?"

Frère Michel turned, smiling gently. "Peace, my son, you are not insane. You are but tired and ill. Rest, now, and in a moment more I shall leave you in a haven of safety."

He touched Grayson's brow and the touch of his hand was soothing. Grayson's panic left him. He slept then, and perhaps in slumber found healing, for when he wakened again his mind was clearer and he heard the words of his companion without confusion.

"We have come, my friend."

Grayson roused himself. "Come? Come where?"

"To the land of the Lusitains. We are on the outskirts of Lisbon. You will find the city without trouble."

Grayson stumbled to his feet. It was as his companion had said. "But—but how did we get here?"

"Through the highway of that which is to be, we have returned to the now," said the old man strangely. "Go now, my son, in peace. And if you will, tell they who tremble and are afraid of that which you have seen. Bid them be of good heart, confident that liberty and justice shall not yet pass. For I, Michel of the tribe of Isaachar, have seen so and now so tell you. Perhaps if you seek in some hidden place you may find written that which I have yet to write. Look for it, my son. It will open to you many doorways of hidden knowledge. And now, farewell!"

He stepped back into the curious metal cage which for a time had borne them both. Then suddenly it and he were gone. A great weakness and a nausea overcame Grayson. He did not remember walking into the city . . .

Grayson stopped. "Well," he said. "That's all. That's the story."

There was a faint half smile upon his lips, but in his eyes a sort of eagerness, a sort of wistful desire for understanding.

I think we all looked at him stupidly for a few minutes. I know I did. Phil Grogan broke the silence. He said, "Damn it, Stu, *what* story? I don't get it. You drew a blank in the south of France, had a delirious dream about an old monk who talked double-talk—and you say that's the greatest story you ever ran into! Am I just plain dumb, or is there something I've missed?"

"I have already told you," said Grayson soberly, "that the story could never be printed. You must make two assumptions before it makes any sense whatsoever. The first is that though I was shocked I was not delirious, and that the things I saw really happened to me. The second—"

"Well?" said Callison.

"I didn't understand the second myself until some time later," said Grayson slowly. "Not until, completely baffled by a mystery I couldn't explain, I did a little intensive research.

"I discovered some rather peculiar facts connected with the town of Salon and the church of St. Laurent. Buried in the crypt beneath that church lie the remains of one who in his day was famed as astrologist, prophet, and seer. A curious, secretive man, descended of the Jewish tribe of Isaachar whose priests—or so the legends tell—during the Exodus bore away something far more precious than silver or gold. The documents from the initiation chambers of the Egyptian temples. All the geometric, algebraic, and cosmographic formulae by which it is said the Egyptian priests could divine the future.

"That's not so funny as it sounds. There are many, even today, who will tell you that in the construction of the great pyramid of Cheops was outlined the trend of human events for more than five thousand years to come.

"This French frère of the 17th Century—suppose he had somehow inherited this now lost secret? Suppose it were not so esoteric as mechanistic? Oh, I know you think I'm talking nonsense, but—I was there. I saw those things myself. And later, studying the rhymed history of the future written by this prophet, I found not only a 'prediction' of those things which he and I had together seen, but read also the actual words we had spoken to one another!"

Crockett stared at him incredulously. "But you're talking about *time* travel, Grayson! You're saying this prophet was no charlatan but a man who had actually gone forward and seen—"

"I'm not *saying*," corrected Grayson, "I'm only—wondering. I think a lot of people are wondering, too, in view of the fact that in this prophet's book, *The Centuries*, appear predictions that one by one, over a four hundred year period, have come true. Complete with names, dates, places.

"It is implausible, yes. But is it impossible that I should have met him on one of his investigatory flights? I think not. I hope not. For if my hunch is right, I have seen in advance that which all of us will rejoice to read of in the days to come. The fall of Rome, the triumph of Britain, the coming of a more peaceful, happier, world."

Crockett said, "But what's this man's name, Stu? I don't remember any Michel—"

"That was not all his name," said Grayson. "There was more of it. I told you his name as I heard it before I had greater understanding. Michel de Nostre-Dame was his full name. We know him by another name today. We call him—Nostradamus."

Pipeline to Paradise

THE TELEPHONE RANG BEFORE DAWN, AND THE CALLER was Marcus Kane. His voice came over the wire long-distance distorted and thin, but gaily ebullient as ever.

"Blake, baby, this is Marcus. How's my good buddy?"

Blake Arnold blinked the sleep from his eyes and fumed.

"Are you out of your goddamn mind?" he asked peevishly. "Do you know what *time* it is? Almost four in the morning! And I just got rid of the grand-daddy of all headaches." He stopped abruptly, petulance melting in a solvent of confusion. "Marcus?" he repeated. "Marcus Kane?"

"Himself," said the far, jovial voice. "In person, and no facsimile."

"But that's impossible," said Blake. "Marco . . . you're *dead!*"

There was a moment of silence. Not really a silence at all; more like a pause for breath before reply. Then the answer, as brightly cheerful as before.

"That's right," said Marcus blithely. "Does it matter?"

"Matter! Does it matter? Marco, where in hell are you calling from?"

"Not hell, sweetheart." Marcus laughed. "The other place. I made it, kid. In spades. The reward for good, clean living. Believe it or not, I'm calling you from heaven."

Arnold lowered the chortling handset from his ear and stared at it incredulously. *This isn't really happening,* he thought. *It's a dream. The damnedest, craziest dream I ever had. Not a nightmare. There's nothing scary about it. You can't be afraid of a familiar voice that chuckles and jokes and calls you baby, just like a lustrum of years ago in Nam. But wild. Insane. Entirely impossible.*

"I'm dreaming," he said aloud. "In a minute or so I'll wake and roll over . . ."

"You'll have to speak up, Blake, baby," clacked the bee-thin voice by his knee. "I can hardly hear you."

Confusion ebbed, and anger flowed back on its flood. Blake lifted the phone again.

"Listen, smart-ass," he flared. "I don't know who you are, but this is one hell of a tasteless gag! If you think it's funny to call a guy in the middle of the night and pretend to be a friend who died five years ago . . ."

"Blake, lover, don't be so hard-nosed," derided the voice. "It's really *me* calling. Just as we pledged, if one of us should go before the other."

The voice went smoothly on, insistently convincing by its very uninsistence.

"That night at the E.M. club . . . remember? A few weeks after the '68 Tet offensive. Whoever goes first will try to get through to the other. And give him the password to prove it?"

"The password," whispered Arnold. *There* was a *password. And only the two of us knew it.* "You know the password?"

"Of course," said the chuckling voice. "I'm the one who selected it. The password, baby, is 'brillig'!"

Now there was silence indeed, but this time the silence of awe, and of dawning conviction. Forgotten was shattered sleep; forgotten the skull-wracking headache that had kept Blake Arnold awake long after the hour of midnight. Forgotten, too, was the hour, and the seeping chill of night on his slipperless feet, and the muted night-sounds from the street below. Blake Arnold was far from the sixteenth floor of his midtown Manhattan apartment. He was back in Da Nang on a sweaty March night, with a tepid beer tin in one hand, his other hand drumming the table in tempo to the jangling juke-box blare of the current Beatles hit, with the smell of warm beer and warmer bodies in his nostrils. And in his ears the singsong monotone of a *mama-san* at the bar, voicing the lyrics of that tune in a curious, mixed garble of French-accented English in an

Oriental chant. *"I'm the Waw-roos!"* And across the scarred table from him a just-barely unsober Mark Kane, fixing him with a faintly wall-eyed stare and repeating, "Brillig, baby . . . brillig. *That* will be our password, when one of us gets to that big, bright, beautiful wonderland beyond the stars, and comes back to tell the other one about it. Brillig. Like 'and the slithy toves.' Can you remember it?"

Arnold shattered the silence at last.

"So you made it," he whispered. "You actually got through. But, Marco, it's been five years!"

"Earth time, good buddy. Earth time. Which doesn't exist in these parts. As a matter of fact," Marcus mused, "I wouldn't have known if you hadn't told me. There was nothingness at first, for God only knows how long. Then awareness again. Then this, here, all about me."

"What?" asked Blake eagerly. *"What's* all about you?"

"Later," laughed Marcus. "I'll paint you the whole picture by-and-by. But not right now. I've only just learned to break through, and I can't stay too long this time."

"But you're really," demanded Arnold, "where you said? In Paradise?"

"Well, let's just put it this way," chuckled Kane. "That's what they *tell* me. And it sure doesn't *look* like the other place. That is, if the other place is like the preachers used to tell us."

He's being evasive, thought Blake. *Is he telling the truth, or lying?* Suspicion burgeoned, blossomed, in his mind. *Suppose, though, he really did get through. But it isn't heaven he's calling from, but the other place. And for some dark reason . . . a reason I possibly know . . . he wants me to think otherwise. I've got to find out,* he thought. *I've got to know.*

"I've got to know," he said.

"To know?"

"Where you *really* are, said Blake. "And aside from the bet we made, why did you *really* break through? What do you want from me?"

"From you? Blake, baby, you've got it backward. I don't want anything *from* you. I want to help you."

"Help me? With what?"

"That's for you to tell me. What can I do for you? I'm in the cat-bird seat now, sweetheart. The good old guardian angel bit. Mark Kane, Incorporated. Apprentice G.A. in charge. Sees-all, knows-all. Instant assistance on the half-shell. You call the shots; I move. Got any problems need solving?"

"Problems?"

"Fame? Fortune? Some secret yearning?"

"You've got to be kidding!"

Mark sounded faintly aggrieved.

"There must be *something* I can do for my old buddy to prove I'm looking out for him from the after-world?"

"It's too camp!" exploded Blake. "This whole damn thing's too corny. Like a cheap fantasy in a paperback. The next thing I know you'll be touting tomorrow's winner at Aqueduct. Then I bet on the horse and he runs last, and it turns out you're calling from hell instead of heaven . . ."

"Cute script," chuckled Kane, "but all wrong. "No, baby, I'm really in heaven. If you don't believe me, ask Eve."

"Eve? Eve who?"

"Aw, come off it, kid! You only know one Eve. Ask her. And I'll be talking to you later. But now I've run out of time." The voice was beginning to fade. "I'll call you again. Soon."

"Marco, wait! Don't hang up. How can I get in touch with you?"

"You can't," said the voice, getting thinner by the instant. "But I'll be in touch with you. Soon, I expect."

Now the voice was a winnowed shred on a wire that spanned the stars. There was a distant click. Then silence. Then the dial tone.

No one knew where Eve was.

Arnold called her at work before noon. The receptionist said, "I'm sorry, sir. Miss Addams is not in today. Can someone else help you?"

"It's a personal call," said Arnold. "Do you know where I can reach her? Is she at home?"

"I really don't know, sir. I could give you her number."

"I have that, thanks."

"Oh, it's *you*, Mr. Arnold?" The formal voice unfroze. "I really don't know *where* Eve is. She just didn't show up today. She didn't call in sick. I do hope she's all right."

"I'll let you know," said Arnold.

He dialed Eve's apartment number and got no answer. He scowled at the phone as he slowly cradled it. *This doesn't make sense,* he thought. *Eve isn't the kind of girl to go gallivanting off into the wild blue yonder without leaving some message, some hint of where she's going.* It had been only twelve hours since they dined together. She had said nothing then about not feeling well, or of going out of town, or of anything that would cause her not to be at home, not to report to work, not even to call her office and say *why* she was not coming in. A steady girl, Eve. Direct and forthright. Never secretive or mysterious.

Until now.

He tried again in an hour. And before he went out to dinner. And after dinner. And numerous times before bedtime. But still no answer. He went to bed troubled and confused, with the ghost of last night's headache tugging at his temples.

In the darkness that comes before dawn the telephone rang, and the caller was Marcus Kane.

"Blake, baby . . . Marco here! Did you talk to Eve?"

"I haven't been able to reach her. Marco, tell me . . ." Blake voiced the doubt that had been nagging him all day. "Tell me the truth. Are you really in heaven, man? I mean . . . *really?*"

Once more that chuckle Blake was beginning to dislike.

"Would I bullshit you, buddy? Of course!"

"But how can you *phone* me? There's no PBX to heaven."

Marcus laughed.

"Blake, baby, this is the twentieth century! I'm using the most direct line available. What did you expect? Table-tappings?"

"Don't joke," persisted Blake. "Level with me. What is this all about?"

"It's all about you and me, pal. And a promise we made to each other. And what I can do for you. Could you ask for a better deal than your own private pipeline to Paradise?"

He's playing me for a sucker, thought Blake, *and he thinks I've swallowed the bait. He's conning me into something . . . I'll find out what later on. When I've gone all out and lost my butt, then comes the switcheroo. The chuckling voice on the wire, and the jeering taunt at the end.* "Of course it's not heaven, pal. It's hell. You mean you didn't guess?" *But I have guessed. In fact, I'm damn near sure. Because why should Mark Kane do anything for me? Especially if he knows . . .*

"Marco?"

"Mmm?"

"What happens when you get . . . over there? Is it true, that bit about omniscience? Do you get a clear view of what was, and what is to be?"

"To an extent," said Mark. "Not altogether. At least, in my case, not yet. I think it's something you grow into."

Then he may not know?

"But Eve? Where does *she* fit into the picture? What has she got to do with you and me? What can she tell me I don't already know?"

"Oh, she can help, believe me. But if you can't get in touch with her . . ."

The voice was beginning to fade. Strange how just before he had to hang up Mark sounded as if he were slipping a million miles, a million years, away.

"If I can't get in touch with her?" urged Blake.

"Try the waitress," suggested Mark. "She knows where Eve is."

"The waitress? *What* waitress?"

"The one at the cafe," said the ghost of a ghostly voice. "The Paradise Cafe." The shadow of a chuckle. "Where else? 'Bye, now, Blake, baby."

Then silence.

The Paradise was a night spot exclusively frequented by the by-no-means exclusive night people who liked good booze and plenty of it, loud music and plenty of it, pink flesh and plenty of it, plentifully displayed. There was no use even going there before ten p.m. Which suited Arnold fine. Because once again, as with increasing frequency during these past several months, around dinnertime he developed another of those devastating headaches. A furious and fiery migraine that picked him up and flapped him like a banner in a gale; that blinded and ravaged and made him physically ill; that caused him half to forget both who and where he was; that made him for bleak, blank hours a tempest-tossed chip on the seething waves of an ocean of pain.

He finally came out of it shortly before midnight, the pain dissipating as swiftly and inexplicably as it had come upon him. He found himself at home, rocking on his bed, head cradled in his hands, though how he had got there, or when, he did not know. But with passing of the pain came recollection of a needful thing undone. And Blake went to the cafe.

Traffic was snarled at the Paradise Cafe. Blake was forced to park more than a block away and shoulder his way through a milling, buzzing crowd to get near the place. There was a patrol car parked before the entrance, and an officer urging the crowd, "Keep moving, folks. This doesn't concern you. Keep moving!"

"You, too," he said to Arnold, who had thrust his way through the throng and was staring with horrified eyes at two white-clad men who were carrying a stretcher to the ambulance at the curb. There was a sheet-covered body on the litter. And the sheet was blotched with red.

"What happened?" choked Arnold.

"Move along," said the cop. "Keep moving!"

A by-stander said, "It's a waitress. Some hippie came in the back door and caught her alone in the kitchen. Stabbed her three times with a knife."

"Move along!" said the cop irately. "Move along!" Then suddenly, in disgust, "Oh, sweet Christ!"

Arnold threw up on the pavement. The crowd in that sector moved swiftly.

And before dawn the telephone rang.

Blake Arnold, who had not slept, snatched it up frantically.

"Marcus," he cried, "is that you?"

"Hey, there's my good buddy!" said Marcus approvingly. "Waiting for me to call? Did you get in touch with the waitress?"

"Marco, she's *dead!* Somebody killed her before I could get to the cafe. Marco, what did she know that I should know? And why are all these strange things happening to me?"

"You're just unlucky, baby," said Marcus soothingly. "Just flat out unlucky. Killed, eh?" *You could almost hear the shrug.* "Well, these things happen. And death isn't all that bad." *His laugh was in shocking bad taste.* "I ought to know."

"But you said she could tell me where Eve is. How do I find Eve *now?* If she was the only one who knew . . ."

"Oh, perhaps not the only one," said Marcus. "The switchboard operator. She probably can tell you."

"Which operator. Where?"

"At Eve's hotel," came the suddenly thinning voice. "The one who put you through the night you dined together. Try her."

Then the distant click again. And the dial tone.

Arnold called the hotel. This operator's voice was one he had never heard before. But then he had never called Eve at this hour. This obviously was the relief girl on the lobster watch. The other girl, she told Blake, went off duty at twelve. If there was anything she could do. . . ?

"No, thanks," said Blake. "I'll call her tomorrow night."

But he didn't call early. For again after dinner his head began to pound. This time he made no effort to fight it off. He had learned the folly of that. He stayed home and took to his bed. If he had to black out, he thought, it was better to do so in safe and familiar surroundings. And black out he did, for a time. But he woke, fully dressed and stretched out on his bed, around ten.

His headache had miraculously cleared. He looked at his watch. It was late, but not too late. Just right, in fact. The girl he wanted was still on duty, and would not be too busy to talk. So Blake drove uptown.

There was unusual activity in front of the hotel. At this late hour no milling crowd had collected. But again, as the night before, there was a patrol car standing before the entrance. Inside, a policeman was scratching notes on a pad. As Blake parked his car at the curb, the officer got out and approached the driver's window.

"Don't park here, mister," he said.

"Beg pardon? Is this a restricted zone?"

"It is now. There's an ambulance due any minute."

The cop's eyes searched his face, half hidden in the gloom.

"You live here?"

"No. Just visiting a . . . a friend."

"Haven't I seen you before?"

Blake thought, *That you have. I damn near threw up on your leg last night at the Paradise.* But he said, "I don't think so. Very well, officer. I'll move." He started the motor again. Then casually, "What happened in there?"

"Girl got killed," said the cop succinctly. "Switchboard operator. We don't know who did it, or why, but she's stiff as a mackerel. Okay, here comes the ambulance. Get going."

Blake got going, the wings of panic hammering at his ribs as if they were the bars of a bursting cage. The policeman stared after him thoughtfully, a frown creasing his forehead. Then he took out his pad and wrote down Blake's license number . . .

Marcus Kane didn't call him that night. Nor the next, nor the next, nor the next. Nor could Blake at any time get through to Eve. Not at her office, where her employers could not explain her absence. Nor at her apartment . . . which he did not try, because for some gut-instinct Blake did not clearly comprehend he feared to call her.

So three days passed in torment. *An undeserved torment,* he thought. *What's happening to me? A week ago I was a happy man with a steady girl, good job, good health, good prospects. Now suddenly the whole world's gone to hell in a giddy hand-basket. And all because the telephone rang at dawn, and a dead man who couldn't be there knew things that nobody could know.*

Except Eve. Or so Marcus had said. *Eve* knew something.

But all leads to Eve had been broken.

All leads?

All leads lost now?

The waitress who could have told him where Eve had gone ... dead now. And the switchboard girl who might have possibly known ... also dead.

But Marcus had said he had to contact Eve.

Thinking was hard, because his head was pounding. But he sat on the edge of the bed and forced himself to think.

Eve Addams. Where would she be if not at her hotel? She had no close friends in the city ... or at least none known to Blake. And her family lived miles away. Somewhere in the Dakotas, Blake recalled. It was conceivable she could have gone to visit them. But not without telling him that she was going.

Where, then?

Then the obvious answer struck him.

"The lodge!" he said aloud. "I gave her a key to my cabin. She's up there waiting for *me!*"

In a burst of excited speed he rose and dressed. His head was still throbbing dully, but the pain was tolerable now that he saw an end to his bewilderment. Sensed a solution to the mysteries that had plagued and perplexed him since that night last week when Mark first called.

Night traffic was slight, and grew slighter. The headlamps of the few approaching cars were dim, then bright, then disappeared behind him in twin Doppler dots. The city turned into suburbs, and the suburbs into country. The concrete turned into blacktop, and the blacktop roughened to a country lane that curled its way up the hills to Blake's lodge overlooking the Hudson.

He arrived at the cabin an hour before dawn. As he neared it a triumphant exaltation gripped him. There was a light on in the cabin's bedroom! Then she *was* here, as he had guessed. He took out his key and hurried to the door ...

The door was open.

"Eve?" he shouted, racing to the bedroom. Eve didn't reply. But what had been Eve was there. Eva was an unfamiliar week-long, long-dead thing stretched on the red-stained sheets, its once-lovely face now a gray mask carven in the agonies of death.

"My God!" choked Arnold. "My God!"

Then the telephone rang.

The telephone rang, and predictably it was Mark. But a Mark whose chuckle was now neither friendly nor gay, but grim.

"Mark!" cried Blake Arnold, "she's dead! Who did this?"

"*I* did, good buddy," taunted Marcus Kane. "But that's not what counts. What really counts is that they'll think *you* did it."

"*You* did this? To Eve? But why? How?"

"One question at a time, sweetheart," chuckled Marcus, the malice of eternity to his laughter. "That's all we allow each customer. Why?" His voice hardened. "You know damned well why! To pay you back for what you did to me. In Nam."

"Then you know," whispered Blake. "And you never forgot."

"Believe it! And neither will you."

Arnold stared with glazed eyes at the hideous thing on the bed.

"But *how?*" he demanded fiercely. "You're a nothing . . . a voice on the phone. How could you . . ."

"Simple, good buddy. The same as I handled the others."

"The others, too?"

"The waitress at the Paradise Cafe . . . through a hopped-up teen-age hippie. The switchboard girl through a sweet little old lady resident the cops will never suspect in a zillion years . . . and who doesn't know herself that she was used. And your sweetie-pie . . . through a sneak-thief who doesn't remember a thing about it, except that a week ago he ripped off a summer lodge."

"But that's impossible," cried Arnold desperately. "You can't control a living person's mind. And body."

"You think not?" Marcus laughed. "You never heard of demoniac possession?"

"Demoniac! Then I was right. You're not in heaven at all! You're . . ."

"In hell," acknowledged Marcus cheerfully. "Right, baby. Right at last. But since they can't get me here they'll need a fall guy. And guess who's elected?"

"You set me up," whispered Blake. "For vengeance, you set me up."

"Ta-da-daah!" chuckled Marcus maliciously. "Fanfare and roll of drums as Blake Arnold sees the light!"

And then light there was in abundance. The harsh white of pocketflash beams, the coarse yellow of auto headlights, the sibling scarlet of revolving bubble-tops. The room was abruptly a kaleidoscope of coldwhite and ocher and red. And the red matched the stains on the sheets.

Arnold slammed the phone down in its cradle and started toward the door. They stopped him there. Hands gripped and held him tight. A strident voice hammered in his ears.

"Hold it, Arnold!"

Then the voice turned rigid with disgust, and icy in the formal words of arrest.

"Read him his rights, and take the bastard away!"

The State appointed counsel, since Arnold did not seem to care. The attorney was young, eager, willing . . . and frustrated.

"Give me something to work with," he pleaded. "They think they have an airtight case. Give me a pin to puncture their balloon. An alibi, a witness. Some proof you didn't commit these awful crimes."

"It was a trick," said Arnold. "From the beginning it was revenge he was after. He was never in heaven at all."

"Who," asked the lawyer, baffled, "wasn't where?"

"It was as I guessed at the beginning. He's actually in hell, where he belongs. And he wants me there, too."

"Who," asked the lawyer again, "are you talking about?"

Arnold said nothing. He sat on the edge of his metal bunk staring blindly into space. Into space beyond space and time. To a realm beyond human concept of sight and sound. To a twentieth century hell with a telephone pipeline to the damned.

The attorney was voluble . . . and helpless.

"Tell me *this*, then," he pleaded earnestly. "Whatever you tell me is privileged, but I've got to know. Arnold, *did* you actually kill those girls?"

"I killed Marcus," said Arnold bleakly.

"Arnold, *please* . . ."

"Marcus Kane. My buddy. We were walking perimeter patrol. They came up at us out of the high grass, the Cong in their black pajamas, screaming like slant-eyed banshees. He had only his M-16, and it jammed. I had an M-30 machine-gun. I could have saved us both, but I panicked and ran. They swarmed all over him. Marco screamed my name once."

"You're talking about Viet Nam . . ."

"I'm talking about the night I killed Mark Kane," said Blake. "My buddy. My best friend. Who has found a way to get revenge."

The lawyer said patiently, "Arnold, *please!* We looked into that. It's all your imagination. There *is* no Marcus Kane. We've checked the records. There was never any such person. Not in the Army, nor the Marines, nor the Air Force . . ."

"I'm sick," whimpered Blake. "And my head is beginning to ache. Would you go away now?"

He lay back and closed his eyes. The lawyer eyed him helplessly. After a while he left . . .

The lawyer was young, and eager, and determined. He called in a psychiatrist who examined Arnold. Then together they went to the District Attorney seeking a deal.

"You can't ask for Murder One," insisted the psychiatrist. "You cannot possibly execute this man. I dislike the word, but he's obviously insane. His whole story proves it. Phone calls from heaven . . ."

"From hell," Arnold's lawyer corrected.

"From heaven . . . from hell . . . from his sub-conscious mind! From the deep-rooted sense of guilt so firmly woven into every fibre of his being that his conscience would not give him any rest.

"Those headaches. Blinding and devastating headaches each time before a victim was killed. Then swift relief when the deed had been committed. The typical reaction of a schizoid paranoiac."

"We have another expert," said the D.A., "who will testify that Arnold is sane enough to know right from wrong."

"His delusion," persisted the psychiatrist, "is a fantasy fabrication from start to finish, keyed to a Biblical motif by happenstance. Eve Addams. The Paradise Cafe. Thus the invented name of his mythical caller . . . Marcus, or Marco, Kane. Mark of Cain! Arnold's verbalization of the crimson sense of guilt so etched in his soul that he felt it etched on his brow. He murdered his Eve, from Paradise, and the mark of Cain became the name of his heavenly accuser."

"Nevertheless," said the D.A., "he must die. He killed Eve Addams . . . only he knows why. Then he started brooding about the trail he had left behind him. A waitress at the Paradise Cafe had served them on the night they dined together, so she had to go. The switchboard operator at Miss Addams' hotel knew Arnold had a date with her that night, so she had to go, too.

"He made six mistakes, classic but fatal. He returned to the scene of every one of his crimes. An officer saw him at the Paradise Cafe the night the waitress was murdered. The same man saw him again at the hotel the night he killed the switchboard girl. He recognized him, and took his license number. That put us on his trail. We followed him. And he led us to the cabin, where we found his first victim."

"That's three mistakes," said the lawyer. "The other three?"

"He murdered three girls in cold blood," said the District Attorney grimly. "And he'll pay for it with his life."

A jury agreed with him. Their deliberation was brief. They brought in a unanimous verdict in record time. Murder One, with no recommendation for mercy. So the sentencing judge showed none.

The attorney was young, and eager, and persistent. He appealed to the Governor himself. His Excellency listened politely but said apologetically, "You see the bind I'm in? We've just emerged from years of a foolish no-execution law. The public is sick and tired of seeing criminals go unpunished. I don't dare interfere."

"You're his last chance," pleaded the lawyer.

"I have no valid grounds for intervening."

"You have the best of all possible grounds: lack of proof. There is no direct evidence that he killed those girls. He only knew one of them . . . Eve Addams . . . and he loved her. The others could be pure coincidence. There are hundreds of unsolved murders in New York every year. All the evidence against my client is purely circumstantial."

"So is a trout in the milk," said the Governor flatly.

"He's a guilt-ridden, tortured soul," said the lawyer. "His cowardice caused the death of his best friend, so he thinks he killed him himself. That's why he makes no defense. Because he believes he should be punished for the death of Marcus Kane."

"There *is* no Marcus Kane. You looked into that yourself."

"We *found* no Marcus Kane. That doesn't mean such a person never existed. Perhaps we didn't check far enough. There were not only American troops in Viet Nam. There were Aussies, too. And American advisors to ROK troops, not on the American rosters. Perhaps Kane was one of *these?*"

The Governor shrugged.

"You can look into it farther if you want. My mind is not closed. If you can establish such a fact it might influence my decision."

"And if I can come up with any such evidence?"

"There is a hot-line from my office to the execution cell," said the Governor. "I will do what is right. That is all I can promise you."

They located no Marcus Kane. At least not before the hour of execution. The grim formalities went through on schedule. There was a choice of menu offered for the prisoner's last meal; Blake Arnold ate nothing. There wás a visit from the prison chaplain; Arnold refused to see him. There was a macabre interlude with a barber who used his razor to shave two small patches of hair, but two only. Then an unhurried march down an echoing metal-walled corridor to a dark door at its end.

In the control room beside the execution cell the warden asked in a husky, half-hopeful voice, "No calls?"

An attendant shook his head. The warden sighed.

"Very well," he said. "Proceed."

A switch was depressed. And raised. And depressed again. The overhead lights dimmed, flared, dimmed, and were normal. The men in the room refused to look at each other, or at the odorous thing that had been Blake Arnold. And then . . .

And then the telephone rang.

The warden's face drained to sand.

"Oh, God!" he said. "Not the Governor! Not *now!*"

He reached for the telephone with a palsied hand.

"Yes, Governor?" he croaked. "Yes, Governor?"

Time trembled and stood in limbo. Then a puzzled look came over the warden's face. He stared at the others in the metal room.

"It's somebody named Mark Kane. And he's laughing his fool damn head off!"

* * *

Postscript to Pipeline

I was greatly pleased . . . nay, let us make that flattered . . . when Roger Zelazny invited me to contribute to this anthology. This for a number of reasons, the main one being that prior to this appearance my last major science-fiction short story was BUTTON, BUTTON which appeared in . . . are you ready for this? . . . the March 1954 issue of BLUE BOOK!

And where, you ask, had I been, and what had I been doing in those intervening forty years? Well, thanks for asking. The sad and simple answer is that around and about that time a noisome upstart y-clept television ceased being a snow-mottled novelty and became America's favorite form of entertainment, subsequent to which one by one the magazines for which I had been so happily and prosperously writing for over twenty years like Longfellow's Arabs folded their tents and silently stole away. So to preserve my economic stability (not to mention my domestic tranquility and sanity), since I could not lick 'em I elected to jine 'em, and I, too, deserted the Happy Hunting Grounds of magazine fiction and started writing both for movies and (culpa mea!) the very monster that had changed my life . . . television.

The rest, therefore, is silence. Unlike many others of my era, I ceased to exist as a science-fiction writer and embarked on a new career of becoming the Forgotten Man.

This sordid situation continued until a year or so ago, at which time a one-time friend wrote a letter to a fanzine confessing that he had once known "the late Nelson Bond." This stunning announcement of my as-yet unaccomplished demise so distressed me that I immediately wrote both to the magazine and to its contributor pointing out that as in the case of Mark Twain the news of my death was grossly exaggerated.

The fan, Russ Chauvenet, was delighted to discover I was still alive and cantankerous enough to kick. And as for enlightened fandom, almost instantly strangely beautiful things began to happen. I got a score of letters from fans in various countries (many of them asking me to sign labels they could place in my books); I received not only a swift nomination but an equally swift election to the enviable honor of First Fandom's Hall of Fame and . . . finally getting back to where we started . . . I received Roger's invitation to contribute to this anthology.

. . . Which now I have done, and all I can add to the foregoing is to say that I hope you will not be disappointed in this late, latest and possibly last short story by the newly revived and, believe me, still very young at heart octogenarian who here subscribes himself . . .

—NELSON BOND

The World Within

SCHLATER HAD MORE PATIENCE THAN HIS COMPANION. His method would have been to tie Alderson securely, then extort his secret in one of the approved fashions. The Gestapo had taught him many pleasant little ways of stimulating conversation. A hot flame applied to bare soles, the mute insistence of a foot of rubber hose, that little trick with fine wire and the eyelids.

But Koshu, being a Jap, was impatient, nervously impetuous. He scowled when the old scientist claimed he had no blueprints for the instrument that stood in the center of the room, and when Alderson staunchly refused to explain its operation, the little man's hair-trigger temper flared. So did the automatic in his yellow fist. A look of stunned surprise came into the American physicist's eyes. He coughed, choked on his own blood, pitched forward, and lay still.

Schlater said ruefully, "That was not too clever, my friend. You should have forced him to explain before you shot him. This looks like no war machine I have ever seen."

"We have no time to waste," hissed Koshu. "Someone may walk in here at any moment. We will not need any diagrams or explanations. We have the machine itself. That will tell us all we need to know. Let us take it to my place and study it. Give me a hand, please, friend? Steady, there! Up with it. *Aie*—maledictions!"

He jerked his hand from the machine, mopping blood from his right palm with a not-too-clean handkerchief.

"Curse it, that metal flange is sharp! Well, let us make haste. We must get out of here. Lift, please!"

Schlater lifted. The hour was late, the sky black, the street deserted. No one saw them carry the odd-looking, projector-like instrument across the pavement, put it into a station-wagon. Schlater lowered the side-screens carefully. Koshu, still nursing his injured hand, waited fretfully. A few minutes later, gears ground; the station-wagon and its mysterious cargo sped away from the quiet laboratory in which lay the body of Dr. Robert Alderson, inventor.

Some time afterward, in Koshu's quarters, they stood before their stolen toy, studying it. Their styles of approach to the new problem were typical of their thought habits. More clearly than their appearances it typified the differences of the races from which they sprang.

Koshu was all feline eagerness as, black eyes gleaming, he strode about the machine in short, mincing steps, lingering here to touch a tube, there a coil, tracing with long, sensitive fingers the path of a wire; delving, conjecturing, leaping to half-inductive, half-deductive conclusions.

Schlater did not finger the instrument. He analyzed it with the cold, mental detachment of the Teuton. He, too, was identifying the purposes of the cryptic parts—but his probing was entirely cerebral. And he, too, was slowly reaching a conclusion.

As he studied, some untouched portion of his brain found time to be scornful of Koshu's nervous concentration. Schlater neither liked nor trusted the Nipponese agent. He collaborated with him only because to do so was in accordance with orders issued to all Nazi agents in the United States.

Inasmuch, read the general orders, *as a friendly understanding exists between our two nations, members of our Intelligence will cooperate, whenever expedient, with agents of the Japanese government. It is recommended, however, that discretion be employed in permitting valuable secrets to fall into the hands of our allies—*

Schlater had followed the first part of his orders. Learning that Dr. Alderson had completed a new war machine, an instrument which the childishly hopeful Americans believed might be the "weapon to end all wars," he had joined forces with Koshu to steal that secret. Their carefully plotted effort had been successful, as was evidenced by the glistening projector that now stood before them. And Schlater wondered how far his "allegiance" with Koshu should now go.

If this weapon were, indeed, all it was rumored to be, and a growing conviction assured him it was, it was "a valuable secret." As such, it should be communicated to the Nazi, and only to the Nazi government. A war weapon shared by two countries is quartered in value. Therefore. . . .

He glanced guardedly at the Jap, just in time to find Koshu's beady black eyes intent upon him. Koshu's voice was high-pitched with the excitement now.

"Well, Schlater? You understand its purpose?"

Schlater did, now. Or at least he thought he did. The curious, parabolic arrangement of the convex lenses gave him the needed key, that and the wiring which determined the concentration of focal radiation on a point established by a series of verniers. It was a staggering conception; one, Schlater admitted reluctantly to himself, of unparalleled genius. It made of this innocent-appearing projector a mighty weapon, a weapon that could, indeed, end wars. Or, in the hands of the proper persons, it could pave smooth the path of conquest.

But he shook his head. He said, "I don't know. We may have been hoaxed. There seems to be nothing dangerous in this maze of wires and coils."

"You think," queried Koshu, "it is worthless?" And a frown creased his forehead; his eyes looked worried. Scorn, mingled with an urge toward laughter, stirred within Schlater. Then he had guessed right. Koshu's intellect was not shrewd enough to grasp this novel, terrifying concept. Such an idea was beyond the yellow man's mental powers.

"Utterly worthless," said Schlater negligently. He shrugged. "We might have guessed as much. You know these *verdammt* Americans. Always straining toward the fantastic, the impossible end. Oh, I suppose there is some slight logic behind the machine. Maybe it could be made to work." He paused. "Suppose we try? Let us attach it. Apparently this is a small scale model, designed to operate on house current. If you will plug it in, *mein Freund?*"

Koshu darted to the wall socket, inserted the plug that fed current to the strange projector. For a moment his back was to Schlater, and the Nazi agent's hand went toward his pocket. He stilled the movement with an effort.

This was, after all, Koshu's apartment. Undoubtedly he had

friends here. The bark of a Luger at this hour might rouse them, end forever Schlater's chance of winning complete possession of the projector. And, there was another way. A better way. If the instrument worked as he thought. . . .

Koshu was again at his side, fretfully eager.

"What now, Schlater?"

Schlater stepped to the machine, pressed a button briefly, experimentally. As he did so, current sang its high, whining song. The muzzle of the projector brightened; from it diffused a weaving spiral of light.

Koshu squealed in delight.

"It does work, Schlater! What is it? A death ray? A sonic beam?"

Schlater snapped off the light swiftly, grateful for Koshu's single-mindedness. The Nipponese agent, fascinated by the spiral of color, had failed to notice the more significant result for which Schlater had been watching. The weird effect the beam had had upon objects on the far end of the room. The Morris chair, that picture on the wall—

He muttered, "A moment, *bitte*. There is an adjustment to be made." He fingered another of the verniers. The scale bore numbers. He set the vernier at the number "4." That, he judged, should be about right. Koshu would be about four feet away when the beam was turned upon him.

The Jap was staring at him narrowly.

"What are you doing, friend Schlater?"

"Just experimenting. You want to find out how the machine works, *nicht wahr?*"

"Yes, but—" Koshu's small hands gestured. In the movement he tensed the muscles of his wounded right hand; the cut split afresh and he winced. "You know more than you have told me. You're hiding something, friend Schlater!"

"Don't be a fool!" Schlater had finished his preparations now. All but one thing. An equalizing correction to be made on the projector lens. That done, it would be but the work of seconds to end this little farce. One swift movement of the projector, the pressure of a finger, and Koshu would be eliminated. The Reich would not have to share this knowledge with a publicly embraced, but secretly detested ally.

It was then that Schlater made his mistake. Eager to complete his task, he stepped to the front of the projector. His hands sought the lens. Then, from the corner of one eye, he glimpsed sudden motion. Koshu, a triumphant grimace on his lips, was leaping forward. Schlater bellowed a harsh warning.

"Koshu — be careful!"

He spoke too late. With a shrill burst of laughter, the Son of Heaven clawed the button. A mist of golden flame flooded the projector's nozzle, suffused Schlater with a fiery pain!

Blinded, dazed, numbed, his flesh acrawl with a maddening sensation of contractile pressure, Schlater fought to stagger from beneath that radiant downpouring. But the golden mist followed him. Koshu, handling the projector, was training it upon his "ally" with deliberate, deadly accuracy. And there was gloating mockery in the Jap's gibes.

"So you thought Koshu a fool, eh, Schlater?"

Schlater screamed, "Turn it off, Koshu! Before it is too late! *This weapon condenses matter!*"

"I know," laughed the Nipponese. "Your Aryan pride did not let you believe another mind could be as quick as your own, did it, Schlater? You underestimated Koshu."

Schlater tugged despairingly at his pocket, but once more the Jap anticipated him. Before he could shoot, Koshu's hand stretched forth and wrenched the gun from him as if it were a child's toy. And Schlater saw now, with a burst of horror, why the weapon had been so easily torn from his grasp.

Because he was shrinking! Koshu's hand was gigantic. The walls were racing away from him at a frightful speed. The eye of the lens now above him was as large as his head, almost as large as his body! The ceiling had disappeared, lost in a vague nebulosity. The soft carpet beneath him seemed to slip in all directions from under his feet. He staggered and reeled, finding he must keep in motion in order to stay upon his feet.

The ray burned down upon him, and through its golden aura he glimpsed the Cyclopian face of Koshu grinning at him. A great, pocked visage, mottled and brownish, coarse with occasional weed-like tusks of beard. Koshu's voice seemed to be deeper. Its taunting was thunder in his ears.

"So, little one, the first man dies before the new weapon that will make *my* nation ruler of the world! How does it feel to be the size of a kitten? Ah, you run? You flee? It is useless. But take courage, Schlater. Koshu will spare you the final ignominy. When you have dwindled to the size of a louse, I will crush you — *like this!*"

A ponderable darkness came between Schlater and the blinding sun; like a colossal Juggernaut it moved inexorably down upon him. He screamed, his voice a high, thin bleating in his ears, and tripped and fell upon a spiny trunk of wool, rose and scampered from beneath Koshu's massive foot.

Fear lent wings to his feet. The Gargantuan boot missed him by inches. Inches that, even as he scrambled, became yards. For that brain-seething pressure still flamed in his body; in some dim corner of his mind he was aware that the beam was still upon him, he was still shrinking. Where this would end he could not tell—nor dared he guess. The carpet that had once been a soft surface beneath his feet was now a granite-strewn plateau, grim-ringed with the leafless spines of fibrous growths. No longer was there a room, walls, or a ceiling, or a machine. There was just this drab, gritty wasteland, and an ochre sky from which hot, wracking beams scorched him deeper and yet deeper into the realms of nothingness.

A remnant of logic made him try to figure his present size, but the thought defied all computation. He was microscopic; that he knew. If grains of dust were, to him, mountains . . . if even now clefts appeared in solid terrain, tumbling him downward to imponderable depths . . .

Countless miles and aeons above him there was a dull and sullen roaring, cadenced but indistinguishable to Schlater. Stark fantasy had its will with him. It was the elder gods he heard, the gods of thunder, and the sun was blotted by their wrath. Actually, it was Koshu who now, upon his hands and knees, was seeking some faint sign of the "ally" whom he had thrust into the unimaginable. The thunder was Koshu's voice, screaming in rage and disappointment. "Then you think thus to escape me, mannikin? But you, shall not. I shall crush the life from your puny body, hammer you to a pulp!"

His voice lifted to a bellow. Heedless of his wound, Koshu beat and pounded on the carpet. Dust rose thickly, and blood stained the dun as Koshu sobbed and cursed and clawed the carpet like a mad thing. But there was no sign of Schlater. He was gone. The Jap rose, weeping with rage, and cut off the current. A moment he stood there, gazing mutely at the empty floor, a long, long moment.

The wrath of the thunder gods howled about him; a typhoon screamed vast winds about his ears, caught and spun him, hurled him viciously into the depths of a spongy thicket. Jet blackness surrounded him, now that the sun had been blotted out. Somewhere above raged the fuller fury of the wind; the ground beneath him trembled and rocked. His world was a madman's dream in which small objects at his side grew while he watched, towered skyward, becoming monstrous, awesome impossibilities. New scenes sprang from nothingness. Valleys became ridges, pebbles boulders, as he slipped and skidded perilously through a treacherous universe.

Schlater dared not guess what yet might lie ahead. All he knew was that the persistent throbbing still tingled in his veins; that with each new breath his body became more minute. A memory came to him of a theory he once had heard; that there might be worlds within worlds, solar galaxies within atoms of the world on which once, a normal human, he had dwelt and dreamed and plotted for glory. If so, he was not far from learning the truth or falsity of this theory.

Out of the darkness came a strange, new feeling of sultriness and increased pressure. Warmth was about him, and movement. His mind reeling under the impact of this new mystery, he cast himself from his latest refuge and ran on tottering legs toward—he knew not what.

He had taken perhaps a half-dozen faltering steps when he felt upon him an insistent, wrenching tug, a sort of dreadful suction from above. He fought against it with the desperate fury of a doomed man, but the violent force became more potent every instant. He tried to cry out, but the cry died in his throat. Pain cut through him with the edge of a honed blade, his muscles knotted in agony, the very marrow of his bones seemed wracked with torment.

Once again, and futilely, he kicked out in a blind panic, but his attempt to free himself was waste and hopeless motion. There came a sense of lifting swiftness. A giddiness nauseated him. His head felt weirdly light; his body sagged with impotence. He had no longer the strength with which to fight his fate. He surrendered, suddenly and completely, and all was black.

It was a strange world in which he awakened. He lay on a narrow shelf, scant inches above the crest of a sluggish stream that poured endlessly down the corridor of a vast, high-domed tunnel. There was no sky above him, no earth beneath; nothing but this plunging stream and the smooth, washed, plastic bore that was its aqueduct. But faint and far-off, in the direction toward which the river coursed, Schlater could hear a sound familiar to his earthly ears. The rhythmic pounding of a machine.

He rose, weak, dazed, uncertain, but taking courage from the fact that he still lived! And in the equally hopeful fact that the scene about him did not change before his eyes. Apparently he had reached the end of his mad journey in size; the period of his diminution had ended.

And if so, hope was not yet dead! What if his adventure had brought him to some microscopic universe? What if there were no beings like himself (Schlater was a logical man) in this murky world? There must be intelligence of some sort. The mathematical perfection of the tunnel argued that; it represented an engineering feat of no mean scope. And the beat of machinery off in the distance—where there were machines there must be thinking creatures to build them. Could he but find these builders, win their friendship.

Well, he had studied the machine of Dr. Alderson. With persistence and effort, Schlater thought he could build its counterpart, return to the world from which he had come, and avenge himself on the traitorous Koshu.

Spurred by this thought, he studied his surroundings more carefully. The ledge on which he now stood was not constant, it was an accidental hardening or encrustation on the wall of the tunnel. He could not, then, walk to his destination as a man might explore the depths of Paris in the bowels of the sewage system. And there were no water craft. All he could do, for the present at least, was trust himself to the mercies of the stream. Swim with the current down the tunnel or feed-pipe, resting whenever opportunity presented itself, until he found himself in a more favorable location.

Gingerly, he lowered himself from the shelf. The stream was pleasantly brackish, and, so near as he could tell in the semi-gloom, a pale, muddy, yellowish color. The air he breathed was heavy and sickly sweet, but it bore no trace of the offal taint he had feared.

Apparently the aqueduct was part of a power plant, not a portion of a drainage system.

The current was deep and strong, the water viscous. It tugged at his foot. He loosed his hold on the ledge, and found himself drifting swiftly down the tunnel. He had but to paddle gently to keep himself afloat.

His eyes were becoming more accustomed to the gloom now. He noticed, with increasing wonderment, several things he had not previously recognized. One of these was the intricate construction of the feedline in which he swam. It was not, as he had first thought, a single, large tunnel; it was a labyrinthine network of small corridors, all leading into this major aqueduct. His sweeping passage bore him, in short seconds, past a half hundred tiny doorways, each sealed with tiny, automatically-operated portals of what appeared to be a plastic substance of some kind. These seemed to move with a predetermined rhythm. As he swam past one, it opened momentarily, and a sudden gout of water cascaded upon him. Something sharp and hard struck him, bruised him. His hand, instinctively leaping to the object, identified it as a bit of spiny bone, like the skeleton of a coral.

It had, he saw fearfully, been gnawed clean, and for the first time a doubt entered his mind. He had placidly assumed himself to be alone in this watery grotto—but could he be sure? There might be other life here, dangerous antagonists. He sought, and found, the case-knife strapped to his calf.

As though his newborn fears had fathered the actuality, he saw, suddenly then, the first of the denizens of this weird place. A trap vent opened in the wall of the tunnel before him, and from it wriggled a creature that brought a choked cry to Schlater's lips.

It was a sallow, slimy, serpentine monster, almost half again as large as Schlater. It had no eyes, but in its thick, wedge-shaped head was a gaping, toothed vent that was its maw; and from the tip of its proboscis writhed two wiry antennae that now stirred inquisitively in Schlater's direction. It spun, a hundred coarse-haired cilia palpitating, and darted toward him.

Schlater, shocked to action, churned the water in a swift, fearful desperation. The creature whisked toward him, its maw opening hungrily. His arm raised, his knife slashed once, twice, and yet again at the blind face of the monster. It recoiled before that biting edge. A thin ichor oozed from the wounds; the water churned and boiled as the injured water-thing sought to close in upon its quarry and still avoid the knifing pain.

Sheer chance saved him then, for suddenly beside him was another rimy ledge, similar to that on which he had found himself at first. With a scrambling effort, Schlater dragged himself onto this. The sea-thing followed his scent blindly, butted its still-dripping head against the ledge a foot below Schlater, then seemed to lose him. A moment it lingered there, its triangular head weaving back and forth in mute querulousness; then it wriggled off to the other side of the tunnel. A moment later it was burrowing, with a series of nauseating snuffles and mouthings, a ragged hole right through the wall of the aqueduct.

To what purpose, for what purpose, Schlater could not begin to guess. All he did know was that his forehead was damp and cold, his body quivering with disgust, his stomach churning with nervous fear. What kind of monster was this that could digest smooth structural plastic—and why?

He saw, then. It did not add to the quietude of his nerves. For before his eyes he saw the snakelike beast curl up within the tiny cavern it had burrowed, proceed to split in half, and vomit up a hundred, tiny, slimy simulacra of itself! The beast's nauseous puppies, each as large as Schlater's hand, turned instantly on their parent, tore it to bits, and gulped every morsel of the rent body!

Nor did their feeding end there. His eyes sharpened by this experience, Schlater saw now that there were still other life forms swarming in the humid cavern. Those pallid objects he had dismissed as stalactite growths, pending from the high, arched ceiling, he saw, now, were living blobs of matter. And in the water itself were still other mobile forms. Some, so tiny that they would have escaped his attention entirely had it not been for this sickening revelation, others very large. There was one form of fish or crustacean something like a clam, except that its "shell" was translucent, its shape that of a roughly hewn crystal. One constant form was a curious, disc-like creature with almost invisible cilia; these were a pale, yellowish color. The serpent puppies seemed to find them a delicacy, diving eagerly into the stream to fish them out, ripping them apart with sharp, hungry teeth. These platter-shaped things were completely defenseless apparently. When torn, they exploded with a sharp, popping sound, and Schlater thought he could detect the faint, ammoniac smell of ozone whenever this happened. They were like the blowfish of Gulf waters, terrifying to look at, helpless in battle.

And as the puppies ate, they grew. As they grew to the size of the parent that had attacked Schlater, they, as had the parent, ceased their feeding, burrowed new cubbyholes for themselves in the wall of the tunnel. Within the space of minutes, the entire chamber was pock-marked with their burrowings; where had been one monster, pregnant with loathesome young, now the corridor seethed with this hateful life form.

The tiny shelf upon which Schlater crouched, trembling, had long since been undermined by this horde of swiftly breeding beasts. It would not be long now, he knew, before it gave way, catapulting him into their midst. And when that happened. . . . He shuddered.

But at that moment a wild activity developed amongst the wedge-headed monsters. A swift current seemed to course through them; then, as if advised by some telepathic warning, as one they turned for flight.

And Schlater saw why. There was splashing movement from the farther end of the tunnel. Out of the gloom appeared a solid host of colorless, transparent creatures that slipped through the water with the fluid ease of gigantic amoebae.

Even before the wrigglers had assembled for flight, the first of the newcomers had invaded their midst. Schlater saw its long, colorless body expand before his eyes, stretch, grow pseudopods, and ingest a wriggler. The transparent body wall veiled, clouded, as strong acids digested the enemy—and the colossal amoeba was twisting toward another of its prey!

Everywhere the same scene was taking place. Here a wriggler, lashing out desperately with its countless cilia, swarmed high to the tunnel wall. Its pursuer calmly, coldly, stretched tactile arms up the wall until it reached its quarry, devoured it piecemeal. There a wriggler, ripping and tearing with that ferocious maw, sliced an invader in two. Imperturbably another of the pale amoebae took up the battle where its slain brother had left off, destroyed the wriggler, then proceeded to devour its comrade's carcass methodically!

Schlater saw, now, that not only from one direction had the tunnel-guardians—for he guessed them to be that—come. Another regiment had swept down from the farther end of the tunnel; still others had entered the battle chamber from the side ports. Flanked thus from every side, with no reinforcements, the wrigglers never had a chance. Within the space of minutes, the river had been swept clean of all wrigglers, the host of pale guardians disappeared to their posts, leaving behind a scattered few scavengers who tidied up by calmly devouring the slain bodies of friend and foe alike. Nothing escaped their painstaking housecleaning save one lifeform, the yellowish, disc-like, harmless creatures upon which the wrigglers had formerly feasted.

So fascinated had Schlater been by this battle that he had completely forgotten his own peril. Now he was sharply reminded of it. One of the tunnel-guards, scavenging the pockmarks beneath his tiny ledge, sensed his presence, quivered delicately, and stretched a pseudopod up toward him.

In panic desperation Schlater screamed and screamed again, hacked at that exploring arm with his knife. The blade passed through harmlessly; where it had gone, new flesh grew instantly. The tactile arm strengthened, crept up and tightened about Schlater, and then slid away again! The guardian, as though completely satisfied with Schlater, went on about his work!

He could not stay here; that was certain. And again hope blossomed within Schlater. Evidently he had been judged by the guardians of the tunnel and found harmless. Schlater wondered for a moment, fearfully, if these weird, amoeboid warriors were the ruling race of this new world in which he found himself. If so, his hopes were in vain. But if not—

Maybe, he thought hopefully, his presence had been discovered from afar by the real rulers? It was evident that they had some means of checking on all parts of their underground aqueduct. How else would they have sent this detail to destroy the invading monsters?

There was but one way to find out. Continue on his self-appointed journey toward the pump, the machine that continued to throb its rhythmic, hollow message of hope through the tunnel.

He hesitated a moment. Then, heart pounding, he dove once again into the racing flood. There was no attack. Instead, a gigantic, amoeboid watch-dog deserted its former tasks, slipped into the stream behind him, and followed him down the tunnel, for all the world like a patient bodyguard.

How many miles he traveled, Schlater had no way of guessing. The traveler marks distance by the passage of time; Schlater wore no watch, and in this murky tunnel, where never occurred a change of light, it might have been night or day, twilight or dusk.

But he had the feeling, as time passed, that he was getting somewhere near his goal. For one thing, the aqueduct down which he paddled was now larger than that in which he had first found himself. The transition had come about gradually, during one of many twists and turns.

For another, he was moving faster now. At first the stream had been sluggish. But now, as the steady pounding of the central power plant sounded deeper, nearer to his ears, the flood waters gathered momentum.

For a time, his logical brain sought an analogy between this place and a possibly similar location on the Earth he had left behind him. But he could find none except in a dimly remembered passage from the poem of a mad Englishman of long ago.

> "In Xanadu did Kubla Khan
> A stately pleasure dome decree;
> Where Alph, the sacred river, ran
> Through caverns measureless to man
> Down to a sunless sea. . . ."

But that, of course, was nonsense. For there were here no "gardens bright with sinuous rills," no "forests ancient as the hills."
Koshu!
The memory of the Jap's perfidy flooded back upon him, stirring him to sudden, renewed anger. Again he was afire with impatience to reach that mysterious, distant chamber where were the engines that utilized this stream. There to find creatures, intelligent inhabitants of this diminutive world. There to begin work on the machine that would bear him back to his own, now macrocosmic universe.

The trip was not without incident. Once, as before, he was attacked by a denizen foreign to this tunnel. This time his antagonist was a creature so contrary to common sense that Schlater had difficulty defining it to himself as living. It was more like an animated problem in higher mathematics. Its form was that of a spiral convolute of the third order; it had no evident organs of digestion, breeding, or sense.

Yet, lacking these things, it gave Schlater a bad moment as it came spiraling toward him like a monstrous corkscrew, studiously intent on making him a *piece de resistance*. This time there was no fortunate ledge on which he could take refuge. Had it not been for his silent follower, his adventure would have ended abruptly there beneath the vaulted roofs of the dim, jointed caverns of the infinitesimal. But even as the looped attacker weaved toward him, the guardian amoeba charged past, brushing him out of danger's way, to fight his battle for him.

It was no battle. At the sight (or sense, Schlater could not guess which) of the pallid protector, the spiraloid spun in panic flight. Futilely, for the gigantic protoplasm swelled to a huge cup, inexorably surrounded its foe, and once more Schlater looked with shocked, wondering eyes upon the filmy acid clouds churning within his guardian as it ingested its prey.

And ever the sound of the motors deepened. For this Schlater was increasingly glad, for now a new factor began to disturb him. Up to this time there had been air space between the surface of the stream waters and the roof of the tunnel. Now this space was being filled, more and more, by the waters, as from the countless tiny sub-passages came minor torrents to fill the aqueduct.

And the air, Schalter noted uncomfortably, was growing thicker, more offensive, less breathable. He had to labor, now, to breath, and in his nostrils lingered an offensive, almost sulphurous odor. A new fear entered his mind. Perhaps he had been too sanguine in presuming that arrival at the mysterious "machine" would mean his salvation? Suppose this feed line led directly into the bowels of some gigantic force-pump performing some fathomless function? What then would happen to him?

But, no, that was unlikely. The builders of this tunnel must have prepared exits. How else to account for the fact of his silent protector. No, soon he would come to an open space. There he would find intelligent creatures. Perhaps not men like himself, but at least reasoning creatures with whom he could make peace, to whom he could explain his plight and his desires.

It happened so swiftly that he was unprepared. Not that he could have done anything about it. He was hopelessly within the grip of the forces that stirred about him, by will or main force he could not have prevented that which occurred.

But one instant he was drifting down the tunnel, the next the throb of the nearing engine had risen to a clamoring roar. A deep, booming torment of sound that threatened his eardrums trembled the fibers of his body.

The flood which bore him swiftened, foamed, became a swirling, churning maelstrom. He saw, with a burst of horror, that what little air space there had been was now vanishing as the frothy waters boiled against the portals of a huge flood-lock!

He had time for one agonized glance toward his calm "protector," time to gulp in one last, lung-filling draught of precious air—then that ponderous plastic gateway throbbed open! From inside came a tumultuous thunder of mighty forces at work, the ear-splitting rhythm of the machinery Schlater had dreaded. And then a terrible suction gripped him and the waters in which he struggled. Beaten, pounded, bruised by the weight of the torrent upon him, he was drawn into the heart of the clamorous chamber!

That he survived those next few seconds was a miracle in itself. The chamber into which the aqueduct fed was gigantic. Schlater caught a fleeting glimpse of tremendous, curved walls meeting in an arched dome over his head, felt, rather than saw, the brain-maddening, angry crimson of those walls. Like the pulsant scarlet drapes on the walls of Poe's *House of Death.*

Then he was being dragged down, down, down, into unfathomable depths. Water boiled and bubbled about him, frightful pressure racked his bones, threatened to force the last ounce of precious air from his straining lungs. All about him strange bodies seemed to live, fighting and struggling; he was tossed and spun like a chip in a steaming cauldron. Hungry fingers ripped the clothing from him, and his flesh was alive with pain from the brutal pummeling.

Then, as suddenly as he had dropped, he found himself rising. And again he was on the surface of the water, a spent tatter of humanity. He panted fresh air into his lungs, struck out violently for the nearest of the ruddy walls, hoping against hope he might find a foothold, a fingerhold on one of those smooth, curving surfaces.

Clawed hands scratched at the wall, but his effort was vain. For these walls, unlike those of the tunnel through which he had entered, were soft and yielding; they seemed made of a spongy, fibrous material. They gave beneath his frenzied attack. In his delirium it seemed that all the walls were suddenly racing away from him now; that the mighty cavern was expanding.

Then one wall sheared away entirely into a gaping vent, the retreating roof of the cavern came pounding down like the crimson gavel of the gods—and again he was seized in a terrific suction, thrust headlong through a second lock, into another thundering chamber.

Down again, down he went into the maelstrom, floundering, fighting, struggling like a madman to sustain that tremendous pressure; then up, up to a breath of air, up to clutch, screaming, at resilient scarlet walls; to claw horribly at barriers that shrugged him off, throbbing, paling, like the huge muscles of some giant.

Muscles!

The simile was born out of Schlater's madness. But the instant it occurred to him, sanity came back to his mind like the douche of icy waters. Muscles! Schlater was a logical man. And now, even though about him beat and thundered a cacaphony that had long since destroyed his sense of hearing, he brought the force of that cold, Teutonic logic into play.

He understood, now, wondering why he had not guessed the

answer before, where he was. He understood the tunnel, the rimy excrescence on which he had found himself, the battle of the monsters.

He understood, suddenly and completely, the chamber to which the aqueduct had borne him, knew the purpose of the "watch-dog," knew what his eventful fate must be. . . .

There was no last, lingering hope now. No chance of ever returning to the world outside. For in these murky caverns were no intelligences to befriend him, no metals with which he might build the machine that would be his salvation. His destruction was a matter of time. Die he must. But with him could, and *must* die. . . .

Schlater was a logical man. And he still had his case knife. He slipped it, now, from its sheath. Strangely, he found strength to do that which he must. Against the incessant pounding of the waters, he fought his way to the wall of the chamber, that great, towering wall of crimson muscle. All his strength, and all the fury of his new vengeance was in his right arm as he plunged the knife again and again into that yielding wall.

He had the satisfaction of seeing the wall rip into jagged shreds about him before the avengers came. The huge, amoeboid forms that had at one time protected him came swirling toward him in hordes as he hacked and carved at the wall before him. Then one was upon him; its mobile body was expanding into the cuplike sac that, Schlater knew, would soon engulf him, burning his body into nothingness with its scalding acid secretion.

Once more and gloriously, with a choked laugh on his lips, he slashed at the faltering, throbbing wall. Then he thrust the knife deep and true into the wall, and turned to face his certain destroyers.

The F.B.I. man nodded toward the odd-looking projector in the middle of the floor.

"Get that out of here, Peters," he said, "and keep it out of sight. From now on, that's government property. We mustn't take any chances on its being stolen again." He turned to the telephone in the room, dialed his superior.

"Chief? Thompson speaking. We found it. It hasn't been damaged. Young Alderson's with me. He says he knows how to operate it. And, Chief, you'd better throw a cordon around the city. The German is missing—Schlater. Apparently he and Koshu had a row. He killed the Jap and skipped. Get on his trail. Okay, Chief. I'll be back with the medical report."

He turned to the medical inspector, now rising from Koshu's side.

"I don't know, Thompson. I'll have to perform an autopsy to make sure. It's the strangest thing I ever saw. At first I thought it might have been death by poisoning—that open wound in his palm, you know. A virulent infection might have attacked him through that opening.

"But that's not it at all. It's some form of heart failure—but the most violent I've ever encountered in all my years of medical experience. His heart seems to have suddenly, and for no reason at all, burst like a rotten fruit! It's ripped into a thousand pieces. Just as if it had been sliced to ribbons—*from the inside.* . . ."

The Geometrics of Johnny Day

OLD MACDONALD HAD A FIRM. IT WAS CALLED THE Northern Bridge, Steel & Girder Co., and Hector MacDonald's boast was that despite a plethora of municipal, State, Federal and other taxes, despite the mad machinations of That Man in the White House, it managed to issue its annual report to stockholders in black ink.

It was also his boast that the N.B.S.&G. operated on a principle of maximum efficiency at minimum cost, a statement grudgingly borne out by those workmen whose sole duty it was to salvage tiny steel shavings from the workshop floors.

" 'Tis braw folly," decided old MacDonald, "to waste gude metal so! And the junkman will pay nowt for't. Shave it fine and scour it. 'Twill make excellent steel wool at a savin' o' three-fufty the carton."

So they did, and it did.

Not that old MacDonald was stingy. He paid his men well—without benefit of unions—and provided comfortable, though not luxurious, working conditions. He was a thrifty man, deploring waste in any shape or form. "Time is money!" was his watchword; to spare himself the expenditure of this valuable commodity, his office was bulwarked by a battery of secretaries employed to protect him from the host of sales, insurance, and contact men who prey on busy executives.

Thus it was, with great surprise that, upon entering his sanctum after an inspection tour of the welding shop, he found awaiting him a young man of whose presence he had not been forewarned.

His first reaction was one of anger, his second was a gesture of dismissal. Spluttering for words, he lifted an arm toward the door. But the young man further confused the issue by seizing the outstretched hand, pumping it vigorously, and grinning.

"How do you do, sir? My name's Day; John Day."

MacDonald retrieved his hand with a snort.

"How," he demanded, "did *you* get in here?"

Johnny Day continued to grin, which was clever. It concentrated attention on his fine, strong lips and jaw line, made the watcher overlook his shortness of stature, the fact that he wore rimless bifocals, and that his hair line thinned back above the temples. He nodded amiably toward the window behind MacDonald's desk.

"Through there," he said.

"*What!*" said MacDonald. He strode to the casement, peered out. His office was on the second floor. But he saw for the first time that the brickwork facing was so arranged as to afford easy hand and footholds to an agile man.

He turned to face Johnny. "Ye clumb!" he said.

Johnny nodded. "I've been trying to get in to meet you," he explained, "for three weeks. Your secretaries have pebbles for hearts. All they can say is, 'Sorry!' I had to find another way."

MacDonald stroked his jaw thoughtfully. "I *should,*" he mused, "ha' ye thrun oot on ye're nawdle. But ye've done me a favver in exposin' a vulneerable spot. Therefore, I'll listen to ye"—he took out his watch—"fr exactly twa minutes. Though, mind, ye're wastin' y'r time! I've na use fr insurance, stocks, nor nowt else. But proceed. What is it ye want?"

Johnny's grin faded, and his lips became as serious as his eyes.

"I want," he said, "a job."

"Eh?" said MacDonald.

"I want to work for you."

"Ye said that," said MacDonald, "afore. The slight change o' vairbeeage doesna' deceive me. Ye want a job, eh? And just what is it that ye do?"

"I draw things," Johnny told him, "and I add things and I say A plus B equals C. In other words, I am—or used to be—a mathematics professor. A geometry teacher. But I quit. I'm tired of looking at faces; smooth, pleasant, dumb young faces. I want a chance to apply my special talents in the business world. There . . . there's another reason, too—"

"The fairst," said MacDonald, "is sufficient." And he shuddered. "My secretaries were richt, Mr. Day. There's na place fr ye in this concairn. If ye were an engeeneer, pairhaps, or even a fairst-class puddler. But a teacher! A hypotheteecal word-mongerer—" He gazed at his watch. "Y'r twa minutes is up, young man. If ye'd be so kind as to shut the door softly when leavin'—"

"Look, Mr. MacDonald," said Johnny Day desperately, "you're making a big mistake. I'll admit that I know little or nothing about the steel-construction business. But I can learn. And while I'm learning, I can be of *some* value. The science of mathematics is useful everywhere, in thousands of little ways—"

"Name one!" said MacDonald.

"I . . . I beg your pardon?" faltered Johnny.

"Name," repeated MacDonald sardonically, "one." He rocked on his heels and smirked. "I'm a fair mon, Mr. Day," he said, "I'm open to conveection: I'll gie ye a chance fr to prove y'r claim. If ye're richt, I'll find a job fr ye. If not, I'll ask ye to remove y'r A's and B's quietly.

"Look aboot ye, Mr. Day. The room we stond in was designed and equipped by efficiency experts whose purpose it was to achieve maximum efficiency at minimum cost. Ye'll see that the office is neat, but not gaudy; complete wi'oot the expense o' needless geegaws.

"However, if ye can show me *one way* in which a cent might ha' been saved in the equippin' o' this room—disregardin' the initial cost of furniture and materials, which I bought at wholesale—I'll put y'r name on the pay roll. Is that fair?"

"Yes, sir," said Johnny mechanically, already scanning the room. The assignment did not sound difficult. But the more he looked, the harder became the test. MacDonald's boast was not a vain one. The arrangement of the office was strictly, maddeningly, functional. Sturdy, but inexpensive, furniture; a hardy fiber carpet, painted walls, plain, unornate lighting fixtures—

"Well?" said MacDonald gleefully.

"The . . . the lamp on your desk!" Johnny's heart gave a lurch; he seized at a timber-sized straw. "The wire which feeds it comes from all the way across the room! Representing a sheer waste of . . . of about forty feet of wire! At nine cents a yard—"

"Forty-two feet," chortled MacDonald, "at eight and a half cents. One dollar and nineteen cents to run that extension. Not bad, lad—"

"Then I get the job?" breathed Johnny.

"Ye dinna! Ye overlooked the trifln' fact that by runnin' yon extension I saved the labor and equipment cost o' puttin' in a second outlet! Wi' the wall plug alone costin' eighty-nine cents, and the labor at least three dollars—" Again he glanced at his watch; this time impatiently. "Well, I maun be askin' ye to leave now. This is all verra gay and entertainin, but time is money, and—"

"*Wait!*" cried Johnny Day.

"Eh? What's that?"

"I've got it!" said Johnny. And swiftly, "What was the cost of that wire? Eight and a half cents a yard? Then two feet would be worth approximately six cents, right? And you said if I could save a single *penny*—"

MacDonald glanced again at the extension under discussion. Simple, cloth-bound cord, it originated from a plug set rather high in the blank north wall, the wall facing his desk, ran down this wall to the floor, along the floor under the carpet, up the south wall to the wainscoting, to connect with a triple socket.

"Well?" he growled.

"Too long!" proclaimed Johnny triumphantly. "Sheer waste! It could be two feet shorter and still do the trick! When do I start work, Mr. MacDonald?"

"Bide a wee!" MacDonald shook his head. "It won't do, lad. I know ye could save a few feet by stretchin' it across the room deerect, but 'twouldna be practeecal! Folks would be forever tanglin' their pates in it. It had to run along the floors and walls—"

"Of course," said Johnny. "I know that."

"Then what're ye blatherin' aboot? D'ye think it's made o' roober? It canna be shorter and yet follow the wall. It touches only twa walls and the floor!"

"That's just it!" said Johnny. "It ought to touch three walls, the floor, and the ceiling!"

"Three walls—" MacDonald shifted nervously. His voice lowered. "Look, lad, ye're a bit excited. Pairhaps a leetle rest . . . a cup o' tea—"

But Johnny's attention was elsewhere. He had moved to MacDonald's desk, found paper and pencil, sketched a pair of diagrams with swift, sure strokes. He thrust his drawing under the older man's nose exuberantly.

"There's the proof. Get your engineers to study it out; they'll agree with me. Geometry is always right. It's your eyes that deceive you. The route of the extension cord is a problem in geodesics—and curiously enough, the *shortest* possible route is one that requires the wire to run upon five of the six sides of the room.

"In rough figures, *my* method of running that extension requires two less feet of wire than the method employed by your efficiency experts. A saving of almost six cents—or six times as much as you asked me to save. And I can"—breathlessly—"I can start work today, Mr. MacDonald!"

MacDonald stared at Johnny, then he stared at the wire, then at the diagram in his hand, then at Johnny again. He said, "Well, I'll be domned!" and his mouth was wry, but it twitched at the corners. His eyes twitched, too. And he pushed a button and spoke sentences into a gadget. He said, "Pearson, I'm sending you a young mon. Put him to work. He says he can lairn the business.... Aye! Verra gude!"

"Thank you, sir!" said Johnny.

"Get along wi' ye," said MacDonald. "Ye're wastin' my time, since ye now work here. I'm a hard mon, but a fair one. Ye passed my test square and honest. Wait a minute!"

Johnny paused at the door. "Yes, sir."

"Ye said ye had a second reason fr wantin' to work fr me?"

Johnny fidgeted. "Well, sir—"

"Speak up, mon! Time is money! Is there something else ye're wantin' beside a job? What is it?"

Johnny's face cleared. The grin came back. "There *is* another thing, sir," he said quietly. "I want to marry your daughter!"

And he ducked out. Quickly. Which was a very wise decision—

So, Johnny Day, one time professor, erst-while follower of Euclid, Lobachevsky, Riemann, Bolyai, transferred his "special talents" to the workaday world.

It was not the easy transition he had hoped for and expected. He soon discovered that there exists a wide chasm between the serene mountain peak of Theory and the harsh plateau of Practice. A specific knowledge of general quintics, he found, did not aid in determining the tensile strength of a new type of girder. By formulae and figures the structure was sound: an actual test found it faulty. Johnny rechecked his computations fretfully; the plant engineers shrugged and called the experiment a "cheesecake cast," and tried another type.

He was assigned to the shipping department. Eager to prove his worth, he spent two whole days figuring out how to most compactly load a freight car with cylindrical cable reels. He drew cubes and squares and cylinders and consumed reams of paper and came within an iota of solving the problem of the squared circle.

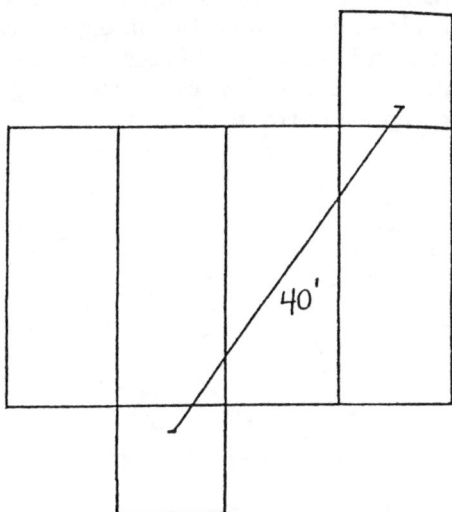

The Day method of running a lamp cord—

He got what he wanted, finally. When he carried it to the loading foreman, gleefully, this worthy—a Bulgarian named Derek, who required assistance in counting his weekly earnings—pointed out that he had been loading freight cars in just that manner for the past nineteen years.

He found a niche, ultimately, in the Estimate Department. There was little opportunity here for the exercise of his "special-talents," his mathematical requirements did not extend beyond the complicated functions of multiplication and division—but it was a job, and Johnny was happy.

He was happy because he was working for *her* father, and because every so often—about five days a week, in fact—*she* visited the office.

She was Peggy MacDonald. She was sugar, and spice, and everything nice; she had hair the color of tarnished sunlight, eyes the color of a Highland loch, and Johnny's heart did things every time she came within a mile and a quarter. The strange and wonderful part was that she felt the same way about Johnny.

"In another year, Johnny," she said. "By that time daddy will realize how brilliant you are, how important to the business. You'll be a vice president, or at *least general manager,* and then—"

"I might as well be a vice president now," Johnny told her gloomily, "for all the good I do around here. The office boy has a more important job than I have. Well, I'm getting what I deserve. I tricked your old—I mean, your dad—into a job, and now—"

"You didn't trick him," declared Peggy indignantly. "You beat him at his favorite trick. And he can growl and grumble all he likes, *I* know he respects you for it."

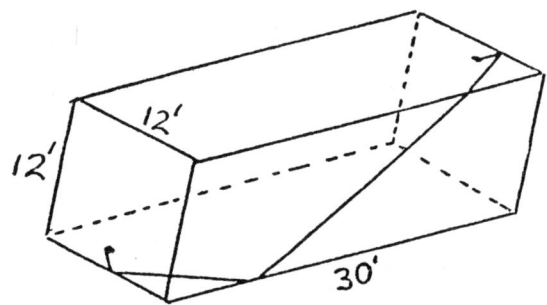

It looks funny, but it's shorter this way—

"M-m-m!" said Johnny.

"And didn't he turn over a complete estimate job assignment to you just the other day?"

Johnny said, "Ye-e-es," grudgingly. "Yes, he did. But what is it? A contract assignment for government steel? The handling of a big corporation job? No! The assignment of constructing a new, all-steel fence around our own company property. Peanuts!"

"It's a beginning," said Peggy stanchly. "It will lead to bigger things. How's it coming?"

"Oh, all right, I suppose. He hasn't complained, anyway. I designed it in the shape of a circle—you know, largest space-inclosure at a minimum cost for materials—and put through an order for the new flexi-steel to be used. He O.K.'d everything. The job will be finished in a day or two, except for the painting, of course.

"And who's going to do that?"

"I don't know yet. I've sent letters to the major paint men in town, inviting their bids. The cheapest—"

Peggy looked thoughtful.

"You didn't write to Campbell, by any chance?"

"Bruce Campbell? Tartan Paint & Varnish? Why . . . why, yes. His company is the largest in town."

"Oh, Johnny, you shouldn't have! Mr. Campbell and daddy are old enemies. I don't mean they'd actually *fight* each other, or anything like that, but—Well, Campbell is a Lowlander and daddy is a Highlander, and you know what *that* means. They spend half their waking hours trying to think of ways to take advantage of each other. If Campbell bids on this job—"

Johnny's neck turned red.

"I don't see," he growled, "where friendship and enmity have anything to do with it. If Campbell's bid is the lowest, and the quality of work satisfactory, he should have the job. Furthermore—"

He never got to mention the "furthermore." For just then the door of MacDonald's sanctum opened, MacDonald strode to Johnny's desk. He glared once at Peggy, then ignored her. To Johnny:

"It has come to my attention, Mr. Day, that ye sent the Tartan Paint & Varnish Co. an invitation to bid on the paintin' o' the new fence?"

"Yes, sir. I was just explaining to Peg . . . to Miss MacDonald—"

"I wush to make it clear," said MacDonald emphatically, "that by makin' sooch a gesture ye are doin' what is known in cairtain caircles as 'leadin' wi' y'r chin.' This I wush to make clear for the pairticular reason that tonicht I am leavin' for Cleveland, and willna be back fr a week.

"Mind, I'm not forbidden' that ye accept an offer from Campbell if by some meeracle the auld tightwad should happen to submit the best offer. All I *do* say is that ye'd best not only be careful, but unco' canny, in dealin' wi' yon penny-clutchin' auld pirate. One slip and he'll ha' y'r eye teeth!

"In which case"—MacDonald's eyes glinted coldly—"Mr. Day, the N.B.S.&G. will most reluctantly be fairced to dispense wi' y'r valleeable sairvices. Do ye oonderstand?"

"Yes, sir," said Johnny.

"Verra well, then. I leave the matter to y'r discretion. If," said MacDonald, "ye possess sooch. Peggy!" He stalked away, then stopped at the door. "Incidentally—when Campbell's estimator cooms, ye might find a way to delay him an hour or so. Nowt breaks that auld rascal's hairt so much as to ha' his men squander gude time. Peggy!"

"Yes, daddy." Peggy's lips framed the word, "Tomorrow!" Then she was gone, and Johnny got back to work.

Thus it was that, two days later, Johnny Day stared thoughtfully at the fistful of estimates submitted by painters who had entered bids on the now-completed fence.

Topmost of these papers was the bid from the Tartan Paint & Varnish Co. It read, "ESTIMATE. For painting, according to approved specifications, exterior fence of Northern Bridge, Steel & Girder Co.—$200.00."

Johnny pushed his hand through his hair and looked again and couldn't believe it. He leafed through the other bids. The lowest of them was $225, the highest, $415.08.

"I wonder why," thought Johnny, "the eight cents?" And discarded the bid. And discarded the others, one by one, until there remained in his hand only the Tartan Co. bid. "It's the lowest!" he muttered defensively. "MacDonald be hanged! There's only one sensible thing to do—"

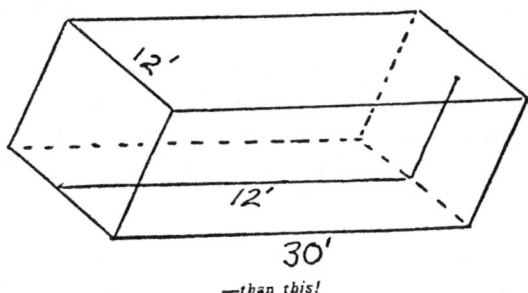

—than this!

And he reached for the phone.

That was on a Tuesday. On Wednesday the Tartan men began work, and young Prentiss, Johnny's companion in the Estimate Department, whistled and said, "Oh-oh! Campbell! The old man's not going to like it, Johnny!"

On Thursday the job was well under way, and Peggy's eyes were as worried as her voice.

"Why did you do it, Johnny? You know how my father feels about Campbell."

"He won't object to Campbell's getting the worst of a business deal, will he?" retorted Johnny. "The Tartan Co. submitted the lowest bid. A suicidal underestimate, if I know paint costs."

"That's just it," said Peggy thoughtfully. Campbell doesn't submit suicidal underestimates, Johnny. He's too canny. Something's wrong—"

"There's nothing wrong," growled Johnny. "Read the contract. The specifications are there in black and white."

"I know, but—"

"Suppose," said Johnny, "you leave this to me. I'm responsible. I'll take care of any trouble that comes up."

Which made easy saying. Because he didn't actually expect any trouble. But it came, ready or not. And sooner than Peggy, or Prentiss, or anyone else, had dreamed. A wad of trouble. The very next day. The foreman of the painting crew came to Johnny's office late in the afternoon. He said, "Well, I think there's going to be about a half gallon of red lead left over, Mr. Day. If you don't mind, I'll leave it here. You can use it for touching up spots later on."

Johnny said, "That's nice. Thanks!" before it made sense to him. Then he started. "Eh!" he said. "What's that? Left over? But . . . but you're not half finished yet!"

"My instructions," the foreman told him, "were to do the outside of the fence. There's just a little bit left to do. We'll finish it first thing tomorrow morning."

"Outside!" yelled Johnny. He yelled other things. Loudly. They had no effect on the foreman, who ducked into a shell of reserve and took refuge behind a single sentence.

"I dunno nothin' about it, you better call the boss."

So Johnny called, and what he heard from the general manager of the Tartan Paint & Varnish Co. gave him that dropping-elevator feeling in the pit of his stomach. Arguing over the telephone got him nowhere, so he went to the Tartan office; there, by sheer belligerence, got to face old Campbell himself.

Which must have been just what Campbell was waiting for, because the grin on his face stretched from here to the Antipodes. He took a duplicate of the original bid from his desk and shook it under Johnny's nose.

"Ye'll notice, yoong mon," he said, "that this estimate calls for the paintin' o' the *exterior* fence o' y'r concairn! There's nowt said aboot paintin' *both* side o' yon fence. 'Tisna my fault ye mistook the meanin' o' the waird 'exterior.' Any gude dictionary will inform ye it means 'outside,' not 'outer' or 'surroundin'' as ye seem to think.

"Furthermore, should y'r employer care to make an issue o' the matter, any court o' law would agree—"

Johnny left. There was no use in arguing the matter any further. Campbell was shrewd, but his logic was unassailable. 'Exterior' did mean 'outside,' therefore just one side of the fence. It did not matter that Johnny had presumed the bid to mean a complete painting of the outer fence. Old MacDonald's prediction had come true.

Johnny went back to his office. Peggy was waiting there. She had heard the bad news from Prentiss.

"Oh, Johnny! What are you going to do now? I knew something like this would happen. You've *got* to make him do both sides of the fence—"

"He offered to," said Johnny gloomily, "for another two hundred and fifty dollars! Your father was right. I'm a hypothetical theorist. I don't belong in a business office. I'd better go back to teaching. 'Special talents'! Huh! My special talent is for allowing myself to be chiseled by the first verbal sharpster who comes down the pike."

"If it were anyone else but Campbell!" wailed Peggy. "Daddy will die! He'd rather lose an arm than lose a trick to Bruce Campbell."

"What is today? Friday? Well, anyway, your father won't hear about it till Monday. Perhaps by that time—"

"But he will, Johnny! I got a telegram this morning. He's finished his business in Cleveland. He's flying back tonight. He'll be at the office tomorrow morning!"

Johnny groaned.

"This is it, then. I had some cockeyed notion about borrowing the money, having the job finished at my own expense so he'd never find out. But I can't do that in so short a time. This is the end, Peggy. The end of my big ideas, my plans for a career in the business world. I've jumped right off the end of that damned fence—"

He stopped suddenly, his mouth and eyes widening.

"The end of the fence!" he repeated. "The end of the fence! Of course! *That's it!*"

Peggy looked startled.

"Wh-what's what, Johnny? Do you feel well?"

"Listen, Peggy—when does the outside of a fence end and the inside begin. Can you tell me that?"

"Why . . . why I don't know, Johnny. When you can't go any

farther without crossing an edge, I suppose. But what's that got to do with—"

"Crossing an edge!" howled Johnny gleefully. "We've got him! Prentiss, there are some men on night duty, aren't there? Well, get 'em—quick! We've got a little job that must be done before those painters get here tomorrow. Hurry up!"

Peggy gasped, "Johnny, what is it? Are you—"

"Tell you later, sugar!" Johnny was scribbling on a scratch pad. He ripped off the sheet and shoved it into Prentiss' hands. "It's a good thing we used that flexible steel. Here, Prentiss. Tell the men to join the fence like this. Get it?"

At eight-thirty the following morning the painters returned to finish their job. At eight forty-one the foreman of the paint crew stalked into Johnny's office, glowering.

"Lookit, mister!" he said, "there's somethin' funny about that there damn fence. When I left here last night I only had about twenty feet left to paint. Now—"

Johnny grinned at him. "I dunno nothin' about it," he said blandly, "you better call the boss."

Baffled, the foreman did so. Johnny listened to his explanation gleefully. "But I tell you they ain't no end to it. Awright, come see for yourself. Send the old man!" And he banged up the receiver. "Campbell's coming over here!" he threatened darkly.

"Good," said Johnny.

Five minutes later, Hector MacDonald arrived at the office. The grapevine telegraph had operated. He wasted no time on preliminaries. He skewered Johnny with a glance.

"So ye done it!" he roared. "In spite o' my warnin' yet let y'rself get bilked by Campbell! Well, ye know what I said. Pack y'r kit, young mon!"

"Good morning, chief," said Johnny.

MacDonald turned a delicate mauve. "Gude mornin'?" he bellowed. "Is that all ye have to say? Ye pull a boner that costs me twa hoondred dollars, make me a laughin' stock in the eyes o' yon thievin' Lowland scoundrel, and ye chirp, 'Gude mornin'!"

"It's a *very* good morning," said Johnny. "The marines have landed, and the situation is well in hand. Ah—there's Mr. Campbell now. How do you do, Mr. Campbell?"

The president of the Tartan Paint & Varnish Co. didn't answer his greeting. He pointed a shaking finger at MacDonald; his voice was shrill with pious wrath.

"What kind o' de'iltry is this, MacDonald? I've seen yonder fence, and 'tis no proper fence a-tall! It coorves!"

"Coorves?" repeated MacDonald dazedly. But Johnny interrupted before he could say anything more.

"Curves, Mr. Campbell Why, yes, I suppose it does. But there's nothing wrong in that, is there? I believe most fences curve to some extent."

"To some extent, aye! Back and foorth! But not oop and doon, like this 'un! And there's no end to't! The ootside's the inside, and the inside's the ootside." Campbell wiped his forehead and glared. " 'Tis skullduggery!" he raved. "I've given my men orders to stop work. I'll not paint bath sides o' the fence fr the price o' one!"

MacDonald could only gulp and stare at Johnny. With rare acumen, he kept his mouth shut. Johnny grinned lazily, but there was an edge to his words.

"You'd better tell them to get back to work, sir. They're just wasting time, and time is money. Because, you see, they haven't finished painting one side of the fence as yet."

"But they ha'!" howled Campbell. "They've painted the entire ootside, now they're *inside*, still paintin'—"

"I'm sorry, sir, but you're mistaken. That fence *has* no inside. They haven't come to an edge yet, have they?"

"Edge! There is no edge!"

"Exactly. No edge, no inside. Both sides of the fence are outside. Therefore, by the terms of the contract, you are bound to continue painting until you reach the spot from which you started."

Campbell snorted. I'll do nothin' a' the sort. I'll take this case to law! I'll—"

"I shouldn't, if I were you," said Johnny pleasantly. He picked a strip of paper from his desk; a long, thin oblong. "Because if you do, we can bring a hundred mathematicians into court to testify that what I've said is true. There is no end to that fence, Mr. Campbell, and it has only one side. It is what is known as a 'Mobius strip.'

"Consider this strip of paper to be the fence. It is so joined that the upper end of one extremity connects to the lower end of the other; thus the fence undergoes a half twist. And that half twist has eliminated one of the sides!

"You don't believe me? Convince yourself by drawing a pencil line straight down the center of the strip, extending it until you return to the point from which you started. Now separate the end of the strip, and you will find that both sides are covered by a straight line, even though in drawing you did not cross any edges.

"I'm afraid, Mr. Campbell"—Johnny tossed the strip of paper to the paint man—"I'm afraid you'll have to continue painting the *outside* of the fence until both sides are painted. I beg your pardon, sir?"

"Nothin'," said MacDonald. "I said nothin'."

Campbell twisted the strip of paper and studied it. He frowned. He retwisted it and studied it again. A look of respect crept into his eyes. He nodded. To Johnny he said, "Verra well, young mon. Ye win. I take consolation in knowin' that yonder auld cow dinna ken any more aboot this bit o' geometrical rascality than I did. Y'r talents are goin' to waste, Mr. Day, in a plant like this. How much is he payin' ye?"

Johnny thought of his weekly salary and started to answer honestly enough. "Twenty-five—" he began.

But MacDonald interrupted hastily.

"—hoondred a year!" he finished. "And I'll thank ye to no' attempt to steal my valeeable employees, Campbell."

"I'll gi'e ye," said Campbell to Johnny, "Three thousand. What d'ye say?"

"We-e-ell," said Johnny.

"But beginnin' today," broke in MacDonald swiftly, "his salary is thirty-fi' hoondred. And"—he cast a sidelong, meaningful glance at Johnny—"and though it doesna concairn ye, Bruce Campbell, I micht add that there are certain pairsonal reasons—havin' my approval—by reason o' which Mr. Day would undoobtedly rather remain wi' this company. Am I right—Johnny, lad?"

Johnny stared at him. Things went round and round for a minute. When they settled down, he was conscious that Campbell, disgruntled, was leaving; that old MacDonald was still gazing at him with an air of benevolent, almost parental, fondness; that entering the office was a reason for staying with hair of tarnished sunlight and eyes the color of a Highland loch. And—

And, "Aye!" said Johnny Day.

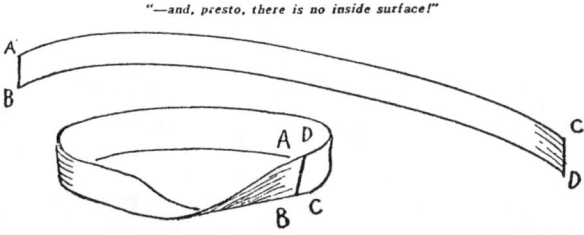

"—and, presto, there is no inside surface!"

"Wild Talents"

When . . . as has oftimes been the case . . . I claim that I do not look upon myself as a science-fiction writer but a fantasist, those to whom I make this protest ask, "But what's the difference?"

"There are many answers. Someone has said that science fiction is the improbable made possible while fantasy is the impossible made probable. But the one I like is to explain that a writer of science-fiction is motivated by the question "What if. . . ?"

What if someone actually did perfect a time machine? What then?
What if we do land a spaceship on Jupiter? What then?
What if the earth really is hollow? What then?

The fantasist is motivated otherwise? The question in his mind is, "But supposin'. . . ?"

Supposin' there really is a centaur . . . a flying horse . . . a snowman? What then?

Supposin' a man could create things simply by thinking of them? What then?

Supposin' the law of gravity were suddenly reversed? What then?

In the stories that follow you will encounter individuals who wittingly or unwittingly possessed one of these wild talents. You will find them totally unbelievable but, I hope, amusing. For that is another attribute of fantasy not shared by science-fiction. Fantasy is tongue-in-cheek, but there's nothing funny about hardware!

Mr. Snow White

TOMLINSON WAS TRYING HARD TO FINISH HIS STORY, but it was the wrong kind of story for this time of year. There were sulphur-men from Sirius in the story—great, yellowish monsters with four legs and a terrific body-odor; and their main objectives were (1) to conquer Earth, and (2) to kidnap the heroine. But somehow Tomlinson couldn't get the story going properly. And that, perhaps, was because its theme of dread and disaster was strangely out of keeping with the season.

It was April outside his office window; April, all green and gold and fragrant. The sun was beaming quietly on a budding, peaceful earth. Little breezes slipped deftly in the narrow crack of window (Tomlinson was susceptible to colds), tugged at Tomlinson's hair, and whispered tempting suggestions—such as, "Come away! Come away!" or, "Wander with us in the woodlands!"

But Tomlinson, with the dogged persistence of all science-fiction authors, dispelled these suggestions and set himself to the task in hand. There must be *some* way for the hero to counter the attack of those Sirian invaders. A gun that bombarded them with *gamma* rays, perhaps? But no—that would transmute them into phosphorus-men, luminous and even more deadly. . . .

It was at this point that Tomlinson heard, for the fourth time within a quarter-hour, the clatter-banging of youthful footsteps downstairs, and stifled, mysterious sounds from the vicinity of the kitchen. Junior again! Tomlinson, his nerves ragged, deserted the typewriter to indulge in some good old-fashioned parental wrath.

"Junior!" he bawled from the head of the stairs.

No answer for a long moment, during which Tomlinson identified the opening of the electric refrigerator, the raw clinking of a cube-box, then the closing of the refrigerator door.

"Junior!"

This time he followed his own shout down the steps, arriving just in time to see Junior, tongue firmly clenched between his teeth, dumping the contents of an ice-tray into a paper bag.

"What in the name of the Seven Saints," demanded Tomlinson, "are you doing?"

Junior said promptly, honestly: "Getting some ice, Daddy."

"I can see that! But why? This is the fourth time you've been into the kitchen for ice!"

Junior clutched the paper bag, already a bit damp, to his breast. "It's for the snow man, Daddy."

"I don't care what it's for!" began Tomlinson. "I have enough bills to pay without— *What!* For the what?"

"The snow man," repeated Junior wearily. Grown-ups, he could not help thinking, were awfully difficult sometimes. Maybe as they grew older, their brains got nearsighted, like their eyes, only they couldn't buy glasses for their brains. "The snow man I built last winter. He's hungry."

Tomlinson closed his eyes and held them shut while he drew a long, deep breath. When he spoke, his tone was gently soothing.

"Junior, old man—suppose you go in and lie down for a few minutes; have a little nap. Daddy's going to send for the doctor—"

"Don't you feel well, Daddy?" asked Junior. And he added candidly: "You don't look so good."

"A snow man—in April!" groaned Tomlinson. "Here, Junior, do as Daddy says. Give me that bag—"

Junior sighed and relinquished the paper sack. "He won't like it, though, Daddy! He's *awful* hungry. And I told him I'd be right back with it."

Tomlinson remembered, then, something he had read in a book on child psychology. All growing children are apt to develop illogical fantasies. The best way to teach them to distinguish between truth and hallucination is quietly to point out their error. He handed the bag back.

"You take it, Junior," he said softly. "We'll go out and visit the snow man—together."

He had almost forgotten the snow man. They—he and Junior—had built it three months ago, during that record-breaking January snowfall. Tomlinson had good reason now to remember the day, because Myra, whose turn it was to entertain the Tuesday Afternoon Bridge and Backbite Club, had forbidden them to build it on the front lawn. Therefore they had built it in the small cleared space behind the garage; a spot invisible from the street or from any curious neighbor's eyes.

But it was strange that Junior should have remembered for so long a figure that must, weeks since, have melted into oblivion. Perhaps, thought Tomlinson with a curious tug of parental pride, Junior cherished the recollection because his Daddy had played so great a part in it. . . .

And then they rounded the corner; and Junior, with a tiny, apologetic murmur, left Tomlinson's side, and Tomlinson stopped stock-still in his tracks, gasping. For there, shiny-white and as firm as the day he had built it, coal-eyed and carrot-nosed, scantily clad in an old hat, a cane and sculptured buttons, stood the snow man!

And as he stared, incredulous, the snow man gravely reached out and took the proffered sack from Junior's hand, muttered, "Thank you, sonny," popped an ice-cube into his pebble-toothed mouth, and turned to grin at him.

"Hello, Maker!" said the snow man.

Tomlinson's knees faltered, but his brain raced at a mile-a-minute clip. It couldn't be the highball he'd had at Tanner's house last night, for that had been extremely mild. And besides, Junior saw the same thing. It might be that insanity had struck them both at the same time. Or it might be a form of mass hypnosis. But—

"I said," repeated the snow man petulantly, "Hello, Maker. I've been wondering when you were going to visit me again. Pretty scurvy treatment, if you ask me. It's damned lonely out here behind the garage, what with only that amorous old tomcat for company—"

"You," Tomlinson muttered faintly, "you're talking!"

"Well?" said the snow man, and crunched another ice-cube.

"You're eating!" said Tomlinson.

"Junior," said the snow man, "does your old man always act like this, or only when he uses the needle?"

"You're *alive!*" exploded Tomlinson.

"I'm not," said the snow man testily, "a mummy. Of course I'm alive!"

"Sure, he's alive, Daddy," said Junior. "I tried to tell you, but you wouldn't listen. His name is Mr.—Mr. Snemon?"

He looked at the snow man questioningly. The snow man shook his head, and his carrot-nose wabbled. "The name," he said, "is Schneemann." Herr Schneemann."

"A Nazi?" Tomlinson questioned suspiciously.

The snow man snorted a fine spray of hoar-frost.

"Don't be silly! If I look that stupid, it's your fault. You made me. But—" There was a certain pride in his voice.. "But I *am* a pure Aryan. The cloud that carried me gathered its moisture from the headwaters of the Rhine. You'll notice the fine contours of my head. *Brachycephalic.* That is the reason—I *beg* your pardon, Maker!"

He snapped the last in a tone of startled reproach. Confused beyond measure, Tomlinson had absent-mindedly drawn a cigarette from his pocket, and even now was preparing to strike a match. Now, apologetically, he thrust both cigarette and matchbox into his pocket.

"You—you'll have to forgive me," he faltered. "I guess I'm a little upset. It's rather a shock, you know. I mean seeing you here—"

Mr. Schneemann smiled condoningly. "Don't mention it. I know how you feel. Upset? Gracious, no one was *ever* more upset than I was the day I tumbled head-over-heels down to earth. Mercy me! I hardly knew my knee from my elbow. To make matters worse, you see, I couldn't very well decide, because at that time I had not yet been molded into either a knee or an elbow— I'm sorry, Maker. What did you say?"

"I said," Tomlinson told him haggardly, "migawd!"

"Quite!" said Mr. Schneemann complacently, sucking the last of the ice-cubes. Tomlinson could not escape the conviction that Mr. Schneemann looked the healthier for his meal. His coal-eyes seemed to glitter a little more brightly, his cane swung from a crooked elbow at a jaunty angle, and there was an indubitable bulge at his waistline that Tomlinson had not noticed before.

Tomlinson tried to reason it out, but it didn't make reason. The more he thought, the more unreasonable the situation became. At last, almost angrily, he said:

"I suppose, Schneemann, you know you're responsible?"

Mr. Schneemann shrugged.

"If you're going to be difficult," he said coldly, "so are you. *Quite* impossible! I must confess. I'm a trifle disappointed in you, Maker.

I hadn't full control over my faculties when you made me; I had a confused recollection of you as a—a sort of super-snow-man. Now I find you're just a warm-blooded mammal, like the tomcat—"

"I mean," interrupted Tomlinson desperately, "you can't exist! Everyone knows that life is the result of the commingling of proteids, compounds, colloidal matter. You contain none of those. You're simply a figure molded out of snow. Frozen water. Hydrogen and oxygen—"

"All right," said Mr. Schneemann a little sulkily, "so I'm all wet. So what? Snow is crystalline, isn't it?"

"Yes."

"Well, rocks and crystals and silicates are crystalline too. You won't deny that *they're* alive. They grow! And so can I—if I want to. My goodness, you should have seen my uncle! He was a little underweight so he rolled halfway down the Matterhorn. By the time he reached the bottom, he weighed three and a half tons!"

"But—but speech!" wailed Tomlinson. "Rocks can't talk!"

"That," sniffed Mr. Schneemann, "is what *you* think! They're regular chatterboxes. Especially the conglomerates. They babble on like—like glaciers!"

"What do they say, Mr. Schneemann?" asked Junior.

"Run along, Junior," said the snow man. "Your old man wouldn't want me to tell you."

Tomlinson snorted savagely. "Hah! Trapped you, didn't he? You were lying! They don't say anything—"

Mr. Schneemann sighed. "Maker, you make me so mad I could melt! What would *you* say if you were a rock? Always being stepped on by humans. And with all the dogs in this neighborhood sniffing and—"

"That will do!" interrupted Tomlinson hastily. He was slowly but surely being forced to the conclusion that he was wrong and Mr. Schneemann right. There was just one thing, however, that didn't make sense—

"This weather!" he said. "You should have melted a month ago. Why, your body temperature is thirty-two degrees Fahrenheit. You can't continue to live with the sun shining like this."

Mr. Schneemann glanced petulantly at the sun. "You have something there," he confessed anxiously. "It *is* getting a little too warm for comfort. Of course this spot is well shaded. I never catch the direct rays of the sun. As for the body temperature—pah! What's *your* body temperature?"

Tomlinson said, "About ninety-eight and six-tenths."

"Disgusting!" shuddered the snow man. "Nevertheless, it proves my point. *You* don't melt when the weather gets a little warmer than that, do you?"

Tomlinson passed a shaking hand across his brow. A defeated man, he stared at the snow man. He knew when he had met his match. Silently he turned toward the house.

"Don't go, Maker!" called Mr. Schneemann. "I want to talk to you!"

His cry raised a stiff, icy breeze about Tomlinson's neck and shoulders. Tomlinson sneezed and moved faster. As he fled, he heard the voice of the snow man admonishing Junior, "Now, mind you get good solid ice, sonny! The last you got me was full of air bubbles. And it tasted like hail—"

Thus Mr. Schneemann became a recognized member of the Tomlinson household—a member recognized, however only by Tomlinson and his son. Myra did not become a party to the secret, for obvious reasons. And though Tomlinson often considered the advisability of introducing Mr. Schneemann to some of his scientist friends, he never could force himself to the point of doing so.

His mind, the evidence of his senses, told him he had seen and talked to Mr. Schneemann. But—could he trust his mind and his senses? Tomlinson wasn't sure. He sought refuge in his encyclopedia, discovered there several anomalies that had never before occurred to him. Under "Life" he found Herbert Spencer's calm declaration that life is the continuous adjustment of internal relations to external relations"—which most definitely did not obviate the possibility of Mr. Schneemann's existence. He also found, to his amazement, that life is as truly a property of crystalline substances as it is of organic ones—the only difference lying in the fact that crystals grow by the superficial apposition of new particles ("Those confounded ice-cubes!" thought Tomlinson) and living substance by intussusception.

He plunged still deeper into his work. But somehow he could not get interested in the adventures of hardy young space-adventurers among the plant-men of Pluto and the taffy-men of Tethys. His work began to slump. Fan mail fell off. His editors wrote him a sharp note of query. And one of his most faithful fans, who was accustomed to awarding him at least four Brazil nuts on each story he wrote, declared that his latest effort was worth, at most, one split goober.

In his office, thinking coldly, logically he would convince himself that Mr. Schneemann was but a figment of his vivid imagination. "Strain," thought Tomlinson. "Overwork. I've been going it too hard. Perhaps my digestion—"

Then, reassured, he would stroll out behind the garage—and nine times out of ten find Mr. Schneemann standing, smiling, sucking on an ice-cube brought him by the obedient Junior, experimentally frosting the leaves of a hapless elm.

"I'm an accursed man," Tomlinson complained once, haggardly. "There's never been another freak like you in the history of the world. *I* have to be the first man to—"

"Stuff!" said Mr. Schneemann roundly. "And nonsense! There have been millions of us. Didn't you ever read about the Frost Giants? They were my ancestors. And the Hyperboreans were first cousins."

"Mere legend!" croaked Tomlinson. "There's never been a living snow man in recent times—"

"Are all humans," asked Mr. Schneemann plaintively, "as stupid as you? I suppose it's the inner heat that makes your mind sluggish. But of course my family has lived in fairly recent times. Once when there was a terrific blizzard in Rome—"

"In—in Rome?"

"Ah, yes! My great-great-great-grandmother used to tell me about that. A terrible blizzard. We tumbled from the sky by the thousands. The streets of Rome were white with us. Scandalous city, Rome. They had just murdered their dictator, a bald little chap named Caesar, I believe. And his friend, realizing that they couldn't give him a big funeral unless we left the city, addressed us. 'Friends, snow men, countrymen—' he said—"

"This," wailed Tomlinson, "is too much! This has to be the end!" And he fled.

But it wasn't the end. Mr. Schneemann remained, a smiling, self-satisfied guest in Tomlinson's back yard, and a menace to the size of Tomlinson's electricity bill.

Until one morning Tomlinson woke to find the sun beaming brightly into his window—woke happily to find that changeable spring had left the earth and that the warm hand of summer had come.

Myra was not home. She had gone to visit her mother. Tomlinson and Junior were alone in the house. Which is one reason why Tomlinson's pleasure vanished in a jolt of sudden fear when he heard Junior's voice raised in an agonized cry: "Daddy! Daddy! He's gone!"

Tomlinson raced into his clothes, downstairs and into the backyard. Behind the garage he found Junior, sobbing uncontrollably, pointing at a damp oval spot on the ground.

"He's gone, Daddy! And he didn't even say good-by!"

A great load seemed to lift from Tomlinson's mind.

"Good!" he cried. "Gone at last! Well, come along, Junior. We're going to celebrate with the biggest, joyfulest breakfast any man ever had— What's the matter, son?"

Junior bit his lip. "N-nothing, Daddy. I just had a little pain in my tummy. It—it's all right now."

Still staring mournfully back at the place where Mr. Schneemann had stood, Junior allowed himself to be persuaded into the house. The boy, thought Tomlinson, was not himself. He was strangely pale and quiet, oddly inactive. But when he'd see a nice glass of orange-juice before him—

He went to the refrigerator, pressed the handle—and frowned.

"Stuck again! I told Myra we didn't need a great big refrigerator like this. Always something getting out of order. Open up, you!"

He tugged again, harder. This time the door swung open reluctantly. And from inside came a plaintive voice:

"Shut that damned door, will you, Maker? I'm running all over the place!"

It was Mr. Schneemann, cheek cuddled close to the cube-box, knees drawn up close to his chin for comfort, his arms wrapped around the vegetable cold-tainer. As Tomlinson watched, one of Mr. Schneemann's toes melted and dropped with a juicy *plop* onto the kitchen floor.

"*If* you don't mind!" said Mr. Schneemann. "Can't you see I'm suffering from heat prostration? I had to come in here for coolth."

"For," repeated Tomlinson dazedly, "coolth?"

"Heat is warmth, isn't it? Well—oh, shut the door!"

That was the last straw. Something clicked in Tomlinson's brain; a red haze danced before his eyes. And rage shook him as a college boy shakes a letter from home. "Shut the door?" he yelled. "The hell I will! I've had enough of you, Herr Schneemann. I'm going to get rid of you right now! I'm going to give you a good punch in the icicle—with *this!*"

And he moved to the stove for the kettle of boiling water he had set there. Mr. Schneemann gasped frigidly.

"No! Not that! Anything but that!"

Then came a startling interruption. From Junior, who had been sitting, white of cheek and hollow of eye, came a frightened whimper. "Daddy! Oh, Daddy—I feel—" And he fell off the chair in a dead faint.

In a single leap Tomlinson was at Junior's side. The boy's pulse was too rapid, his cheeks pale, his mouth contorted with pain. Tomlinson loosened his son's belt, and as he did so Junior stirred from his stupor, winced, loosed a tiny moan. Tomlinson sprang to the telephone.

Dr. Newton snapped, as soon as Tomlinson described the symptoms:

"Appendicitis, Tomlinson—acute. I'll be right there with an ambulance. Put a cold pack on his abdomen until I get there—" Then he hung up.

Tomlinson brushed Mr. Schneemann's elbow roughly off the ice-box, yanked out a cube-tray, and—

"I'm sorry, Maker," said Mr. Schneemann apologetically, "I—I ate them all. This morning. I—I was hungry!"

"You *ate* them!" Tomlinson aged ten years in half that many seconds. "Then what are we going to do? My son—if anything happens to him—"

Then: "Get out of the way!" said Mr. Schneemann.

Laboriously he clambered out of the ice-box. As he moved into the kitchen, a warm breath of summer air stirred through the open window; a faint fog rose around Mr. Schneemann, and he shivered. But he did not hesitate. On slippery feet he moved to Junior's side, bent over and placed both hands upon the suffering boy's abdomen.

Tomlinson cried, "What are you trying to—" then stopped. For with that cool caress, Junior's labored breathing had slowed, his mouth stopped twisting and he lay still. Mr. Schneemann said simply: "Someone *had* to do something!"

The next ten minutes were like a nightmare to Tomlinson. The hands of the kitchen clock crept like listless shadows across the dial; the room was alive with a dreadful silence. And before his eyes as he stood there helpless, impotent, was being enacted a strange, weird drama.

Mr. Schneemann, heedless of the cold perspiration that poured off his head, his neck, his shoulders, remained with his snowy hands pressed to Junior's body. A puddle grew beneath his feet; once there was a muddy *gloop* as Mr. Schneemann's left leg fell off. The snow man turned to Tomlinson pathetically. "If you don't mind?" he said.

Tomlinson pressed the leg back into place. But it felt weak and watery beneath his fingers. It wouldn't be long, in this heat, before Mr. Schneemann—

For Mr. Schneemann's shape was sadly altered now. His hat had long since caved in over his ears; his pebble-teeth had one by one dropped from his mouth; his carrot-nose drooped, and only in his coal eyes was there any spark of intelligence. The kitchen floor was a rivulet. And from the melting ball hunkered over Junior came a thin, faint voice:

"I—I can't last much longer, Maker."

Then came a welcome sound. The sound of a siren screaming up the street, halting before the house; footsteps pounding up the walk. With a swift, decisive gesture, Tomlinson scooped up the dwarfed remains of Mr. Schneemann, crammed them recklessly into the refrigerator and slammed the door. Dr. Newton came in, cast one bewildered glance about him, and bent over his patient.

He rose finally, nodding to the orderly, who bore the youngster away, to the ambulance, to the hospital, to a swift, assured recovery.

"Quite a mess you made around here, Tomlinson," he said. "Lord, man, you must have had that icebox *filled* with ice! A good thing. It saved the boy's life. A messy first-aid—but effective."

"He'll be all right?" asked Tomlinson—his voice hoarse with anxiety.

Dr. Newton nodded comfortingly.

"Perfectly. We've caught it in time. He'll be up and around again in a week or ten day—thanks to you."

"Not thanks to me," breathed Tomlinson gratefully. "Thanks to Mr. Schneemann."

"Eh? What's that?"

"Nothing," said Tomlinson. "Nothing at all, Doctor."

Afterward, with the refrigerator dial turned to "Quick-Freeze," Tomlinson opened the door for a moment. Mr. Schneemann was still weak; but that he would recover, Tomlinson saw at a glance. For the snow man had devoured every container of frozen food in the box; and now, with aplomb, was remolding his somewhat bedraggled features. He smiled at Tomlinson cheerily.

"Junior all right, Maker?"

"Fine, thanks. And you?"

"A little underweight," admitted Mr. Schneemann ruefully. "And I miss that left leg. Maybe you'd build me a new one, come wintertime? And my face— I can't seem to get my nose on straight—"

Tomlinson shook his head slowly.

"You won't be here, come wintertime, Mr. Schneemann."

"Won't be—" The snow man's coal eyes bugged with horror.

"You mean you're still going to pour hot water over me? Oh, please, Maker—"

"You won't be here," continued Tomlinson, "because I've made arrangements to send you somewhere else. Somewhere you'll find peace and happiness, and perhaps others of your own kind.

"I've a friend who is leaving Marcus Hook tomorrow to join the Byrd Expedition at Little America. He's promised to take you along—if you want to go. I think you'd like it there, wouldn't you?"

Mr. Schneemann's look was answer enough. There was radiance in his face as he replied: *"Like* it! Oh, Maker!"

And two great drops of water rolled down Mr. Schneemann's face. But maybe he was still melting a little.

The Unpremeditated Wizard

> For who the dangerous path can shun
> In such bewildering world as this?
> Crabbe—Meeting

OF COURSE, IF YOU DON'T BELIEVE IN MAGIC, YOU MIGHT as well stop reading this story right now. Because from here on, this is a tale of magic. Universal magic. It could even happen to you . . .

It all began with the coffee. The coffee was bad. So bad that it gave Arthur Abbot hangovers. The difference between a coffee hangover and one of the more familiar type is that in garnering the Brazilian variety you don't have nearly so much fun the night before. No one really *wants* throbbing temples, or a mouth that tastes like the fringes of a boiled horse-blanket, but if you must endure these discomforts it's better to get them in a cafe out late than from *café au lait*.

Arthur Abbot realized this. But he didn't seem to be able to do anything about the headaches.

Arthur was a bachelor. Which means he did his own cooking.

Which, in turn, meant he was unable to discern any fault in his practice of the culinary art. Being thus myopic, he blamed his bad coffee on every reason but the true one—which was that he always permitted the brown effusion to boil vigorously for any haphazard length of time from five to ten minutes while he was bathing, shaving, dressing, and (all too frequently) soaking his head in cold water in vain attempt to get rid of the headache caused by last night's bedtime cup of caustic lye.

Coffee is not, after all, the only mealtime potable. So Arthur Abbot, without loss of face, might have given up the battle. But those same qualities of methodical persistence and dogged determination which held him to his overworked and underpaid post at the Warner Loan Company—a stubbornness that did not permit him to acknowledge defeat in any situation—kept him from taking the coward's way out.

He liked good coffee. He intended to learn how to brew a good cup of coffee or die in the attempt.

The morning on which this story properly begins was like countless other in that Arthur woke with a coffee hangover. It is unlike others in that he arrived at a conclusion as to the reason for his chronic headaches. He made this discovery quite by accident as he was tidying up his kitchen after breakfast. He had just finished washing the dishes when his gaze alighted on the dishrag. A mild frown creased his forehead.

"Hmmm!" he said.

He turned and stared at his current coffee-making apparatus. It, too, utilized a scrap of cloth, a fragment of linen as a filter. This strainer-cloth, noted Arthur, was as dingy and stained and unsightly as that with which he had just scrubbed the dishes.

"Hmm-hmm!" murmured Arthur Abbott.

A concept, dazzling in its mathematical perfection, blossomed in his mind. Dishwater was a notoriously unsavory concoction. His coffee tasted like dishwater. Dishwater and coffee had one thing in common; *i.e.*, segments of discolored cloth. Things equal to the same thing equal each other. It was as simple as that.

"Filters!" said Arthur Abbott. "That's it! I need fresh filters!"

With singing heart he finished his household chores and set forth for his place of employment. And on the way, he stopped at the only shop open at that early hour of the morning.

It was a curious little shop, upon the windowpane of which appeared the unusual name: *Odds & Ends, Incorporated.* The window-well was evidence that the name was not selected without reason. In it were displayed an incredible number of dissimilar objects, a mad mishmash of merchandise piled in a hopeless jumble, ranging in alphabetical heterogeneity from an Abysses abacus to a Zulu zither.

As Arthur entered the shop a concealed bell tinkled greeting, and up from behind the counter—as if worked by springs—popped a cheery little man with cheeks the color of ripe cherries.

"Good morning!" cried this chubby little merchant. "Good morning, good morning, good morning, sir! What can I do for *you* this lovely, lovely, morning?"

Among other things, decided Arthur with a certain understandable dourness, he could refrain from being so disgustingly happy. It was not *that* good a morning; not by a long shot. In fact, it was a particularly loathsome morning, what with this headache and all . . .

Arthur shrugged and answered.

"Filters," he said. "Do you sell filters here?"

"Yes, indeed. Plain or fancy?"

"Eh?" Arthur's wandering gaze had ranged the rows of wares displayed on the shelves and counters of the store. They were even more amazing than the merchandise that littered the window. Broomstick, candles, incense-burners; all these items commonplace enough. Less usual—and considerable less comprehensible—were the other surprising objects with which he found himself surrounded. Such things as crystal balls and astrolabes, planchettes and iron cauldrons and grinning masks like those worn by African witch-doctors. In an umbrella stand was racked a supply of freshly peeled willow and hazel wands. What might be their purpose, or why anyone in his right mind should want to buy them, Arthur did not know. In a shadowed corner of the shop stood a wicker cage filled with—of all things!—cats. Arthur could see no reason why any place other than a pet shop should stock cats. Especially cats so uniformly black and truculent.

But his not to reason why; his but to brew, or try. He regained his aplomb with some effort.

"Why," he said, "plain, I suppose. I hardly know."

"It all depends on the purpose," smiled the little man who, inexplicable, had drawn from his pocket a small brass telescope, through the wrong end of which he was thoughtfully appraising his customer. Now he collapsed the tube, thrust it into a loam-filled flowerpot, and poured over it a beaker full of some strange silky fluid. "You have some *reason*, of course?"

"Well, in a sense," acknowledged Arthur. "You see, I love good cc——"

He choked in mid-sentence. From the pot into which a moment before the telescope had been thrust now was writhing a faint green tendril, a stalk. This sprouted before his eyes, grew leaves, blossomed, and bore a small but perfect rosebud! The proprietor bent over, sniffed this incredible flower appreciatively, plucked and placed it in his coat lapel, then smiled at his startled audience.

"I see. I don't know who *Kaw* is, but——"

Abruptly he darted to the rear of the strange shop, returned with a handful of paper envelopes. Through he leafed with brisk intensity.

"Do you know what kind you need?"

Arthur thought ruefully of the many coffee-makers cramming his kitchen shelves. They were all sizes, shapes and styles; probably no two were identical. And many of them used filters.

"I'm afraid not. But I've got to do *something*. I get these awful headaches——"

"I see. Assorted then." The little man's nervous fingers deftly sorted packets into Arthur's outstretched hand. "*These* are the usual kind. These others are special, for use as noted on the wrappers. You'll be careful, I hope?"

"Careful?" repeated Arthur, who was staring wildly at the remarkable convolutions of a piece of twine the store owner had tossed on the counter. Like a drowsy serpent, this bit of cord had first coiled itself; now it was sinuously unwinding to balance on its nether tip.

"*Please* be careful! urged the shopkeeper. "There are certain complications——But of course you understand?"

"Oh, but of course!" gulped Arthur. "Certainly!"

Which was a doubtful statement. He knew just one thing certainly—and that was that he wanted out of here. He had experienced many coffee hangovers before, but never one complete with hallucinations. He groped in his pocket.

"How much do I owe you?"

"Oh, that's all right!" disclaimed the store owner amiably. For reasons known only to himself, he had suddenly donned a conical black hat embellished with the signs of the zodiac. He tapped this headpiece with a silver tuning-fork, and from its volcanic peak began to spiral a spume of spark-flecked, turgid smoke. "Perfectly all right. No charge to fellow craftsmen. Will there be anything else today? Eye of newt or toe of frog? Bat's blood? Perhaps a nice——"

"No, thanks!" gasped Arthur Abbott—and departed with unseemly speed. He was several blocks away, entering the portals of his own office building, before it occurred to him that he had been mistaken for someone else.

And also that *Odds & Ends, Incorporated,* was a very peculiar place.

And also that the door of the shop though which he had so precipitately fled had been opened for him by a deferential old gentleman only two feet tall, inexplicably garbed in a bottle-green swallowtail coat and bright purple pantaloons!

For once, Arthur was glad that among his many duties was that of opening the office, and that he was, therefore, first to arrive in the morning. He had left home physically disturbed; now he was emotionally ditto. He felt the need of a good, strong lift—such as a cup of coffee might provide. Either that or an examination by a psychiatrist. And Arthur distrusted psychiatrists. He thought that anyone who would to go a psychiatrist should have his head examined.

The Warner Loan Company's ultramodern offices included a small lounge room complete with kitchenette. It was to this last that Arthur betook himself, and hastily set to brewing a pot of his favorite drink. His usual bad luck prevailed. Just as the coffee came to a boil, the telephone rang. By the time Arthur had returned to his unwatched pot the liquid within it looked like the dregs of a roofer's tar-barrel.

It tasted much the same.

After one shuddering gulp Arthur realized, somewhat belatedly, his present acquisition. Deciding to change the filter on the office coffee-pot right *now,* he drew the packets from his pocket, opened one—and stared in baffled dismay at its contents.

No filter, this, of cloth or fine mesh paper. The envelope contained an ounce of soft, white, granulated powder! Puzzled, Arthur looked again at the notation: *Standard. For best results, stir into the boiling effusion.*

Arthur pondered briefly, then shrugged and obeyed the instructions. It was possible, he decided, that this was a new wrinkle in coffee-making technique. Perhaps the powder acted as a catalyst, straining or settling down the brew. Arthur knew a woman who always put egg shells in her coffee. Maybe this was something that worked along the same lines.

At any rate, it was worth trying. *Anything* would be an improvement over his present methods, therefore anything was worth trying. So Arthur dumped the powder into the pot. He had just stirred the augmented potion and poured himself a cup when he heard behind him an ominous "Grrmmph!"

He turned to find his employer glaring at him from the doorway.

"Well, Abbot!" growled Horace A. Warner. "Is this what you call getting on the job?"

Arthur stammered, "G-good morning, sir. I—I was just making myself a cup of—"

"Dolt! Idiot! Numskull! I see what you're doing. And it's not what I pay you for. You're supposed to be at your desk at nine o'clock sharp. Do you realize it is now sixty-three seconds past that time?"

"But-but, Mr. Warner, I've been here since—"

"Get," commanded the boss grimly, "to work!"

"Y-yes, sir," said Arthur meekly. He squeezed past his employer, scurried to his desk. His last glance over his shoulder showed Horace A. Warner reaching for the steaming cup Arthur had just poured for himself . . .

Lois glanced up as Arthur slipped into his swivel-chair. Lois was Arthur's secretary. She was also Mr. Warner's secretary. She was also the bookkeeper, file clerk, telephone operator, receptionist, and stenographer of the organization. She was, in brief, the feminine personnel of the Warner Loan Company, just as Arthur was the sum total of male employees.

"Good morning, Mr. Abbott!" she greeted cheerily. "I've finished sorting the mail. Here's a letter from—"

Then a look of concern touched her eyes.

"Why, Mr. Abbott—what's the matter? You look awful!"

Arthur said patiently, "One of my headaches, Miss Lane. I was making myself a cup of coffee, but Warner came in and caught me. So I've got to do without, I guess."

The girl bridled.

"Ooh! That old H.A.! He makes me so mad—"

"Please, Miss Lane!" reproved Arthur gently. "He's our employer, you know."

"I know. But the way he treats you! And the way you *let* him treat you! I don't know why you stand for it. I wish you'd—"

"What?" asked Arthur wanly, as she faltered to outraged silence. "What would you like me to do?"

"A *lot* of things!" declared Lois, with a thoughtful sidelong glance at her companion-in-bondage. "Maybe some day I'll tell you all of 'em. But one thing for sure—"

"Excuse me," interrupted Arthur. "Client." And he rose, for into the office had just stepped the day's initial visitor. A worried looking man, as all who were reduced to entering the web of the Warner Loan Company.

Arthur stepped forward to meet the newcomer, but a step too late, for the boss had emerged from the kitchenette, and it was he who moved in on the hapless client, face alight with crocodile cordiality.

Arthur sighed and sat down again. A tender-hearted soul, it always grieved him to see a client fall into Horace Warner's clutches. Had *he*—Abbott—waited on this man, the poor fellow might have succeeded in paying off his obligation a day or two before Gabriel tooted his trump. But with H.A. handling the affair—. Arthur shook his head. The visitor had come in for a business loan. He would probably get the loan. He would *definitely* get the business!

Lois Lane, who knew what he was thinking, reached forth impulsively and touched his hand. It was an odd fact that for some reason or another Lois frequently contrived to touch Arthur's hand gently. It was an even odder fact that for some reason or another Arthur had never noticed this.

"Too bad!" she whispered softly. "But never mind. Maybe's got a rich uncle who'll die and—"

Then she stopped abruptly, and Arthur stiffened in sudden astonishment, because from across the room the voice of their employer lifted in unbelievable words.

"Three hundred? But of course, my dear sir! We'll be delighted to advance you the money. Are you sure that's enough? How about five hundred?"

Arthur stared at the gasping girl, then at Warner, incredulously. Warner *never* acceded to a first request. It was his custom to beat his clients down to half their original demand, then compute the interest rate on the amount first mentioned.

There was a mumble from the visitor, then Warner's voice again:

"No, no, sir—I insist you take five hundred! In the present emergency you'll need all you can lay your hands on. Oh, Mr. Abbott—"

"Yes, sir?" managed Arthur.

"Please make out a check to this gentleman for five hundred dollars, and record the loan on our books."

"Yes, sir. And the—interest rate?"

"Interest rate? Oh, tush! No interest. He only wants the money for a few months."

The floor rocked beneath Arthur's feet. As from a vast distance he heard Lois' frightened whimper. "Mr. Abbott, *quick!* What's the telephone number of Bellevue?" Then, as the world continued to spin in giddy circles, again came the voice of Warner!

"Well, Abbott? Let's not keep the gentleman waiting all day!"

Insane or not, the boss had issued an order. Arthur sprang into action. He leaped forward with checkbook and ledger. A few minutes later a dazed but happy client was walking from the office, the loan company's check for five hundred in his wallet.

Warner gazed after him, beaming fatuously.

"A fine chap, that. Lovely fellow! Like to have a man like that for a friend. A dear, dear friend."

Then his turning gaze lighted on Arthur; his smile faded.

"Well, Abbott? What are you standing there gaping for? Get to work, you slack-jawed idiot!"

"Y-yes, sir!" gulped Arthur, and tottered back to his desk. With some surprise he discovered that his mouth *was* open. With some difficulty, he closed it. But for half an hour thereafter, it kept drooping open again . . .

By ten o'clock, activity in the office had settled down to a semblance of normality. Three more customers had come and gone. Arthur had attended two of these and approved their loan requests at the Warner Loan Company's unusual (*i.e.,* maximum legal) interest rates. Warner had served the other, turning him loose with half the amount he had asked for, and a life-sentence to penury.

Within the hour, Warner had barked four times at Arthur, and sworn at him twice. He had thrice criticized Lois for doing things he had yesterday told her to do, while six times he had criticized her for *not* doing things he had forgotten to tell her. At odd moments he had complained about (a) the weather, (b) the high cost of living, (c) incompetent help, and (d) the Federal government. In between times, he had waged violent telephonic warfare with an assortment of victims ranging from the janitor to the head of a rival concern. He had threatened nine persons with lawsuits, and challenged one to a duel. It was, for him, a placid ante-meridian.

But at ten o'clock the door opened, and in strolled the two persons in the world whom Warner dared not bulldoze. They were Mrs. Horace A. Warner and Miss Janice Warner. The first-named of his duo was built on the general lines of an aircraft carrier: deep of keel, wide of beam, and equipped with a voluminous landing-deck. Her daughter was a lighter craft—a torpedo boat, perhaps—lithe, slim, gracefully mobile, and dangerous.

To the discerning eye, there was a vague resemblance between these two. A connoisseur of womankind, viewing them together, might have predicted the coming day when Miss Janice would look too grimly like her mother. But Arthur Abbott was no expert in such matters. All he knew was that whenever he saw Warner's daughter his heart went *pitty-pat*, and weird things happened to his basal metabolism.

As now. Right now he was simultaneously hot and cold, mute and voluble, shy and excited. He rose eagerly to greet the pair, and with a strangled effort gargled phrases intended to convey his pleasure.

"Good morning, Mrs. Warner. Miss Warner—I'm glad to see you. Is there something—"

Miss Warner dismissed him with a frosty nod. Her mother's words were of the same temperature.

"Where," demanded the head of the Warner household, "is he?"

"In his private office. If you'll be seated, I'll tell him you're here. He—"

With a sniff and a snort and a swish the aircraft carrier brushed by him. The torpedo-boat followed in a low gliding maneuver that left poor Arthur wallowing in its wake, utterly submerged in waves of hopeless yearning and *Toujours l'Amour*. Eyes glowing like stars, he floated back to his desk, where Lois stood glowering at him petulantly.

"Do we," she demanded caustically, "go on with our dictation? Or do we take time out to pluck petals off the daisies?"

"Eh?"

" 'She loves me,' " sneered Lois, " 'she loves me not.' So *that's* why you continue to work in this moth-eaten modern version of a Carthaginian galley? Because that padded blonde is his daughter?"

Arthur shuddered at the blasphemy.

"Miss Lane—*really!* You have no reason to say such things about Miss Janice. She is a lovely, sweet, and gentle creature. Furthermore, she's not—er—"

"She is, too! It sticks out all over her! Oh—you men! Of all the stupid, blind, ignorant—"

Arthur scarcely heard her irate ranting. From within the chief's office came the muted clink of china. A smile touched his lips, and he sighed.

"Listen—they're drinking coffee. *My* coffee! *She* is drinking a cup of the coffee I brewed myself!"

"With your own dainty lily-white hands?" Oh, goody! Maybe after you're married she'll let you make her a platter of nice gooey fudge—to match that icky look on your face!"

"Married!" Arthur crimsoned. "My dear Miss Lane, aren't you leaping to conclusions? I'm sure Miss Warner has never *dreamed* of marrying me."

"Oh? And are you equally sure you've never dreamed of—Oh, you have, have you? Never mind trying to hide that guilty look! Well, how about it? Was I right? *Is* she padded or, or isn't she?"

"Miss Lane," said Arthur with great dignity, "you should be ashamed of yourself. Such thoughts, such words, ill befit the lips of a modest young lady. I'd thank you to—"

"I'm *not* a modest young lady! And I'm darn sick of trying to pretend I am. I'm a fullgrown, healthy, normally-developed young wench, sound of body and limb! I don't have to drown myself in gallons of ten-dollar-a-dram come-hither to make myself attractive, and I don't have to wear a lot of slinky Mainbocker gowns to show off a figure I bought at the dry goods counter, and I don't dye my hair, and I—I—I can get all the men I want, anyway, and I wouldn't have you if you were the last man on earth, and I hope she does marry you, and you'll be sorry, so *there*, Mr. Starry-Eyed Abbott!"

"But—" said Arthur dazedly.

"And I've been a doggone fool long enough, sticking around this dirty old clip-joint working my fingernails off in the hope that some day you'd notice there was something behind my typewriter beside dust, and you're just a simpering, stuffy, meaky-mousey *sample* of a man, anyway, and I'm sorry I ever looked twice at you!"

"But—" said Arthur.

"And I'm getting out of here right now, and I don't care if you get down on your hands and knees and *beg* me to stay, because I'm not going to do it. And if I ever see you again in my life, Mr. Coffee-I-Brewed-Myself Abbott, it will be too soon!"

"But—"

"Good—" said Lois Lane at the doorway—"*by!*"

The door slammed.

It opened again immediately. Lois stuck her head in. Abbott noticed with stunned concern that she was crying.

"Forever!" she yelled.
And the door slammed again. Violently.

"Well!" said Arthur Abbott. Then, recognizing that under the circumstances the expletive seemed hardly expressive enough: "Well, *really!*" he elaborated.

He was experiencing emotions which he found utterly chaotic. There was a sort of tingling which he tentatively identified as pleasure. After all, it is not every day that a man—especially an Arthur Abbott—learns that he is the object of a lovely girl's affections. And it dawned on Arthur belatedly that Lois was a lovely girl. Immodestly outspoken as might have been her self-appraisal, it was accurate. Moreover, it was illuminating. And interesting.

Arthur was not quite sure what he should do. Mixed with his exhilaration was a goodly amount of doubt, uncertainty, and outright fear. He could, of course, follow Lois. But if he did so, and caught up with her—what could he honestly say? That he loved her? Or even liked her deeply? No man who has steadfastly fixed his eyes on one star for months can suddenly transfer his interest to another. And there was no doubt that Janice Warner was the shining star of Arthur's life. A golden star, bright and alluring, hopelessly beyond reach.

Which was an excellent reason for shifting his field of interest to Lois. She was not, by her own admission, half so inaccessible.

"Still," mused Arthur, scarcely realizing he spoke aloud, "if there were any chance of winning her—"

Then a swift chill touched his spine, tingled up his backbone, and stirred horripilations on the nape of his neck. For suddenly there was a cool, soft hand on his forehead, and a voice which—until this moment—had only in his dreams been so sweetly intimate, asked:

"Of winning whom, Arthur, dear?"

He rose and turned slowly. Fearfully.

It was not hallucination. It was Janice!

Arthur took a deep breath, squeaked an incoherent syllable, took a second deep breath and bleated, "Did—did you call me dear?"

"I did," answered the girl smoothly. "You are my dear, aren't you?"

"But—" gulped Arthur. "But—but—but—"

"That is," amended the girl "when you're not playing motorboat?"

"B-but, Miss Warner—"

"Janice," breathed the angel of the same name. "My darling, let me hear you speak my name."

"But, Janice—I didn't think you'd ever *noticed* me. I mean, I've loved you for months and months, but you've never looked at me, spoken to me—"

"Oh, that!" said Janice. "What do we care about a little thing like that?" Nevertheless, a small frown creased her perfect forehead. Arthur thought, and instantly reproved himself for entertaining the thought, that for an instant she looked amazing like her mother. "Now that we've finally discovered how we feel about each other—Kiss me, darling!" she demanded suddenly.

"Er—here?" asked Arthur feebly.

"What better place?"

"N-now?"

"Why wait?"

"Well—" said Arthur. He took her into his arms. He hadn't far to reach. He lost himself in the depths of an electric shock. A tingly, mingly, technicolor electric shock that culminated in a blasting road from not too far away.

"Abbott! Janice! What's going on here?"

Dreamland faded suddenly, and the land of nightmare took its place. Arthur disengaged himself and turned to face his employer. In a curious detached mood he noted that Warner's face was an unusually vivid shade of lavender.

"Oh, hello, Mr. Warner," he said. "I've got a surprise for you. Janice and I—"

"And I've got a surprise for you!" roared the boss. "You're fired—effective the week before last. Your two weeks are up and you've overstayed your leave! Now, get out of here!"

"Father," cried Janice coolly, "you're being ridiculous!"

"Eh? I am nothing of the sort. I'm—"

"You're exactly what she said," assented Mrs. Warner, entering from the kitchenette. "What did she say? Oh, *now* I see! This young man with the lipstick on his nose, eh? Well, Janice, darling—I must admit you have good taste."

"Good taste!" bellowed H.A. "You mean you approve of her smooching with this—junior clerk in my office?"

"But of course," giggled Mrs. Warner. "If I weren't old enough to be his mother, I could go for him myself. Your name is Arthur, isn't it, young man?"

"Y-yes, Mrs. Warner."

"You can call me Agnes. Now, Horace—as for Arty being a junior clerk, I'm sure we can easily fix *that.*"

"I've already fixed it," commented Warner sourly. "He is now eligible for unemployment compensation."

"Your mistake, Horace. I'm hiring him again."

"You!"

"Precisely. I am the treasurer of this organization, am I not?"

"No! I mean—Well, yes. But that was solely for the purpose of incorporating. Your title, and the one held by Janice, are purely fictitious—"

"I'm sure the income tax authorities would love to know that," said Agnes Warner archly. "Come, Horace, try to be reasonable. Would you rather have Arty as your executive vice-president or—" Her jaw hardened—"would you like to spend six months in the clink?"

"Well, I—I—" Horace Warner knew when he was licked. He nodded meekly. "Very well, my dear. Arty—er, that is, Arthur—shall be my executive vice-president. But as for his marrying Janice—"

"Oh, don't rush things, Daddy," giggled the erstwhile cool and aloof Janice. "There's no hurry. Next week will be time enough."

Arthur heard this conversation, but as through the folds of a soft, woolly blanket. To him the events of the past fifteen minutes were one big baffling mass of confusion. It is true his heart was pounding with excitement. But something else was pounding, too. His head. More than ever before in his life he needed something to clear the fuzz from his brain. Coffee. The cup in Agnes Warner's hand reminded him of coffee. He went to the kitchenette.

But there disappointment met him. The pot he had brewed was gone—all gone. As swiftly as he could, Arthur prepared a fresh one. As it brewed, he remembered his powder filters, took them from his pocket. Most of them were labeled *Standard,* like the one he had first used. But there must be others. The shopkeeper had said this was an assortment.

He found the one he wanted. It bore the inscription: *Special. To Clear the Brain.* This must be the one the dealer had given him for his headaches. Arthur dusted the powder into the boiling pot.

A moment later the coffee was ready. Arthur poured himself a full, steaming cup, sipped it. It tasted good. He took another sip. And another. And then. . .

Then suddenly his headache was gone—vanished completely, as if by magic. And in its place was a strange new sensation utterly unlike anything he had ever experienced before. A feeling of confidence, of knowledge and power, of understanding. A magnificent clarity of thought.

He took one step toward the outer office, then cried aloud, abruptly, "Wilkinson!"

"Eh?" gasped H. A. Warner, appearing in the doorway.

"Wilkinson! You've been trying to remember the name of the man who witnessed the Southern Realty Corporation contract. That's it!"

"By Jove, you're right!" explained Warner. "Good for you, Arthur. Maybe you're not as big a dope as I thought you were. Now we can get a judgment against Southern."

"Boiled!" shouted Arthur, his brain still seething with that strange new intelligence. *"That's* the trouble!"

"With you?"

"With my coffee. In the past I've always boiled it too long. That's why I got those headaches. Now that I've discovered the reason—"

"Darling, whatever *is* the matter?" demanded Janice anxiously, giving way before him as he strode into the outer office. "You're talking wildly. Really, my sweet—"

"Don't!" roared Arthur. "Don't call me your sweet. Shouldn't marry, you and I. Big mistake. Incompatible."

"What? But, Arthur, darling—"

"Wouldn't work out. Wouldn't work out at all. Infatuation. Divorce in six months. All a mistake. All the result of—"

He stopped, confused. Agnes Warner asked, "Yes?"

"Filters?" said Arthur on a puzzled tone. "Seems like the answer is filters. But *that* can't be right. What could filters—" He snapped his fingers, a light dawning in his eyes. "Great guns! Of course!"

"Of course *what?*"

"Philtres!"

"But that's what you said before, sweetheart."

"No. Same sound, different spelling. I asked him for *filters—* with an eff. He gave me the other kind—with a pee aitch. Case of mistaken identity. Probably thought I was a fellow magician, or warlock, or wizard, or whatever he is. Those powders are *Magic!*"

"Quite so!" acknowledged a new voice. "So you've discovered that?"

Into the office sauntered the little gnome who had waited on Arthur at *Odds & Ends, Incorporated.* He was wearing a long black robe emblazoned with gold designs which the eye strained to follow. They seemed to writhe and twist off the robe into some dimension invisible to human optics.

"I just learned you were the wrong person," said he apologetically. "I came as soon as I could. May I have the philtres back?"

"Back? Do you think I'm crazy?" demanded Arthur.

"Not necessarily. Not unless you insist on keeping them. They really won't do you any good, you know. The results aren't lasting."

"They're not?"

"Oh, goodness, no!" The small man smiled amiably. "I know this girl now thinks she's in love with you. And her mother thinks you're wonderful. But that's just because you were the first person they saw after they drank the love potion. I don't know *who* he saw," he added, staring dubiously at Warner.

"Wonderful chap!" murmured Horace A. Warner. "Delightful fellow. Must call him tomorrow and see if he needs another five hundred. Didn't lend him enough."

The shopkeeper smiled faintly and shrugged. To Arthur he said, "Tomorrow he'll probably try to have the man arrested for obtaining money under false pretenses. Because, as I told you, the effects aren't lasting. So if you'll be kind enough to return the powders to me—"

"Then my love affair," groaned Arthur, "is just a magic shell? And my promotion to vice-president—"

"Well, you had already figured the love affair for yourself before I got here. As for the promotion—that's up to Warner. Personally, I think it was a good choice. I don't know what *he* thinks."

Horace Warner said reluctantly, "Well, it might not be a bad idea at that. Arthur *does* know the business almost as well as I do. And I'm getting on in years. I'd enjoy the opportunity to get away from the office more often. For golf, and all that sort of thing. If he'll guarantee not to marry my daughter—"

"Father!" wailed Janice. "What are you saying? I love Arthur. Adore him! I can't live without him!"

Arthur looked at the little man appealingly.

The shopkeeper smiled and cocked an eyebrow.

"Give her a sip of your coffee. The brain-clearing brew," he suggested.

Arthur did so. After a pause!

"Well?" queried the tubby one. "How about it? Do you still want to marry him?"

Janice eyed Arthur wistfully. Then somewhat more thoughtfully. She said, "We–e–ll–"

"Have another sip," suggested the shopkeeper.

Arthur said, "If you want to go through with it, I will. I think it's a mistake, but I don't want to break your heart—"

"Break my heart!" sniffed Janice Warner indignantly. "Good gracious! I hope you don't think I *meant* all those absurd things I was saying a few minutes ago? Don't you know a joke when you hear one? Marry you, indeed! Do you think I'd marry an employee in my father's office?"

Agnes Warner glanced regretfully from her daughter to her briefly-intended son-in-law. Then, being an eminently sensible woman:

"Arty, dear," she sighed, "let *me* have a sip of your coffee, too, will you? I *still* think you're wonderful!"

Arthur smiled—not without a small pang of regret—and passed her the cup that cleared. He said wistfully, "It's all for the best, I suppose. You may have the philtres back. But it is disappointing to lose the love of people seemed to—"

Then suddenly remembrance struck him.

"Lois! he cried. "*She* didn't drink my coffee!"

"Lois?" queried the shopkeeper.

"My secretary. A slim, dark-haired girl. A lovely girl. A *beautiful* girl," explained Arthur, warming to his description.

"Oh, yes! She must be the one I saw in the hallway as I entered. I suppose she's still there. She—"

That was all Arthur heard. In three swift strides he was across the room, through the doorway, into the outer hall. Miraculously, Lois was still there.

Arthur said, "Lois—"

"Go away!" came the muffled answer from the huddled figure by the window.

"Lois, darling!"

"Go—" began the girl, then stopped. "Lois *what?*" she faltered.

"Lois, darling," said Arthur firmly, "I've been an idiot. A blind, foolish idiot. If you'll give me a chance to prove I've come to my senses—"

"You've got another headache," declared the girl. "A bad one. You're talking wildly again."

"It's not a headache. It's a heartache. Oh, Lois, my dear—"

"I—I can make good coffee," ventured Lois. "If that's any recommendation?"

Then Arthur was lifting the head of the one woman in the world who did not need a magic potion to make her love him . . . was gazing into the eyes of a girl who momentarily blossomed with new beauty as her lips raised to his . . . he was feeling for the first time the warmth and pressure of her soft arms about her neck . . .

Of course, if you don't believe in magic, you might as well stop reading this story right now. Because from here on, this is a tale of magic. Universal magic. It could even happen to you.
  If you're lucky.

The Secret of Lucky Logan

WELL, WE LOST BUB WATSON AT MARS CENTRAL SPACEport. I didn't think it was in him, but somehow or other he managed to wriggle through his exams, and the night before the *Sirius* was scheduled to lift gravs for her return trip to Earth, Bub came by to say so long and pick up his ditty bag.

We had three or twelve drinks all around, according to custom, and we handed the chit to Bub, which was only good common sense, and as he paid the bill for our D.T's, he said, "Well, O.Q., it's worth it to get off this void-perambulating madhouse. Goodbye, you space-happy lunks, and good luck!"

Joe Sanderson, our First Mate, hiccoughed delicately and said, "So you're going into the Patrol, eh? So you're going to become a great big two ray-gun he-man with a Lens on your wrist and hair on your chest? Well, best o' luck, chum! Think of us when you're dying in agony in some filthy Outland pesthole."

"Not him!" sniffed Rube Ballard, the Second. "If I know Bub, he'll put in for a nice, easy lightship post, where he can catch up on lost sleep and press waffles on his aft in a cane-bottom chair. Good old Bub!" he added affectionately, and reached for the bottle.

Bub just grinned.

"You're just jealous," he said. That's what's the matter with you.

The whole damn bunch of you are mad because I'm finally getting into active service, and you have to stay here and play nursemaid to a bunch of pipsqueak passengers."

"The Passenger Service," I said with quiet dignity, "is the backbone of the interplanetary space fleet—"

"Comets to you, Jimmy!" mocked Bub. "You know what a backbone is, don't you? A long and dreary necessity with a headache at one end and a kick in the pants at the other. It isn't so bad for *you*, maybe. You're not a brevetman like Joe and Rube and Tommy—" He nodded at each of his former mates in turn. "You're the moneybags. A civilian officer. But *I* know, and *they* know, how monotonous bridge routine becomes on a passenger liner. No thrills, no excitement—"

"—and no early graves," concluded Tommy Randolph, the Third, "on hostile planets. Give it a rest, Bub. If you want to play hero, that's O.Q. with us. Only thing we'd like to know is—who's your replacement? If he's as bad a Fourth as *you* were—"

Bub said peevishly, "That's a hell of a way to talk about an officer of the Solar Space Patrol. But, oh, well—never mind! I don't exactly know who he is, Tommy. A fellow named Hogan, or Grogan, or something like that."

"Old hand?" asked Sanderson.

"Uh-uh. Cadet."

"Out of the frying pan," groaned Ballard, "into the fire! Hold your hats, boys, here we go again! A nice little pink-cheeked recrooty, fresh from the Space Academy. I never saw one yet who didn't think he knew more than—whuzzat?"

"That" was the intercommunications audio humming to life. The visiplate glowed and upon it appeared the all-too-familiar features of our skipper, Capt. Benedict Burke, known throughout the spaceways as "Hurry-up" Burke for reasons too obvious to mention. For a moment he glared at us, then:

"*Mister* Lincoln!" he snapped.

"Y-yessir?" I said.

"Stop trying to conceal that bottle and come to the bridge immediately! The new Fourth has come aboard. You are to show him to his quarters. Hurry up!"

"Yessir!" I said. "Right away, Capt—" But I was talking to myself; the panel was already dark. There was one good drink left in the bottle. I threw it down the hatch and galloped topside.

* * *

Bub Watson hadn't known the new Fourth Mate's name. I still didn't know it after Cap Burke's introduction.

"Mr. Grrzzlph," he growled, "this is Lt. Smlgp, our new Fourth. Please show him to his quarters, so he can get a good night's rest. We lift gravs for Earth in the morning."

"Very good, sir," I said, "This way, Lieutenant—"

"You'd better stop by the Officer's Lounge," warned the Old Man, "and suggest to my alleged aides that they break up their little brawl. The same advice, I might add, applies to you, Mr. Lincoln. You have a passenger list to make up in the morning, and manifests to clear. Well, run along! Hurry up!"

We said, "Aye, sir!" and left. In the corridor, my new acquaintance looked at me sidewise and grinned. "Quite a man, eh?" he said. "Crusty old character, no?"

"Don't mind him," I said. "His Burke is worse than his bite. Only thing is, the Old Man doesn't approve of 'the Cup that cheers'. He's a strict teetotaller—"

Lt. Whatever-his-name-was looked down at me, a huge chuckle on his lips. When I say "down" I mean just that. He was a big youngster, three or four inches over six feet. But he wasn't lanky or gangly. Studying him for the first time, I saw that he was stacked up like the retouched photograph of a professional strong man. Strong, muscular throat ... shoulders like T-beam girders ... narrow waist and flat thighs ... all this surmounted by a large, well-shaped head crisp with tiny black curls, gray-eyed, lean-nostrilled, with features as clean-cut and regular as those of any Greek god. He was a handsome lad—and I don't mean just pretty. He was the stuff!

But he was chuckling now. He said, "A teetotaller, eh? You wouldn't care to lay a little bet on that, Lincoln?"

"Bet?" I repeated. "I don't understand."

"I've got a hunch you're wrong," he laughed. "As a matter of fact, I've ten credits that says the skipper is having a wee, private snifter right now, at this moment."

I stared at him for an instant. I could hardly get my hand into my pocket quick enough. "Ten credits?" I cried. "I'll take that, pal! That's what I call easy money. Here's where we have to do a little justifiable spying, though. How about this keyhole? You peek first. It's your party."

"No, you go ahead," he said. "Quietly, though. He probably wouldn't like it if he knew we—"

It's a good thing he warned me to be quiet, because I was on my knees, now, before the door. And what I saw made me gasp like a mermaid on a sandy beach. The Old Man had his head tilted back. There was a bottle in his hand, the bottle had a label—and the label *didn't* say "Cough Medicine." The label said OLD MARINER. It also said, "Guaranteed nine years old . . . Bottled in Bond, Galactic Distilleries, Inc." It said, "90 Proof!"

My new friend smiled at me pleasantly. "Satisfied, Lincoln?" he asked. "Ten credits, please—"

I dug the bills out of my moth-proof wallet, handed them to him with shaking fingers. I stared at him. "But how did you know?" I croaked. "I would have sworn on a crateful of invoices the skipper never touched a drop! How—"

He shrugged.

"Call it a hunch. I'm pretty lucky, I guess. They all used to think so at the Academy—"

Academy! That did it. The names by which Bub Watson and the Old Man had called him paraded suddenly before my memory. "Lt. Smlgp"! Hogan! Grogan! Came the dawn. And I yelped my astonishment.

"Logan!" I hollered. "You're 'Lucky' Logan!"

And the new Fourth nodded pleasantly

"Why, yes, he acknowledged. "That's my name."

Well, hell, I should have known! Should have known the moment I clapped eyes on that build, that handsome pan of his. I had heard —and what spaceman had not?—plenty about Christopher "Lucky" Logan who, though still a space fledgling barely over his majority, was already on his way to becoming something of a legend to the men who go out to the stars in ships.

Lucky Logan—acknowledged to be one of the finest athletes ever to win five Academy letters, alleged to be the smartest gambler to ever lay a wager, rumored to be the wildest, whackiest, brain-stormingest youth to ever wear blues—*he* was Bub Watson's replacement!

Logan's outrageous luck was the talk of a universe. It wasn't even *logical* luck. When he played football, people said the holes opened before him miraculously every damn time he toted the leather. Three times during his college career he was guilty of screwball conduct that should have cashiered him into the discard —but each time Lady Luck tossed the die his way and saved his neck. Once when, taking an examination, he based his entire thesis on the possibility of faster-than-light radio transmission, a theory at that time contrary to every known fact. Since passing or flunking depended on this one question, he would have been booted out of school for his crackpot assumption—had not that very week *another* nutsack, Lt. Lancelot Biggs of the space-lugger *Saturn*, invented a new type of uranium speech-trap that proved Logan's theory right!

Then there was the time when, in direct violation of orders, he changed course on the schoolship he was piloting. They yanked him before a drumhead courtmartial for that little act—and two winks of an eyelash before the Commander could strip him of his rocket, a terrified lookout burst into the room and informed all and sundry that a black rogue asteroid had just smashed by within three hundred miles of their course, and that if the course had not been changed by Logan, every one of them would now be frozen spacemeat!

Well, I didn't know whether to bubble with glee or despair. But I did know that if I let Logan get to his berth without having met his fellow officers, my position as Purser and Supercargo on ye goode shippe *Sirius* would be comparable in comfort to the position of a Hindu yogi slumbering on his bed of red-hot needles. So I grabbed Adonis' arm and tugged him toward the lounge.

"Come on!" I pleaded. "It ain't beddy-bye time for you yet! You got things to do and folks to meet!"

Thus we burst in on the boys unexpectedly. Nor had they exactly abandoned the party simply because I had gone. To compensate for my absence, they had opened up a few more bottles and now they were concentrating on emptying 'em. As we entered, Bub and Rube Ballard were attempting a little bit of murderously close harmony on "Venus Nell," while Sanderson was painstakingly explaining to Tommy Randolph the Jones-Hake theory of intragalactic spore permeation. Which was rather a waste of time, I thought, inasmuch as Tommy was busy in a far corner, trying to stand on his head.

Four heads swivelled around as we entered, though, and eight eyes stared at us owlishly as I introduced my find.

"Boys," I chortled, "put on the rubber gloves. Get ready for a shock. I want you to meet the new Fourth Mate—Lieutenant 'Lucky' Logan!"

It took a few seconds for that to seep through the alcoholic mists, but when it did, the result was worth waiting for. The four men stiffened like strychnine victims, and Randolph spoke for the crowd when, in an awed voice, he said, "Lucky Logan!"

"Himself," I said proudly, "in person, and not a disney. Logan, these are Lieutenants Sanderson, Ballard and Randolph, your future bridge companions. The soggy looking thing at the table is Lt. Watson, whose place you are taking. My advice is to greet him now and forget him instantly."

Logan said, "How do you do, gentlemen?"

Tommy was still very, very spiffed. Otherwise he'd not have said what he did, because he's a nice youngster. He gazed at Logan open-mouthed and open-eyed. And, "Great balls of fire!" he said, "the synthetic superman himself!"

The minute he said it, he flushed scarlet. Silence fell over the room; awkward silence; and I suddenly remembered another of the whacky tales people told about Lucky Logan. His old man, Dr. Theophilus Logan, had been something of a wingding himself. A brilliant man, his mind had apparently been affected when his wife died in childbirth; he had taken the newborn child and moved bag and baggage to Mars Central, then a desolate frontier outpost of civilization.

There he had raised his child according to certain secret theories of his own. No one knew about this, you know, until years later. Then Dr. Logan had indiscreetly revealed that in Christopher's diet had been planted certain formulae, in his training certain psychological novelties had been used, that made the boy "—a forecast of the superman who someday shall rule the universe" was the way Logan had phrased it.

Well, the newspapers and telecasters got hold of the story, and they gave it the merry-go-round. They hooted and hollered, they employed famous psychiatrists and alienists to study Christopher Logan. When it turned out that he was just another very frightened, very sadly confused boy, they turned the full battery of their scorn on old man Logan. For a year or so, life must have been unbearable for both father and son; then the affair had died down, as things have a habit of doing, and their lives had reverted to normalcy.

But every once in a while some idiot—like Tommy now, or like the sportscaster who went haywire when Lucky scored eight touchdowns against Fontanaland University in the Earth-Mars annual Bowl game—cracked wise with a reminder of this unhappy interlude in Logan's past.

And it must have been embarrassing to Logan, too—because

glancing at him I saw that his cheeks were as crimson as Tommy's. But his gray eyes remained calm, and he tried to pretend he had not even heard the remark.

"I'm very glad to be here with you gentlemen," he said. "The *Sirius* is a fine ship. I'm proud to be one of her officers."

"And we're glad to have you, Logan," said Sanderson. But you couldn't much blame him for being curious. After all, a man with Logan's reputation—"But tell me," asked Joe, "is it true that you're blessed with amazing luck? That's what people say, you know."

Logan smiled. "Blessed," he said, "or cursed. It's hard to say which. Well, yes, Lieutenant, I suppose I am an exceptionally lucky man."

Bub Watson was just bleary enough to be belligerent. Over in the corner he was mumbling. Now he said, " 'Sa lotta hogwash! Don' b'lieve a word of it. No sush thing's luck!"

Logan glanced at him shrewdly. He said, "No, maybe not. You're Watson, aren't you? Mmm-hmm. Well, Watson, some people call it luck; *I* prefer to call it—well, hunches!"

Bub grunted. "Don' b'lieve in hunshesh! No sush thing—" he persisted doggedly.

"For instance," said Logan, "there's a little hunch I happened to have right now. There's no logical basis for it, you understand—but when I get these things, I simply can't control them. I have a strong hunch that *you*, Watson, have a physical peculiarity—"

Bub started. "Huh? Whuzzat? 'Sa lie!"

"I have a hunch," continued Logan suavely, "that on your left foot you have six toes. You'll admit I have no way of knowing whether or not this is so, but—"

Bub's grumble turned to a howl. "Sixsh toesh! 'Sa *damn* lie! No such thing—"

"—and furthermore, I'm willing to back my hunch," Logan offered, "with a little wager of—oh, let's say twenty credits—"

Oh, boy, did he get takers! We all hollered at the same time. I'd seen Bub Watson in the showers a dozen times. I knew there weren't any extra toes on either of his feet. So did the others. Quick as I was, Sanderson and Watson got the jump on me.

"I'll take it!" they yelled in unison, then looked at each other. Joe backed down ungraciously. "Oh, all right. It's your foot, Bub."

And triumphantly, Bub Watson sat down and stripped off his left boot, his left sock, wriggled his foot before Logan's eyes for the lucky lad's inspection—

There were exactly five toes on Watson's left foot!

Gleefully, Bub tucked away the bills Logan handed him. He wouldn't have been human if he hadn't gloated a bit over his victory.

"Looksh like your luck ran out that time, Logan," he taunted. "Guessh that'll teach you not to make foolish bets any more. Twenty nice fat creditsh—"

But the smile had not faded from Logan's eyes. It was even more serene than before. He said, "Yes, I guess so, Bub. Do me a favor, will you? Don't put your shoe on—"

He stepped to the wall audio, pressed the button to the bridge. An instant later the face of Captain Burke shone down on us. "Well, Logan, what is it?" he demanded. "Didn't you go to your bunk? What are you doing in the Lounge? What do—" Then his jaw dropped, his eyes jolted open. A bellow split his throat. *"Watson!* Am I seeing things? Do you have your *shoe* off?"

"Yesh, shir!" chortled Bub proudly. "Lucky Logan's luck ran out on him, shir. I made 'im a lil bet—"

Cap Burke turned to Logan numbly. His voice was an empty husk. "I—I'll see you first thing in the morning," he said—and blanked out.

Sanderson stared at Logan curiously.

"What's this all about, Logan? What did he mean?"

The new Fourth smiled modestly. "Well, you see, it seems Captain Burke had heard of my—er—luck. When he welcomed me aboard, he undertook to advise me against gambling. He wanted to teach me a lesson, so—"

"So?" I prompted.

"So before I left the bridge," explained Logan, "he and I made a little bet. A hundred credits. I—er—I bet him I could make Bub Watson take his left shoe off within five minutes after meeting him . . ."

Well, if that's "luck," I'm a monkey's uncle—and no cracks, please! When you give twenty to win a hundred, it ain't luck, it's logic.

But do you know, the boys wouldn't take that bit of finoodling as conclusive evidence that Logan was the wise lad he was supposed to be? I don't know why it is, but let a man get a reputation in some line and immediately every Tom, Dick and Harry wants to try to beat him at his own game. Look how stumblebums fall all over themselves trying to get into a ring with fight champions, and watch the suckers lining up in front of a dice table.

During the next three or four days, Sanderson, Ballard and Randolph spent all their waking hours trying to prove they were just as clever, and just as lucky, as Lucky Logan. All they proved is that a fool and his money are soon parted. Because Logan simply couldn't be beaten at any game of skill, chance or logic. He took 'em at stud and at craps, at high-low and at matching coins.

Me, I didn't get sucked into any of this craziness. As combined Purser and supercargo aboard the *Sirius*, I've got all the job I can handle once the ship lifts gravs. I had to make out passenger lists, prepare invoices and port clearance statements, arrange for freight transshipment and quarantine inspection—all that stuff.

So I was as busy as a hound in an apple orchard for the next few days. Meanwhile, the *Sirius* plowed ether like a dream, maintaining her routine cruising speed of 200,000 mph. and Earth, as viewed through the observation chamber panels, was daily becoming larger, greener, nearer.

It was on the evening of the fifth day that I stood in the observation chamber, looking out upon the never-ending marvel of star-spangled space, when Lucky Logan came to stand beside me. All the passengers had turned in; save for us and the night-watch, a pilot on the bridge and an engineer in the motor-room, every other living soul aboard was asleep.

"Lovely, isn't it, Jimmy?" he said.

"If you mean that the way it sounds," I replied cautiously, "the answer is yes. But if that innocent-appearing opening remark is the prelude to a little bet of some kind—"

"Oh, don't let's talk about bets, Jimmy," he sighed. "Let's not talk about luck or bets or hunches. Sometimes I get so weary of pretending—"

He stopped suddenly. I stared at him.

"Pretending?" I repeated.

"Skip it, Jimmy. It was a slip of the tongue."

"I know all about them slip of the tongues," I told him sagely. "They've usually got something behind them more than mixed-up vocal cords. Maybe it isn't any of my business, Lucky, but—come clean. What's on your chest? Maybe you'd feel better if you told somebody."

"I told you," he said half-angrily—and I couldn't tell whether his anger was directed at me or at himself, "it was merely a slip of the tongue. Forget it, please. Let's just look at the stars and lose ourselves in the beauty of—*Hey!*"

"What's the matter?" I asked.

"Look! That way. Off to the right and a little below Alioth—"

I looked in the direction designated. To the right and a little bit below Epsilon Ursae Majoris there was a dot, a bright gleam of light that shouldn't be there. I gasped.

"A nova! Boy, what do you think? Hey, I bet the Old Man would like to see this! I'm going to wake him—" I started for the doorway. But Lucky stopped me.

"Wait, Jimmy! That's no nova; that's a new comet! And unless I'm very much mistaken—Come on! We've got to get down to the radio turret!"

Sparks was drowsing in his chair when we highballed into his turret, but five minutes later the last vestige of sleep was banished from his eyes as we dictated our message to Lunar III and waited for a reply. He looked at Logan admiringly.

"Gee, some guys have all the luck! I'll bet a hat you were the first guy to see this. Now they'll name it after you, and—"

Lucky said tightly, "I'm not concerned about that. What I'm wondering is how a comet should appear so suddenly, without its presence ever having been suspected. We didn't get any observatory reports on this one. Which means it must have appeared without warning. And *that* means—"

"Speed!" I broke in. "Tremendous speed!"

"Right! And it's moving in the general direction," said Logan worriedly, "of our Solar System!"

Then before the full import of his words struck me, Sparks' receiver started chattering, and our answer came back from Lunar III. And the answer justified Logan's fears by a thousandfold.

"Position of new comet verified," read the message, "by three Lunar, seven Earth observatories. Mass and weight not yet ascertained, but speed determined as highest ever yet recorded. From initial observations, Prentiss of Copernicus Observatory fears comet will approach within three degrees of Earth's sun. Further reports later."

That was all. It was enough. I'm not a trained astrogator, nor is Sparks, but both of us had enough space-learning to know what that meant. We looked at Lucky Logan with haggard eyes, and his answering gaze was equally dismal.

I said, "Three degrees! But, Lucky, that means—"

And he nodded slowly. "Yes, Jimmy. The death of an empire—Man's empire! The destruction of the Solar System!"

I can't tell you exactly what happened then, because everything happened at once. I remember racing down to Capt. Burke's quarters, rousing him, bringing him to the bridge. I guess Logan must have audioed the other officers, for they all were there; Joe and Rube and Tommy, even Chief McMurtrie and his Assistant Engineer, Bob Evans.

Swiftly, Logan explained the situation. His statement was greeted with blank dismay. Then, because spacemen do not meekly surrender, even in the face of insurmountable odds, suggestions started pouring forth.

Cap Burke stoutly refused to believe that the situation was as dire as it had been painted.

"Nonsense!" he declared. "The Solar System has endured for aeons; it will live for aeons more! Just because a new comet has been sighted is no reason for falling into panic. Anyhow, this is all a matter of snap judgment. Astronomers are always crying doom. After they've checked their figures, they'll probably decide the comet won't come any nearer than Pluto. Or if it does come nearer, what then? The Sun is so large that it will shrug it off—"

He was whistling in the dark, of course. He knew as well as we did that if this weird extra-galactic visitor were to approach within three degrees of Sol there would be a duplication of that horrendous event which, untold ages ago, had brought Earth and the rest of Sol's cosmic family into being.

Two mighty, flaming monsters brushing each other in space. Great arms of fire, tidal waves of scorching death and destruction, stretching toward each other. Tremendous flames hurtling from comet to Sun, from Sun to comet; all ether ruddy in that seething cauldron. Little Mercury plummeting into the fiery bosom of the Sun ... Venus' steamy jungles parching, the volcanic core of Earth bursting its thin skin in a thousand places, mighty Jupiter reeling in its course ... these were but a few of the lesser things that *might* happen.

The chatter of the receiving set put the lie to his guess. Joe Marlowe was reporting again from Lunar III. There was something like hysteria in his call.

"Previous information on comet now verified. Earth doomed. Entire Solar System liable to destruction, scientists claim. Terrestrial, Martian, Venusian governments organizing all available spacecraft for evacuation to outer planets.

"*Flash!* All craft in space! Proceed instantly to nearest colonized planet, take aboard full complement of refugees and sail top speed for New Oslo, Uranus! Keep tuned to this wavelength. That is all."

Tommy Randolph stared at us starkly.

"It's impossible!" he choked. "There aren't that many spacecraft. They can't save one man out of a hundred thousand. But—but we've got to do our share. Skipper?"

"It's a toss-up," said Burke grimly. "We're as far from Mars as from Earth. We might as well go on into Luna."

Chief McMurtie nodded dourly.

"We'll have to, Captain. We haven't enough fuel to reach Uranus unless we restock. Even so, it will take us ten weeks or more to reach Uranus. In that time—" He shrugged.

"Ten weeks!" That was Lucky Logan. "But certainly it won't take us that long, Chief! Surely the *Sirius* is equipped with one of those new velocity-intensifiers?"

"If you mean the experimental V-1 unit," glowered McMurtie, "invented by that Biggs chap, yes, we have one. But we were issued strict orders not to attempt to use it. Both times he tried to use it on the *Saturn*, something happened to the ship. The last time Biggs was killed, Heaven rest him."

"But this is an emergency! We've got to use it! I have a hunch—" A look of calculation come suddenly into the young Fourth's eyes. "I have a hunch that if we stepped up our velocity, went out to meet—"

"*Mister* Logan!" Cap Burke's temper was frayed. He whirled on Logan determinedly. "I'll ask you to remember you are fourth in command aboard this vessel. This is no time to listen to your 'hunches'. It will take more than mere 'luck' to get us out of a perilous situation."

"But, sir—"

"That will do! Now, gentlemen, here are my orders. We will not inform the passengers of this emergency. There is no reason for creating amongst them the confusion and despair we ourselves have been made subject to.

"We will proceed as swiftly as possible to Luna, and there assume whatever part in the evacuation plan is allotted to us. I see no other course to pursue. Now, I advise all of you to go to your quarters, get as much rest as possible. You will need all your energy and vitality in the evil days before us. Goodnight, gentlemen!"

"But, Captain—" tried Logan again.

"Goodnight, Lieutenant!" said Burke again firmly. And that was all Lucky could get out of him. We retired.

* * *

We retired, but we didn't sleep. How could we? The Earth doomed, our loved ones in danger, Man's hard-fought-for civilization, his empire of the stars destined to die beneath flames of a holocaust—how could we sleep?

But orders are orders. When I awoke the next morning I found that so far as the passengers were concerned, nothing had happened in the night. They were still laughing, playing, flirting, enjoying themselves as passengers on a luxury liner will.

But I glanced through the observation panel and saw that the comet, which twelve hours before had been but a dot, was now a blazing orb. And when I visited the radio turret I learned from Sparks that our period of grace had been computed. Ten days! Ten days before the comet should sweep the skirts of Sol, raising the flaming tides that spelled death to Earth and its sister planets. . . .

It was that afternoon that Lucky Logan came again to Captain Burke with a suggestion. Burke was in no mood to hear him, but Logan's sheer persistence won him an audience.

"Make it short, though!" warned the skipper. "And I warn you, I want no crazy plans such as that you suggested last night. I have troubles enough—"

"No, sir," said Logan mildly. "This is something entirely different, sir. It's about the passengers. They don't know about the comet, sir, but they're sort of nervous. Maybe they feel there's something wrong from the way we've been acting. I thought perhaps some form of entertainment might quiet them, sir."

Burke pursed his lips, then nodded slowly. "Well, I don't see anything wrong with that. Matter of fact, it's not a bad idea. What form of entertainment did you have in mind, Lieutenant? A dance—"

Logan said politely, "That would be very nice, sir. But what I *really* had in mind was something a little more unusual. Everyone is interested in mesmerism. And it so happens that I have a—er—trifling skill at the art of hypnotism. I thought it might amuse our guests to watch an exhibition—"

"Very good!" grunted the Old Man. "Like to see that myself. But you'll need a subject—"

Logan said, "Yes, sir. I was going to ask Jimmy to act as my subject—"

I yelped, "Who, me? Oh, no! Leave me out of this! I've got enough worries, without—"

Cap Burke frowned me into silence.

"That will do, Lincoln. I heartily approve of Lt. Logan's plan. Lord knows this may be the last entertainment any of us get for a long while. You will act as his subject. That is not a request; it is a command."

Lucky said, "Thank you, sir. And—er—I believe you expressed some interest in watching the exhibition? If I might make the suggestion, sir, you might watch it through the audio-visiplate. And whatever others are on duty might also be advised of the hour—"

"I'll do that," approved Burke. "We'll make it for eight o'clock, Solar Constant Time, O.Q.?"

And so it was decided. And of course I was the victim. As if *that* were unusual!

Thus it was that a few minutes after eight o'clock Lt. Christopher Logan and I were standing on the platform of the main ballroom in the *Sirius* before the assembled guests and officers of the ship. The audio-visiplates were turned on, and our little act was being watched not only by those before us, but by Capt. Burke and Lt. Ballard on the bridge, by a crew of wipers in the boiler room, by Slops in the pantry, a storeroom guard—oh, everyone on or off duty.

Logan had made a few introductory remarks concerning hypnotism, sketching in a brief history of it from its early discovery as "mesmerism" or animal magnetism up to its acknowledgement as a true force in the latter part of the 21st Century, and now the main event was to begin.

"Mr. Lincoln," Logan concluded, "will be beguiled into seeing things that do not exist, performing operations that he is normally incapable of performing, hearing sounds that are inaudible to our ears. In short, while under the influence of the hypnotic spell, he will live in a world all his own; a world in which we do not exist, or, if we do, we will exist only in some distorted version of his own mind.

"Now, Jimmy—"

I sighed and faced him. His fine gray eyes were friendly, but there was a compulsion in them I had never before noticed. He rearranged our positions so that he could face me and at the same time face both the audio and the men and women of his audience. Then he began to speak in a firm, low tone. His words were strangely soothing and gentle.

"There is quiet falling over this room," he intoned, "and in that quiet is the peace and forgetfulness of sleep. You are becoming drowsy . . . drowsy . . . drowsier by the moment. A great weight is upon your eyelids . . . you want to sleep. . . ."

Oh, yeah? I stared at him amazedly. I had never felt more wide awake in my life.

"The soft fingers of sleep close down upon you," he continued. There were little beads of sweat on his forehead, now; his eyes were grave and intent with concentration. "You will forget the toil, the trials, the troubles of the world, and relax completely. Let sleep claim your mind, let gentle slumber overwhelm you. Sleep . . . sleep . . . sleep. . . ."

This was getting whackier by the moment! Sleepy! Me? Why, hell's booming gongs, I had no more desire to go to sleep than a hungry cat in an aviary. I wet my lips and gave him the high-sign out of the corner of my mouth.

"Ixnay, alpay!" I whispered. "It ain't orkingway!"

But he paid absolutely no attention to my pig Latin. His eyes were gray clouds of strain, now; the perspiration was staining his cheeks and throat as he bent forward, looking not *at me* but over my shoulder and his voice which had been low and soothing, was raised now in sharp, ringing command.

"Sleep! You will all sleep till I bid you awaken!"

That was the last straw. I shook myself and stepped forward, grinning. I said, "Sorry, pal, but it's no go. I'm afraid you'd better pick yourself a new subject."

Then Lucky Logan relaxed, took a handkerchief from his pocket and wiped his brow. And a broad smile came to his lips. He said, "New subject, Jimmy? I've got plenty of subjects. Take a look, friend—"

I turned, following the wave of his hand. And when I turned, I yelled my shock out loud. *Every single soul who had been watching the exhibition was fast asleep!*

Get that straight! I don't mean some of 'em. *All* of them! The passengers, the crewsmen—even those who'd been watching through the visiplates. I glimpsed Cap Burke in the control turret, his head had fallen forward onto his arms and his eyes, wide open, were vacant pools. The black gang down in the engine room were slumbering like contented cats. The cook was snoozing in his galley. It was—

"M-mass hypnosis!" I gasped. "You gave 'em all the works at once!"

"Right!" acknowledged Lucky grinning. "All but you, pal. I needed someone to help me, and I figured you had as much good all-around commonsense as any of 'em. We've got plenty of work to do. Come on, let's get started!"

I edged away from him cautiously.

"Now, wait a minute," I said, "if this is some plan of mutiny—"

"Don't be a damned fool!" he snapped. "This is the only salvation for ourserves and our world. The Old Man was too stubborn to listen to me last night, so I had to cook up some scheme to try out my ideas.

"Now, look—these folks are going to stay asleep for the next couple of hours. We've got to work fast. Where is that velocity intensifier unit McMurtrie was talking about?"

"In—in the storeroom."

"Well, get it for me. I've read about it. I think I can make it work." A frown creased his forehead. "I hope I can make it work," he gritted. "Because it's our last chance!"

So we got busy. And he made it work. It wasn't any breeze, because the V-I unit was based on an entirely radical system of atomic transformations than any machine either of us had ever seen before. But Lucky Logan had gray matter behind that Adonis phiz of his. He puzzled over it for a while, then said, "O.Q. This wire goes here, that shunt ties in there . . . we connect this . . . and this . . ."

I said, "Maybe if we move some of these Sleeping Beauties out of the way we can work easier, hey, Lucky?"

He stopped me. "No! Don't touch them, Jimmy! We mustn't ever let them know what happened. You and I are the only ones in the universe who will ever know the truth."

"And unless you give out," I complained, "you'll be the only one. What *are* we doing?"

He finished tying in the last coil of wire, lifted, stared at me soberly. "We're going out to deflect that comet, Jimmy," he said. "We're going out into space to meet it—at a speed greater than that of light!"

"What?" I yelled. "Us—in this little band-box of a spaceship? Going out to deflect— You're crazy!"

"Maybe," said Lucky Logan softly. "But I've got a hunch it will work, Jimmy. You see, size doesn't matter. The only thing that matters is *mass*.

"You studied Einstein's general theory in college, didn't you? And you know the Lorenz mass-energy transformations? Mass increases as speed approaches the velocity of light, until at light-velocity mass is infinite. And mass has tremendous gravitational influence, attractive power.

"Therefore, if we can approach anywhere near that comet and stabilize our speed at 186,000 miles per second, the *Sirius* will be an object of infinite mass. Its force will divert the comet from its trajectory—and the measure of its deviation will save the Solar System!"

It was at that moment I knew he was right. And it was at that moment, too, I realized something else. I was in the presence not of the luckiest man alive, nor the whackiest, but of *genius!*

I said soberly, "How long, Mr. Logan? How long will it take us to get out there and do our stuff?"

"Not very long. Because we'll be travelling at the rate of approximately five hundred million miles per hour—"

I gulped. "W-we will?"

And he smiled. "No, we already are! I cut in the V-I unit five minutes ago!"

I suppose I should tell you how it feels to travel that fast. Well, I can't because it simply didn't feel a bit different. That was, Logan explained to me, because we were a "closed universe" in ourself. Time and matter and speed being purely relative, it didn't matter a particle to us how fast we were travelling; things looked just the same. Though we would have been, Logan said, completely invisible to an outside observer. "We contract" he explained, "along the line of our flight in geometric ratio to our increased speed. At the speed of light we have zero dimensions and infinite mass. We are already warping the space through which we travel. By my calculations, we need only get within three billion miles of the comet to disturb it sufficiently to turn it completely off its course."

"Three billion, you said?"

"That's right."

Well, that was a break for our side. I had feared we were what you might call a sort of "suicide expedition." That we would have to destroy ourselves by approaching the comet closely enough to divert it. I sighed and said, "When do we know we've done the trick?"

"By watching. Look through the visilens, Jimmy. You'll notice that space doesn't look the same as you're accustomed to seeing it. Instead of it being made up of black background and white dots which are the stars, it is a crazy quilt of flickering gray, crossed and crisscrossed with lines of lights.

"Those lines are the stars, viewed at our frightful speed. You see that one broad yellow line? Well, that's the comet. Watch that closely. When you see it 'break' suddenly and seem to veer off away from us, our task is done."

"Away from us? But it should be toward us. If we attract it."

"No," said Lucky, "because I'll be watching, too. And the moment I see the line shift, I'll throw the ship in a Loernberger loop, returning to our former course. Thus the stars will be running away from us, and the comet's path will seem to break the other way."

And it was just as he had said. For a little more than an hour (the comet had been deeper in space than we had imagined) we sat there at the controls, grimly watching that yellow line move smoothly on in a straight direction. Then, suddenly, it gave a little wriggle.

I yelled. But even as I yelled, Logan was tugging on the control levers, the *Sirius* pulled around with a jerk, and we were flashing back toward our own little sector of familiar space.

And it was then that Lucky Logan rose with a sigh of relief.

"It worked, Jimmy. Earth is saved. And now, let's get this mess cleaned up.

"Cleaned up?" I yammered. "You mean you're not going to leave the V-I unit connected?"

"For a little while, yes. But I've got some other things to do—"

And he disappeared.

After a while I got curious. I switched on the visiplates until I caught sight of him. He was in the ballroom, bending over one of the passengers, apparently whispering something into the sleeping man's ear. As I watched, he moved on to the next person . . . then the next.

Then he returned, and I confronted him indignantly.

"What's the big idea, pal? Secrets, hey? What were you whispering to those people? I saw you. You even visited the bridge and told bedtime stories to the Old Man—"

Lucky shook his head.

"I'm sorry, Jimmy, but that's the one thing I can't tell you. Anything else, yes. But that's one little secret you must always allow me to keep. And now, we're approaching our regular Mars-Earth quadrant. So if you'll help me detach the V-I unit—"

I did. And when it was finished, so accurate had been his

calculations that the *Sirius* was sailing through the exact sector in space it would have been at had not we taken our wild flight to the comet. And Lucky said, "O.Q., Jimmy, our little game is over. Let's go back to the ballroom."

We went back. And we stood once more on the dais. And Lucky leaned forward suddenly, passed a hand across my eyes, and I swear that for a moment everything went dizzying black. There were great bells gonging in my ears ... the bell sounds faded, and I heard a voice calling:

"Waken! Waken from your slumbers, Jimmy Lincoln!"

And I opened my eyes to hear riotous laughter ringing in my ears! I stared about me, dumbfounded. Everyone in the ballroom was on his feet, laughing—at me! Several of the passengers were running up to the platform, were patting Lucky on the back, saying, "Congratulations, Lieutenant! Excellent performance . . . excellent!"

I looked into the visiplate. Captain Burke's face was wreathed in grins. He said, "How do you feel, Jimmy, all right? Nice exhibition, Logan." And he blanked out.

And Sanderson and Randolph were at my side. Tommy was doubled over with mirth. "Boy, I thought I'd die at you, Jimmy!" he chortled. "You really were a caution! Tell me, how did it feel to be hypnotized? When you let on you were a big game hunter chasing elephants with a pea-shooter—"

"What I liked best was when he thought he was a lady fisherman," chuckled Joe, "baiting his hook with a worm. Pretty good, Lucky, old boy! You really had him under control!"

I stared at them wildly.

"Had *me* under control!" I yelled. "Why, I was the only one aboard the ship who was awake! Every darned one of you was as dopey as a—"

But that only made the laugh the louder. I thought Sanderson was going to fall right out of his boots. "Listen to him! He thinks *we* were asleep and he was awake! Oh, what a party! Oooh—" Then his face sobered. "If only this—this other thing weren't hanging over our heads—" he said.

I realized suddenly I could still convince them! I knew one thing they didn't.

"If you mean about the comet," I bawled, "it might interest you guys to know that—"

But I was not destined to finish my proof. For at that moment the visiplate flashed on, and a happy Cap Burke beamed down upon us all. "Ladies and gentlemen," he cried in a triumphant voice, "I am happy to report to you that a peril which threatened all our lives and homes has been successfully averted.

"A tremendous comet, information concerning which was withheld from you in order not to occasion undue alarm, caused great fear throughout the Solar System. But I have just now received a radiogram from Lunar III advising me that one hour ago the cosmic visitor mysteriously changed its course, swept toward outer space, and is fast disappearing. Observers are of the opinion that its course was deflected by some hithertofore unsuspected dark body, search for which will be made."

I groaned. With that statement went my last chance of ever proving that they—not I—had slumbered through the wildest experience any man had ever known.

And do you know what one damned fool said? One of the fat, foolish passengers? He yawned and said, "Listen to that! Isn't that just like a professional spaceman! Always trying to pretend their job is more hazardous than anyone else's. . . ."

Afterward, I got Lucky Logan alone in his cabin. I didn't mince words. I said, "O.Q., pal, thanks for the buggyride. You certainly made me look like a Grade A dope. Next time you want a sucker, please get somebody else to do your dirty work for you. I don't mind saving a few universes before breakfast—just to keep my hand in, you know—but it's not my idea of appreciation to have everybody think I'm the world's prize nitwit when I do it."

He said, "I'm sorry, Jimmy."

"Sure, you're sorry. So what? So the hell with *you*, Mr. Logan. You had me buncoed. I don't know what to believe, now. For a while I thought you and I had saved Earth, while everyone else slept. Then I wake up to find I was the Snow White and the universe was saved by a dark star—hell, I can't even trust the evidence of my own memories. Because maybe we never used the V-I unit, maybe we never made a wild flight into outer space, maybe it was all one of the hypnotic dreams you forced on me. Which was it? Am I right, are they? Was it a dream or—"

He said, "I'm sorry, Jimmy, but I—I can't tell."

"You mean you *won't* tell?"

His eyes were gray and calm as he lifted them to me. Surface-calm, that is. But behind their shadowy depths there was a sort of desperation.

"*Can't* tell, Jimmy. Don't you see that if it were ever to become public knowledge that I—"

And he stopped abruptly.

But this was the second time that Christopher Logan had almost spilled the beans to me. And maybe I am a little slow on the uptake, but I'm not ripe for the Paper Doll Class yet. This time I put two and two together. And got something more than four. I stared at him. And then, slowly:

"I think I'm beginning to understand, pal," I said. "So you're 'Lucky' Logan, hey? You get 'hunches,' and those hunches are always better and more accurate than anybody else gets. You never lose at games of chance . . . you seem to almost be able to read minds . . . you 'guessed' the secret of faster-than-light radio transmission and without previous instruction were able to put together a velocity intensifier unit you had never seen. You saved a ship, once, by disobediently shifting it off its course. . . ."

"What do you mean, Jimmy?" he demanded nervously.

"You know damn right well what I mean, Lucky Logan!" I said. "Let's suppose, just for the hell of it, that your father was a smarter man than anyone gave him credit for being. Let's suppose that he took his infant son off into the wilds and fed him a special diet, trained him in special ways, and educated him along certain lines known only to himself—"

"Leave my dad out of this!" he said.

"Oh, no! Because he's very much in it, my friend! Let's further suppose that the old man did do exactly what he aimed to. He created a new type of superhuman. A sample of the 'superman' to come. A man with tremendous extra-sensory abilities that would enable him to unerringly guess the fall of cards, dice, any gambling device. A man with great mechanical ability, strong physique . . .

"That's *you*, Logan! You are a superman! But you're afraid to reveal it to the outside world. Maybe because Man looks with suspicion upon any life form more intelligent than himself. Maybe because that examination in your childhood was such an embarrassing, terrifying experience to a sensitive person. But *I* know! You're more than a plain man. You're a superman. That's the secret you conceal behind a wisecracking exterior. Now, isn't it?"

But Lucky Logan had completely regained control of himself. The tortured look had left his eyes, and there was the ghost of a smile on his lips. A smile in which—perhaps mistakenly—I thought I could read a subtle meaning. Maybe I was completely wrong, and he was laughing at me. Or—maybe I was right. And he was happy that in all the world, at least, *one* person understood him. And he was less lonely.

Anyhow:

"Is it?" he laughed. "Why, I wouldn't know, Jimmy. Say, how about a drink?"

And that's all I could get out of him. Except the drink. I had three of those . . .

The Fertility of Dalrymple Todd

I WAS HAVING A HELL OF A TIME WITH MY CARTOON STRIP that day. I had a central figure, something about a Philadelphia lawyer who could put two baseballs in his mouth, but I didn't have a single oddity for the border spots. It was hot, and I was tired, and getting sorer by the minute. I guess I was pretty curt when someone knocked on the door.

"Come in?" I yelled, and this stranger eased into the room.

Hell's bells, what a man! Gargantuanly fat; so fat that the Beef Trust gals would have been pygmies in comparison. He goggled at me wistfully for a moment, sliding from one foot to another like a jittery elephant. Finally he piped,

"Are—are you the man who draws the cartoon, 'Ain't It The Truth?'"

"That's me," I told him. "Why? Who sent you here?"

"Nobody. I just came. I think I've got something for you."

Another one of those phony screwballs. They pop in all the time. Probably his name was "I Bark," or something like that, and he drew it so it looked like a dog. I chucked him a pad and pencil, and turned back to my board. I said,

"Draw it on there, pal. And don't forget to close the door as you go out."

For an instant he stood there, the drawing pad and pencil in his hands, staring at me with a vacuous expression on his pan, as if I'd thrown the Gordian knot in his face. Then his lips opened and his face turned red.

"Oh, no!" He looked indignant. "It's not that at all. You don't understand. I—I can grow things."

"Grow things?" I said. "Brother, are you trying to pull my leg?"

He folded himself into a chair, collapsing at the joints like a carpenter's rule. He took off his hat, unveiling a mop of scrambled hair that looked like a bewildered black chrysanthemum. He leaned forward; stared at me with big, humid eyes.

"Yes. In my hair. Do you want to see?"

I stood up, forcing a grin. I said, "Why, of course!" heartily—and edged toward the door. "Wait a minute. There are a couple other guys outside who'd like to—"

"Oh, *don't!*" he cried. There was a look of despair on his cadaverous features. "You're just like all the rest of them. You won't even give me a chance to—look! Peas!" he said.

I gulped and started. For there, right smack in the middle of that unruly tangle he called his hair, were a half-dozen green, marblelike objects. He shook his head, and they fell off. One of them rolled across the floor to my feet. I stopped and picked it up. It squashed in my fingers. I looked at it; smelled it.

Undeniably—it was a pea! He smiled triumphantly.

"See?" he said.

I said, "Hey—do that again!"

"What would you like to have? A fruit? A vegetable?"

I said, "A—a tomato."

"All right," he said. "Tomato!"

And there was a ripe, rosy tomato, coyly nestling in his hair! He handed it to me.

"Taste it!" he said. "It's good. See, I can grow anything. Apples, turnips, beans—"

Things started plopping on the floor squishily. It looked like bank night at a fruit stand. But now I got it. I strode across the room, grabbed him by the collar, and yanked him to his feet.

"Okay, pal!" I snarled, "Trying to make a sucker out of me, eh? Well, it doesn't work. Now—beat it!"

He was big, but not strong. He pushed easy. I got him all the way to the door before he managed to yelp.

"But I'm not trying to make a sucker out of you. I really *can* do it! I—"

"Sure," I said. "And Thurston could make drayhorses float in mid-air. So what? I'm not using my cartoon to give publicity to any tinhorn sleight-of-hand expert. Scram!"

He piped vexedly, "*Oh!* Oh, if you only knew what I *think* of you—"

"Leave it outside!" I said grumpily. "I've got work to do." I shoved him, and he went flying. I returned to my board.

I heard him fussing and fiddling around out there for a few minutes; muttering under his breath. Then his footsteps slap-slapped down the hall. I scratched into my files and found a few items to use. One was about an armless Alpine guide; another on a two-headed pig from a farm near Keokuk, Iowa.

Just as I was putting the final curlicue on the pig's tail, Willy Cardell came in. Willy is copy boy for the Art Department. He looked like he'd been wading around in a bowl of overripe Jello. His shoes were dripping juicily, and his trousers were stained to the calves. He glared at me angrily.

"Hey, Michelangelo!" he yelled. "What's the big idea? You going huckster on us?"

I said, "Why? What's the matter?"

"Matter! Look at this!"

He held open the door so I could see. Outside, where my visitor had stomped around muttering his opinion of me, was a pile of fruit, knee deep! About four bushel baskets of—raspberries!

Well, that was that. I wondered about it for a while, then finally forgot my raspberry-sprinkling visitor. I might never have thought of him again had I not gone to Pete's Chili Kitchen one midnight for a jolt of liquid cayenne.

Pete himself served me. And while he was dunking his thumb in the goulash he mourned,

"Noive of the guy! A bowl an' a spoon, he says, an' fill the bowl wit' hot water. Hot water! They's a hell of a lot of profit in that, now, isn't they?"

I agreed, "They isn't!" cheerfully. "What's he want to do, Pete? Take a bath?"

"Ast him!" Pete jerked a thumb toward a booth in the back of the joint. "Me, I don't want no truck wit' such cheap skates!" He waddled off.

It was late, and Pete's place was lonely. Beside, I was curious. So I strolled back to the other booth and found—my erstwhile visitor! He was placidly spooning a thick, steamy potage. He looked up as I approached; smiled amiably.

"Hello!" he said.

"So!" I said. "Fancy meeting you here, pal. Thanks for the berries."

He said, "Oh—*them!*" and flushed. "I'm sorry about that. But I was a little peeved when I left, and I couldn't help thinking—"

I sat down. I said, "That's all right, bud. I don't blame you for getting sore. I was out of sorts that day. And that trick of yours *was* clever. I still can't see where you got all those damned raspberries. I know they weren't up your sleeve."

"Of course not," he said plaintively. "They're never up my sleeve. I told you—they're in my hair."

"Now," I grunted, "you're getting in mine again. I'm not asking how you do it. All I want to know is—"

He said, suddenly, "How's your chili?"

Well, I didn't blame him for not wanting to explain. I grinned, and ladled up a mouthful of the stuff.

"Okay," I said. "A little thinnish, maybe. A few more kidney beans—"

"Kidney beans!" he said.

And there they were again—a whole darned handful of kidney beans, all tangled up in his curly locks. He reached up and unsnagged them.

"You'll have to shell them," he said sheepishly. "I'm sorry about that."

I stared. I said hoarsely, "Where did you get those things? I was watching your hands. They were on the table!"

He looked mildly reproachful.

"But of course! Where else should they be?"

I rose angrily. "Fun's fun, guy. I like a joke as much as the next man. But when a fake magician starts mixing business into everyday life, I say he's going a little too far. So good night, and the hell with you, Mr.—"

"Todd," he said. "Dalrymple Todd."

"*Who*-rimple Todd?" I demanded.

"Dalrymple. D for dates. A for apricots. L as in lemon. R for—"

Something went *splash!* in his soup. I yelled. As he spoke, things started popping out of his hair. Dates and apricots. A lemon. A rutabaga. Common sense told me to beat it. But my legs refused to move. My spine felt like the spiral binding on the back of a looseleaf notebook.

I moaned weakly, "Todd—stand up, will you?"

He did. I looked on the seat, under it. I patted his pockets, his sleeves, his trouser legs. He didn't have a thing on him but the things a man normally carries—a handkerchief, watch, billfold, some loose silver. Pen and pencil.

I choked, "Todd—say 'alligator pear.'" Alligator pears were out of season. I wanted to know, once and for all—

"Alligator pear!" he said.

We both grabbed for it at the same time. It writhed out of his hirsute jungle, fresh, green, appetizing. I slumped back into my seat.

I groaned, "All right, Todd, you win! Tell me. How do you do it?"

His brow furrowed. "I don't know. I just say the name of any growing thing and—there it is!"

"But," I expostulated, "it's mad! Preposterous! If I hadn't seen it with my own eyes, I'd say impossible! Contrary to every law of chemistry, physics—"

"I know. When it first started, several months ago, I was frantic with fear and wonder. I visited a doctor—"

"What did he say?"

Todd shuddered. "He tried to take a section from my scalp flesh. Just as he made his incision, I happened to think what a dried-up little prune he was. A prune popped out and hit him in the eye. He screamed for the police. I had to run."

"And then?"

"Well, I've never gone to see another doctor. But I read every book I could find on gardening, soil culture, heredity. They tell me nothing except that it's impossible. And it can't be *that*, you know"—he looked at me sadly—"because it happens."

I suggested, "Maybe it's the way you wear your hair."

"Frowzy like this, you mean? I can't help it. If I went to a barber, I might start thinking about a flower or a fruit, and scare him to death. I trim it myself. And even that's a task. I get the comb halfway through, and start thinking what a peach— *Whoops!* There it goes again!"

He stared woefully at the peach which lay between us. I picked it up; tasted it. It was perfect.

I said, "You realize, of course, that I can't feature this in my cartoon strip."

"I suppose not," he agreed dully.

"I'd be hooted off Broadway. The people in the sticks would call me the biggest liar since Ananias. But, say—" I got a sudden inspiration. "Do you want to commercialize your ability?"

"How?"

"The stage!" I said. "Vaudeville's almost dead, but there's enough left to give you a start. And there's Hollywood, and the radio—"

He unfolded his lanky length from the booth. His big, watery eyes were wide with excitement.

"I *could*, couldn't I?" he said. "My goodness! Why didn't *I* think of that? How can I ever thank you!"

"Don't thank me. Make me your agent. For ten percent of your earnings—"

"Ten!" he piped. "Make it twenty! Why, the pair of us—*Oh!*"

So a pear hopped from his head. I put it in my pocket. I thought I might get hungry later on . . .

Thus began Dalrymple Todd's rise to fame. We opened in Brooklyn—and he was terrific. We went to Philadelphia, and he rolled 'em in the aisles. Broadway demanded a look-see. We went to Radio City. And wowed 'em there. The crowd didn't unthaw till he walked down the aisles, giving customers whatever fruit, vegetable or flower they named. Then they went nuts. They thought it was a hoax—but *what* a hoax!

A lawsuit shoved us on page one. A guy from the Bronx claimed his son got indigestion on a Todd-grown apple. The suit was tossed out of court when our lawyer discovered the judge was an orchid fancier and Todd gave him a whole armful.

Then Hollywood beckoned, putting on a bidding spree that made the chant of the tobacco auctioneer sound like an Alabama drawl. We signed, finally, with Superba films—for a salary that looked like a three months' WPA appropriation.

Todd's first short, "Hearts and Flowers," outdrew the most ballyhooed melodrama of the year. There was some talk of giving him an Academy "Oscar." DeMille wanted him for an extravaganza, "Forbidden Fruit." Disney pleaded frantically for the privilege of caricaturing him in a retake of "Ferdinand."

Everything was fine. Everything was super-colossal. And then—Todd fell in love!

I learned it at the set. This picture we were filming was based somewhat nebulously on the legend of Merlin, magician of King Arthur's court. Bolski, the director, was preparing to shoot the love scene between young Merlin and the witch-queen of Umbria, Morgan le Fay.

"Awright," he said. "Now in this scene, Mr. Todd, you an' the dame are showin' off your magic. She waves her hand an' comes up with a bracelet—you got that bracelet up your sleeve, Miss Honeycutt?"

"Yes, Mr. Bolski."

"Good. Well, she dares you to beat her trick. Then you bring an apple outa your hair. Miss Honeycutt, you're startled, see? You think it's a phony. You make your maid take a bite outa the apple. Got it?"

They both nodded.

"Awright. So we're shootin'. Camera!"

The Kleigs went on, and the "take" signal flashed. Morgan le Fay smiled langorously from her nest of cushions.

"We have our own magicks in Umbria, Merlin, my pertling," she said. "Say—couldst match *this* with thy guile?"

Her arms made a weaving motion. The bracelet sprang into view. "Merlin" Todd smiled serenely. Two grand's worth of voice culture hadn't taken the squeak out of his pipes, but it got by.

He yipped,

" 'Tis a gay ruse, my queen. Yet man hath wrought that bauble. Couldst conjure from thy very self a fruit of freshest growth?"

His eyes met those of the queen; turned to the serving maid beside her. His lips wrestled with a word. Then—

It was flowers! Peonies. Larkspurs. Daffodils. A regular all-fired bouquet of flowers!

"Cut!" screamed Bolski. He raced onto the set, his pudgy hands pawing the air. "Not flowers, Todd. An apple! The script calls for an apple!"

Dalrymple Todd flushed miserably. "I—I know."

Bolski looked panic-stricken. He hushed, "Can't you—can't you *make* an apple?"

"Yes, sir." Meekly.

"Then do it! An apple it must be. Could the maid eat maybe a flower?"

Why waste words? They tried it again. And again. They tried it until Morgan le Fay trembled so, she could hardly draw the bracelet out of her sleeve. Until perspiration made Todd's greasepaint streaky. But it was no go. Every time the maid stepped into the picture, Todd's eyes lit strangely. And—more flowers!

I was the first to catch on. I grabbed Bolski's arm, yelled,

"Look—have you got another girl to play the part of the maid?"

"Millions!" he moaned. "Billions, maybe. But only one Merlin, and he can't make no apple!"

"Then get another girl!" I snapped. "Put her in that part. I'll bet my last buck you get your apple!"

He did. *And they did!*

But on the way home, Todd raved at me. "Her first real part in pictures," he stormed, "and you took it from her!"

"If I hadn't," I told him, "it would have been your *last* part. You're in love with that girl, aren't you?"

His long legs twined about each other like reluctant corkscrews. He blushed.

"How did you know?"

"How could I help knowing? Does she love you?"

"She doesn't even know I exist. Worse than that, she thinks I'm a sort of freak." He shook his head mournfully. "And she's right, too. No girl would marry a human hothouse like me."

"How do you know?" I countered. "Have you asked her?"

"What's the use?" He muttered fatuously, "Roses are red, violets are blue; I grew this bouquet, dear, just for you!" And started picking up the flowers he'd sprinkled as he spoke.

I yelled, "Stop it, you dope! Don't waste energy like that! If you love the girl, tell her so!"

Two big tears rolled down his cheeks. "I know what she'd say. No, I'm doomed to live alone, unloved, for the rest of my life—"

A bright blue flower floated gently to the floor of the sedan. It was a bachelor's button. . . .

That was the beginning of the end. Since the girl had been taken from the cast and another substituted, things had gone along smoothly enough, but Dalrymple Todd's heart wasn't in his work. I could tell that by the quality of his botanical subjects. The lilies he provided for Guinevere's wedding were scrawny. The scene where he supplied a legion of besieged knights with fresh fruits and vegetables almost caused a revolt among the extras, who had to eat the stuff. The fruits were bitter. And the vegetables were—well, what's a polite way of saying "rotten?"

Then I found out why. A guy named Ethelred R. Clutz visited me one morning to voice a grievance. Todd, Clutz insisted, was unfair. His attack on the American Brotherhood of Florists and Horticulturists must stop. It was deliberate restraint of trade. The ABF&H lawyers had studied the facts of the case. Since some of the flowers had been sent to a Miss Smythe when she was outside the State of California, the Interstate Commerce Commission would be informed—

I said, "Wait a minute! You mean Todd has been sending flowers to this girl?"

By the crate and truckload, stormed Mr. Clutz. Out of season, too. Flowers that honest, hard-working dealers could not hope to duplicate. Moreover, Mr. Todd had been producing these flowers himself. Since each home-grown blossom represented a loss of revenue to the members of the ABF&H, the union—

I soothed him and booted him out. But when Todd came home, I relayed the accusation. He flushed guiltily.

"Yes, Len." That's me, Len Wright. "I have been sending Susan flowers. Every day." He lifted wistful eyes to mine. "I can't make her notice me any other way. I thought that if I—" He faltered. "They say flowers are the way to a woman's heart . . ."

"They're the way to the poorhouse!" I howled. "You can't do your best work at the studios when you stay up all night growing flowers for *her!* I don't know how that fertile knob of yours operates, but—but think of your future!"

He sighed, "Future, Len? I have no future without—her!"

We had another visitor, too. A short, grumpy-looking chap whose card read, "Hepplewhite Frey, FFCB." He stalked to Todd's side; studied his scalp thoughtfully.

I said, "Yes, Mr. Frey? What can we do for you?"

Frey jotted a note in a small book. Then he drew an imaginary line down the middle of Todd's cranium.

"Here!" he said. "This is your boundary. The Government can't permit further cultivation."

"Permit *what?*" I demanded.

"Overproduction. I'm from the Federal Farm Conservation Board. Crop control bureau. There've been complaints about this man. He'll have to plow the left side under. Is this your total acreage, Mr. Todd?"

Todd said faintly, "Huh?"

"You don't cultivate your chest?"

"No-no."

"Very well." Frey snapped his book. "Have no fear. You will be compensated for the uncultivated area. Uncle Sam will allow you —let me see—thirteen cents, four mills, for your plowed-under domains. The Government"—he smiled majestically—"protects its agriculturists. Good day!"

He left. I stared at Todd with horror. "Dal—will a haircut really stop it?" I asked.

"I don't know. I honestly don't know."

"Because if it doesn't—" I began. Then I stopped. For the first time in weeks, I was viewing Dalrymple Todd's black mane at close range. And making a horrible discovery. His temples were farther back than before. His hairline was receding. Dalrymple Todd was—going bald!

His movie picture was almost completed. There was just one final scene to shoot: that in which Dal Todd as the aged Merlin, demonstrates his magical powers by creating a watermelon. Don't ask me why Bolski wanted a watermelon. I pointed out to him that the Round Table lads had never heard of them. But that didn't matter. A watermelon was big. A watermelon was impressive. And this was Hollywood. So a watermelon it must be—no? Yes!

During rehearsals, Bolski let Todd produce little things, like grapes and kumquats. But finally he said,

"Now we shoot, Mr. Todd. Remember, it gives a watermelon— an' a big one—for the final scene. Get it?"

Todd nodded wearily. The cameras started grinding.

The scene rolled along smoothly. Then came the part where a smart-aleck young magician derides Merlin as being a has-been. Merlin, now old and gray, sinks into his chair—

Todd sank to the chair. I saw his lips frame the word, "Watermelon!" A huge, green crest bulged from the thinning tangle of his hair. It grew and grew. The cameras ground on. Beside me, Bolski watched with bated breath. Even the actors' eyes bulged with unfaked astonishment. This was Todd's *coup;* his greatest effort. The melon grew. Half-grown, now . . . almost three-quarters. And then—

Todd stopped. He groaned.

Bolski forgot the sound warning. Excitedly he yelled,

"Go on, Todd! Don't stop now!"

Dalrymple Todd raised tortured eyes to us.

He moaned, "I can't!"

I leaped forward. I said, "Dal—what do you mean?"

"It—it won't grow any more."

Bolski yipped, "But you gotta! Just a little more. Please! Another thought, maybe!"

Todd shut his eyes; knotted his fists. His face was white with concentration. His lips moved. Then, weakly—

"It's no use. I can't. And—and I've got a splitting headache!"

No wonder! I yelled, "Get a doctor! Get a—a botanist. A tree surgeon! Get *somebody*—quick!"

People scurried and yelped. The place was a bedlam. Then, suddenly, there was a quiet voice at my side. A voice that said:

"Dalrymple—"

Todd looked up, his eyes widening in gladness.

"*Susan!*" he cried.

Bolski and I saw it at the same time. We both high-tailed it out of the scene.

Bolski screamed, "Camera!"

For the watermelon bulging from Todd's conk had suddenly altered. About the great, green semi-globe, sprang a veritable garden of gorgeous flowers. Fragrance flooded the set. Roses, geraniums, orchids, snapdragons—oh, name anything you can think of—poured from Todd's fertile scalp in mad profusion. Chief of all wonders was that amazing sight: a thing half watermelon, half lilac bush . . .

Susan and Dal Todd locked in each other's arms. They were kissing.

"I had to come, my dear," she was murmuring. "When the flowers stopped coming, I knew you must need me—" Blossoms cascaded about them, a jungle of riotous beauty.

Bolski yelled, "Cut! Cut!" and smacked me on the back. "Terrific!" he squalled. "Magnificent! Another triumph for Superba!"

But that was the swan song of Dalrymple Todd. For suddenly the blooms stopped falling. And in the unimpassioned glare of the Kliegs, I saw another glow that made me weep out loud. Todd's scalp. He was as bald as a mirror. His labors had finally destroyed him. He was just another victim of—soil erosion!

That's about all. Susan and Dal Todd have been married now for a year. I'm back at my job drawing "Ain't It The Truth?" But my office isn't in New York. I'm sticking pretty close to the Todds.

Because, you see, there's a youngster now. A cute kid, too. Named Len, after me. And I'm still young enough to be the kid's manager when—. No, of course, I don't expect he'll inherit his old man's strange fertility. That was a freak; something that happens once in a millennium. But at the same time—

Well, I'll tell you. The other night when we went into young Len's nursery to look at him while he was asleep, we found him clutching a bright, new, shiny toy automobile. Susan hadn't given it to him. His Daddy hadn't given it to him. Nor had I. And there had been no other visitors.

A thing like that makes you wonder, doesn't it?"

The Man Who Weighed Minus Twelve

IT SERVED JACK DAMN GOOD AND RIGHT FOR TALKING SO much. I finished the last handful of salted peanuts while he was telling the one about the old maid school teacher and the stammering salesman. After that we took a gander at the refrigerator and discovered we'd polished off all the beer, so Jack said let's go to bed. So we did.

It was plenty drowsy and the bed felt good. But I still had my worries, you understand. In spite of Jack and his friendly chatter, there was still the Gold Stakes for me to fret about. And my nag, Printer's Ink. And the idiotic 126-pound impost the track officials had slapped on him.

I lay there for awhile, though, thinking what a swell guy Jack was, and wondering what in hell he had been so mysterious about. He'd said he had figured the way out for me, and he'd laughed when he said "way." So I'd spent all that day waiting, and now I was waiting for sleep to come and get me.

And then suddenly I heard it. A little pitty-pat sound from the room below mine. No, not the room. It was more as if someone were scraping the ceiling.

I thought, "Mice?" But I knew it wasn't mice. So I thought, "Rats?" But that was wrong, too. Then I thought, "Hey, burglars!" and sat up in bed. I yelled, "Jack!"

Jack stopped sloshing water around and came out of the bathroom. "Whazzup?" he said.

"Listen," I told him, "there's somebody downstairs. You got a gun? It sounds to me like—"

Jack cocked his head and listened for a second. Then he grinned. "Oh, that? That's just Uncle Herman."

"Uncle Herman? I didn't know you had an uncle."

"Can I help it if I have relatives? He came here to live with us a couple of months ago."

I said, "What are you trying to do, kid me? Uncle Herman wasn't at dinner tonight. And besides, if that's his room below mine, he's either nine feet tall or he has wings. Those sounds are coming from the *ceiling* of that room!"

Jack looked embarrassed. "Yeah," he said.

"What do you mean—yeah?"

He said, "Look, Bill, I'll tell you all about it in the morning. That's the answer I had in mind for you, only I couldn't do anything about it today. You see, Uncle Herman is a little—well, odd."

"Oh," I said. "I'm sorry, Jack. I didn't know."

Jack's face darkened. He said stiffly, "Don't be a dope. He's not off his button. He's perfectly normal mentally. His trouble is— well, I guess you'd say physical."

I agreed with him. "You've got something there, pal. He's twelve feet tall and folds up like a jack-knife. What's he doing now? Standing on his head and tap-dancing on the ceiling?"

"He's—" began Jack. Then he shrugged. "Oh, to hell with it! Come along!"

"Where?" I asked. "It's getting kind of late."

"You wouldn't believe it if I told you. And I'm as impatient as you are. Come on!"

So we went downstairs. Jack knocked on the door of the room just below mine and a pleasant voice called:

"Come in! Come in!" So we went in.

That is, Jack went in. I *fell* in. It hadn't occurred to me that there might be anything abnormal about the doorway, so I didn't even notice that it began about a foot above the floor level. As a result I took a nosedive over the portal and made a three-point landing on my puss.

It knocked me groggy for a minute. That's the main reason why, when I staggered to my feet, I went panicky over what I saw. I took one horrified look around me, then made a flying tackle for the only substantial thing in a cockeyed universe—the chandelier a few feet before me.

I wrapped my arms around this and held on for dear life. I guess I must have yelled, too. If I didn't, someone else must have been squawking.

"Jack! For God's sake get me down out of here!"

Then Jack's size twelves were beside my nose, and he was lifting me up, saying:

"Take it easy, guy. It's all right."

All right! All I could figure was that either I had suddenly become drunk, or that the world had gone haywire, or that Congress, in secret session, had repealed the Law of Gravity. Because the room was upside down! Completely, perfectly, illogically upside down!

The "floor" on which we stood was actually the ceiling. It was neatly papered to match the walls. The room had two windows, and in each of these the curtains were carefully draped skyward. Some pictures on the walls were topsy-turvy, the light fixtures were reversed.

And up above— Well, if you want to know what it looked like, stop reading this and stare at your ceiling. Try to imagine you're up there looking down. Get it? That's what the furniture looked like to me. I hollered again and grabbed at Jack, ducking out from under a divan that looked like any second it would drop and smack me on the conk.

Then came the killer-diller. The same voice that had asked us to come in now spoke again, this time somewhat petulantly.

"John, what's the matter with your friend? Is he intoxicated?"

I looked up. There, calmly seated in one of those upside-down chairs, staring down at me with an expression of mild annoyance, was a chubby, pink-cheeked elderly gentleman in dressing gown and carpet slippers.

Jack said, "Uncle Herman, this is Bill Harkness, my friend. He runs horses. He's spending the weekend with us."

Uncle Herman said, "Well, he doesn't have to be so noisy about it, does he?"

But he rose and took three steps across the floor—I mean the ceiling—no, I mean the floor—oh, to hell with it! Then, gravely, he leaned down and shook my hand.

For an instant I had a sensation of curious lightness. I didn't know whether he was going to pull me up with him, or whether I was going to drag him down to my level. But nothing happened. And then Jack said:

"Bill heard you walking around, Uncle. He couldn't understand it. So, knowing you were still up, I thought I'd bring him down to meet you."

Uncle Herman nodded, beaming. "Quite right, John. Very thoughtful of you."

He smiled at me. I guess it was a smile. From my angle, the corners of his mouth turned down instead of up. He said, almost proudly:

"I suppose you are wondering about—all this?"

I was indeed. I was wondering about a room which had on its ceiling chairs, tables, bookcases, divans—all carefully bolted and fastened. More particularly, I was wondering about a man who could live in such a room.

I said, "If you don't mind, I'd like to know how the—I mean, what causes—"

"To be honest," confessed Uncle Herman, "I don't know myself. That is, not yet. However, I've been working hard on the problem, and have several theories." He nodded toward his bookcase. "You see, it all began about three or four months ago. Until then, I was just the same as other men. Wasn't I, John?"

"Hm-m," said Jack.

Uncle Herman folded his newspaper loosely, laid it on his knee. Instantly it cascaded toward the floor. I grabbed it and handed it back to him. This time he tucked it into his bookcase.

"Thank you, Harkness. As I was saying, it began about four months ago. I was doing some research in my laboratory—I am, or was, an experimental chemist, you know—when suddenly I experienced a strange, lifting sensation. I distinctly felt my feet move a few inches off the floor.

"In a few seconds the feeling passed. Naturally I said nothing about it to my associates. I assumed it to be merely a giddy spell, a moment of vertigo. But a few days later—"

"Yes?" I said.

"A few days later, While having dinner at a downtown restaurant, it happened again. This time I floated a full twelve inches off the floor. It was only by exerting a strenuous effort that I succeeded in pulling myself down.

"In the course of this—er—unfortunate incident, I upset a glass of water. Thus I attracted some attention to myself. I assure you, it was most embarrassing. Most!"

He looked at me as if expecting some comment. But I said nothing. How the hell can you tell a guy you're sorry he's a human blimp?

Uncle Herman shrugged and continued. "The restaurant incident caused me some alarm. I visited a physician, who assured me I was in perfect health. But at his office, during the examination, I discovered one other peculiar fact. My weight. I weighed only one twenty-four!"

I said, "One twenty-four? But surely, sir—"

Uncle Herman beamed. "I know. I look much heavier, don't I? My build is that of a man of one seventy-eight; which, in fact, was my weight before this—er—all began.

"But apparently some strange chemical reaction, possibly the result of my experiments, had assumed control of my body. For as the weeks passed, I experienced with increasing regularity these spells of 'falling upward'. And after each spasm, I found that I had lost a little more weight! I dropped to ninety-three, then to seventy, to thirty-one. Until, finally—"

"But, sir!" I interrupted. "That's impossible! Why, your bones alone would weigh more than that!"

"Until finally," continued Uncle Herman imperturbably, "I attained my present weight. Which, for some weeks now, has remained static. And that weight is—*minus twelve!*"

I rose. I must have looked sort of grim. I was fed up with this nonsense and more than a little bit sore at both Jack and his precious "Uncle Herman." How they had devised and accomplished this trick, I had no idea. But I knew it *was* a gag. Clever, yes—but a trick. And a dirty one. Robbing a guy of a night's sleep—

I said, "Well, thanks for the bedtime story, boys. Now, if you'll excuse me—"

Jack looked at Uncle Herman and said, regretfully:

"I'm sorry, Uncle. I thought he'd understand."

Uncle Herman looked none too pleased. "I wish you would select your friends from the more intelligent—" He sighed. "Oh, well. I'll show him, if you wish."

I said, "Show me what? What's the next act?" and reached for a cigarette.

Jack stopped me. He said, "If you don't mind, Bill—Uncle detests the odor of tobacco smoke."

So I shoved the fag back in my pocket and Jack disappeared. When he returned he was lugging the bathroom scales. He put them on the floor—our floor, you know, not Uncle Herman's. And he reached up a hand to Uncle Herman.

"All right, Uncle," he said.

Uncle Herman said, "The weight first, John."

"Oh, yes." Jack disappeared again. This time he brought back a big weight, the kind they use in warehouses.

He said, "Look, Bill!" and placed it on the scales. The dial spun to read "20."

I said, "Ta-da-*daaah!* So it weighs twenty pounds. So what?"

"Well," said Jack, "here's what. Ready, Uncle?"

He handed Uncle Herman the weight. Immediately the chubby little man began floating floorward, turning as he came down. He landed, puffing slightly, on his feet before me. I saw then that he wasn't a tall man; just an ordinary, friendly looking little old Dutchman. He was holding on to the twenty-pound weight for dear life.

He said, "I believe this will convince you, Mr. Harkness, that my story is no exaggeration—"

And he stepped onto the scales.

I took one look, then gulped. Then I looked again and gulped some more. Because the dial of that instrument hovered, despite the twenty-pound weight and the additional weight of Uncle Herman, at the figure "8"!

I said, "Hey! But that's impossible! Nobody can weigh less than—"

"Oh, yes," interrupted Uncle Herman pleasantly. "I can. As a matter of fact, I do. Here, John."

He handed back the weight, and immediately floated ceilingward again, somersaulting very capably as he went so that he was finally upside down to us again. His voice continued as rationally as if everything were quite in order.

"You see, there are several possible theories to explain my—er—peculiarity.

"As I told you, this unusual trait first manifested itself as a result of some chemical experiments I was conducting. Unfortunately I have no idea just which experiment was responsible for my—er——change."

He paused a moment. "I had made several small experiments on the day in question. One involved a study of lighter-than-air gases, another had to do with magnetic inductions, a third was concerned with the isolation of neutronium particles.

"It is possible that I in some way counter-magnetized myself against the attraction of Mother Earth. As you undoubtedly know, Earth is a strongly charged electronic particle in the macrocosmos.

Einstein* has shown us that electricity, magnetism and gravitation are three manifestations of one underlying principle. Therefore it is possible that I received a charge opposite that of Earth's polarity—you understand?"

"No," I said.

He sighed. "Well, there is another possible explanation. It may be that in some way, one of the chemicals I was dabbling with acted as a catalyst, altering the chemical structure of my body—perhaps I should say the ionic structure—so that the atoms which are a part of me became neutronium atoms."

"New—new what?" I asked him.

"Neutronium. A—er—fearfully heavy condensation of matter. You see, if by some necromancy my bodily atoms had been converted into neutronium, I would have a potential weight equal to that of Earth, despite my lesser mass. In other words, my gravitation would counterbalance that of the Earth itself. I would weigh—"

"Wait a minute," I gasped. "You mean you'd actually weigh as much as the Earth?"

"A trifle more. I would weigh, in round figures, six thousand million, million, million tons and—er—twelve pounds."

I glared at him, but he didn't even crack a smile. The little twerp was serious about all this! I said, sort of hoarselike, I guess.

"And the third possibility?"

He smiled beatifically. "Now we come to the most likely of all. It is my honest belief that in some unusual fashion, the nitrogen elements of my physique have been superseded by elements of helium—thus making me considerably lighter than air! I have not yet been able to prove this to my own satisfaction. Nitrogen only accounts for two and one-half percent of the human body. It would, seem that—"

"It would seem that," I interrupted him dizzily, "I lost track of what you're talking about a half hour ago! If it's all the same to you, I think I'll go back to bed."

So I did. And this time, leaving the room, I was careful to step over the sill as I went out.

I didn't sleep very well that night. I finally got to bye-bye land about three-thirty, but even there I had no release from the

---

* A refugee from Nazi Germany, Dr. Albert Einstein, discoverer of the theory of relativity, is now living in Princeton, N.J., where he is a member of the Institute for Advanced Study.—*Ed.*

tormenting thoughts Uncle Herman's tale had inspired. I dreamed all night that I was falling into the sky, grabbing at treetops and mountain peaks as I soared starward. And even my unconscious was wondering what Jack had meant by saying that he had my way out. He hadn't told me yet, and I had been too dizzy to ask. Just that damned mysterious smile lingering on his good-natured face . . . and there was Printer's Ink running fourth, fifth . . . lingering on his good-natured face and now it was merging with a lunar crater that was coming up to swallow me whole.

"Jack!" I was yelling, suddenly, sitting up in bed.

He came running down the hall, his robe half off. "Told you not to eat so fast," he said, sleepily. "Indigestion?"

"Only mental," I said. The sweat was running down me. "Listen, if you don't come out with an answer or two, I'm going to leave here in the morning for a sanitarium."

"I know a good one," he answered. "Specializes in horse players." He yawned and sat down on my bed. "Here, wipe that honest perspiration off your brow. Now then, the trouble with you is that impost, isn't it?"

"Oh-h-h," I groaned, "that impost. A hundred and twenty-six pounds. Damn those stewards."

"Let me get it straight again. They put that impost on, which means that your horse has to carry 126 pounds, either in the jockey's weight, or in some other additional weight to reach that figure?"

I nodded, dully.

"Ever think what Uncle Herman could do to weight requirements?" said Jack, idly.

It was as if somebody had jabbed me with a live wire. "What?" I screamed. "Do you mean—"

"Take it easy," said Jack, sitting down on me. "No, Uncle Herman can't ride. I said take it easy. Let me finish. I said I had the way out, though, remember? Way: w-e-i-g-h," he spelled, laughing. "I've worked out the most sensational gag you ever heard. See how you like it."

Still sitting on me, and I confess it was necessary, he outlined his idea to me. When he finished I had a fever. "It can't work," I said, almost crying. "It's fantastic. It can't possibly—"

"You still don't know Uncle Herman," Jack said, gravely, with that lousy twinkle coming back to his eyes. "In the morning, we'll ask Uncle Herman if he'll play with us. He's a nice egg."

Nice? He was wonderful. I didn't sleep any more that night, if you want to quibble and call what had happened to me before, sleep. But in the morning we all had a short talk. And then we made plans.

You know the Gold Stakes. It's the second richest race in the United States. $75,000 added. Limited to those thoroughbreds selected by the Stakes Committee as the "outstanding racers of the year."

My horse, Printer's Ink, was one of the invitees by virtue of victories in the Rose Challenge, and at Narragansett and Churchill Downs. The other dangerous entries were Freda, the gallant filly who had won the Pimlico Special, and Jolly Tar, victor at Saratoga and the Flamingo.

The trouble was the handicapping of the stewards. The filly, Freda, had been assigned only 112 pounds. Jolly Tar had been imposted with 120. And here I was—or rather here Printer's Ink was—spotted against the finest field in horsedom with a top weight of 126!

That in itself was enough to lengthen odds against him. When we reached the track the afternoon of the big race, the pari-mutuel boards told the story. The public had established Jolly Tar as the favorite at 3 to 2. Freda was 5 to 2. And Printer's Ink was barely ahead of the ruck with a wager rating of 4 to 1.

Uncle Herman, who was sitting in the back seat of our car, bundled in an overcoat the pockets of which we had loaded with shot to keep him stable, glanced at the boards and cluck-clucked.

"Dear me, Harkness! It doesn't look as if your horse is strongly favored."

"Why should he be?" I asked. "He's carrying a top load. But we'll fix that! Let's go to the weighing room."

We found the Committee sitting in judgment on the jockeys soon to ride in the big race. My boy, little Teddy Symes, saw me and came over disconsolately.

"I've weighed in, Mr. Harkness. I tipped the scales at one hundred, so I've got to carry twenty-six pounds on the side." He was far from happy about it. "They shouldn't oughta do us like this. Geez—"

"It's okay, Teddy," I told him. "We're winning."

I went to the table just as a burst of cheering from outside told that the fourth race had ended, that the Stakes was to begin within a few minutes.

I said, "Well, gentlemen, you are quite satisfied with my jockey?"

The chairman nodded. "Quite, Mr. Harkness. I'm sorry we found it necessary to burden Printer's Ink with so great an impost, but—"

"Oh, that!" I grinned and waved a hand in what I hoped was an airy fashion. "Think nothing of it. Matter of fact, you didn't give Printer's Ink *enough* weight to keep him from winning. You underestimate my horse, gentlemen. He's a real champion!"

That staggered 'em. Stewards are accustomed to being bawled out by owners, not praised. They cheered up. I continued:

"By the way, there's nothing in the rule book to prevent a horse from carrying *more* than his assigned weight, is there?"

They stared at me. Finally the chairman said:

"I—er—I'm afraid I don't understand, Mr. Harkness."

"I mean, it is my privilege to let my horse carry a double weight if I want to, isn't it?"

They all looked nervous. One of them started leafing through the code book hastily. He spoke for the entire Committee.

"There's nothing against it, no. But why should you—"

"Call it just a whim," I said. "Coupled with a desire to prove to the public what a really great horse Printer's Ink is. Very well, then. You may wish to make the announcement that Printer's Ink will carry, in addition to his regular jockey, a *second* rider. Uncle Herman, here."

They looked at Uncle Herman, chubby, pink-cheeked, smiling, an obviously middle-aged and obviously heavy man. Then they looked at me. The chairman's face darkened.

He said stiffly, "My dear Harkness, if you think this is funny, if you're trying to turn the Stakes into a comedy—"

"Far from it!" I said. "I believe I'm within my rights, gentlemen. Come on, Jack. Come on, Uncle Herman."

Uncle Herman had no right in the tackroom. So we met the horses as they marched through the chute toward the track. There we stopped Teddy Symes, and to his great amazement I told him to move up and make room for Uncle Herman.

The kid's eyes almost popped out. He wailed:

"But, Mr. Harkness!"

"You do as I say," I told him, "and everything will be okey-doke. Okay, Uncle Herman—off with the overcoat. Up you go!"

He dropped the lead-weighted coat and zipped onto the rump

of Printer's Ink. A couple of handlers standing nearby gasped. Uncle Herman wobbled. For a minute I thought he was going to lose his grip and float right on up to the flagpole. Jack grabbed his leg quickly.

"Hold on tight, Uncle Herman. Don't let go of the jockey; not even for a second."

"All right, boys," grinned Uncle Herman.

Honest, he was having the time of his life. Teddy Symes still looked as bewildered as a cross-eyed drunk in a mirror maze, but he was a good jockey. He had felt—even though he could not explain it—the sudden lifting of weight from Printer's Inks' back, as Uncle Herman hoisted.

And then the bugle blew "Boots and Saddles" and the public address system blared the announcement of the richest race in the East, and the horses moved toward the barrier. And I grabbed Jack and started running.

"Come on! I yelled. "The odds will be going up like a skyrocket, and I want plenty of 'em!"

I was six hundred percent right. The public took one look at Printer's Ink out there carrying double jockeys, then surged like one man for the betting windows. Those who had bet on Printer's Ink were frantically covering their wagers with equal amounts on Freda or Jolly Tar. Those who had backed the other two favorites were increasing the size of their bets.

In sixty seconds the odds on Printer's Ink were up to 7-1. In another minute the machines were offering 11-1, and no takers!

Except us! Jack was in for fifteen C's of his own and an extra five of Uncle Herman's; I was in hock for every last cent I had, twenty-five hundred simoleons. Baby! And at an average of 10-1!

It's a shame to tell the next part. After all the buildup, it should be one of those thrillers you read about. Like, "At the quarterpole it was Freda and Jolly Tar neck and neck. At the half the outsider, Frenzy, led by a nose. Thundering down the stretch it was Freda and Printer's Ink—"

But it wasn't anything like that. Printer's Ink was a good horse. More than that, he was a great horse.

Even with a full 126-pound impost he would have had more than a fighting chance to win—but with Uncle Herman astride his rear quarters, hanging on to Teddy Symes for dear life, adding his minus-twelve weight to the race—

Well, at the quarterpost Printer's Ink led by two lengths. It was four at the half, six at the three-quarters. Coming into the stretch Jolly Tar made a bid. It was a good bid. It was so good that when they crossed the finish line Printer's Ink led by only five lengths. Jolly Tar was second, and an outsider, Laughing Girl, came in to show. Freda was way back in the ruck, probably nursing a broken heart.

Then everything was bedlam. The crowd went stark, staring mad, of course. While a radio announcer yammered incoherent sentences of praise into his mike, the mob burst through the barriers and out onto the track to surround this magnificent horse which, carrying two riders, had showed clean heels to the best thoroughbreds in the nation.

At the head of that mob were Jack and I. Jack had the all-important overcoat flung over his arm. We reached Printer's Ink first, tossed the coat up to Uncle Herman. As soon as he put it on, Printer's Ink sagged a little, but no one noticed that in the excitement.

Reporters were crowding us, demanding Uncle Herman's name; asking why we had chosen to pull this spectacular stunt; asking a million other questions. Cameramen were clicking shutters, popping flashbulbs like firecrackers. A handler was trying vainly to lead Printer's Ink to the winner's circle.

I whispered swiftly into Jack's ear. "Get Uncle Herman out of here before somebody gets hep. Here, take these—" I handed him the handful of tickets I'd bought on Printer's Ink. "And change 'em for mazuma. As soon as the excitement's over I'll join you."

Then Tippy Malone, a camera hound from International Press whom I had known for years, struggled through the mob, grabbed my arm beseechingly.

"Bill, for gosh sakes, gimmie a break! Some damned fool busted all my bulbs and I didn't get a single picture. I had to dig this old flash unit out of my kit. Please—"

I said, "I'm sorry, Tippy, but—"

"You've got to, Bill! This is the biggest sensation since Upset beat Man-o'-War. If I don't get a picture I'll be fired!"

I said, "Well, all right then. But make it snappy. Uncle Herman!"

He took his pose; not on the horse, but standing beside Printer's Ink, pudgy and smiling in his heavy overcoat. He stroked the horse's nose. Tippy poured powder in his old-fashioned pan, set the box.

"All right. Smile. *Now!*"

A streak of white flame flared. Everybody blinked. There was a sudden wailing bleat.

"Wait a miiinnn—"

Then it died off into the distance, and there came a hollow, puffing sound—a pint-sized burst of thunder from our very midst! Printer's Ink neighed and bolted. The mob howled. Tippy looked up from his box, scowling. He said:

"Hey, where the hell did he go? That's a fine way to treat an old pal, Bill! Tell him to come back!"

But Uncle Herman hasn't come back yet. His room, that elaborate upside-down room in Jack's house, is still waiting for him. His pipe is there, his carpet slippers and dressing gown. And a pile of banknotes that he won riding Printer's Ink to victory.

But Uncle Herman hasn't come back. We don't know exactly why. Or how he disappeared. Tippy Malone showed us the picture he snapped just as Uncle Herman disappeared in a wailing bleat. It doesn't make sense. It shows Uncle Herman, overcoat and all, surrounded by a filmy halo, scooting hell-bent-for-election skyward with something that looks like streamers shooting from his mouth, ears and nostrils.

Jack says maybe the excitement caused still another chemical change in Uncle Herman; that his weight diminished to the point where even lead weights wouldn't hold him down. I have another thought.

Maybe I'm wrong. I have a sneaking hunch that Uncle Herman's reason for being lighter than air was not that he was filled with helium, but that he was loaded to the gills with *hydrogen!* And—well, you know what happened to the *Hindenburg*. And Tippy Malone's old-fashioned flash box emitted a spark—

Anyhow, Uncle Herman hasn't come back yet. We are still waiting and hoping. So keep in touch with me. I'll let you know if we hear from him. . . .

Occupation: Demigod

WELL, THE OLD GENTLEMAN IN THE STAR-SPANGLED topper was getting ready to draw capsules out of his fish bowl, which made some seventeen million annoyed Yankees between the ages of twenty-one and thirty-five eligible to spit in Herr Hitler's eye, so since I'd served two semesters in the Federal Writers' College, it won me a berth on the registration board. So I went, and it was just like I thought it would be.

First thing in the morning, the jernt was jammed to the rafters with "gotta-get-to-work" boys, but the crowd let up about eleven o'clock, and by two in the afternoon we were almost lonesome. I don't know how it was in your big towns; I'm just telling you how it was where I evade my taxes.

Anyhow, things were pretty dull until some sterling genius remembered that every true American cherishes the inherent right to lose two things: his life in battle, and his shirt at poker. After that, time whizzed by to the cheerful clack of chips, and whenever a late registrant straggled in, the holder of the high spade had to go snare his J. Hancock.

So, of course, everything happens to me. I had to be showing the ebony ace when this johnny marched in. I moaned and flipped over the matching one-spotter in the hole, and I got lots of sympathy—like hell! And naturally I wasn't the nation's Sweetest Disposition Registrar as I waved the new signer-upper to a seat and grabbed a form.

"Park it!" I said, and punched the inkwell with the spray gun our post-office department laughingly calls a pen. "O.K.," I said. "Your name, please?"

He was a big jasper. Big and broad and blond, with china-blue eyes so placid they almost soothed you. At first I figured him for one of those "strong-back, weak-mind" lads—bovinely stupid and complacent. Then I looked again and wasn't so sure.

It wasn't that at all. The quietude of those pale washed-blue orbs was not born of a low I.Q. rating; his ease was that of confidence, of a sort of *knowingness*. For a strange, strained moment I felt tiny and unimportant as I sat there facing him; I felt somehow humble in his presence. Then I thought, "Hey, wait a minute! What makes here?" And I said again, "Your name, please?"

He carried one of those bulgy leather cases used by musicians and gangsters to conceal their lethal weapons. He set this on the desk between us, handling it carefully, gingerly. His voice was deep and rumbly and pleasant.

"Ayres!" he said. "T. Marshall Ayres."

"Don't be formal with Uncle Sam," I told him. "The front handle?"

"Theritas," he said sheepishly. "My friends call me Teddy."

Well, it takes all kinds to make a world. You'd be surprised how many Marmadukes and Algernons are living under aliases of Butch and Spike. I made him spell it for me, and it looked as silly as it sounded. Then I said, "Very well, Mr. Ayres. Now your address?"

He fidgeted, and for a moment there was uncertainty in his preternaturally calm eyes. "I . . . I don't exactly know how to answer that," he said slowly. "I . . . that is—"

"It's very simple," I told him. "Where do you hang your toothbrush? That's home, be it ever so humble. You *do* have a toothbrush?"

"Oh, yes. But what I mean is—I'm not living anywhere just now. I've just left one place, and I'm on my way to another—"

He seems to want to explain, but I was thinking of those wired aces and cut him short.

"Skip it," I said. I wrote "transient" and went on to the next question. "Give me the name of someone who will always know where you are."

"Amaltheia," he answered promptly.

"Amaltheia, *who?*"

"Just Amaltheia," he said.

"Your wife?"

"My fianceé. We're going to be married next week."

I said, "Oh, hell!" and wrote in Amaltheia Ayres," because the United States government is funny about last names. And I said, "Her address?"

"Olympus," he said.

"Olympus *where?* What State?"

"Just Olympus," he said.

This was getting monotonous. And I was getting an itch to throw things. I said savagely, "Look, Ayres—it's *got* to be somewhere! Now, where is it?"

"We-e-ell," he said dubiously, "some think it's in Greece. Of course it isn't, really, but—"

"What's good enough for Rand & McNally," I snarled, "is good enough for me." I put it down that way, then shot him the rest of the quiz program. "Age—height—weight?" I filled in the proper blanks, finally reached the last one. "Occupation?" I asked. "Business or profession?"

He looked at me calmly. And—

"God," he said.

The pen leaped and spluttered in my hand. I shoved my chair a few inches clear of the desk for a quick getaway. "I . . . I beg your pardon?" I said.

But there was no trace of laughter on his lips, and his eyes were gravely courteous.

"Perhaps," he amended, "I should say *demi*god. I'm not quite sure yet. The matter hasn't been finally decided. That's why I have to go to—"

Well, he looked harmless enough, at any rate. So I picked up my pen again. I said soothingly, "Don't look now, pal, but isn't that profession a little out of the ordinary? Maybe we ought to write you down as something less unusual?" My eyes lighted on the leather case, and inspiration burned. "That's some kind of musical instrument, isn't it?"

He nodded. "A horn," he said. "The horn of—"

"Then suppose I put you down as a musician? Understand," I hastened, "I don't *doubt* you. But—"

"I guess that would be all right," he approved. "I *was* a musician, you know. Until I found—*that.* The horn." I couldn't help thinking that, for a deity, he was curiously sheepish. There was a pathetic eagerness in his voice. His eyes shone with a sort of wistful puppy-dog desire for understanding. "That's what started all this. I'd like to tell you. That is—if you'd care to hear?"

I glanced across the room. The poker chips clacked merrily. Somebody said, "Up five!" and somebody else said, "I'm in." There was a hell of a lot of money in the pot. I was nuts to waste time on this tow-headed wacky. But there was something about him— Oh, I can't explain it! Anyway, I settled back.

"Sure," I said. "I'd love to. Go ahead," I said.

He leaned forward, fingering the leather case as he talked. His story was fantastic, of course, and no sane man would believe a word of it. But his tongue had not the ease of glibness of that of the congenital liar, and there was a pleading look of truth in his eyes.

"I was walking down a small side street," he began, "when first I saw it—"

He was walking down a small side street when first he saw it in a pawnshop window. It rested between a battered microscope and a slightly used set of uppers. Like everything else in the window, it was covered with a fine film of dust, but the moment he laid eyes on it, he knew it was just the thing he had been looking for.

He went in. The room was small and dark and musty, and though a tiny bell jangled somewhere in the back of the shop, no one appeared.

Teddy waited. Nothing happened.

He called, "Hey!" Still nothing happened.

The display counter, with its grilled arch and long, dirty-paned showcase, was deserted. He took out his watch, glanced at it—

And instantly a gnomelike creature, all belly and beard, popped out of nowhere to talon the timepiece from his grasp, squint at it suspiciously, and rasp, "Two dollas!"

Teddy said, "B-but—"

"*Tree* dollas!" said the pawnbroker with an air of finality. "Tek it or leave it!"

Teddy said, "Look, Uncle, I want to see that—"

"A customuh! Vy didn't you say so?" The pawnbroker proprietor thrust back Teddy's watch. "Yessir! Vot vill it be? Name it, I got it. Rinks, revolwas, fishinks, taggles, box-fighting gloves for the liddle boy, *nu?* Diamints—fine all-wool suets and ovacodes— typeridas—all on gendle time payments—"

"—that horn in the window," persisted Teddy.

"Hawn?" The broker looked blank for a moment, then beamed. "Ach, yes, the hawn!" He waddled away, returned in a moment, vigorously puffing dust from the object of Teddy's interest. "Movvless, ain'd it Genuwine antigg powda hawn. Rewolution period, maybe sooner. Only a collector of relics like yourself should know the true value, *nu?*" Hopefully he studied Teddy's impassive face, surrendered the oddly shaped convolute of keratin and carried on stanchly. "Vas a powda hawn, maybe a dringink cup, who knows? Is now a fine awnament for the home liberry or den—"

Teddy raised the horn to his lips, tongued it. As he had hoped, it was pierced. The proprietor shifted verbal gears without missing a syllable.

"—and is *also* a hundlike hawn of eggsellent tone and qualidy!"

"How much?" asked Teddy.

The uncle scratched his beard speculatively. "Ten dollars?" he hazarded.

"I'll give you two."

"Is a boggin at eight. Six?"

"Two fifty," said Teddy. He laid own the horn.

"Faw fifty, and I'm losing money."

"Good-by," said Teddy. He started for the door.

The gnome moaned faintly and waddled after him.

"Waiddaminute! You want the hawn or don't you? So I'm going broke. Whose worry is that? Tree and a half, you said? Take it?"

Teddy grinned.

"You're a chiseling old scoundrel. If it cost you a penny more than one buck, I'll eat it. But all right, I'll take it for three fifty." He laid down three one-dollar bills and a fifty-cent piece, picked up the horn. "You got a case for this thing?"

"Tree," counted the pawnbroker absently, "and fifty cents, righd! Vot? A case? No, sir."

"I wish it had a case," said Teddy petulantly. "I'm going to look silly carrying an old cow's horn up Broadway— Hey! What's that?"

"That" had toppled from a shelf above his head, had fallen at his feet. It was a leather case of the type used by musicians, bright and new and shiny. In the fall its hasps jarred open; Teddy stared at the velour-lined interior with amazement.

"It's the case for this horn! Look, it fits perfectly!"

The proprietor's jaw gaped for a moment. He stared at the dimmed shelves perplexedly, then snapped back to normal.

"For the case," he wheezed, "only one dolla. It's a boggin."

"Half a buck," snorted Teddy, "and it's a windfall! You didn't even know you *had* a case!" He flipped a coin at the little man, turned to the door again. In the gloom his foot missed the sill. He stumbled and barked his shin, and said, "Damn! I wish you'd get some lights in this dump!"

And he left. On the street outside, for some reason he never could afterward explain, he turned to look back upon the shop he had just quitted. And he witnessed a surprising thing. Despite the fact that it was still daylight, the pawnbroker had taken him at his word.

The little shop was ablaze with lights!

"It was all lit up," said Ayres, "like a Christmas tree. Do you understand? That dirty little shop with its miserly proprietor—"

I said, "But what's so unreasonable about that? He may have had work to do after you left. And if the shop was as dark as you say—"

Ayres shook his head.

"I didn't think you'd get it—yet. I didn't. It took me quite a while to realize the truth. Of course, the meaning was staring me right in the face. I should have understood right then. And afterward, when I was practicing—and when *she* came in—"

"She?" I said. "Practicing?"

"Here's how it was," he said. "I went home—"

He went to his lodginghouse. It was only six in the evening, which is a professional musician's noon. He didn't have to go to work until nine o'clock, which left him three full hours in which to eat, bathe, shave and dress before he reported to the Kangaroo Klubbe where currently, and probationally, the dance band of which he was a member, was appearing. "Rusty Roberts' Rollicking Rhythm Rogues," they called themselves.

He drew the cow's horn from its case and looked at it admiringly. Perhaps a little hopefully, as well. He was not any too sure he could push music through it, but he was game to try. Anything that has a mouthpiece, a tube and a bell can be made to elicit sounds if the blower knows how to lip it. If Bob Burns, thought Teddy, could squeeze melodies out of a length of lead pipe and a funnel—if that gobble piper in Krupa's band could swing out on an old-time marine foghorn—surely he—

He lifted the thing to his lips—and blew.

Its bleat was piteous to hear. Low and mournful as the plaint of an agonized soul. And it didn't take the wind very well. Teddy got out his knife, cut a wider lip to the horn's end, tried it again. And again. After a while he succeeded in modifying the bleat into a series of ascending-descending notes. The range was short, but the sound was—well, unusual!

He smiled, satisfied. Rusty Roberts would approve of this. Rusty had been a little critical of his playing of late; had, in fact, made several caustic comments featuring the words, "corny" and "schmaltz." But wait till he let go with a hot lick on the old cow's horn. It would wow 'em!

He leaned back in his chair and patted his foot—*oompah! oompah!*—and jammed "China Boy" through the twist of horn. A perfect performance. He never hit the theme once, but succeeded in glissading perilously about its edges with minors and fifths that yearned toward barrelhouse chords. Heaven was in and about him, his heart was at ease, and his eyes were rapt. The bleating soared and quavered. And so did an irate voice.

"*Mister* Ayres!"

The screaming reproof finally broke through Teddy's mantle of deaf contentment. He came to with a start to find his landlady standing in the doorway, eyes stormy, her hands pressed hard against her ears.

"*Mister* Ayres—how many times must I ask you don't blow them awful things here in my house?"

Teddy said, "I'm sorry, Mrs. McClanahan. I hope it didn't disturb you."

"It ain't me I'm thinkin' of. It's the rest of the lodgers. Poor Mr. Drake, him which has to sit up all night, watchin' at the Apex Luggage factory, and not gettin' a wink of sleep with you makin' them ungodly sounds—"

"I'm sorry," said Teddy again. "I'm stopping now, though. I've got to get dressed."

The word woke an echo in Mrs. McClanahan's memory. Her errand came back to her. Her broad hands sought broader hips, and her elbows arched dangerously akimbo.

"Dressed," she snorted, "is right! And so, if you ask me, should *she!* The nerve o' that hussy—"

"Eh?"

"I'll ask you to remember, *Mister* Ayres, that this is a respectable lodginghouse! Things is come to a sorry state when young ladies— only *she* ain't no lady, as anyone can plainly see—comes boldly callin' on menfolks in . . . practically nothing!"

Her broad face reddened, whether with shame, fury, or indignation Teddy could not guess. He said, "But . . . but I don't understand, Mrs. McClanahan. A young lady? To see me? Where—"

"And where else should she be but downstairs? I'm not one to dictate right an' wrong to my roomers, Mr. Ayres, but it seems to me there are certain limits—"

Teddy pushed past her, out the door, and leaned over the stairwell. What he saw in the narrow hallway two flights down brought a gasp of surprise to his lips.

"Why . . . why she's wearing a *chiton!*"

"Sheet on," stormed the landlady furiously, "or off, I won't have her in my house! You'll be kind enough to make her leave immediately, Mr. Ayres! And" —darkly— "yourself with her if she so much as sets her nose inside my house again!"

"A *chiton,*" said Teddy impatiently, "is a costume, Mrs. McClanahan. The style of garment worn by ancient Greek women. As to whom this girl is, or what she wants here, I'm as much in the dark as you. But if you'll excuse me—"

He raced down the stairs. He was almost at the bottom when the girl turned and looked at him.

And then—

Well, those things happen. They happened then, all of them and suddenly, to Teddy Ayres. There was no *ping!* of a straightening bow chord, there was no *whiz!* of an arrow—but Teddy was a gone goose, instantly and completely.

His footsteps faltered, his hand on the balustrade trembled with an unwonted ague. His tongue felt like a wad of throbbing cotton, and his heart boomed and pounded like a set of timpani. He stared, speechless and shaken.

Hair the rich, ripe sheen of sunlight on soft gold, eyes the calm, sweet blue of high lake water, lips warm and red as—as—Teddy's descriptive powers failed him. She was a dream walking. A melody wakened to vibrant life. An—an eight-bar break on a tenderly haunting tune.

"Hello," she said. Her voice was like the laughter of mellow wood winds. "Hello. Are you Teddy Ayres?"

Teddy stared, entranced. No breeze wafted through the dim and fusty hallway, but she seemed to bear along with her a sweet and secret, personal and private, woodsy scent of her own. The flowing edges of her classic garment clung to the perfect lines of her figure; her hair was a cascade of molten bronze.

Then the cat relinquished his tongue. Partly. And he gulped, "Y-yeah, I'm him. B-but who—"

"I'm Amaltheia," she said. "Where did you find it?"

"It?" said Teddy.

"The horn, of course. We've been looking for it *so* long. Ages. Ever since that perfectly foul Italian barbarian got Donny whiffed on ambrosia and stole it from him."

"And then—" She smiled, and Teddy's heart did a nip-up. "And then, of course, you used it—and we knew at once someone had found it. So we came."

The carbon of emotion was still clogging the motor of Teddy's brain.

"H-horn?" he said.

"Yes. *My* horn! Oh, please don't be difficult. We know you have it, and—it's *very* important, you know. What with the way things have been going lately, we're likely to need it almost any day. Where is it?"

"The horn!" said Teddy suddenly. "Oh, you mean the *horn?* The old cow's horn? Why . . . why it's upstairs. But I don't see how you knew—"

Amaltheia's eyes glinted, and a swift pink suffused her alabaster cheeks. She stamped her foot.

"*Cow's* horn indeed! Why . . . why, you impossible mortal! Aren't you ashamed to talk that way about—"

"And a fine one," interrupted a strident tone. "You are to be talkin' about shame! Mr. Ayres, didn't I ask you to get this creature out of my house immediately?"

Teddy's patience snapped. He turned on his landlady angrily. "Oh, go hide your head under a rug!" he snapped. "This lady and I—"

He stopped stricken. For Mrs. McClanahan was nowhere to be seen. And at his elbow, where she stood a moment before, now stood an incredible figure. A creature half man, half goat, bearded of lips, furry of thatch, thigh and chest, grinning—and bearing in his hands the horn!

"O.K., sis!" said the amazing apparition. "I got it. Shall we go?"

All else was forgotten in Teddy's swift panic for his new-found instrument. He reached out angrily.

"Hey! Gimme that!"

Amaltheia said dubiously, "Achelous—I don't think we should take it without giving him some compensation. After all, he found it for us—"

"Aw, come on!" chuckled Achelous. "We'll send him a million *mina,* or whatever they use for money nowadays." He started for the door; Amaltheia moved after him uncertainly.

But Teddy was not through yet. Anger welled up in him like a dark flood, his brow contracted and his usually placid eyes flamed. He leveled a warning finger at the disappearing satyr. "That horn comes back to me this minute," he roared, "or else—"

He never finished his threat. For at that instant occurred a breath-taking finale. The cow's horn seemed to give a little shrug in Achelous' hand, wriggled free—and flew across the hall to Teddy. It nestled there securely, even though Teddy's fingers were too nerveless with surprise to grip it.

Amaltheia cried, "Oh!" in a hurt little voice, and what the satyr said was archaic, but still very obvious. He stared at Teddy glumly.

"You bought that thing," he moaned, "with *silver!*"

Teddy nodded, dazed.

"Why . . . why, yes. A fifty-cent piece—"

Achelous growled and stomped his hoof bitterly.

"I might have known it! Now we can't get it unless you give it to us of your own free will! All right, mortal! How much?"

Too many things had happened to Teddy. A half-hour ago he would have been willing to turn over his little "find" at any reasonable profit. Even five minutes ago he would have gladly given it—and his right arm along with it—to the girl now standing wide-eyed and pleading before him. But he was dazed with incredibility, now, and bewildered and more than a little frightened. And a frightened Yankee is a stubborn Yankee. His might tightened like a steel vise.

"It's not for sale!" he said.

Achelous stroked his beard pettishly.

"I see. Know a good thing when you have it, don't you? All right—two million *mina?*"

"It's not," said Teddy grimly, "for sale!"

Amaltheia moved forward softly, placed a warm hand on his elbow. "But it means so much to us, Teddy. You don't know, of course, but we do. They're rearming, you know. I think they're dreaming of the old days of Empire. They're not content to rest and dream as we are. They want to rise and rule again. They want to take our last refuge from us—put it under their dominion. They've even gone so far as to ally themselves with those other horrid creatures—the hairy ones from the North—and very soon—"

"I don't know what you're talking about," broke in Teddy rudely, "and I don't care. I bought this horn to use in the band. And I'm going to use it. Now—"

A late shaft of evening sunlight, dying, entered a chink in the doorway and fell slantwise across Teddy's face. It was that which caused Amaltheia to gasp suddenly, clutch her brother's arm.

"Achelous—that jaw! He looks like—"

Achelous, too, had seen it. Astonishment shone in his eyes; he fingered his beard nervously. "Mortal—what is your name?" he demanded.

"She knows my name," said Teddy fretfully. "Ayres. Theritas Marshall Ayres—if you want to make anything of it. And now—"

"Theritas!"

"And now, I wish the two of you would run along and leave me alone!"

For the briefest instant there hovered in the air a dying whisper of Amaltheia's startled exclamation. "Ther—"

And then they were gone! And Teddy was shaking himself, wholly unable to assure himself as to whether this affair had been hallucination or verity.

He stared stupidly at the horn in his hand, then at the door. The door had not opened. How, then, had his visitors—if, indeed, he had had visitors!—left? Was it all some feverish dream? If so, it was a dream that, departing, had left behind one heart-stirring essence of charm. For in the musty hallway there lingered the delicate woodsy scent of the nymphlike creature he had seen and loved on sight.

Muffled sounds from the living room roused him from his mental meanderings. He stepped to the door, pulled it open. And a strange sight greeted his eyes.

Stern lifted to the ceiling like that of a sinking ship, hands pawed wildly at the scuffed floor boards, voice muffled by a thick and dusty layer of woven fabric, his landlady was kneeling on the living-room floor—*with her head hidden under the rug!*

Ayres paused dramatically, looked at me as though expecting some comment. I shook off the inexplicable sense of eerie that had engulfed me as he talked. I lit a cigarette. I said, "Ostrich, eh? Well, it's fashionable these days. Even governments do it."

"Don't you see," he said, "what it meant?"

"Hm-m-m," I told him. "It meant you weren't the only hinkey-pate in that lodginghouse. Did you take turns on the needle, or did you all have your own?"

The moment I cracked smart, I could have pulled my tongue out and stuffed it in my vest pocket. Because somehow my alleged humor didn't seem funny. I think it was his eyes that put the freeze on me. They were cold and stern, and at the same time judicial. I got a creepy feeling that if he should at that moment decide to give me the old eenymeeny, I'd all-of-a-sudden be out, and I *do* mean *woosh!*

Then the glaciers melted. Once again his eyes were wistful, friendly, anxious. He said slowly, "Don't you see? I told her to go hide her head under a rug. And she *did!*"

"I realize that," I said, "but I still don't get it. Who was this Amaltheia doll? And what and who was she talking about? And that hair-on-the-hoof she called her brother—what was he doing there? and how does the horn fit into the picture?"

"I was beginning to understand," said Teddy Ayres, "faintly. But I wasn't convinced. It was all too incredible. The clincher came later. That night, at the Kangaroo Klubbe."

That night at the Kangaroo Klubbe was like any one of a thousand other nights at any one of a thousand other small, hopeful, frayed-at-the-cuff night clubs in Manhattan. Dismal-looking waiters scurried fretfully back and forth between wan-looking tables and a drab kitchen, carrying lugubrious trays of victuals; an obese M. C. with a flatulent smile waved a wet fish at newcomers; bus boys dropped dishes; the hat-check girl gnawed gum viciously; the foods were cold and the drinks were hot and the ventilating system had already been closed tight, in anticipation of a lovely, suffocating evening.

It was early; the orchestra had not yet assumed its place on the dais incresting the four-foot circle known as a "dance floor," and a discouraged-looking piano player noodled casually through a retinue of old, and sometimes indistinguishable melodies.

In a back room Rusty Roberts eyed his trumpeter dubiously and said, "Novelty? What kind of novelty, Ayres?"

Teddy smiled mysteriously.

"Look, Rusty, don't make me tell you. Just take my word for it, won't you? It's a whipper, I'll guarantee that. Just give me eight on the second chorus of *China Boy* and I'll show you—"

Rusty Roberts said, "I don't know, Buster. The M. C. ain't been any too friendly lately. If you start sprinkling corn around here again tonight—"

"Corn!" said Teddy aggrievedly. *"Again!"*

"You heard me. Trouble with you, Ayres, you've got the idea you're a gut-bucket. The truth of the matter is you're strictly springtime. Maybe you better forget this idea. If you've got anything hot, trot it out and let's have a listen. But I'm not giving you any blind licks without knowing—"

"O.K.!" said Teddy sulkily. "O.K.! Just skip it!"

He glared at the band leader, but Rusty didn't even notice. He had turned and was waving the boys from the room. "All right, gang, let's go. And give out tonight, hey?"

One by one they filed from, the room. Teddy was the last to leave. He stood staring moodily at his horn, anger and disappointment mingled within him. "For two cents," he muttered to himself, "I wouldn't—"

But his pride was stronger than his petulance. He carried two cases into the club with him. His trumpet and his curly horn. The first he displayed prominently; the second was slipped under his chair until an auspicious moment should present itself.

Then the evening settled down to routine. Roberts' scale-rangers jumbled 'em up, old and new, sweet and hot, as is the custom of night-club bands. The dinner crowd dwindled off, and the after-dinner crowd ankled in. The air became staler and bluer and smokier, the food colder and more expensive, the drinks warmer and weaker as the café habitues got tighter and tighter.

And, somehow, it was eleven o'clock, then twelve, and almost one. And still Teddy had not taken the horn from its case. And then, new numbers having been dragged through the mill till they were tattered, Rusty Roberts gave the uncork sign for old favorites. And tapped the stick for "China Boy."

It was then that his impatient dream wakened again in Teddy Ayres' mind. As he tongued the opening blaze chorus with the band, he was remembering, swiftly, the routine Rusty always followed on this number. He always turned the third chorus over to the percussions. The skins took up the dying beat, began to hammer around it. Then the doghouse came in; finally the piano, playing a bass fugue around the tempo.

It was a natural set-up for his little curly horn. Its melancholy wail would sparkle like a diamond against that throb setting. He bent over slyly, loosened the hasps of its case. He waited anxiously. And finally it came. The reeds dropped out. The brasses faded. The skins took up the time and started rumbling softly—

Teddy picked up his horn. He glanced once, and nervously, at Rusty Roberts. "I hope he doesn't notice," he whispered to himself. "I hope he doesn't notice till I get going—"

And, surprisingly, Rusty didn't. He stood there on the podium, beating the time, smiling mechanically, eyes fastened directly on Teddy—but he didn't seem to notice as Teddy lifted the curly old cow's horn to his lips.

Teddy swung out.

What happened then was baffling, for everything happened at once, and everything that happened was completely illogical, but no one in the night club seemed to think so except Teddy, and he was so intent on forcing music through his horn that he had little time to wonder.

For with the first wailing note of the horn, every bit of din and clatter in the club ceased, and all eyes came to the bandstand. Waiters paused with trays still poised above their heads, diners stopped eating, drinkers—incredibly!—neglected their drinks; even the manager of the club came from his office to listen, nodding with approbation.

The dancers stopped dancing, moved closer to the stand. And it was then that, even as he kept on playing in a sort of glow, Teddy saw something which made his pulses leap. Into the small cleared space stepped a familiar, and already dear figure—followed by a creature half man, half goat. And—

"Teddy!" called Amaltheia softly. "Teddy—play *our* song!"

It was impossible, of course. Impossible and fantastic. There was no reason for Teddy Ayres to know what she meant by *our* song—but curiously, he did! An instinct, deep, intuitive, guided his lips as he played the tune. And like the dim, incessant surge of white waters breaking on a golden, sandy beach, the drummer beat the time for him. All the other musicians had stopped playing; their mouths hung openly agape, their eyes were dull and pleased and vacant as the polite and empty eyes of figures painted on canvas.

And the song rose and wailed and filled the little room. And even as he played, Teddy found himself thinking that this setting was all wrong.

"It shouldn't be like this," he thought. "I should be in a shaded dell—warped, stunted trees, laden with rich, purple olives should surround me—green grass beneath my feet—and an azure sky—"

And it was so! Suddenly there was no longer a drab, ill-lighted night club. He played in the center of a shaded dell, encircled by slim trees laden with purple fruit. The fresh, green grass was spongy beneath his feet. And before him, light as a tossing leaf in an April breeze—Amaltheia was dancing!

Amaltheia, then Achelous. And their dance was that of the woodland nymphs and satyrs. She laughing, taunting, chaste and fleetingly evasive—he the capering, grimacing would-be captor beating the turf with his cloven hoofs, breaking his half-beast heart in an ever-unattained pursuit.

That was the song, and the song had words, but the words were not those of an ancient race. They were English words, and where Teddy had heard them he could not at first remember. High school, perhaps—or college. Keats, maybe. "What men or gods are these? What maidens loth? What mad pursuit? What struggle to escape? What pipes and timbrels? What wild ecstasy—"

But the miracle of it was no one save himself seemed to see the marvel of this moment. The drummer beat his hides, the slim, piercing-thin note of a pipe had crept in from the background, Teddy's music sobbed and cried, but his audience did not see how the walls of the night club had vanished, exposing a horizon and wildwood and sky, against which, like a huge and snow-capped backdrop, was outlined a lofty, cloud-garmented mountain peak.

And Amaltheia spoke to him again.

"The other song, Teddy! The song of Theritas!"

But he had anticipated her. Already his lips had found the new theme. No longer was the music soft, musing, pastoral; it was the skirling of pipes, now, the clash of steel on steel, the roaring of a thousand voices raised in just outrage. It was the tramp of men's feet, the valiant farewell of women to men in arms. There was glory and power and courage in this new but ancient song. A message and a warning. A defiance—

It was over! The music ended in a final, defiant note. The drummer sat stupidly before his instrument, his eyes dull, uncomprehending. The horn fell from Teddy Ayres' lips. He stared at it, shaken. Then at the girl, who had come to his side.

"But I don't—" he whispered, "I don't understand?"

Her hand was a gentle compulsion on his arm.

"Achelous was right, Teddy. You *are* his son. You *are* one of us. Now do you understand?"

"*His* son?" repeated Teddy. "One of . . . of what?"

"His other name," said Achelous, "is Theritas. The Spartans called him that. Your father. I suppose you never saw him?"

Teddy shook his head.

"He . . . he disappeared before I was born. My mother waited, but he never came back. It was the war, you know."

Amaltheia nodded indignantly.

"Yes, that sounds like him. He *would* be there, of course. And he's been lolling around, ever since. Oh, I'll tell him what I think of him when we get back. But at least he gave you his name. That's more than he usually does, the scoundrel!"

"My name?"

"Ayres," said Achelous impatiently. "Or Theritas. He's your father, you know. And I suppose that makes *you* a god, too. Or a demigod, anyway. We'll have to ask Father Zeus about that. I wouldn't be surprised if he granted you full rights and privileges. You found the horn, you know, just when we needed it."

He took the horn from Teddy's unprotesting hand, lifted it. For the first time, Teddy noticed that Achelous had only one horn; that there was a broken stump on his left forehead. The satyr pressed the horn to the stump. It fitted reasonably well.

"Chipped," said Achelous pettishly, "and, of course, *you* had to bore a hole in the end of it. Oh, well!"

Teddy stared at him numbly.

"It's your horn?"

"Certainly it's his," said Amaltheia. "Or mine, to be accurate. Father Zeus gave it to me for helping him. He gave it the Power, you know, to grant any wish to its owner. That's why—"

"Amaltheia!" Light dawned suddenly upon Teddy as he remembered almost-forgotten legends. "Amaltheia's horn! The Horn of Plenty! Cornucopia!

"Then that's why I got the case. And the pawnshop lights came on. And the landlady hid, Rusty didn't notice, and—" He stared about him wildly, groaning. "Look what I've done here! I wished this night club would turn into a wooded dell!"

Achelous said, "Oh, change it back and let's get going! Don't you know every minute is precious? I can hear the drums rolling now. First thing you know, that blasted Mars is going to be rolling his chariots over *our* hills—"

"It's war again, Teddy." said Amaltheia seriously. "The Roman gods. They're restless; they wouldn't sleep and dream, as we have. Now they've joined forces with those vile, hairy gods from the North. Woden, or whatever his name is. And Hermes says they're planning to attack us. The Horn is our rallying horn."

"Already it is late—too late. We'll probably have to leave Olympus for a while. Not that those stumble-witted Roman gods could ever drive us out, but the cold, dark gods they've called in from the North—

"We'll rally at Olympus now, and then . . . then perhaps the Old Ones of Egypt, slow as they are to waken, will answer the Horn. We'll have to go there, I think, and rouse their aid—"

For a long moment, Teddy stared at her. Logic still told him that this was impossible—but the hour for logic was past. And instincts deeper and more certain than mere reason guided him now. He turned to Achelous.

"The Horn, Achelous!" There was a new imperiousness to his tone as he faced the weirdly quiet, weirdly motionless night club. "When we have gone," he said gravely, "let this place return to normal in all save one thing. That no man remember what took place here tonight; that I, Teddy Ayres, be completely forgotten by those people and by all mortals who ever knew me—"

"They went back to Olympus," said Teddy Ayres, "in the . . . the usual way. I couldn't accompany them because I've not been given full rights and privileges yet. I have to go as a mortal. So I'm on my way South to New Orleans. I can get a steamer, there, for Greece.

"But I thought I should register before I left. I am—or was—an American citizen, after all. And who knows? Perhaps we may yet—"

I shook myself. Dark evening had fallen, and the poker game was breaking up. I'd wasted a whole afternoon on this crazy, towheaded lug and his fantastic lies. I said, "Well, guy, I'll say one thing for you. You're the most convincing crackpot I ever met. Are you sure there isn't a P.S. to that story? About how you personally created the Universe and started it spinning like a top?"

"Then you don't believe me?"

"Me?" I laughed shortly. "Oh, yes! I can swallow anything. I'm Old Man Gullible himself. Look, pal, why don't you go home and—"

"Wait a minute!" he said quietly. He snapped open his music case. Nestled against the velour was a small and curly horn. "Put your hand on it," he said. "Wish for something. Anything."

I grinned at him derisively.

"Anything for a laugh, eh, pal? O. K.—I wish I had the ten bucks you've cost me this afternoon. If I'd stayed in that poker game, I'd eat steak tonight. And I wish you'd get out of here—"

Well, I knew he was sensitive. But I didn't know he was that sensitive. I must have hurt his feelings pretty badly with that last crack, because he didn't even stop to say good-by. As a matter of fact, he was gone before I finished talking. Funny about that—I didn't see him go. And the music case, the horn, seemed to slip from beneath my fingers as if by magic—

Still, it wasn't logical, and I'm a logical man. I did my best to forget about Mr. Theritas Teddy Ayres as soon as possible. And in the hurly-burly of registering America's militant manpower, I would have succeeded pretty well except for two things.

First was what happened a week or so after Registration Day. You know what I mean. We woke one morning to find that crack troops of the Italian army had marched from Albania into Greece. Purely a defensive movement, of course. The Greeks, it seems, were plotting to annex Albania, raid Rome and use Il Duce as a pincushion.

Only the Roman legions advanced swiftly to the rear, and the Germans finally came down. They took Olympus finally—but not before those who wanted to had left for Egypt, nor before they'd learned a wholesome respect for the fighting power of the Greeks—

And the other thing!

Well, figure it out for yourself. It happened just about two minutes after Teddy Ayres and his magic cow's horn disappeared. Johnny Baldwin sauntered over to the desk. He said, "Thanks, friend!"

"Thanks," I asked him, "for what?"

"The chips," he said blithely. "I ran out of cash, and since it didn't look like you were coming back into the game, I used yours."

"Well, of all the—" I began.

"And I won," he continued hastily. "Twenty smackers. So here's your split. Ten bucks."

I stared dumbly at the crisp ten-dollar bill he laid in my hand. And I felt a tight little chill run up and down my backbone. It was coincidence, of course. But he had said, "Wish for something. Anything. The thing you want most—"

And I still think he was a wackypot. But—I wish I'd wished for a million!

Epilogue

"**B**UT WHY," YOU MAY ASK, "DID YOU TITLE THIS BOOK The Far Side of Nowhere?"

I offer two answers.

One of the questions most frequently asked an author is "Where do you get the ideas for your stories?" I know not what others may reply, but my answer is, as it truthfully must be, "Out of nowhere." One day, one moment, I have no story; then suddenly there it is, complete and whole in my mind from the opening sentence to the last, and all I have to do is put down the words. In short, a story comes to me from the far side of nowhere.

And my second answer? From the word nowhere itself, which defines its location in the very spelling of the word.

For nowhere is that tiny spot of space between now and here.

Two thousand five hundred copies of this book have been printed by the Vail-Ballou Mfg. Grp., Binghamton, NY using Garamond Antiqua typeface on 50# Maple Antique Shade 86 paper. The binding cloth is Arrestox B grade. Typesetting by The Composing Room, Inc., Kimberly, WI.